WOMEN on WOMEN 3

A New Anthology of American Lesbian Fiction

Edited by Joan Nestle and Naomi Holoch

A PLUME BOOK

PLUME
Published by the Penguin Group
Penguin Books USA Inc., 375 Hudson Street,
New York, New York 10014, U.S.A.
Penguin Books Ltd, 27 Wrights Lane,
London W8 5TZ, England
Penguin Books Australia Ltd, Ringwood,
Victoria, Australia
Penguin Books Canada Ltd, 10 Alcorn Avenue,
Toronto, Ontario, Canada M4V 3B2
Penguin Books (N.Z.) Ltd, 182–190 Wairau Road,
Auckland 10, New Zealand

Penguin Books Ltd, Registered Offices:
Harmondsworth, Middlesex, England

First published by Plume, an imprint of Dutton Signet,
a division of Penguin Books USA Inc.

First Printing, June, 1996
10 9 8 7 6 5 4 3 2 1

PERMISSIONS AND ACKNOWLEDGMENTS

"Why I'm Here" Copyright © Lucy Jane Bledsoe, 1996
"The Gift of Wholeness" from *The Gifts of the Body* by Rebecca Brown. Copyright © 1994 by
    Rebecca Brown. Reprinted by permission of HarperCollins Publishers, Inc.
"blueberry" Copyright © Clover L. Cannady, 1996
"The Vanish" Copyright © Mary Beth Caschetta, 1996
"The Woman Who Plays Trumpet is Deported" from *Bodies of Water* by Michelle Cliff.
    Copyright © Michelle Cliff, 1990. Used by permission of Dutton Signet, a division of Penguin
    Books USA Inc. and Methuen London.
"An American in Chiapas" Copyright © Nisa Donnelly, 1996
Selection from *Riverfinger Women* by Elana Nachman/Dykewomon. Copyright © Elana Nachman/
    Dykewomon, 1974. By permission of Naiad Press.
"One Day at the Mace Factory" Copyright © Leslie Feinberg, 1996
"Flossie's Going" Copyright © Ellen Frye, 1996
"Salisbury Jo" Copyright © Frankie Hucklebroich, 1996
Selections from *Spoken in Darkness* by Ann E. Imbrie. Copyright © 1993 Ann E. Imbrie.
    Reprinted by permission of Hyperion.
"The Printer" from *My Jewish Face and Other Stories* by Melanie Kaye/Kantrowitz. Copyright ©
    Melanie Kaye/Kantrowitz, 1990. By permission of Aunt Lute Books.
"Garden Blues" Copyright © Sarah Lane, 1996
"A Room, in a Stone House, in Spain" Copyright © Jenifer Levin, 1996
Selection from *Dry Fire* by Catherine Lewis. Copyright © Catherine Lewis, 1996. Reprinted by
    permission of W. W. Norton & Company, Inc.

(The following page represents an extension of the copyright page.)

34 FINELY CRAFTED STORIES
BY TALENTED WOMEN WRITERS

"A Woman Who Plays the Trumpet is Deported"
by Michelle Cliff

A black woman musician doesn't have much of a chance to make it in America in the 1930s, so she flees to Europe—but suffers more serious racial consequences there, in a powerfully imagined story by o

Dramatic comments
on the con dangerous
netherworl

" wn

The depth strength are
gracefully caring for
others is t

My Book

A bare n a home for
the narrat okes images
of the str

Joan Nestle is co-founder of the Lesbian Herstory Archive in New York City. She is the editor of *Persistent Desire: A Femme-Butch Reader* and co-editor, with the late John Preston, of *Sister and Brother: Gay Men and Lesbians Talk About Their Lives Together*. **Naomi Holoch** is a novelist and professor of French Literature at SUNY-Purchase. Together, they have edited all three volumes of Plume's *Women on Women* series.

REGISTERED TRADEMARK—MARCA REGISTRADA

LIBRARY OF CONGRESS CATALOGING-IN-PUBLICATION DATA

Women on women 3 : an anthology of American lesbian short fiction/
edited by Joan Nestle and Naomi Holoch.
    p. cm.
    ISBN 0–452–27661–6
     1. Lesbians—United States—Social life and customs—Fiction.
2. Short stories, American—Women authors. 3. Lesbians' writing,
American. I. Nestle, Joan. II. Holoch, Naomi.
PS648.L47W67   1996
813'.01089287'086643—dc20   95–50787
                                  CIP

Printed in the United States of America
Set in Kabel and Times Roman

Contents

Editors' Preface ix

From *Riverfinger Women*
    Elana Nachman/Dykewomon 13

From *Sita*   *Kate Millet* 23

Home   *Barbara Smith* 27

Flossie's Going   *Ellen Frye* 34

Salisbury Jo   *Frankie Hucklenbroich* 43

A Woman Who Plays Trumpet Is Deported
    Michelle Cliff 66

One Day at the Mace Factory   *Leslie Feinberg* 72

Preface from *Spoken in Darkness*   *Ann Imbrie* 77

The Printer   *Melanie Kaye/Kantrowitz* 96

Crystal Ball   *Lu Vickers* 104

Convoy *and* And the Skies Are Not   *Sheila Ortiz Taylor* 112

blueberry   *Clover L. Cannady* 118

Why I'm Here   *Lucy Jane Bledsoe*   121

Phase Two   *Catherine Lewis*   142

Leap of Faith   *Hilary Mullins*   155

The Gift of Wholeness   *Rebecca Brown*   172

Sign *and* I Wanted to Add   *Linda Smukler*   179

Garden Blues   *Sarah Lane*   182

The Vanish   *Mary Beth Caschetta*   189

To Be Like That   *Leslie Pietrzyk*   202

Vera   *Minnie Bruce Pratt*   215

There's a Window   *Sapphire*   218

The Faintest of Rumbles   *Cynthia Lollar*   223

A Kosher Megila   *Lexa Roséan*   243

Julie   *Susan Fox Rogers*   254

A Room, in a Stone House, in Spain   *Jenifer Levin*   270

What We Do in Bed   *Lydia Swartz*   281

The Vale of Cashmere   *Gerry Gomez Pearlberg*   286

Lines in the Sand, Cries of Desire   *Riki Anne Wilchins* 298

Killer in Love   *Sarah Schulman*   310

An American in Chiapas   *Nisa Donnelly*   316

Family Reunion   *Ann Allen Shockley*   327

Author Biographies   341

Editors' Preface

Joan Nestle

For a very long time, lesbians were trapped in the narratives of others. Through centuries of fiction and poetry, the Sapphic woman was used as an exotic or monstrous element, adding sensuous color or moralistic punch to racy texts. In the "true" stories of doctors, lawyers, and clerics, the mannish woman and her childlike lover were represented as a dangerous distortion of human sexual nature. But when we started writing our own stories, particularly in the second half of the twentieth century, it became clear that, for the lesbian writer, fiction was a way to be real.

Whatever fictional stance is taken by the lesbian author, whatever stylistic innovations she uses to break the conventions of the "expected," and however far removed the characters are from herself, her fiction carries the authority of a true story—because it is. A story told because no one else could do it, a voice created because no one else cared to do it, a language honed because so much was useless, a body delineated because it was at the heart of the story. Lesbian literature becomes a homeland because so much is still in battle, so much is still not possible.

When I wrote the afterword for the first volume of *Women on*

Women in 1989, gathered around me were the shadows of all the lesbian stories that had never found life in print. Of course, a few had occasionally come to light in small journals, shimmering with homoerotic hints, like Helen Essary Ansell's "The Threesome" in the 1962 edition of *Story* Magazine. In that afterword, I thanked lesbian pioneers like the editors of *The Ladder* and Elly Bulkin, one of the first anthologizers of lesbian short fiction.

Now, just seven years later, a full and lusty crowd of lesbian anthologies thrive in a wide variety of bookstores. For this third volume alone, we received close to three hundred submissions. The lesbian short story is on its way to becoming a literary tradition, a narrative form that allows for complex, completed moments of insight or disturbance, of passion or subversion. A new generation of writers has won for us a territory of possibilities, a place to be real in the most fictional of ways.

Naomi Holoch

Is it possible that there is a kind of freedom in the very absence of a tradition of stories and histories? After all, as Elana Dykewomon wrote in 1974, ". . . being unable to find catchwords in newspapers or the books we read in our dormitories, for *that*, for what *that* meant, women loving women—in *that* we could have no fads." As we have written more, spoken more, resisted more, as "community" has become more visible, so sidestepping and resisting our own "fads" has sometimes proved difficult. The ways in which we view and judge one another can be as complex and constraining as the ways in which we are viewed. The danger from "inside" as well as "outside" is in telling only *a* story, instead of stories. Happily, as witnessed by the ever-increasing number of lesbian writers being published, and by the diversity of narratives included in this volume alone, there is little such danger now.

But it is not only the telling that is important; it is also the listening. Too often, when confronted with diversity, we choose to hear only what is familiar, comfortable, reassuring; resisting a story perhaps because its content evokes a brutally painful reality, or because it critiques a political stance or institution with which we identify or have viewed from a discreetly respectful distance. Or because it paints in words fantasies or acts, sexual or otherwise, that ignore the boundaries of the "acceptable."

When the writer breaks with traditional storytelling, style and form may also ask the reader to "listen" in a different way. This sometimes requires a certain imaginative effort on the part of the reader, though the freshness of voice and image offers its own rewards. Without the attentive, adventurous reader, a text, any text, runs the risk of existing as a lonely shut-in.

Without listening there is no love. There is nothing. Doc knew this. He hated interrupters. He despised them. They don't let other people say their words. They lock them up, wrote Sarah Schulman in her novel *Empathy.*

It is our hope that readers find themselves at home in some of these pages, but on the high seas in others; and that our selections will prove to be an invitation to a freeing and open-ended voyage for the readers, the authors, and the stories themselves.

From *Riverfinger Women*
Elana Nachman/Dykewomon

Lucy Bear and Rainbo Woman have disappeared. Therefore I, Inez Riverfingers, set down this, the pornographic novel of my life, with no regrets. The dough rises anyway, pierced as it is by arrows, and bleeding small bees that hover about the kitchen, searching for honey.

I have wondered what people who don't make love all the time do with their lives—and I have wondered this even though I have made love only six times this year, and was interrupted by the police one of those nights. They must have mistaken my abandoned Sunday school, with its red urinal, for the abandoned birth-control clinic down the block. Or possibly, they were agents of the Committee (my friends tell me that's paranoia, and maybe it is, and maybe it's not).

They say it's sex that makes everyone crazy, and I believe it, though I am not quite sure how it happened.

End of Introduction. I am Inez Riverfingers, and I come complete with a vast family of the same. Some of their names: Ratatoville Riverfingers, Little Noodles Riverfingers, Natasha Riverfingers, Gabi-dog Riverfingers, Eulalee Riverfingers, Delphine Riverfingers, Holly Riverfingers, Bruce and San Fernando Blondie Riverfingers, Maggie and Al Bear Riverfingers, Peggy Warren (a closet Riverfinger), and Abigail, otherwise known as

Abby Riverfingers (who chastises me now, years after, in her letters from Jerusalem, for not taking another steady lover—god knows I've tried, but it's not an easy life for a dyke). Pickpockets, poets, acrobats, sociologists, tough street women, farmers and friends.

This list-making reminds me of the *Iliad*. Homer squatting to take a shit on a hot day in the Aegean counting off the names, as his fingers rubbed the white rocks near the water-on-fire-beneath-its-blue-skin that he could not see, rambling on about many-horsed whomever.

"Who's that old fart, daddy?"

"Traveling storyseller son, one of that degenerate kind that go around buggering their own sex, relieving themselves on other people's lawns, blind to the beauty of the true cosmos, telling lies and getting drunk shamelessly on other men's hard-earned drachmas. Don't bother with him. On to the Agora."

Inez Riverfingers the first. Vital Statistics: 5'3", 160 pounds approximately, 22 years old, lesbian, fresh scar on left wrist, old scar over left eye, appendix scar, light scar on bottom chin from times it was knocked in ten-year-old rage on the pool edge, scar at base of throat from almost successful thirteen-year-old suicide, brown eyes, huge breasts, brown hair down to same, fair & smooth-skinned, limps on left foot, small hands, bites nails, has never been known to mess with explosives, needs new boots and a dog of her own.

Living patiently in the abandoned Sunday school. Stuck here to tell the stories. Of Abby who was her steady true love for over two years, starting ten days before they graduated from high school. Of Peggy Warren who is friend to both of them and queen of the slightly seamy. Stuck here, at the end of another atypical early seventies college career, with only the memory, the smell of memory, of Rainbo Woman and Lucy Bear.

It's quiet in the abandoned Sunday school, living with straight women, unformed women. Only the two-dimensional canvas comforts the hungry eye: young girls, summer, 1971; summer, '67; summer, '54; summer, '48; summer, '32—the young girls, the summer, the Scottish love songs, the young men getting their trousers sewn while the trousers are still on them, these years and the young girls sending boys away in the middle of the night, the hesitant one A.M. conversations:

"Well, what are you doing Monday night?"

"How should I know?"

"Well, I'm having a birthday party in the mountains, and I'd like it if you could come."

"Oh—oh, in that case, sure, if I can get back by Tuesday—I'm running off to join the circus, seriously, and learn trapeze, and I have to train on Tuesdays."

The young girls, their hair pulled back, their flannel nightgowns, their dogs, their kittens—their eventual marriages, their eventual children, their eventual returning and saying to the odd person out: "What happened to us? We did not mean to squander our world as we saw the world squandered. We did not really mean to give up so much of our young lives to raising children, to all the problems of having children, to reading Dr. Spock, making contracts with our husbands about the kitchen. We meant to live in the Eye of Art, live by danger and by cunt cunning, by sharp pleasure and deep understanding—then how did we end up with these frog eyes with their filmy lids, tell us, tell us!"

I have not always been in these rooms, listening to and telling these stories. I have traveled in great arcs across the big cities of America and Europe, and the arches were always her legs.

For when she moved on top of me, sleepily, I thought: a giant ant lives inside her skin, ready to pop out any second devouring and I am frightened of her I cannot understand how it is, that we are all in such different bodies.

Girls in boarding schools, years with sadists, black leather jackets worn self-consciously, men picked up on Greyhound buses, one-night stands, Baltimore slums, New York and S.F. gay bars, hashish-smuggling out of Tangiers, sisters and brothers in their underwear (looking at each other, listening to grandmother snore in the next room), funerals, acid and mescaline,

the first promise of an armed women's nation, the coming together and the dropping away, days on the road, police in the
night, taking over city hall in Oregon, planning the deals right,
pimping on the side, code after code, a different language for
everyone and everything—it is all true, and there are some
who'd give large amounts for definite verification.

In a moment I will conjure Abby Riverfingers and Peggy Warren and the burden of inventing myself again will wear off, the
story will begin. Peggy who is somewhere in Michigan or Minnesota, or was two weeks ago, making her way across to this
coast; and Abby, one and one-half years distant, only letters in
the space between San Fernando Valley and the Promised Land.

Moments have passed, and I will make Abby reappear. It is
as easy as this, a voice squeezed from black plastic keys, telling
stories in bed. The hammering of myself into the background
will seem to be over. This hammering, this background—the
language of our getting older, the time of our being no longer
children but young women, that is to say, forming into identifiable shapes, it is not simple. From time to time you will hear
that faint tackety-tackety-tackety, like kids at summer camp,
making bronze name plates in relief dot by dot:

these are our lives, these are our lives, these are our lives.

"Once upon a time there was a wonderful bear, named Lucy.
She lived in the deep magic forest, on the other side of Talking
River. What made Lucy wonderful was not only how strong she
was, not only how beautiful—all gold and orange-colored in the
early sun—but how kind she was, gentle with all the other animals in that forest no man has ever found. She never ate fish
the way bears in the world do, she would sing duets with them
instead as they swam along Talking River. She helped the bees
scout for good clover, and had learned the secret bee dance, so
she could tell them where it was. The bees rewarded her by
giving her all the honey she needed, which she would eat along
with all the other wonderful berries that grew all year long. But
there weren't many other animals her size in that place, so she
grew lonely and restless. One day the River noticed that she was

singing fewer and fewer duets, and peering farther and farther over the River's edge.

" 'What are you looking for, Lucy?' the River asked.

" 'I'm looking for someone big enough to dance with me,' she said. 'I'm thinking of crossing to find others more like myself.'

" 'Oh no, Lucy!' the River cried. 'There are dangerous men on the other side, who will capture you and dress you in ridiculous skirts and charge a price for your dancing and make you eat flesh, and keep you locked up for their own amusement—either that, or they'll shoot you outright.'

" 'But there must be another kind of people besides these men.'

" 'There is. There is another kind that walks, called women, but they're mostly afraid—afraid of each other and the men and of what the men tell them. Among them there are some who aren't afraid, who are trying to know something different, but they are outlaws and in hiding. One, called Rainbo Woman, is heading this way alone. Wait for her to come.'

" 'Okay,' said Lucy. So she waited, and began dancing the bee dance again, to pass the time.''

"Will she have to wait a long time, for Rainbo Woman to come?'' asked Inez, rubbing Abby's neck with her nose.

"I don't know yet. Stop that, it tickles, bum,'' Abby said.

"And when Rainbo Woman comes, will she turn Lucy Bear into a beautiful woman, will they live happily ever after?''

"Well, now, kid, I don't rightly know. You're getting ahead of the story. Maybe Lucy Bear will turn Rainbo Woman into Rainbo Bear, and they'll spend the rest of their nights growling at each other, their stomachs full of blueberries.''

Abby turns to look at Inez in the Colorado street light, in their first apartment, a two-room converted attic. Peggy Warren sleeps in the other room, which is also the kitchen. Inez is curled on her side, cuddled into the hollow of Abby's thin arm, looking up. They fit. Seventeen, eighteen, thin to fat, not self-conscious, pleased to be there, seam against seam. Their hands trace each other, begin to touch as leaves touch in first summer winds.

Unbelievable. All the forces of civilization had worked against this, still it happened. They made love again that day, the last time before falling asleep. They had the freedom to touch while they were still children. No one had given them permission. They just made it all up, taking their freedom with their hands in front.

There was nothing in either of them that was older than seven, except that they knew how to do it, finally, after five weeks they had figured one hole from another. There were no movements putting pressure on their consciences, only safety in being two together. There was only the fairy tale, being seventeen and sleeping in each other's arms in Colorado. These small protections they wove like nets, to keep away what they understood perfectly.

They understood perfectly about names and rumors, psychiatrists and angry fathers, perverts, rotten ungrateful selfish vain children, disgust and fear, more fear, self-hatred, confusion, no women will let us baby-sit for their children if they find out.

They were beginning to learn to protect themselves by never touching or looking at each other in public. By waiting until they got into gas-station restrooms when they wanted to kiss each other. By calling themselves roommates. By watching other people very carefully. By being children only together, in their first double bed. Sometimes they were open with Peggy, who never told them until three years later that she was jealous, for wanting to join them.

Abby accepted it, because it was safe and at the same time exciting, a little dangerous—she knew it felt good, and she wanted it. She was very stubborn about what she wanted, when she was positive that she wanted it.

She had been stubborn with her parents for two years now about her independence. About not going to a Long Island suburban high school anymore after tenth grade. Her mother had screamed and cried, and her father had consoled her mother by sending Abby away to boarding school—first to an experimental school in the South which Abby had hated almost as much as the suburban one, and then to Highland Hills in Massachusetts, where she met Peggy and Inez. She was also stubborn with her

parents about not taking any more money from them, except for
school. She was stubborn to be on her own, to start really running, to build muscles at least eight ways. The plans for the
octagonal cabin she was going to build in the wilderness were
all drawn up, down to even which way the doors would slide.
There would be room in her life to travel cross-country on horse-
back, and there would be room for horses to live inside her cabin
in the cold mountain winters. She would take care of all the
animals that would come to her, and she wouldn't bother with
people.

Back on Long Island her family was saying: She'll grow out
of it. It's a phase. So we spoiled her a little, because she was
our youngest daughter, we let her be a tomboy, and she got a
little willful. But she's young still, there's plenty of time for her
to get married, like her sisters.

Whether or not they'd drag her back if they learned about
Inez, about what was going on, was a question Abby was not
about to risk answering.

She knew better than to trust almost anyone. She almost knew
better than to trust Inez. What she saw was that Inez was a little
crazy. Many a woman has been a sucker for that one. Feeling
protective. If only you would stop looking at your eyes reflected
in windows, if only you would be happy, Inez, and ride horse-
back across country with me. We could take care of stray animals together.

Abby picked up worms so they wouldn't get run over in the
middle of the street. She began to see Inez the same way she
saw her cat, or the horses in her fantasies. To have that feeling
about Inez, that she needed and would simply accept protection,
returning simple sexual affection, was to come very close to
trust.

Still Abby wasn't sure. What is this sex and living together?
What is going on here? She knew it wasn't wrong, it couldn't
be wrong, to feel this. But what do the words mean anyway?

She knew that she would not let Inez hurt her, that no human
being would get that close to her. She knew people wielded
power over each other, seeing how her mother and father, good

middle-class Jewish people, controlled each other with the power to make each other miserable. She saw all people trying to get that edge, parents over children, teachers over students, bosses over workers, lovers over lovers. She didn't understand why it was, but she knew she did not want it. She would go alone into the mountains first, with her camera, and be with the animals.

Inez heard Abby when she said, "I don't like people, I am better company for just myself, I'd rather be a hermit." But Inez knew that she could get Abby to follow her, just the same.

There are powers, there are ways, and Inez knew about them. Guiltily she extended a paw toward Abby, saying: I too am a creature, I am a wounded creature, nurture me. There was just enough attraction in their bodies and confusion in their heads to bind them.

A thousand fantasies multiply in that feeling—of marriages, weddings, houses hung with ribbons of safety. Abby was the first person who didn't hurt Inez—didn't make her feel freakish and clumsy. Inez knew what that meant, what the game was, how you had to hold onto it, opportunity only knocks once, she had read about it in books, she had read a lot of books, now it was her turn to play, to use her real body as a marker in the game. It would be good, it would be gentle, it would be so tender that they could make a movie, and get someone else to play her part (who wasn't quite so heavy). They could make a movie about Inez and Abby, so that people would see that lesbians are beautiful, there is nothing, nothing at all unnatural about them, they too can have weddings and be in the movies.

Some pornographic novel! Some novel! What's going on here anyway? Where's the sex, where's the action, the angst?

Let me try to make it clear. In 1967 we still wanted to repeat the same straight story. But we knew even then, in our careful duplications (toasters, laundry, feeding the cats, a whole inventory of living together), that we were pornographic because we were both women.

Nothing else—we were too modern already to believe that one

of us was the man and the other was the woman. We felt like neither men nor women. We were females, we were queers ("but I'm not a lesbian," Abby said in Colorado, "I just love you, Inny."). We knew we had the right to love whomever we loved—it was part of the amorphous thought of a sexual revolution we found ourselves in the middle of. It was very democratic, theoretical, and very, very personal. And we knew that when we made the movie about how good it was, how after all lesbians could live normal lives, have jobs, go to college, how they were the same, the same, really the same as straight people, only they were both women, but that was just—an accident—a matter of—chemistry—we knew that when men came to see the movie we would make, the men would come because it was pornographic, that's all, baby, sinful, immoral and certainly absurd for women to think they could do it without them.

Let me try to make it clear. There is Inez. There is Abby. They became lovers when they were seventeen. This is the story of what it means to be women and lovers when you are seventeen, with the years just behind (moving them toward it), and the years just ahead, with everyone waiting to say, uh-huh, just as we thought!

There is Peggy Warren. She is smuggling hash from Tangiers, accumulating a thousand tattooed stories behind her eyes like veils that keep even her old friends away. She's been sleeping with every kind of man there is, sadists, baby pimps and North Pole engineers. She comes to speak about heroin and the (real) 42nd Street porno trade, massage parlors and organized crime. She is an old friend of Abby and Inez.

There are all the places where these stories touch each other and make the start of a common life, the beginning of an idea about community. There are all the places where the story falls apart and something else shows through—an isolation, a terror, a hunger to shape that isolation and terror into some kind of love for ourselves.

A hunger for each other, two hungers, three: one out of fear; one for metamorphosis (to be girls no longer, to be women, and

serious); one for actual love, whatever it is. There is a first pow-
erfulness in knowing what our hungers are, that they may not
be taken from us and be sold by Tampax or Pepsi-Cola.

When you're talking about someone's body, that's about as
close as you can get. This is how it worked in our bodies, how
our hungers worked into our bones. There was authority at every
pressure point, trying to direct us (for our own good). We fought
back with fads that nearly killed us. And slowly in our bodies
words grew, formed a strength against both the fads and the
pressures of our mentors.

We thought we were very special then, we thought we were
hot shit, for being perfectly existentially unique, reading all the
books by men about ultimate aloneness and the isolation of mass
man.

We were exactly like millions and millions of others in the
sixties and seventies and long before and after, self-important
with big words like alienation and technological elite. It's the
same story for every girl and boy adolescent who knuckled under
waves of words they couldn't own: sexual revolution and hard
rock and LSD. We were scraped along the sharp stones of those,
where the undertow dragged us.

But in being faceless unmentionable nameless lesbians, un-
approved by Ann Landers or Jerry Rubin, in being unable to find
catchwords in newspapers or the books we read in our dormitories, for that, for what that meant, women loving women—in
that we could have no fads. That was where some of us began
our resistance, learned to change (acid on stone) who we thought
we were doomed to be into who we are. Tough, strong, proud:
free women.

From *Sita*
Kate Millett

Unexpectedly, I remembered what it was like. Realizing only through the contrast. In the coffeehouse last night, one of my students reading a poem describing some lovers. It was all there again, the frankness, the joy, the ease and intimacy of bed. Sitting up and chatting, laughing, getting up for coffee, diving back into the flesh again. As the poet read I could feel the sliding fabric of sheets, mornings of lovemaking, coffee cups, whole afternoons of sex, sunlight that is luxury and time without hurry, without goals, only the goal of living in that high moment which is forever, both past and future, that second which expands to fill the world, blotting out childhood and old age, transforming each segment of life into the refracted light of now, the moment to which all others led and can only follow.

And I thought of our taut and nervous bodies now, like two long, gray metal bars laid parallel in bed. Suddenly it seemed curious that we can sleep at all, our flesh now so without ease or spontaneity. So out of touch and harmony. But it did happen once. And that's what I remember now, having almost forgotten it. How we sat up in bed and chattered, drank wine, smoked. Sacramento those first dawns, making love before classes or as soon as the world released us into evening. The speed and grace with which she removed her clothes, how it always astonished

me. Quite wonderfully, without shame or hesitation. Her arms
removing a blouse on entering the room. And suddenly she
would be there in her brown skin and flanks, the great brown
circles of her nipples. And we had all that, that ease, the freedom
of feeling, quick and alive, young in our joy, our frank knowing
of each other in flesh and spirit and talk. Such a feast of talk,
endless talk. Our naked bodies moving between bed and bath
and kitchen, downstairs to the coffee or the plants, the talk con-
tinuous, witty and relaxed, intimate but objective, or gossiping
or partisan, lofty or flippant, talking of a book or a meeting or
a personality. How it all flowed.

The little bedroom there, its shadowy light of candles the
nights she visited, its pearl-gray mornings after I had stayed up
all night reading for a class, having to cram because we had
spent the evening in lovemaking. And then she would sleep
while I kept vigil, doing the two hundred necessary pages before
a nine o'clock. I cross the hall from my study, sensing the
strange pale light, knowing that now I must wake her. Hesitating,
hating to do it. But after a moment, there is no sorrow at all—
we were never tired. Sita waking to love again and a shower and
coffee. Mornings when her presence, her great happiness was
like a song through the house, through the coffee, through the
clean early sunlight. How different we are these mornings.
Strained little moments at the dining-room table, each reading
the paper. Or if she does not read, I also forbear in courtesy.
And the hope of a moment's attention. But I lust for the paper,
the opiate of it, the cover to our emptiness, our so obvious
emptiness.

It is the distance of our bodies. That more than anything, that
is the index, that our bodies no longer know each other in the
same way as once, are no longer friends. It is the distance in our
bodies. And our minds and our souls. But you see it in the bodies. If you can even remember, of course. But I remembered
it in the poet's phrase, a certain piquant image of lovers and
their bodies, the good friendliness of their bodies in bed, their
good will, their excited, almost childlike escape from all self-
consciousness, their special camaraderie. Only then did I feel the

loss, the difference, and understand the terrible change. As lovers how our movements now are curtailed. It is difficult for us to be ample, attend to the whole body, be generous with care and attention; I cannot throw back the covers and find her thighs with my mouth. Our lovemaking is cut-rate now, short of fabric, skimpy. Like girls in boarding school fearful of waking a house mistress, campers sly not to arouse the counselors—no, they all enjoy themselves—like prisoners, then. Like prisoners, stealthy and adroit, minimal. Sly we are, secretive. As if we were ashamed.

Once how far otherwise, free with our flesh, our bodies nude from room to room, unconcerned about our cries through the thin little apartment walls. And now, merely this hasty little act below the covers, this mockery. Hidden, out of sight. Is it always so, the end of love? Always that abbreviation of the former drama, its play and invention and embroidery, its long serene caresses snipped, eliminated, pruned, divested of their ritual, leaving only a quick push for orgasm—the goal, the finish, the having it over?

It was not a remarkable poem, only that it conveyed the magnetism between bodies; together with their innocence, their friendliness even. And that made me understand, with one blow, measure the distance and be appalled. What do you do then, when you realize you have fallen so far, when you can calculate and must admit it, like an account finally investigated by a bank auditor, the evidence confounding you? What do you do? Admit it's gone? Leave? Or relapse into vacancy, into not knowing, into hope, into expecting change? Do you confer? But conferences are already admissions of failure, and our failure is too ominous to withstand a conference. If I take a hard line, if I say it is over, she will agree. If I do not, she will go on about the years ahead, how I "will always be a part of her life," how we are in a "stage," a particular "moment of growth." And say that she loves me, with that diluted, almost sisterly affection she now considers love. But we are not lovers, our flesh has lost its knowledge of each other. Not only that glorious electrical affinity that kept us up all night, but even its relaxation, its contentment, its friendship. And you cannot define something so nebulous as the trust between bodies. Or restore it merely by taking note of its absence.

If I had not listened to this poem. If I had not remembered. If I had not realized. If I did not know.

Home
Barbara Smith

I can't sleep. I am sitting at an open window, staring at the dark sky and the barely visible nighttime gardens. Three days ago we came here to clean and paint this apartment in the new city we're moving to. Each night I wake up, shoulders aching, haunted by unfamiliarity. Come to this window. Let the fresh air and settled look of neighborhood backyards calm me until exhaustion pulls me back to bed.

Just now it was a dream that woke me. One of my dreams.

I am at home with Aunt LaRue and I am getting ready to leave. We are in the bedroom packing. I'm anxious, wonder if she can feel a change in me. It's been so long since I've seen her. She says she has a present for me and starts pulling out dozens of beautiful vests and laying them on the bed. I am ecstatic. I think, "She knows. She knows about me and it's all right." I feel relieved. But then I wake up, forgetting for a minute where I am or what has happened until I smell the heavy air, see Leila asleep beside me. The dream was so alive.

I felt as if I'd been there. Home. The house where I grew up. But it's been years since then. When Aunt LaRue died, I had to sell the house. My mother, my grandmother, all the women who'd raised me were already dead, so I never go back.

I can't explain how it feels sometimes to miss them. My child-

ish desire to see a face that I'm not going to see. The need for
certitude that glimpsing a profile, seeing a head bent in some
ordinary task would bring. To know that home existed. Of course
I know they're gone, that I won't see them again, but there are
times when my family is so real to me, at least my missing them
is so real and thorough, I feel like I have to do something, I
don't know what. Usually I dream.

Since we got here, I think of home even more. Like today
when we were working, I found a radio station that played
swing . . .

Every so often one of us sings a few lines of a song. I say,
"Imagine. It's 1945, the War's over, you've come back, and
we're fixing up our swell new place."

Leila laughs. "You're so crazy. You can bet whoever lived
here in 1945 wasn't colored or two women either."

"How do you know? Maybe they got together when their
husbands went overseas and then decided they didn't need the
boys after all. My aunt was always telling me about living with
this friend of hers, Garnet, during the War and how much fun
they had and how she was so gorgeous."

Leila raises her eyebrows and says, "Honey, you're hopeless.
You didn't have a chance hearing stories like that. You had to
grow up funny. But you know my mother is always messing
with my mind too, talking about her girlfriends this and her
girlfriends that. I think they're all closet cases."

"Probably," I answer. We go on working, the music playing
in the background. I keep thinking about Aunt LaRue. In the
early fifties she and her husband practically built from scratch
the old house they had bought for all of us to live in. She did
everything he did. More, actually. When he left a few years later
she did "his" work and hers too, not to mention going to her
job every day. It took the rest of her life to pay off the mortgage.

I want to talk to her. I imagine picking up the phone.

Hi Aunt LaRue. Ahunh, Leila and I got here on Monday. She's
fine. The apartment's a disaster area, but we're getting it together. . . .

Leila is asking me where the hammer is and the conversation in my head stops. I'm here smoothing plaster, inhaling paint. On the radio Nat King Cole is singing "When I Marry Sweet Lorraine." Leila goes into the other room to work. All afternoon I daydream I'm talking with my aunt. This move has filled me up with questions. I want to tell someone who knew me long ago what we're doing. I want her to know where I am.

Every week or so Leila talks to her mother. It's hard to overhear them. I try not to think about it, try to feel neutral and act like it's just a normal occurrence, calling home. After battling for years, Leila and her mother are very close. Once she told me, "Everything I know is about my family." I couldn't say anything, thought, "So what do I know?" Not even the most basic things like, what my father was like and why Aunt Rosa never got married. My family, like most, was great at keeping secrets. But I'd always planned when I got older and they couldn't treat me like a kid to ask questions and find out. Aunt LaRue died suddenly, a year after I'd been out of college and then it was too late to ask a thing.

For lack of information I imagine things about them. One day a few weeks ago when I was packing, going through some of Aunt LaRue's papers, I found a bankbook that belonged to both my mother and Aunt LaRue. They had opened the account in 1946, a few months before I was born and it had been closed ten years later, a few months after my mother died. The pages of figures showed that there had never been more than $200 in it. Seeing their two names together, their signatures side by side in dark ink, I got a rush of longing. My mother touched this, held it in her hands. I have some things that belonged to Aunt LaRue, dishes and stuff that I use around the house, even the letters she wrote to me when I was in college. But Mommy died so long ago, I have almost nothing that belonged to her.

I see them the day they open the account. Two young Black women, one of them pregnant, their shoulders square in forties dresses, walking into the cavernous downtown bank. I wonder what they talk about on the bus ride downtown. Or maybe my mother comes alone on the bus and meets Aunt LaRue at work.

How does my mother feel? Maybe she senses me kicking inside her as they wait in line. As they leave she tells my aunt, touching her stomach, "I'm afraid." My aunt takes her hand.

I wonder what they were to each other, specifically. What their voices might have sounded like talking as I played in the next room. I know they loved each other, seemed like friends, but I don't have the details. I could feel my aunt missing my mother all through my childhood. I remember the way her voice sounded whenever she said her name. Sometimes I'd do something that reminded her of my mother and she would laugh, remember a story, and say I was just like Hilda. She never pretended that she didn't miss her. I guess a lot of how they loved each other, my aunt gave to me.

But I wonder how someone can know me if they can't know my family, if there's no current information to tell. Never to say to a friend, a lover, "I talked to my mother yesterday and she said. . . ." Nothing to tell. Just a blank where all that is supposed to be. Sometimes I feel like I'm frozen in time, caught in a nightmare of a hot October afternoon when everything changed because my mother stopped living.

Most of my friends have such passionate, complicated relationships with their mothers. Since they don't get married and dragged off into other families, they don't have to automatically cut their ties, be grown-up heterosexuals. I think their mothers help them to be Lesbians. I'm not saying that their mothers necessarily approve, but that they usually keep on loving their daughters because they're flesh and blood, even if they are "queer." I envy my friends. I'd like to have a woman on my side who brought me here. Yes, I know it's not that simple, that I tend to romanticize, that it can be hell especially about coming out. But I still want what they have, what they take for granted. I always imagine with my aunt, it would have been all right.

Maybe I shouldn't talk about this. Even when Leila says she wants to hear about my family and how it was for me growing up, I think sometimes she really doesn't. At least she doesn't want to hear about the death part. Like everyone, a part of her is terrified of her mother dying. So secretly I think she only wants to know from me that it can be all right, that it's not so bad, that it won't hurt as much. My mother died when I was nine. My father had left long before. My aunt took care of me after that. I can't prove to Leila or anybody that losing them did not shatter my life at the time, that on some level I still don't deal with this daily, that my life remains altered by it. I can only say that I lived through it.

The deaths in your life are very private. Maybe I'm waiting for my friends to catch up, so our conversations aren't so one-sided. I want to talk like equals.

More than anything, I wish Leila and I could go there, home. That I could make the reality of my life now and where I came from touch. If we could go, we would get off the bus that stops a block from the house. Leila and I would cross 130th Street and walk up Abell. At the corner of 132nd I would point to it, the third house from the corner. It would still be white and there would be a border of portulaca gleaming like rice paper along the walk. We would climb the porch steps and Leila would admire the black and gray striped awnings hanging over the upstairs and downstairs porches.

The front door would be open and I would lead the way up the narrow stairs to the second floor. Aunt LaRue would be in the kitchen. Before I would see her, I'd call her name.

She'd be so glad to see me and to meet Leila. At first she'd be a little formal with Leila, shy. But gradually all of us would relax. I'd put a record on the hi-fi and Ella would sing in the background. Aunt LaRue would offer us ''a little wine'' or some gin and tonic. I'd show Leila the house and Aunt LaRue's flowers in the back. Maybe we'd go around the neighborhood, walk the same sidewalks I did so many years ago. For dinner we'd have rolled roast and end up talking till late at night.

Before we'd go to bed, Aunt LaRue would follow me into the bathroom and tell me again, shyly, ''Your friend's so nice and down to earth. She's like one of us.'' I'd tell Leila what she'd said, and then we'd sleep in the room I slept in all the while I was growing up.

Sometimes with Leila it's like that. With her it can be like family. Until I knew her, I thought it wasn't possible to have that with another woman, at least not for me. But I think we were raised the same way. To be decent, respectful girls. They taught us to work. And to rebel.

Just after we met, Leila and her roommate were giving a party. That afternoon her roommate left and didn't come back for hours so I ended up helping Leila get things ready. As we cleaned and shopped and cooked, it hit me that almost without talking, we agreed on what needed to be done. After years of having to explain, for instance, why I bothered to own an iron, it felt like a revelation. We had something in common, knew how to live in a house like people, not just to camp.

When we first started living together I would get deja vu, waves of feelings that I hadn't had since I'd lived in that other place, home. Once Leila was in the bathroom and I glimpsed her through the door bending over the tub, her breasts dropping as she reached to turn off the water. It was familiar. The steady comfort of a woman moving through the house.

I don't want to lose that moving here. This new place is like a cave. The poverty of the people who lived here before is trapped in the very walls. Harder than cleaning and painting is altering that sadness.

Tonight we made love here for the first time. It was almost midnight when we stopped working, showered and fell aching into the makeshift bed. When I started to give Leila a single kiss, her mouth caught mine and held me there. Desire surprised me, but then I realized how much everything in me wanted touch. Sometimes our bodies follow each other without will, with no thought of now I'll put my hand here, my mouth there. Tonight there was no strategy, just need and having. Falling into sleep, holding her, I thought, "Now there is something here I know." It calmed me.

But I have been afraid. Afraid of need, of loving someone

who can leave. The fear makes me silent, then gradually it closes my heart. It can take days to get beneath whatever haunts me, my spirit weakening like a candle sputtering in some place without air, underground. And Leila has her own nightmares, her own habits of denial. But we get through. Even when I'm most scared, I knew when I first met her that it would be all right to love her, that whatever happened we would emerge from this not broken. It would not be about betrayal. Loving doesn't terrify me. Loss does. The women I need literally disappearing from the face of the earth. It has already happened.

I am sitting at a table by a window. The sky is almost light. My past has left few signs. It only lives through words inside of me.

I get up and walk down the hall to the bathroom. If I can't get back to sleep, I'll never have the strength to work another fourteen-hour day. In the bedroom I take off my robe and lie down beside Leila. She turns in her sleep and reaches toward me. "Where were you?" she asks, eyes still closed.

I answer without thinking, "Home."

Flossie's Going

Ellen Frye

One look at White River Junction, the twins agreed: it was the
dirtiest, the darkest, the gloomiest old place they ever imagined.
No lights at the station—just train smoke and soot, screeching
wheels, and a conductor shouting an English they couldn't understand.

Millie was in tears, a cinder in her eye. She wanted to find
the next train to take them right back to Logieville—never mind
the forty-seven hours and five station changes. All the years she
lived in Vermont, she never forgot that first memory. After the
trains stopped running, you could at least see the sun when it
shined, and they paved over the mud. But mornings, she'd look
out the window, see hemlocks where there ought to have been
ocean, and wonder, What if we'd never left New Brunswick?

Flossie felt the same, but she had a different way to go. They
were fifteen when they came in on that midnight train. A redcap
was shouting, "Junction House! Junction House Hotel!" but that
wasn't where they were going. Two men were cussing a drove
of pigs. Flossie muttered, "That's as good a welcome as this
town is going to give us, pig shit and goddamns!" Millie
shushed her, but the mother was busy arguing with a man in a
taxi. A whistle blast drowned out the pig squeal; then they were

in the cab jolting over the tracks, mother and cabbie still debating the fare.

The father and brothers were already living in a boardinghouse on South Main, taking the Wells River local every afternoon for the graveyard shift up at Olcutt Falls. After Mr. Logie closed the mill, the three of them had walked across Maine and New Hampshire looking for work. Olcutt was the first place hiring, and they sent word for the women to pack their bags. Flossie and Millie dragged until the mother threatened the willow switch. Then one morning they were Sunday dressed and waiting at Delbert's Crossing. Delbert flagged the train, and that was the end of their childhood.

White River Junction is indeed a junction. Tracks for the Boston & Maine and the Central Vermont cross and crisscross. In 1915, fifty-five trains a day wheezed into that station. You could barely see the sun for all the soot and smoke.

The village had other charms, too. Springtime, the mud in the streets was ankle deep. You had to step on boards laid to the side. If somebody came the other way, you squeezed by. Some men pushed out their bellies, let their elbows just happen to brush your breasts. You'd lean as far as you could and pray to keep your balance. They'd laugh and leer.

Flossie took to wearing pants. By that time the family had rented the house on Green's Flat. Flossie came puffing up the hill one day, and Millie hardly knew her—braids stuffed under the father's cap, Wilbur's knickers hitched with a rope. "They don't do it," she snarled, "if you're not a girl!"

It wasn't the first time Flossie had dressed like a boy. Back in Logieville she loved a hand-me-down sailor suit the brothers had outgrown. The first time she fetched it from the rag bag, she couldn't have been more than seven. The raggedy shirt fell over her frame like a patched sail on a windless day. The mother had sent them down to the harbor to see if Uncle Jack was in yet on the morning mail run. He wasn't. They waited for him sitting in an old skiff on the beach. The tide came in, water lapped the stern. Flossie jumped out and started pushing. "Heave, ho!" she

hollered. The boat didn't move, but the tide kept coming in and
eventually they floated. They slapped the oars on the water and
played pirates, their schooner gliding over the boundary maine.
They didn't notice the leak until the water was over the floor-
boards. By that time they'd drifted almost to the harbor mouth.
The mail boat was just coming in, and Uncle Jack made the
rescue, but when they got home the mother sent them out back
to cut willow switches. The sailor suit she tore into pieces and
stuffed back into the rag bag. Flossie rescued it and pieced it
together with big loopy stitches. She hid it in the chicken coop
and only brought it out when the mother was taking tea with
Mrs. Fletcher down at the general store.

In White River Junction, Flossie hung her knickers and shirts
under a dressing gown on the back of the bedroom door. She
and Millie had claimed the third floor attic as their own, so the
room was safe from inspection by the mother. Flossie took to
trading the shopping for Millie doing the ironing. She liked
meeting the neighbors downtown, wishing them good morning
and watching them wonder who she was. One day she reported
to Millie how she'd helped Mrs. Closky with her groceries all
the way home. The old lady gave her a nickel and said, "Thank
you, young sir! So many have no manners these days, I wish
there were more boys like you."

"Boys like you!" Flossie giggled, then let her giggle turn into
a chortle, low, like Wilbur's. "Boys like me," she almost
growled. She stared out the kitchen window into the woods. It
was mostly birch out back, a few skinny walnuts. The hill was
all trees and ledge. Millie was pushing the iron across Clarence's
blue striped shirt. Flossie pulled a towel from the basket and
started folding. Four wild turkeys came out of the woods, picking
their way across the crusty snow. "Starving beggars!" said Millie, but Flossie scooped up a handful of wheat berries and flung
them out the back door. "No more than us," she said, still mad
at the father for not giving them nickels for the Lyric matinee.
"We work hard and beg for scraps." It'd been a morning of
hauling buckets and filling the washtub and bending over the
scrub board, so Millie didn't disagree. Flossie kept muttering,

folding the towels. The turkeys picked through their dinner. Millie handed Flossie the shirt to hang up, but Flossie held the shoulders to her own and eyed the fit.

"If that old biddie thought I was a boy and every jacknabber on the street thinks so, too, then why not?" Why not what? Millie started to say, but Flossie was already pulling her up the stairs. "Watch this," said Flossie. By that time, she had acquired a whole wardrobe—knickers, overalls, even a pair of long pants with suspenders. Millie watched the transformation from errand boy to sporting young man. "What do you think?" asked Flossie. "I think you're going to get a licking," said Millie, but she eyed Flossie's lean front with envy, her own bosoms a heavy embarrassment to her and nowhere to hide her fanny. "What's it like," she asked, "being a boy? I mean, besides not getting pinched."

"The best part," said Flossie, "is the running. You know how the deer lope when you startle them drinking at the lily pond? Running's like that. The wind rushes by your face, the ground goes thwack against your boots. Nobody cares if you're sweating. You can grin and belch all you want, it's like they don't see you, they don't hear you, you're invisible."

Millie knew invisible. It was what she always felt at the dinner table when the father and the brothers shoveled her cooking onto their plates and reached for the salt. But out in the world, longing for invisibility, she felt everyone's eyes were on her. Did her skirt hang right? Would anyone see the mending under the arm? Was a strand loose from her braids? She brushed a thread from Flossie's collar. "Where are you going?" she asked.

"I'm going to get paid for my work," said Flossie. "I'm going to get a job."

The bakery wasn't hiring, and the candy factory said come back in the spring, but the copy boy at the *Landmark News* had just run off to Canada to join up for the Great War. "Two dollars a week and all the coffee I can drink, if you call that boiled piss coffee," she announced to Millie. Millie could see the whole laundry'd be hers.

Flossie was careful not to let the mother see her going or

coming. "I raised you to be ladies," they were always hearing,
"and even if this town is rough and dirty, ladies you are going
to be." The mother wasn't native to Logieville. She'd been born
in Boston. Her father worked in the Post Office, her mother was
a milliner. She used to tell the girls about the dresses she wore
when she was their age—brocade, embroidery, braided button-
holes. She had black leather boots that buttoned to her knees.
And hats—every Sunday she and her mother would stroll
through Boston Garden just to show off the feathers.

When she met her husband-to-be, he was a dashing young
Canadian on holiday. Her father told her that calloused hands
meant a hard life but she said she didn't care about brocade and
embroidery. Later she cared. Two boys, two girls, and then, after
they got to White River Junction, another pair, one of each. The
twin factory, the father joked, but the last pair wore her out.

That was how Flossie got away wearing pants. The mother
would be up by dawn baking biscuits for the men to eat on the
train. She'd get the babies up and the day's work going and then
she'd just seem to wind down. She'd brush her hand in front of
her eyes as if black flies were at her, and her cheeks would draw
up, pale. "I've got a bit of a headache," she'd say. "I'll just lie
down for a minute." The longer they lived in White River Junction, the more the minutes became hours. Flossie'd be pantsed
and off to her newspaper job by eight, leave Millie the whole
house on her own. If the mother got up in the afternoon, Millie
would say Flossie was out shopping. The mother never seemed
to notice that the shopping always took until dinnertime. Meanwhile, Millie fed the Chubb stove and kept the babies out of the
clabbering milk and scrubbed the everlasting soot from the
windowsills.

Down at the *Landmark*, Flossie went by the name of Floyd.
She carried copy from the editor to the rewrite man and remembered who liked sugar in their coffee. She learned how to use a
typewriter, how to make the a's and the semicolons as dark as
the f's and the j's. She rifled the files for fillers and obits. She
waited for copy in the composition room, watching the lead slugs
drop into their places, the ink-smelling sheets emerge from the

machine. She reveled in the noise of the copy room, the panic when a big story clattered out of the teletype just before deadline, the editor's thundering until the front page was rearranged and the headline reset. She eyed the reporters, wondering what it would be like covering events and writing a story to fit the column inch. She never guessed her own chance would come, but it did.

It was a bright orange day, autumn's first woodsmoke in the air. Flossie came home early, talking a mile a minute about suffrage. Millie thought she said "women suffering," and said, "Of course, women suffer, look at our mother," but Flossie wasn't talking about headaches.

"We have got to have the vote," she said, waving her finger as if she were a schoolmarm, sleeves rolled up at the cuff. "If we're working women, like those women in the mill, then we have got to have our say about the laws of the workplace. If we're mothers, we have to control the conditions of health and education that affect our children." Millie stared at her, mop in hand. Even the babies stopped their jabber to listen.

Flossie had just come back from the packing-box factory. One of the reporters had been out sick, and the editor had sent her there to report on a disturbance. The disturbance turned out to be four women, one from Boston, the others from Montpelier. The Boston one talked from a soapbox. The others passed out handbills.

"Listen to this," said Flossie. She unfolded a paper, but she didn't get to read it. The mother stood in the kitchen doorway, her face holding back a storm. She snatched the handbill and tore it to shreds. The babies tried to catch the fluttering pieces.

"There'll be none of that talk in this house!" The mother's eyes were snapping. "No daughter of mine is going to be an unsexed freak." Just as she said that, she saw Flossie's pants. She blinked, brushed at her invisible black flies, turned heel, and left the kitchen.

Flossie took off her pants, but not for the mother's sake. Dorothy Hanscombe was the Boston suffrage lady, and Flossie was under her spell. She'd invited her to dinner, along with her three lady cohorts. All Millie had going was hog's head stew, but Flossie told her not to worry, the suffragists dressed like ladies but were everyday nice. She changed into her Sunday dress and made Millie change, too. Ironed fresh shirts for the father and the boys when they came in from the mill. The mother didn't come down all evening, but she would have been proud of the table Flossie set. The good silver with the forks and knives in their proper places, the Bavarian china—the mother's dowry— or at least as much as had made the move uncracked. Cattails from the lily pond filled the good blue vase. Flossie kept running to the window every two minutes, asking Millie did she think they'd be able to find the house, Green's Flat way up on top of the hill and the road so roundabout. But they did. Clarence and Wilbur couldn't get over a flivver parked at the foot of the street. They pestered the women about cylinders and spark plugs and how did she handle on the road. Dorothy impressed them with a story about taking apart the carburetor after driving through a puddle up to the hubcaps.

At the table, Flossie served the hog's head as if it were tenderloin. "Tell us about how women can make a difference," she urged Dorothy, but Dorothy was asking the father about conditions at the pulp mill. She smiled at him and patted her mouth with the napkin. She agreed that ripping logs was a man's job and that it was the man's job, too, to provide for the family. She invited the father to come to the evening rally, down in front of the Junction House. "Come," she said, "you'll hear how men and women can work together for a better society."

Flossie went to the rally in style, squeezed into the horseless buggy with Dorothy and her friends. The father and Millie took the footpath down the hill. A lot of people turned out and not just working women. A few of the parish ladies came and the three girls who lived across the street and even some of the Italian women from South Main, although the father whispered that they probably didn't know enough English to understand what Dorothy was saying. Men came, too—some to heckle and some because their wives or daughters made them and some just curious to see a lady on a soapbox.

Women's rights! Dorothy made it sound like history in the making. "Women must become, in the fullest sense, citizens of this nation." She told everyone that the female vote would put an end to war, to drug trafficking, to prostitution. It would better the health and welfare of every one. Especially mothers and babies. Millie thought about the mother and her headaches, lying so many hours in a darkened room, wincing at every bright light. How was voting going to stop that? But Dorothy's voice rang out through the night air, and even the hecklers listened.

Flossie didn't come home from the rally until after midnight, and then she kept Millie up until dawn talking women's rights. Dorothy had told her that you didn't have to be a man to work in a newspaper, that women could be reporters and even editors if they wanted. So the next day she put on a dress and marched down to the *Landmark*, said to the editor, "You know that story you published in this morning's edition about the rally? And the interview with the four suffragists?" As far as he was concerned, he'd never seen the girl before in his life. "Well," she said, "I wrote them and I'm going to write more for you." The old guy didn't bat an eye. "Twenty cents an inch!" crowed Flossie when she went home, "and my own byline." She didn't know every other reporter there had started on salary.

She liked writing her stories and seeing her name in the paper, but it wasn't enough to keep her there. Flossie wanted to fly, and White River Junction kept pulling her back to the ground. She tried to be a one-woman suffrage committee, getting one of the typesetters to show her how to run the compositor so she could publish her own handbills. All winter she trouped in and out of the twenty-two Italian markets on South Main Street, trying to edge her way past the counter to get to the women in back. Or up North Main she'd trudge to canvass the workers in the Vermont Bakery. The women of White River Junction just didn't seem to care. The girls across the street turned out to be "ladies of the night," dead set against suffrage. "Put an end to prostitution!" one of them scoffed. "And what are we to do then, work in the mill for a dollar a day?" And the women who worked in the woolen mill for a dollar a day asked what was the point in voting, their men voted and they all coughed blood anyway.

The only person who listened to her was the cook in the Greek restaurant, a woman called Nella who told her she'd been born a slave and always wondered why the Emancipation Proclamation let her walk free anywhere but into the voting booth. Flossie asked her to join in the cause, but Nella pointed to her swollen feet. "These hoofers carried me all the way from Virginia to Vermont. Now they hold me upright while I cook, get their rest while I balance the books. I've been through one freedom fight, missy. It be your feet that find the way for this one."

One March day, after the bakery foreman chased her out saying a woman voting was like a dog walking on its hind legs, she slogged home through the mud and told Millie, "That's it. I can't do this alone." She got her editor to send a teletype down to a pal of his on the Boston *American* and started packing.

"What about me?" cried Millie.

"Come with me, then."

Millie bit her lip. How can I? she thought. By then, the mother wasn't even getting up to bake biscuits, and Sammy and Hannah were almost toddling, and who'd put dinner on the table? Flossie left. Millie didn't cry, there was too much to do. But it felt like the earth had cracked open, so she stepped careful, trying not to fall in.

Salisbury Jo
Frankie Hucklenbroich

I was eight years old the summer Jo Koerner came home to Salisbury Street in St. Louis. I must have been, because it was the year I was confirmed and made my First Communion. I remember I still felt very holy and much inclined toward becoming a nun, preferably a Carmelite or one of the other glamorous orders in which you knelt around all day contemplating God and having visions and not being able to talk to anyone but Jesus and your Mother Superior (and you could only talk to her if she spoke to you first).

That year, the year that Jo came home, I was pretty well convinced I had what the Church calls a "true vocation." There were a lot of pluses to this: Besides a sure ticket to Heaven, I thought having visions would be very interesting, and since Papa's prejudices didn't allow me to play with anyone but my sister Sandy, I doubted I would miss the absence of a social life. Jesus had to be a better conversationalist than my harried mother, my father who spoke only to order or complain, or Sandy, who was only four; my father's mother lived with us, but to my child's mind she didn't count; after many years in this country, Bapcha's Polish accent was still so thick she could barely be understood, and she hated being asked to repeat things. And I rarely saw my mother's mother; Bapcha didn't like her, so Papa didn't like her either and wouldn't let her come to see us, although she lived only a few blocks away. Papa always got grumpy when Mama went over to see Grandma Chaney, especially if she took us kids with her, so we didn't go often.

I was very lonely, and I envied the Franciscan nuns who ran Holy Trinity, where I went to church and school; they seemed to me to be so serene and elegant, gliding rather than walking, like great black cats with starched white chests and faces, unruffled by the world around them, as though they had the answers to a whole set of questions most people weren't smart enough to ask. But I had noticed that the really spectacular nun-saints were usually Carmelites, like St. Theresa of the Little Flower.

I was going through a real identity crisis, except that nobody knew about identity crises in the mid-fifties.

Then Jo came home.

I lived with my father and mother and Sandy in the big flat above my father's barbershop; Papa's mother lived, like the witch in the attic, on the third floor. The Koerners owned the house across the street and two doors down from mine. I must have seen Jo passing by, before she went away to the WACs and came back queer; perhaps when I stood on the tips of my toes, looking down at the street from the big bay window on the second floor. Or maybe I saw her through the plate-glass shopfront on some afternoon when the barbershop was empty and my father left me to watch things for him while he went to share a beer with my mother.

"Call me if I get a customer," he would say. Then he would go through the back room behind the shop, where it was dark and hot and filled with the brooding shapes of old furniture, and climb the stairs up to the kitchen. Sometimes a customer showed up right away, but sometimes it would be an hour or more before one of the neighborhood men or one of the men who worked at Falstaff Brewery or Krey's Packing Company wandered in and I ran to the bottom of the steps and yelled "Papa, customer!" as loudly as I could.

I must have seen Jo Koerner, for I watched all the comings and goings on Salisbury Street. But when she went away to join the WACs the war was still going on, and I was probably too small or she too innocuous for me to remember. Then, one summer day, there she was.

That afternoon, I was on my way home from Perkie's with a bag of groceries for my mother, hurrying up the sidewalk because even though Perkie's was only half a block from our house I'd been gone too long. There was a Kroger Store nearby, but Perkie's was the *neighborhood* store, a place where you could buy everything: paper umbrellas and rubber balls, comic books and pickled pigs' feet, pumpernickel bread and hamburger run fresh through the grinder while you watched. You could get writing tablets and eggs, coffee beans and corn on the cob, nails and hammers and chewing tobacco, crepe-paper streamers, buttercake and Oxydol, Eskimo pies, kites, and buckets of lard, and old Mr. and Mrs. Perkins, who took turns presiding over this jammed and cool and redolent place from early morning until late at night, seemed to me like a neighborhood king and queen. I always dawdled there without meaning to, and I always got slapped for it later. So that day, breathless and sweating, both arms clutching the heavy bag to my bony chest, I was trotting along when a cab pulled in to the curb across the street and stopped in front of the Koerner house.

I stopped in my tracks.

On that street, in that time, a taxi was an event. Except for people like my father or the Perkinses, people who owned their own small business or shop, nobody had a car. Monsignor Lubelei drove around in a great, dark-blue sedan, but even his car didn't count, as it really belonged to the Church, just like the priesthouse did. Anybody else, you walked or you took the streetcar everywhere. Taxis were an unheard-of luxury.

The person who emerged from the backseat of that taxi, tugged a suitcase out, and paid off the driver was even more of an event. On that sticky afternoon so long ago, Jo Koerner, stepping from her cab in all innocence and coming home, stunned Salisbury Street.

My father and his friend Yop had come out of the shop to see who was arriving at the Koerner place in a cab. Above the barber sheet, Yop's face was half clean shaven, half lathered, and I saw his mouth drop slowly open. Papa lowered his hands to his sides; the straight razor in his right hand glittered in the sun. Mrs. Cukierski and Mrs. Prater both stood out on their stoops, frankly staring. Yop said something to my father, and Papa laughed. Down the other way, Mrs. Perkins had come out of the store to look. In that fragile year, in that place, Jo Koerner could not have been more shocking than if Mrs. Cukierski, say, notorious for her piety, suddenly peeled off her clothes and strutted down Salisbury naked.

For the woman who stood on the sidewalk in her rumpled WAC uniform, gazing at the front of the Koerners' house, looked very different from the domesticated women of Salisbury Street. This woman, even to me, looked a lot like a man; a man in a skirt.

She was tall and lean and didn't have a whole lot "on top." The legs showing beneath her skirt were also lean, and calfless; her feet, in her thick Army shoes, looked huge. She wore no lipstick or powder that I could see, and her hair was so short it barely touched her collar, barely showed beneath the smart WAC hat. She looked as though she'd tried to cut herself sideburns. And she was smoking. On the street. Like a man.

Suddenly Jo seemed to notice her audience. She turned and glanced at us, and I saw a dark-red flush climb her neck and seep beneath the skin of her face. Her mouth moved as if she was going to say something. Instead, she shrugged, picked up her suitcase, and mounted the white stoop to her door.

We had just gotten our first telephone. I can still remember the number: Chestnut 2756. After supper that night, my mother, who seldom used the phone herself, got call after call; Salisbury Street's wires were buzzing. Once I heard her say, "You don't know that for sure," and another time she said, "No, I *don't* know what the Service is like! How could I? All I've ever done is take care of Johnny and raise his kids!" She came back into the kitchen, where Papa sat finishing his coffee and I was work-

ing on a book of follow-the-dots, and her mouth was all pinched
up the way it got when she was getting ready to be mad. She
plopped down at the table, across from my father, and patted her
forehead with the back of her arm. Moths were battering themselves to death against the window screens and it was so hot that
the fan on top of the icebox just rolled the warm air around us.

"Johnny, I don't think it's right, what they're saying about Jo
Koerner," Mama announced.

My father looked at her and grinned. "Right, my *ass*!" he
said. "Right that she *is*, or right that they're sayin' it?"

Mama shrugged. "I don't believe it," she said.

"You seen her yet?"

Mama looked sideways at Papa. "No," she admitted.

"Well, *I* saw her." Papa slurped the last of his coffee, and
put the cup down. "Believe me, Rita, she's a real he-she."

I kept my head low, and started on another picture. A *heeshy*!
Jo Koerner was a heeshy. . . . What was a heeshy?

"How do you know that?" Mama said. "How do you *know*
that? She went away and helped in the war. I don't think it's
fair to talk about her the minute she gets home! She's bound to
be odd for a while, being gone so long. Why can't people mind
their own business? Give her a chance to settle back into civilian
life." Mama shook her head. "Meet some nice boy," she finished weakly.

My father hooted. "Wait'll you do get a look at her! She was
never a beauty queen, but *now*. . . . Even if she did want a man,
there's no man gonna want her. *Believe* me!"

Mama made a disgusted sound with her teeth. "All the more
reason to let her alone," she said.

Now it was Papa's turn to sound disgusted. "I'm tellin' you,
Rita, the woman's a queer!" Then he leaned forward and his
voice got very low and soft. "Do you *know* what they *do*?"

I gripped my paintbrush and held my breath.

But I never found out what they did or if Mama knew about
it, because just then Mama remembered I was there and saw that
I was listening with avid, if uncomprehending, interest. Mama

looked at me and said, "Go get Sandy, and get ready for bed."
As I walked down the hall, I could hear Papa's voice rumbling.
The next day, Mama told me never to talk to Jo Koerner.

But I watched. And I wondered what really made everybody
in the neighborhood not like her. Surely, looking like Jo Koerner
couldn't be *so* bad. One night, in the bathroom, I tried pulling
all my hair back from my face. "This is how I would look if I
was Jo Koerner," I thought, staring into the mirror. I thought I
looked pretty good. I thought I looked like Huck Finn.

I pictured Jo married, in a housedress like my mother always
wore, maybe with some kids, and I decided she would look like
herself no matter what she did or wore. She looked like she
looked, like Jo Koerner, that was all. Jo came home nights carrying a lunch pail and dressed in a shirt and overalls and her
Army shoes. I heard Papa say she was working in the factory
down at Continental Can Company. She looked less like a regular, everyday woman than ever, except her hair was growing
out.

By now, people didn't talk to Jo, and Mrs. Koerner wore an
air that was half-sad, half-defiant. Papa said it was a good thing
Mr. Koerner was dead, or Jo would have broken his heart. Papa
said Mrs. Koerner should have kicked Jo out.

Now there was a thing that people did on Salisbury Street in
the late summer evenings when it was too hot to sit inside or
even to sleep, a social thing that knit many neighborhoods in
a way that has vanished along with those gone times. All the
families would come outside and sit on their front stoops for a
couple of hours every night. While kids whooped and hollered
and played tag up and down the block, the men—and even
the women—would drink cold beer, the women gathering on the
stoops in some unspoken hierarchy of chumminess while the
men strolled from group to group, talking about work or rising
prices (coffee was over sixty cents a pound) or whether Harry S
Truman was right to drop the atomic bomb on Japan (most of
them thought he was) or how there'd never be a president to
touch old F.D.R. And sometimes a knot of men drew together

to whisper, and then a low, ribald laughter would spread among them like brushfire and the women on the stoops would get a funny look on their faces and start to speak loudly of domestic things.

Mrs. Koerner no longer came out to sit on her stoop. I noticed but didn't talk about it: When I'd asked Mama what queers were and what they *did*, I got a good slap. I wasn't about to risk another.

Then, as the days drifted on toward summer's end, I forgot about the Koerners and their troubles. Jo, coming home, was just a figure in the corner of my eye. Other things were on my mind.

That summer, a lot happened. We went on a rare family outing, to the circus in St. Charles. And one terrible morning my dog Pudgie got hit by a meat truck right in front of the shop, dead before her indignant howl fully left her mouth. Mama told Sandy and me there would be a new baby when winter came. At supper one night, Mama and Bapcha got in a big argument over how much paprika Mama was supposed to put in the chicken and dumplings and my grandmother threatened to change her will and to start charging Papa rent for the barbershop and our part of the house, besides. Uncle Quentin, my mother's brother, ran into Papa down at the Turner Hall tavern; they drank together for a while, and then they got in a fight. Uncle Quen broke one of Papa's ribs and blacked his eyes, and Papa had to stand and cut hair for weeks with his chest taped up. After that, Mama couldn't take us to see Grandma Chaney at all anymore, or even go herself; Papa wouldn't allow it. I got a new puppy, and named him "Dickie."

Jo Koerner was a small spot in the back of my brain.

Then one day Papa called me in from the yard to watch the shop. All morning he'd been busy with haircuts and shaves, and men hanging around and gabbing with each other like they always did on Saturdays; around noon, the shop emptied out and Papa grabbed his chance to go upstairs before another customer showed up.

"Sweep the hair," he said, "and get started on the spittoons."

I sighed, got the broom and dustpan, and swept slowly, making the job last. The hair I didn't mind; it was fun piling it up in front of the broom, sweeping it into the pan, watching the gray and brown and blonde and sometimes red mix and make patterns according to how straight or wavy it was. It was fun climbing into the white marble chair with its padded black leather seat and arms and the big chrome lever for raising or lowering it, setting the huge chair to spinning crazily around in circles, making it go faster and faster by pushing the broom against the floor, then leaning back and letting the chair spin itself down like a top until I could jump off and stagger dizzily across the room.

But I hated the spittoons and the smelly, sopping mess they held. I had to do them every Saturday. Papa's day off was Sunday and he wanted the spittoons clean and fresh for the new week. There were four of them scattered around the shop; they all had to be emptied into a bucket he kept just for that. Then I lugged the bucket to the ashpit in the backyard and dumped it out. After that, the bucket was hosed out, put away, and the spittoons washed under the faucet, dried with rags, and polished. Papa liked them shiny enough for his face to glow in the brass.

The ugly part was finished. I was sitting on the floor with my can of brass cream and my clean rags and a spittoon in my lap, working away, when the bell on the screen door tinkled and Jo walked in. Like an idiot, I sat gaping up at her.

Jo smiled, and nodded at the spittoon. "Nice job you're doing there," she said. "I used to have to polish a lot of brass, too. Buckles. Insignia. I was in the Army."

Numbly, I nodded.

She took her hands out of her jeans and squatted down by me.

"But you're doing it the hard way," she said, picking up a rag from the floor. "Now watch." Expertly, she wound the rag around the first three fingers of her right hand, scooped a bit of brass cream from the can, picked up a spittoon, and rubbed its side in a slow, circular motion. Then she stopped. "See? You don't have to scrub at it. Just let the chemical do the work. See how it dries to a haze? *Now* you polish it.'' Jo was right; the place she'd done burned like gold. She set the spittoon down and rose to her feet.

I still said nothing. I wasn't supposed to talk to Jo Koerner.

"You must be Johnny's oldest girl,'' Jo said, glancing idly around the shop. "Where's your dad? I need a haircut.''

I looked at her hair, lank and stringy on her shoulders. "I guess he's upstairs,'' I muttered, trapped, and kept on polishing.

"Is he closed?''

"No, ma'am.''

Jo looked up at the ceiling. "Well,'' she said, rocking back and forth on her heels, "can you get him for me?''

Right then, Mr. Hardnacki walked in, stopped, and looked at Jo, who gazed back at him. Mr. Hardnacki got a funny expression on his face. Jo smiled a little. It was Mr. Hardnacki who cleared his throat, and looked away first.

"Your dad around?'' he asked me.

"Yes, sir. Ow!'' I'd scrambled up so quickly, I banged my knee against the edge of the sink. "I'll call him right now!'' I ran to the back, but this time, after I called my father I waited at the bottom of the steps. For some reason, I felt I had to warn him. My heart pounded, and when he came clattering down, I grabbed his hand and tugged. He stared at me, surprised; in our family, touching was reserved for punishment.

"What's the matter with you?'' he said.

"Papa, Jo Koerner's out there! She wants a *haircut*!''

"*What?*''

"Mr. Hardnacki's out there, too!''

Papa said "*Jesus Christ!*'' and hurried into the shop, with me right behind him. Jo and Mr. Hardnacki stood on opposite sides of the big room. Hands deep in her pockets, Jo nonchalantly examined the startled deerheads my father had bought to hang along the back wall; Mr. Hardnacki was assessing the potted geraniums and rubber trees that had been in the windows for as long as I could remember.

" 'Lo, Art!'' Papa said heartily, acting just as if he didn't notice the tall, skinny woman in shirt and jeans right in front of his face. "What can I do ya?" He whipped out the barber sheet and snapped it smartly in the air. "The works?"

Jo said, "Excuse me."

Mr. Hardnacki and Papa both froze as if some masked and slit-eyed hoodlum had come in and said, "This is a stick-up!" Mr. Hardnacki still had one leg, the leg he was going to use to step up into the chair, in the air. Slowly, both men turned their faces to Jo. Slowly, Mr. Hardnacki's foot lowered.

Jo stepped forward, smiling. "I think I was first, Johnny."

Papa looked mad and scared at the same time. "First? First? What for?"

"Why, for a haircut." Jo passed her fingers through the lank strings along the sides of her head. "Sure am getting shaggy."

My father drew himself up. With great dignity, he said, "Jo, I can't cut your hair. Why, you oughtta know better than that!"

"Why? I need a haircut. This is a barbershop. You cut hair."

"Well, because this is a *man's* shop, Jo. You don't *belong* in here!"

Jo's face went white. "Since when is hair male or female?" she said. "Lord, Johnny, I just want a haircut, and I'll be on my way!" Her voice had sharpened; even I knew there was something going on here that had nothing to do with haircuts. "If you're worried about rough talk, I won't cramp your style; I heard plenty in the service and I don't have lily ears."

Papa shook his head. "I'm not doin' it, Jo. I don't *cut* ladies' hair. Why can't you go on down to Doris' on Vandeventer?"

"Because I don't want my hair permed or pommed or curled!" she answered, and her hands were out of her pockets now and hung loose and big and red at the ends of her bony wrists. "I don't want my hair *bobbed* or *tweaked* or *twisted* or *styled*! I just want a plain old haircut. Just a haircut. Like you give."

"Go someplace else for it. You can get one someplace else. Cheaper, too." (My father charged sixty-five cents, but he was a Union man.)

"I don't care about the money!" She flung an arm up and

pointed out the window. "Why should I have to go somewhere else? Look! You're right across the street! We're *neighbors*!"

"Sorry," Papa said. "No can do." He turned to Mr. Hardnacki. "C'mon, Art, get up in this chair."

Jo Koerner threw her arms wide, muttered "*Dammit* to hell, anyway!" and stalked from the shop.

Mr. Hardnacki giggled. "That beats it! That really beats it!" he cried, laughing out loud now.

"Got a foul mouth fer a woman, don't she?" Papa grinned.

When he told Mama, however, Papa acted solemn and weighty, as though he'd successfully turned aside some danger. He tsk-d, and shook his head. "It ruined her, the Service," he said. "Women have no business in there."

"Oh, Johnny, lots of women went. You can't tell me they all came back strange! Besides, she *was* helping out our boys."

"Our *girls*, more like it!"

"*Shhh!*"

"Art says his cousin's girl came back that way from the WAVES. It ruins 'em, the Service."

My mother, who spent what little leisure time she had in reading all kinds of books bought from the Goodwill for a quarter a box, leaned her chin on her hand and said, "Maybe the Service doesn't *change* them; maybe it's just getting out of *here*. Maybe they go off to do one thing and while they're doing it, they *learn* something about themselves. Maybe they're already that way and just don't know it or know how to *be* it." She looked at Papa's frown. "Not that I think it's right!" she finished quickly.

"That kind of learning nobody needs! She shoulda stayed home and gone to work at the airplane factory, if she wanted to help out in the war so bad! Now she's walkin' around lookin' like Little Abner, askin' me for haircuts. . . . Jesus!"

Mama, eminently practical, said, "Well, we could have used the money, Johnny." She patted her swelling belly.

Papa stared at her. "You know, Rita," he said, "sometimes you don't have any sense at all! I don't want her in my shop, get me?"

"Sixty-five cents," my mother said. "A pound of coffee, and three cents change." She could be stubborn sometimes.

But, like a bad penny, Jo came back.

This time I wasn't around, but I heard all about it in bits of gossip from the stoops, in snatches of conversation between my parents, in tag ends that Papa and Mama told Aunt Lottie and Aunt Irene and Uncle Ted and Aunt Jennie when they came for their weekly visit to Bapcha.

Jo came back the Friday after Papa sent her away. She must have picked late Friday on purpose, because Friday evenings were Papa's busiest time; on Fridays, Papa kept the shop open until nine to accommodate all the neighborhood men who wanted sprucing up for the weekend but didn't want to interrupt their weekend free-time, especially if they only had a half-Saturday off. Fridays, from five o'clock on, there would be as many as nine or ten men waiting their turns inside, and sometimes two or three more sitting comfortably on the long iron step that ran across the front of the shop, and the shears and clippers and razor would be silver blurs in Papa's hands. On Friday evenings, Sandy and I couldn't play downstairs until the shop was closed; things got too raw, what with all the cigars and chewing tobacco and swearing and "man talk."

Into this fifties bastion of maleness, Jo Koerner bravely strode. And once again, everything stopped.

Jo went to the cash register on the back bar and laid a half dollar, a dime, and a nickel on the top of the brass drawer. "I need a haircut, Johnny," she said. "I'll wait my turn."

Papa glanced around the room, embarrassed and mad, but before he could say anything, Dale Otto called out, "What about it, John? Should I give the little lady my chair?" Some of the men laughed, and the ugly feeling that had begun to loom in the corners of the room fell back a little. Yop stood up; with a flourish, he offered his seat: "Miss Koerner, *ma'am*? Would ya care t'park yourself?" Now all the men were laughing; it was going to be all right.

Jo said, "No thanks. I'll stand."

Someone said, "Those are goodlookin' pants, Jo. Where'd ya get them pants? I might buy me a pair." Somebody else said, "Them yer Army pants, Jo? Or didja hafta look for 'em?"

Hee hee! the men went. *Haw haw!* they brayed. Mr. Prater wiped tears from his eyes.

Jo stood there and took it. She looked straight ahead of her, the way a cat does when it's looking at something people can't see.

Papa was laughing, too, but he said, "Come on, Jo. Take your money and go. You're not gonna get a haircut here."

Yop hollered, "Give 'er a shave, while she's at it, Johnny!" He collapsed into guffaws.

"I want my hair cut," Jo quietly repeated. "Short all the way. Clippers on the back." She nodded right at Yop and his fresh do. "Like his."

"Hey!" Yop cried, his laugh fading out.

Papa said, "Jo. Come on. Go home, okay?"

"I don't think I will just yet," she said amiably enough. "I want you to cut my hair. My money's as good as anyone's."

None of the men were laughing now. Jerry Haney, who worked in the slaughterhouse at Krey's and always smelled faintly of blood and strongly of chewing tobacco, heaved himself to his feet and walked over to stand facing her.

"Look, girlie," he said, "I dunno what you think yer doin', but why don'tcha do us all a favor, *includin'* yerself, an' get the hell outa here?"

Papa said, "Jerry, she's a woman. I don't need trouble."

Haney swung his bull's head toward my father. "I *know* she's a goddamn woman! Been a *man*, she'da had some *business* in here!" He turned back to Jo. "Now, I dunno what *you* think you are, but since yer a woman I'm askin' you. Nicely. Take yer money an' go, okay?"

"No. I need a haircut."

Haney stepped back, aimed, and let a thick stream of spit and tobacco juice fly from his mouth. The wad landed on Jo's right shoe and ran slowly down to the tan linoleum. *"Get out!"* he cried.

Jo looked at her shoe and then back at Haney. "After my hair gets cut," she answered, but there was a fine tremor in her voice.

"A-AH!" Haney bellowed, his neck swollen, his big face purple. He grabbed Jo's collar and right arm and spun her around toward the door; as he did so, her face cracked into the coatrack and blood suddenly bloomed on her mouth. "I *warned* ya!" Haney muttered, and then he said something that I would hear over a decade later, and more than once: "You wanna *act* like a man, I'll *treat* ya like a man!" And he half pushed, half flung her through the door.

Jo staggered, her arms pinwheeling, but she didn't fall; she stood on the sidewalk, panting, holding her hand up to her bloody mouth and looking in at the shop.

"Goddammit, anyway!" Haney said. He scooped up Jo's haircut money and flung the coins at her from the doorway; they rolled across the sidewalk and spun into the gutter. Haney sat back down grumbling, "I didn't mean t'hurt 'er," and began to whistle softly.

Papa said, "Hell, Jerry!" and shook his head.

Eugene Sie craned his neck past the plants in the window.

"She still there?" Papa asked.

"Naw, she's gone on home, I guess."

There was a little silence, a little sound of shoes scraped on wooden chair rungs and change jingling in pockets as men shifted in their seats. Then Yop brought some humor back.

"Josephine!" he grinned. "Oughtta be Joseph! Then we could call 'er Jo, awright. With a 'e' on the end of it!"

Papa laughed uneasily. "Well, I dunno why she's pickin' on *me*!" and his scissors wove deftly around Dale Otto's head, clipping at the clumps of waxy hair growing from Mr. Otto's ears.

Yop chuckled. "Maybe she *likes* ya, Johnny!"

They all laughed then. Mr. Sie said, "Playin' around, huh? Rita's gonna *kill* ya, John!"

In high spirits now, Haney settled cozily, spat a brown string

into the nearest spittoon, and said, "Well, 'at's that, I guess."
But it wasn't over.

I'm not sure why Jo chose to make her stand against the whole
neighborhood, or, having done so, made it at Papa's barbershop;
maybe she just wanted a haircut and when she was refused, bris-
tled with the injustice and had to try again. Maybe there was
more to it. By throwing out her challenge, though, Jo Koerner
turned an uneasy truce into a situation of gleeful and scandalized
harassment. Now when she passed, the women muttered
"Shame!" or hissed at her back, or loudly called their little girls
to their sides and put protective arms around them. Men catcalled
or whistled at her, or cried "My, my! Ain't that *sweet*!" or
sometimes, "Hey, *fella*! Where ya goin'?" Jo would set her
angular jaw and keep on walking; what else could she do?

The neighborhood boys soon saw nothing would happen if
they tormented this odd-looking adult; when Jo was foolish and
uppity enough to buy a secondhand Buick, some of them snuck
out one night and wrote dirty words in soap on all its windows.
Next morning, there she was with a bucket and rags, scrubbing
away so that she could drive to work. A few mornings later, the
words were back. Mrs. Koerner rarely came outside, not even to
go to Mass or the store. Jo stayed away from church; she did
their shopping on Saturdays, going to Perkie's like everyone
else. Food and haircuts were different. Anybody had the right to
buy food, after all.

Jo's hair was crudely hacked off at the ears, now. It looked
awful. She had taken to wearing a striped engineer's cap all the
time, the bill pulled down low over her nose; the cap and the
way she wore it made her lean face cocky and unreadable. Papa
said Mrs. Koerner must have cut Jo's hair, as no real barber
could do it that badly even if he tried. He wondered if she wore
her railroad cap while she was working; then he said he was
surprised she still *had* a job. Mama said maybe Jo was just a
very good worker. Then Papa said maybe they didn't know she
was a woman at the can company, or how could they give her
a job with so many veterans out of work?

Patiently, Mama pointed out that Jo was also a veteran.

"Goddammit, Rita, you know what I mean!" We were all at the supper table. "I never knew anybody like you for stickin' up for underdogs. Niggers an' hoosiers 're bad enough, without you takin' up for queers! What's the matter with you, anyhow?" He jerked his head toward Sandy and me. "How'd you like t'be Mrs. Koerner, an' wind up with a kid like that?"

Mama regarded us calmly. "That could never happen," she said.

Forgetting myself, I spoke up: "A kid like *what*, Mama?"

Papa, head dog, growled at me from across his plate: "When a puppy eats, it doesn't bark!" Faced with the logic, as well as the warning, in this familiar maxim, I shut up. In sympathy, Sandy reached over and dumped a spoonful of her gravy on my peas.

"Johnny, can we drive out to Irene and Lee's this Sunday?" Mama suddenly asked, changing tacks. She lifted her dark red hair away from her neck with both hands. There were blue circles under her eyes, and her pale, freckled skin was moist. "It's so hot!" she complained. "Maybe it's cooler in the country."

"We'll see." Papa reached for more bread. "We'll talk about it Sunday." Papa never liked to go very far from Salisbury Street, unless it was with his friends from the shop; just to get him to go for a drive to Fairgrounds Park or to the river, Mama had to start laying her plans well ahead of time.

But by Sunday, Papa had something else on his mind, and even Mama admitted this was important: Verldean Prater, of the ripe buttocks and insolent breasts and Betty Grable legs, Verldean, who was still single at twenty-three while all the neighborhood swains pined for her, Verldean, with a good job at Stix, Baer and Fuller's department store downtown, whose least trip to Perkie's was gratefully noted by every male within range, who went out alone and returned home alone several nights each week but who stubbornly refused to accept a date with any of the local men, Verldean, to whom all the women were always so sweetly polite, Verldean Prater quit her job, packed her bags, and boarded the train from Union Station for California.

Mrs. Prater was at home, crying. Papa and Yop and some of the other men took Mr. Prater over to East St. Louis, where it was legal to drink on Sunday, and went out drinking to console him.

Mr. Prater must have needed a lot of consoling, because when Papa rolled in that night he made so much noise that Sandy and I woke up. Papa seemed to be having a hard time getting in the house; it sounded like Mama was helping him up the steps and trying to shush him at the same time. Once he said, "Son of a *bitch*!" and once he said, "Get away from me, Rita, or I'll break your arm off!" Finally Mama calmed him down; we heard his body hit the mattress in their room. Then he groaned and muttered for a while, Mama making soothing noises, and then we heard what must have been his shoes falling, one by one, to the floor.

Above our heads, Bapcha's feet shuffled; then her rocker began creaking hard. A chain of Polish words drifted down to us; Bapcha was praying for the soul of her son, who would surely be a paragon of virtue if he had not, in some madness of heart or loins, married the Irish woman. Down in the backyard, Papa's watchdogs were barking hysterically.

Under the glow from the streetlamp outside our window, Sandy and I knelt in bed, our knobby knees touching, and stared at each other. "Drink of water?" Sandy pled; she always wanted a drink when she woke up at night. I sighed and took her hand; together we trailed down the long hallway to the kitchen. I reached up and pressed the button for the light. Mama was sitting at the table, holding her head in her hands. She looked at us standing there in just our panties. "What?" Mama said. Overhead, the old lady's rocker creaked on.

"Sandy wants a drink."

Mama nodded, went to the sink, and filled a cup. Sandy took a few swallows. "Now, go to bed," Mama said, taking the cup. "Go on." On our way back down the hall, we heard another noise; it sounded scary. It sounded like Mama was crying.

The next day, Papa opened the shop an hour late. First he sat at the kitchen table, drinking cup after cup of black coffee. His eyes were red. His hands shook. Mama told us to stay out of his way, don't make noise, and don't say *anything* to him unless he talked to us first. I thought of the fat razor strop hanging under the counter in the shop, and nodded quickly.

Verldean's exodus, so abrupt and so dramatic (not at all like moving into her own flat, which would have been bad enough), kept Salisbury Street occupied in the days ahead. Some people thought she was ''in trouble'' and abandoned; others opted for elopement with a secret beau. The phone wires and the front stoops crackled with conjecture. Monsignor Lubelei, who hadn't touched the subject of Jo with a ten-foot pole, preached a sermon on the Prodigal Son at eleven o'clock Mass which set Mrs. Prater to openly bawling. In the shop, Mr. Prater was the object of solemn sympathy. Jo was shoved to a back burner on the scandal stove.

Later that month, when a FOR SALE sign bloomed gaudily on the front wall of the Koerners' house, it was noted with satisfaction but little comment. As for Papa, all he said was that Jo and her mother were probably moving downtown, where the gypsies lived and anything went. People were still busy gabbing about Verldean.

In the next days, a thin but steady parade of prospective buyers trudged up Mrs. Koerner's snowy white stoop, spent twenty or thirty minutes inside, then trudged down again; mostly, these were very young couples, sometimes with a child in tow. Then one couple returned, but this time they brought an older man and woman along.

From where I was busy drawing a picture of Straight Arrow on the sidewalk with blue chalk, I watched them enter. A long time went by; I had finished Straight Arrow and was working on his horse Tony when the young couple, the older man and woman, and Jo came outside. They stood talking for a few minutes; then Jo and the men shook hands. The strangers piled into a big sedan and drove away. Jo pulled the FOR SALE sign down from the wall; carrying the sign, she went back into her house.

I ran upstairs. Mama was feeding clothes through the wringer.

"Mama! Mama! Some people were at the Koerners' house for a long time, and when they left Jo took the sign down!"

Mama dried her hands on a rag and hurried to the front room, where the sofa and the two big chairs stood. She leaned out the bay window and stared across the street.

"See, Mama? The sign's gone. Is the house sold?"

My mother nodded. "I guess so," she said slowly, and looked some more; then she sighed and said, "It's best."

"Why is it best?" Nobody had ever, ever sold their house on Salisbury Street; not that I could remember.

"It just is," she answered, turning away from the window.

It was almost time for school to start. Sandy would be in kindergarten and I was starting third grade. Mama took us down to 14th Street and bought us new shoes. Sandy got two new dresses. I didn't get a dress because from first grade on at Holy Trinity, girls wore navy-blue pleated skirts, white tops, and red ties, all bought from the Church; the boys could wear whatever they wanted. But I did get a schoolbag and a new pencil box, so I was happy.

One Saturday morning, Jo walked back into the shop. "Morning, Johnny," she said. She nodded to the men sitting around, then she turned to my father. "Guess you know we sold the house."

Papa nodded warily.

"Reason I'm here, the truck'll be by this afternoon. We'll be gone by tonight." She smiled. "I really don't want to leave without one of your famous haircuts." Her right hand went up to pull off her railroad cap. "I look so *bad*!" she said.

Papa shook his head. "You know better, Jo."

"How about if I give you something extra? I do admire your cuts." Jo reached into her jeans and pulled out a handful of silver dollars. The men watched quietly as she laid three dollars on the counter. "How about it, John?"

Papa looked at the money, then at Jo. He didn't say anything.

Jo waited a second, then added two more coins. "Five bucks, Johnny. Whaddaya say?"

He looked at her butchered head, then at the waiting men. "I can't, Jo," he said. "I don't cut ladies' hair."

Slowly, Jo added five more coins. "Ten dollars, John. Almost fifteen haircuts."

Helplessly, Papa eyed the money.

Then Yop spoke up: "Hell, if she wants it that bad, *give* it to 'er, Johnny! A haircut, I mean."

Jo smiled.

Another man said, "Ten bucks is ten bucks. Lotta money fer a haircut, John!" Someone called out: "Hell, *I'd* do it! Go on!"

Papa, absolved of guilt by a jury of his peers, shrugged and scooped the coins into the cash drawer. "Okay," he said, "but all these guys are ahead of you." Jo nodded but the man Papa had been working on stood up and took the barber sheet from around his neck. "Do me later, John," he said. "I wanta see this."

Jo climbed up into the chair. Papa whipped the barber sheet around her neck. "How do ya want it?" he said, all business now.

"Short. Clippers in the back. Burns. Can you repair the mess?" she asked, squinting into the big mirror over the back bar.

Papa laughed. "Sure. I'm the best there is. I'll give you the best cut you ever had. Girl, you just paid me for fifteen haircuts." He looked around at the men. "Hope you guys don't mind, but this'll take a while." His thumb indicated the cowlicks and the unruly patches, and the places where scissors had cut deeper than the surrounding hair. While he worked, the men watched with real interest. The shop was very quiet.

Papa had become the consummate professional. His fingers flew. He grimaced with concentration. Now and then he stood back from the chair and closed one eye; then he would step forward, take a tiny *snick*! here, tuck a hair into place there, and go on. Thirty minutes later, when Jo finally stepped down from

the chair, the top of her head was crowned with a perfectly an-
gled crew cut, tapering beautifully down into a close, shaped
back and sides. In front of her ears, her high cheekbones sported
sideburns that looked like they'd been drawn and not clipped
there. Papa had outdone himself: Jo looked sleek, arrogant, and
a little bit dangerous.

Jo stood in front of the big mirror, gazing at her profile and
at the back of her head, angling the hand mirror Papa offered
her. She grinned. "I like it. It's good, Johnny!" she said.

Papa, pleased by his work and by the money in his till, was
inclined to be friendly. "So where you moving to?" he asked,
using the whisk broom on her shoulders and back.

"Oh," she waved a vague hand, "out a ways."

"Well, no hard feelings, okay? Say hello to your mother."

"No hard feelings, John." Jo pulled out yet another silver
dollar, and this dollar she pressed into my father's hand.

Papa stared down at the coin. "What's this for?"

"Your tip. Take it." Jo smiled. "It was worth it."

That afternoon, a truck pulled up to the Koerners' and three
men climbed down and went into the house. They began hauling
boxes and trunks and mattresses and furniture out to the truck.
By dusk, they were done. Jo came out and spoke with them for
a few minutes, and then the truck lumbered away. Jo's Buick
still sat at the curb.

A couple of hours later, when people filled the stoops and the
kids ran back and forth, when Papa had just closed down, joined
Mama on our own stoop, and opened his first bottle of beer, Jo
Koerner came out of her house again.

She wore a navy-blue pinstriped double-breasted suit over a
white shirt and a plum-colored tie. Her black wingtip shoes were
polished to a high gloss. The cuffs on her trousers broke just
right over her insteps, and a white handkerchief drooped rakishly
from her breast pocket. A carnation rode her lapel. On the sidewalk, Jo paused, struck a match and lit a cigarette, then dropped
the pack and matches into her jacket. Still standing in the wide
white glow of the entry light, making dead sure everyone could
see her, Jo took a deep inhale of smoke. Then she put her hands

in her trouser pockets, and with the cigarette dangling from the corner of her mouth, Jo Koerner strolled down the block.

Past the knots of silent men and women, Jo Koerner ambled. At the corner, under the streetlamp, she stood for a moment as if drinking in the fine, soft, late-summer night. Then she crossed the street and strolled back up the other side of the block. When she reached the barbershop, she nodded at us and went on. Under the streetlamp at our corner, Jo stopped again; raising her head to look at the sky, she turned in a full circle. She leaned one arm lazily against the lamppost; her other hand snapped her cigarette away. The cigarette made a high, bright arc in the air, and came down in a mist of sparks. After a bit, Jo straightened her shoulders, looked up and down the block, and crossed the street at an easy lope. When she reached her own house, she went swiftly up the steps and inside.

The street was so still, you could hear the cicadas chirring from the little park a few blocks away.

A moment later, the door to the Koerner house opened again. Mrs. Koerner came out, followed by Jo, who carried a suitcase.

Mrs. Koerner walked to the Buick, her freshly permed head held high. Jo opened the door for her mother, threw the suitcase into the backseat, and went around to the driver's side. She slid under the wheel, started the car up, switched on the headlights, and pulled out. At the end of the block, she gave a couple of farewell beeps on her horn. Stunned again, Salisbury Street watched until Jo's red taillights winked out in the distance.

Sometime that fall, the mailman brought an envelope to the shop, addressed simply to Johnny the Barber, 2027 Salisbury Street, St. Louis, Missouri. When I came home from school, the men were passing it around; they didn't look happy.

As I walked through the shop on my way upstairs, Jerry Haney dropped the envelope. Automatically, I stooped to retrieve it and the snapshot that slid from inside. Though Papa snatched them from my hand, he wasn't quick enough. I had already seen.

In the picture, Jo Koerner's Buick was parked somewhere with a beach in the background, with people in bathing suits laying on towels. Beyond was water, and there were people swimming in the water, and a far-off sail. In a blinding white T-shirt, her short hair sleek, her face tanned, Jo Koerner leaned against the front fender of her car. Her left arm lay draped across her mother's shoulders. Her right arm was around the waist of Verldean Prater.

The camera caught their smiles perfectly.

A Woman Who Plays Trumpet Is Deported

Michelle Cliff

This story is dedicated to the memory of Valaida Snow, trumpet
player, who was liberated—or escaped—from a concentration
camp. She weighed sixty-five pounds. She died in 1956 of a ce-
rebral hemorrhage. This was inspired by her story, but it is an
imagining.

She came to me in a dream and said: "Girl, you have no idea
how tough it was. I remember once Billie Holiday was lying in
a field of clover. Just resting. And a breeze came and the pollen
from the clover blew all over her and the police came out of
nowhere and arrested her for possession.

"And the stuff was red . . . it wasn't even white."

A woman. A black woman. A black woman musician. A black
woman musician who plays trumpet. A bitch who blows. A lady
trumpet player. A woman with chops.

It is the thirties. She has been fairly successful. For a woman,
black, with an instrument not made of her. Not made of flesh
but of metal.

Her father told her he could not afford two instruments for
his two children and so she would have to learn her brother's
horn.

This woman tucks her horn under her arm and packs a satchel and sets her course. Paris first.

This woman flees to Europe. No, flee is not the word. Escape? Not quite right.

She wants to be let alone. She wants them to stop asking for vocals in the middle of a riff. She wants them to stop calling her novelty, wonder, chasing after her orchid-colored Mercedes looking for a lift. When her husband gets up to go, she tosses him the keys, tells him to have it washed every now and then, the brass eyeballs polished every now and then—reminds him its unpaid for and wasn't her idea anyway.

She wants a place to practice her horn, to blow. To blow rings around herself. So she blows the U.S.A. and heads out. On a ship.

And this is not one of those I'm travelin'-light-because-my-man-has-gone situations—no, that mess ended a long time before. He belongs in an orchid-colored Mercedes—although he'll probably paint the damn thing gray. It doesn't do for a man to flaunt, he would say, all the while choosing her dresses and fox furs and cocktail rings.

He belongs back there; she doesn't.

The ship is French. Families abound. The breeze from the ocean rosying childish cheeks, as uniformed women stand by, holding shuttlecocks, storybooks, bottles. Women wrapped in tri-color robes sip bouillon. Men slap cues on the shuffleboard court, disks skimming the polished deck. Where—and this is a claim to fame—Josephine Baker once walked her ocelot or leopard or cheetah.

A state of well-being describes these people, everyone is groomed, clean, fed. She is not interested in them, but glad of the calm they convey. She is not interested in looking into their staterooms, or their lives, to hear the sharp word, the slap of a hand across a girl's mouth, the moans of intimacy.

The ship is French. The steward assigned to her, Senegalese. They seek each other out by night, after the families have retired. They meet in the covered lifeboats. They communicate through her horn and by his silver drum.

He noticed the horn when he came the very first night at sea to turn down her bed. Pointed at it, her. The next morning introduced her to his drum.

The horn is brass. The drum, silver. Metal beaten into memory, history. She traces her hand along the ridges of silver—horse, spear, warrior. Her finger catches the edge of a breast; lingers. The skin drumhead as tight as anything.

In the covered lifeboats by night they converse, dispersing the silence of the deck, charging the air, upsetting the complacency, the well-being that hovers, to return the next day.

Think of this as a reverse middle passage.

Who is to say he is not her people?

Landfall.

She plays in a club in the Quartier Latin. This is not as simple as it sounds. She got to the club through a man who used to wash dishes beside Langston Hughes at Le Grand Duc who knew a woman back then who did well who is close to Bricktop who knows the owner of the club. The trumpet player met the man who used to wash dishes who now waits tables at another club. They talked and he said, "I know this woman who may be able to help you." Maybe it was simple, lucky. Anyway, the trumpet player negotiated the chain of acquaintance with grace; got the gig.

The air of the club is blue with smoke. Noise. Voices. Glasses do clink. Matches and lighters flare. The pure green of absinthe grows cloudy as water is added from a yellow ceramic pitcher.

So be it.

She lives in a hotel around the corner from the club, on the Rue de l'Université. There's not much to the room: table, chair, bed, wardrobe, sink. She doesn't spend much time there. She has movement. She walks the length and breadth of the city. Her pumps crunch against the gravel paths in the parks. Her heels click along the edge of the river. All the time her mind is on her music. She is let alone.

She takes her meals at a restaurant called Polidor. Her food is set on a white paper-covered table. The lights are bright. She sits at the side of a glass-fronted room, makes friends with a waitress and practices her French. Friends is too strong; they talk. Her horn is swaddled in purple velvet and rests on a chair next to her, next to the wall. Safe.

Of course, people stare occasionally, those to whom she is unfamiliar. Once in a while someone puts a hand to a mouth to whisper to a companion. Okay. No one said these people were perfect. She is tired—too tired—of seeing the gape-mouthed darky advertising "Le Joyeux Nègre." Okay? Looming over a square by the Pantheon in all his happy-go-luckiness.

While nearby a Martiniquan hawked *L'Étudiant Noir*.

Joyeux Négritude.

A child points to the top of his crème brulée and then at her, smiles. Okay.

But no one calls her nigger. Or asks her to leave. Or asks her to sit away from the window at a darker table in the back by the kitchen, hustling her so each course tumbles into another. Crudités into timbale into caramel.

This place suits her fine.

The piano player longs for a baby part Africaine. She says no. Okay.

They pay her to play. She stays in their hotel. Eats their food in a clean, well-lighted place. Pisses in their toilet.

No strange fruit hanging in the Tuileries.

She lives like this for a while, getting news from home from folks who pass through. Asking, "When you coming back?"

"Man, no need for that."

Noting that America is still TOBA (tough on black asses), lady trumpet players still encouraged to vocalize, she remains. She rents a small apartment on Montparnasse, gets a cat, gives her a name, pays an Algerian woman to keep house.

All is well. For a while.

1940. The club in the Quartier Latin is shut tight. Doors boarded. The poster with her face and horn torn across. No word. No word at all. Just murmurs.

The owner has left the city on a freight. He is not riding the rails. Is not being chased by bad debts. He is standing next to his wife, her mother, their children, next to other women, their husbands, men, their wives, children, mothers-in-law, fathers, fathers-in-law, mothers, friends.

The club is shut. This is what she knows. But rumors and murmurs abound.

The piano player drops by the hotel, leaves a note. She leaves Paris. She heads north.

She gets a gig in Copenhagen, standing in for a sister moving out—simple, lucky—again. Safe. Everyone wore the yellow star there—for a time.

1942. She is walking down a street in Copenhagen. The army of occupation picks her up. Not the whole army—just a couple of kids with machine guns.

So this is how it's done.

She found herself in a line of women. And girls. And little children.

The women spoke in languages she did not understand. Spoke them quietly. From the tone she knew they were encouraging their children. She knows—she who has studied the nuance of sound.

Her horn tucked tight under her armpit. Her only baggage.

The women and girls and little children in front of her and behind her wore layers of clothing. It was a warm day. In places seams clanked. They carried what they could on their persons.

Not all spoke. Some were absolutely silent. Eyes moved into this strange place.

Do you know the work of Beethoven?

She has reached the head of the line and is being addressed by a young man in English. She cannot concentrate. She sweats through the velvet wrapped around her horn. All around her women and girls and little children—from which she is apart, yet of—are being taken in three different directions. And this extraordinary question.

A portrait on a schoolteacher's wall. Of a wiry-haired, beetle-browed man. And he was a colored genius, the teacher told them, and the children shifted in their seats.

Telemann? He wrote some fine pieces for the horn.

The boy has detected the shape of the thing under her arm.

She stares and does not respond. How can she?

The voices of women and girls and little children pierce the summer air as if the sound was being wrenched from their bodies. The sun is bright. Beads of sweat gather at the neck of the young man's tunic.

It should not be hot. It should be drear. Drizzle. Chill. But she knows better. The sun stays bright.

In the distance is a mountain of glass. The light grazes the surface and prisms split into color.

Midden. A word comes to her. The heaps of shells, bones and teeth. Refuse of the Indians. The mound-builders. That place by the river just outside of town—filled with mystery and childhood imaginings.

A midden builds on the boy's table, as women and girls and little children deposit their valuables.

In the distance another midden builds.

Fool of a girl, she told herself. To have thought she had seen it all. Left it—the worst piece of it—behind her. The body burning—ignited by the tar. The laughter and the fire. And her inheriting the horn.

One Day at the Mace Factory

Leslie Feinberg

The factory loomed above me, grim and filthy, each window painted dark brown. The plant was tucked away on the East Side of Buffalo, the heart of the African-American community.

I ground out my cigarette in the gravel with the toe of my work boot and turned up the collar of my denim jacket. My stomach twisted and knotted; I dreaded the first day on any job. I was sick of always being the outsider, the strange stranger. I fished around in my pocket for the time card from the temp-labor agency, took a deep breath and walked into the plant.

The noxious smell inside made me gag. Then I immediately forgot the odor and relaxed; there, clustered around the time clock, were most of the other butches I knew. The agency had sent us all to the same factory assignment. My friends greeted me with slaps on my back and shoulders and mock hook punches to my gut. Maybe this job wouldn't be so bad after all. Maybe it would turn out to be a permanent assignment.

We stood around the time clock, raising our voices to make our stories heard. The foreman's growl silenced us. "Get to work, you fuckin' he-shes."

We had been making a ruckus. Now we settled in quietly, respectfully finding our places on the line with the women who sat across from us, the permanent employees. As we sat in two rows facing each other, the method to the hiring told me a lot about the place. On one side sat the permanent workers: all African-American women. On the other side were the temp workers: all white butches. I had been working this sweatshop circuit for years, so I knew what this all added up to. My eyes and nose and throat were already burned raw from the fumes. This hellhole was probably dangerous. And the wages would leave my stomach growling. I'd bet my first paycheck there was no union to turn any of that around.

As the machinery began to hum, we gradually understood the task. This sweatshop produced bottles of mace. A funnel-shaped spigot filled little metal canisters with the potent chemical. Rather than a conveyor belt, the cans floated down a moving stream of water toward us. Two women at the top of the line inserted the plastic aerosol tubes inside the cans. The rest of us put the little white spray tops on the flexible plastic tubes to complete the aerosol apparatus. Near each of us were piles of spray tops, warming and softening under infrared lamps.

It took a few minutes to realize the hazard of this job. If you put the spray top on clumsily, or pressed down too hard, you maced yourself or the woman across from you.

Gerry found out the hard way. She sprayed the woman across from her in the face. The woman leaped up and began to writhe and claw her eyes as other women urged: "Don't rub, baby. Don't rub it, honey." She gagged, heaved and threw up on the concrete floor.

"Leave her alone, sit down," the foreman shouted. "Jimmy, get a mop and clean this shit up," he said, pointing to the puddle of her vomit. I felt the woman's shame deep in the pit of my stomach. "Take her to the bathroom and wash her eyes out," he ordered an older woman.

We had been working here less than an hour and already we hated the foreman, Frank. We took a vote with our eyes; it was unanimous. "Get back to work," he yelled, as he climbed back up to his perch—the elevated office that allowed him to study us as we worked.

We sat back down, stunned. Gerry looked like she was going

to cry. The woman across from me told us not to worry, it happened a couple of times a day. "It's gonna hit you or me or the woman next to you, honey," she whispered to Gerry. "There's only four directions."

After a few minutes you could see that we had all made a mental note to point the spray tops at ourselves.

In ten or fifteen minutes, the young woman Gerry had sprayed came back and sat down. She looked embarrassed. The woman on her right kissed her lightly on her cheek, "How you feel, baby? OK?" She nodded.

"I'm so sorry," Gerry said. You could tell from her voice she really meant it.

"That's all right," the young woman answered gently, "it happens here all the time." Then, just as she went back to work, she glanced up at Gerry and flashed the sweetest smile. It only took a split second, but everyone noticed it, except the women on the farthest ends of the line, and they got a poke in the ribs to pay attention.

Gerry blushed. From the way she glowed I think her toes got pink. Then she did what most all butches do: she figured she must have been mistaken. She looked as though she was silently kicking herself as she dropped her eyes and worked feverishly.

After a few moments the young woman lightly tapped one of Gerry's boots with her foot. "What's your name?" she asked. Gerry looked helplessly from side to side and swallowed hard before she answered. "I'm Monica" was Gerry's reward. They dipped their heads and worked.

We looked around at each other with a disbelief born of dashed hopes. Could it be? It seemed so. All morning long we watched them both. Occasionally one of them would glance up when the other's head was turned. We'd bow our heads and pretend to be working, while we nudged each other. But even when they weren't looking up you could feel their awareness of each other. A current of electricity sizzled between them.

We were all beside ourselves with pleasure. When the lunch whistle shrieked, we punched out and asked the other women

for directions to the nearest bar that served sandwiches. There
was one on the corner.

"You coming, Gerry?"

Monica had offered to share her lunch with Gerry. "Naw, you
guys go ahead without me," Gerry called out to us as nonchalantly as she could. She narrowed her eyes at us to demand we
not embarrass her. We wouldn't have for anything in the world.
In fact, what was happening with Monica and Gerry made us
feel good about ourselves. It was a reminder for us that this
hostile world still held the possibility of unexpected moments of
intense joy.

So we waited till we got outside to explode with loving guffaws and shouts of "Did you see that?" No matter what we
talked about at lunch over beers and roast-beef sandwiches, we
always came back to the subject of Monica and Gerry. We shook
our heads again and again. "Ain't it fuckin' great?" we agreed.

We were still shaking our heads from side to side in wonder
as we headed back as a group into the plant. We took our places
on the line. Gerry looked sheepish. The butches sitting on either
side patted her affectionately on the back.

The shrill plant whistle cut through me like a knife. Canisters
started coming toward us again. That's when Frank pointed
wordlessly to Gerry and curled his finger to beckon her. "Keep
the line going," he ordered the rest of us. Gerry followed him
to a corner of the shop floor.

We all tried to concentrate on those damned little plastic tops,
but we wanted to figure out what the hell was going on. Open
canisters of mace began clustering and bobbing around danger-
ously in the water in front of us as we strained to hear what
Frank was saying. I noticed it was Monica who had the nerve
to punch the red button that stopped the assembly line. The machinery whined to a halt.

"Why me?" Gerry shouted. "Why am I the only fuckin' one
to get laid off?" Frank must have warned her to keep her voice
down. "No," she yelled. "I don't have to shut up. Why the hell
are you pickin' on me all of a sudden?"

"I don't have to give you a reason," he snarled. His voice rose menacingly, "Get the fuck out of here, you fuckin' *freak*!" The word had been spoken out loud. Gerry immediately looked at Monica to see if she had heard. She had, of course. Gerry looked away, ashamed, before she could have seen the tenderness in Monica's eyes.

Gerry stormed out of the plant. We all stood up, unsure of what to do next. After a quick consultation between the butches, I told Frank that we quit, we were all going back to the temp agency to demand another assignment.

"Hell if I care," he snorted. "One phone call and I can replace all of you, easy."

We turned to the women who couldn't afford to quit a steady job, and said our good-byes. Monica smiled at me, wistfully.

"Hey, Gerry. Wait up!" we called to her when we got outside. We ran to catch up with her. "C'mon, we'll buy you a beer."

"Fuck him," she shouted. "Goddamn him. I should have . . ."

"Yeah, yeah," each of us murmured reassuringly. We all understood. I put my arm around Gerry. "Forget it," I told her, "he's a foreman!"

We walked for a moment in silence. I pulled Gerry closer. "You know, Monica really took a likin' to you."

Gerry pulled away from me. "Don't be stupid. She was just makin' a fool of me." With a sweep of her hand she negated all the sweetness that had happened, and she meant it. She was protecting herself.

I understand. I do that too, all the time. Still, it's a damn shame.

Preface from
Spoken in Darkness
Ann Imbrie

1975

Who murdered her was never the mystery. We might have made a mystery out of it, wondered what became of the doctor's daughter who, in the twenty years she lived among us, had left town only briefly now and then. But by 1975, no one whispered her name anymore over kitchen counters, across backyard clotheslines. No hand reached across a bridge table to touch another woman's arm, to interrupt the photos of children and grandchildren, to pose the worried question. No flyers tacked up on telephone poles counted the time. *Disappeared six months ago. Missing now more than a year.* As it happened, and hardly by accident, we shrugged her absence away, if we noticed it at all. Then we discovered her missing and we discovered her dead in the same moment, her name linked with her killer's name on the same page of the newspaper.

I was off in graduate school in another part of the world when I heard the news from my mother, over a cold telephone. I see myself standing in a dark hallway, the telephone on a small table under recessed lights, a chic design, up to the minute when the house I then rented was new.

My mother hasn't called to tell me. She has called to chat

with the one daughter who, for a time, is also a wife. We speak
of wifely things. The weather turns warm, the laundry piles up
and starts over, the husband works on the nerves. Where one
path splits off from the other, the talk crackles and puts us on
edge.

"How's school?" my mother says.

"It's June already. The semester ended a month ago."

At my objection she withdraws the question. We are still on
trial with each other.

"So, how's the vacation?" she asks instead.

"I don't get one this year." I laugh. "I have comprehensives
in the fall."

"Does that mean you won't make it home this summer?"

"I don't know, Mom." I want to tell her, *my life is more than
an interruption of yours.*

Then she eases in, sheltering and uncertain. "You remember
Lee Snavely?"

The casual mention of her name takes me back to the county
in Ohio where Lee and I grew up. It is crisscrossed by railroad
tracks and lonely country roads, the perfect setting for impossible
accidents, disasters that cannot happen and do. Cars hurtle into
each other at intersections, couples are obliterated at railroad
tracks. Stretched taut and unwavering on all sides, the landscape
explains the mystery to me. You misjudge distance, speed, shape,
everything, across those open fields. Accustomed to seeing nothing for miles around, you won't see something when it's right
on top of you, even if it's a train about to run you down.

Since I left home, I have lived among hills, near rivers, on
the other side of mountains that focus the view. For the years
before that, Lee Snavely, the doctor's dark-haired daughter, was
the only difference I had to look at. Without her, I might have
gone blind.

"She was my best friend," I say.

"That was a long time ago," my mother reminds me, as if to
say, protective of me still, *who could Lee be to you now*?

The stranger I was taught to fear. My mother's daughter. I
have long since stopped holding Lee in mind.

"Whatever happened to her?" I am ashamed to ask.

"The papers are full of it," my mother sighs.

She sketches the grim details: the small town in Michigan, the pieces of identifying jewelry, the man whose life drifted from trouble to trouble, the estranged wife who notified the authorities more than a year after the fact that her husband had buried several bodies in garbage bags under a bedroom window.

My mother shivers on the far end of the line. "It's awful," she says, and there is nothing else to say.

Later, in the other room, I draw back the drapes and stare blindly into the yard through the plate glass window. Without the curtains, the birds can't see the glass for the air. They misjudge distance and space, lose their bearings, and fling themselves against the startling glass. I find them later, hardly a trace of the collision in their bodies, except a ruffle about the neck and a dull quiet in the eyes. Now, my standing at the window warns them away.

A car rounds the corner, and honks its horn farther down the street. The woman across the way comes out for the mail, her cat on a leash. I stand there, watching, as late afternoon wears down to evening, until I can name the noise I do not quite hear.

The memory of Lee beats its wings in my heart.

My mind spins back to the fairgrounds, to the farm machines, to an August day, hot and humid and still, when I first met the dark-haired stranger from another church and another elementary school.

1962–1964

Lee had a beauty mark on her cheek, like Elizabeth Taylor's. She was not like anyone I had ever seen before, exotically beautiful, her hair a dark circle around her face, her eyes dark as well, her eyebrows shadows against the light of her skin.

That day at the fair Lee wore blue knit shorts, and a white, short-sleeved top with a scalloped collar trimmed in pink. I stared, fascinated and alarmed, at her chest.

Like me, I thought, facing seventh grade, *she needs a bra and isn't wearing one.*

My father, innocent of the world, said Lee shouldn't have been at the fair at all that week, her own father buried less than a week before. My mother said it was no wonder, after a funeral like that.

Lee's father, the doctor with the big house in the country, wanted no mourners. At the committal a band played "Oh God Our Help in Ages Past" Dixieland style—saxophones, clarinets, trumpets, and one banjo. The people gathered in a half circle on a little rise near the back of the Oak Grove Cemetery. When the music started, one head turned to another, a question in the eyes. A nervous fan disturbed the air before a woman's face. A man, another doctor, shifted his weight, uncertain where to put his large, gentle hands. A child giggled at a squirrel that darted behind a headstone. No toe tapped. Cheerful syncopation bounced around the grave and the saints came marching in.

My father, a Presbyterian minister, shook his head over the whole business. No local preacher should have allowed such a thing, he said. People are helped by the sadness of funerals, sorrow is the order of the day. But Loyal Bishop, the Lutheran pastor, was new in town, and he agreed to the dying man's request. Maybe, fresh out of seminary, he was still young enough and handsome enough to think there were many ways to make a joyful noise unto the Lord.

The scandal of her father's funeral was the first thing I knew about Lee, before I'd even met her, and the information set me up right. As I came to know her, I figured the tough spin she gave everything spun right out of her genes.

Two weeks after the start of seventh grade, Cheryl, a popular eighth grader and out of my ken, asked three or four of us to meet her for lunch in the school cafeteria. Other small groups of my friends clustered around other eighth-grade girls seated at various points on the cool side of the lunchroom.

"About the dress code," Cheryl began.

The student handbook spelled that out: girls had to wear

dresses or skirts and blouses to school. No pants, no cut-offs, no sloppy sneakers, no halter tops. They wanted us to look like girls without causing a distraction. It was a fine line to walk.

"When Miss Cook pulls the chairs into a circle," Cheryl continued, "keep your knees together at all times."

Miss Cook, young and blond and fresh out of college, taught American history. She announced on the first day of school that she didn't believe in lining up chairs in rows, no sooner a good idea than it turned dangerous.

Rule #1: Knees together.

"When you're changing classes," Cheryl said, "walk up the middle of the stairs. Along the railing, the boys on the next flight down will look up your skirt."

Rule #2: Middle of the stairs.

"Don't hang around with boys who wear white socks."

"Why not?" one of us asked, bravely. Most of the boys we knew wore white socks.

Cheryl rolled her eyes. "White socks are queer," she said.

Rule #3: No white socks. I was beginning to think I should take notes.

"Try to get to school fifteen minutes early, and check your locker before home-room."

This rule I already understood. Cheryl's invitation had been written on notebook paper and stuck in the ventilator slits of my locker. I didn't know how she figured out which locker was mine. Eighth grade was full of mysteries, the next magical link in the chain of command that stretched all the way past the other side of high school to our mothers. We learned what we were to become, step by step.

"And you girls can't walk around holding hands anymore. That's sixth-grade stuff. You want people to think you're lesbians?"

We girls eyed each other suspiciously and shook our heads. Of course not, I thought, but I didn't have any idea what Cheryl was talking about.

"Tell your parents it's time you had your first boy-girl party," Cheryl added, conspiracy in her whispered tone.

An older girl named Linda came up behind Cheryl and tapped her on the shoulder.

"You about finished here yet?"

Cheryl rose from her chair and leaned on the long table to look at us sternly.

"If you guys have any questions," she said, "ask Mrs. Wynn or one of the other gym teachers. I don't want to get a reputation for hanging around with seventh graders."

Linda and Cheryl walked off together, their arms wrapped around their books.

Our town organized children under the age of twelve into five different elementary schools, all of them named for the streets they were built on. Those streets wandered past churches and shops and grocery stores with wide, clean aisles; past houses hidden behind rambling front porches, shaded by maples and dying elms in the center of town; past duplexes crowded together, separated by narrow, gravel driveways or paltry gardens; past brick houses farther out in the subdivisions, slung low to the ground, stretched out on green swaths of lawn. Eventually some of those streets wandered out to the country, where they turned into roads and cut wide strips between miles of soybeans and tomatoes and corn, farms with red barns and white silos. This was our Eden: at twelve, all of us converged on one junior high school, trailing our neighborhoods behind us, and we didn't know it yet.

The eighth-grade girls didn't ask Lee to join in those little talks. She grew up in the country, like a farm kid, although her father had run with the country-club set. She didn't fit with the crowd, lived on the outside of the circle. The eighth-grade girls probably didn't know who she was. Lee, I thought, was safe to ask. From where she stood, she couldn't blab about how dumb I was to the whole school.

I met her at the bus stop at the end of the day, before I caught up with my real friends down at Rogers Drug where we bent our heads over *Seventeen*, played discreet transistors under the tables, and drank Coke out of shapely glasses. In mid-September, the maple trees along Grove Street where the buses waited in line to pick up their children had already started dropping leaves. Crimson and yellow swatches stuck to the sidewalk with the recent rain. I had a lot to learn in a hurry, and I wasn't going to learn it at Rogers Drug. I decided on the direct approach.

"She's a woman who loves other women instead of men," Lee said.

"You mean girls can be queer?"

Lee nodded. "It's like a medical word," she said. Lee wanted to be a doctor like her father had been, and she already had a head start on a technical vocabulary.

"So you've had the talk, huh?" she added.

I looked up at her, surprised at how word gets around, and scooted a maple leaf into the gutter with the toe of my saddle shoe.

"Pretty scary, isn't it," Lee said. "All those rules."

"Yeah," I said. Junior high was full of dangers I hadn't dreamed of.

The door of her bus jerked open, and, twirling her skirt in the air, Lee stepped into the doorway. She turned toward me, pulled her skirt up above her knee, and did a little can-can kick from the first step.

"What happens," she said, "when you *want* boys to look up your skirt?"

Then she disappeared down the dark corridor of the bus.

I hadn't thought of that possibility yet. All at once I saw how easily you could get trapped in the rules.

Early fall in the eighth grade, just after school started, I helped Lee plan a pool party. We wanted that party to be perfect, and we spent a lot of time setting it up, picking out all the best slow songs, trying on different outfits. It was a good thing we worked so hard on it, because as it turned out, it was the only party Lee ever had.

The week before, I stayed over at her house, and we sat up late in her bedroom wearing shorty pajamas, writing and revising the guest list. We marked off two columns on a piece of paper, one labeled "Boys" and the other "Girls," and started by listing

the couples. Tom and Lee. Ann and Sean. Jim and Maggie. The
other Ann and the other Tom.

"They broke up last week," I said.

"But we can invite them both, don't you think. I mean, they'll
be *civil*."

"Oh sure, they can be the extras."

"So, what about Mike?"

Lee was doubtful. "He wears white socks," she said.

"Yeah, but he's a good dancer. And cute, too. And there's
Joel." I was running through the list of extras.

"And Carla," Lee added. "Wouldn't Carla and Joel make a
good couple?"

"Oh, let's see."

I wrote their names down on a piece of paper, crossed out the
letters their names had in common, and worked the lottery we
used to determine our romantic futures: love, hate, friendship,
marriage, one possibility for each uncrossed letter until you ran
out of them, and the last uncrossed letter spoke the truth. This
particular matchup ended in "love," but if it hadn't, we would
have added middle names and started over, a way of cheating
fate. It was an odd little ritual, since both compatibility and in-
compatibility depended ultimately on what the names *didn't* have
in common.

"We can change into our bathing suits if it's warm enough,"
Lee said.

"And we can dance out by the pool," I said. "Isn't that romantic?"

"Plenty of dark corners for interdigital contact and oscula-
tion," Lee said. "That's making out."

"What about your mother?" I could never have a make-out
party at my house.

"She won't even notice," Lee said.

Once we had our plans in order and called everybody on the
list, the mothers took care of their own plans. They hooked into
the telephone network to figure out whose mothers would drop
us off, in clumps, out of station wagons, and whose mothers

would pick us up when the party was over. They'd learned their lesson the past summer, when my whole gang of girls spent our Saturday nights at the Little League park. We climbed out of the station wagon and told the mother driving that some other mother was bringing us home. Then we met up with the boys and rode home on the handlebars of their bicycles, our hair flying out in the wind.

After that summer, our mothers didn't leave the arrangements up to us.

By halfway through the party, things were going pretty much as we'd planned. About the time Joel and Carla started falling in love, Lee and I took a break, and slipped into the bathroom together to congratulate ourselves. The orchestra behind Bobby Vinton's "Blue on Blue" was swelling up, the sounds drifting in from poolside. I approached the mirror to put on my lipstick, smoothed a little of it into my cheeks for color. Lipstick came in flavors that year, and my flavor was Coca-Cola.

"I don't get this song," I said.

I often heard the words wrong, converting the real thing to the image of the world I had in my head. For years I thought Tammy Wynette fit right in with my social studies lessons, singing about some guy named Stan from New Orleans, "Stan, Bayou Man." *Guantanamera* sounded in my ears like *one ton of manna*. Biblical words seemed right at home on the Top Forty charts. Now I thought I heard Bobby Vinton singing about something from *Ephesians*.

Cool little 'Phesian. That's what it sounded like to me.

"That's *cruel little teasin'*," Lee said, and rolled her eyes.

Even after Lee set me straight on the words this time, I didn't get what Bobby Vinton was talking about. *Cruel little teasin'?* A tease was my big brother, tickling his little sisters until we almost suffocated. What could that possibly have to do with Bobby Vinton breaking up with his girlfriend and being blue on blue?

"I'll show you," Lee said. "You be the boy."

She made with her arms like she wanted to dance with me. I

dutifully slipped my arm around her waist, and started leading her around the tiny bathroom. Right away, I noticed the difference. My knees didn't knock against hers once, the way they did when I danced with boys. She nestled up to me a little off center, our breasts alternating, and every step we took, her thigh pushed between my legs. When we stopped, she left me dizzy and aching and dumb.

"*That's* teasin'," Lee said.

I stepped back from her, barely recovered, relieved under the circumstances to have played the boy. "Some trick," I said, when I had my breath again.

"It's not such a useful skill," Lee shrugged, "when you're a one-man woman."

She turned quickly out of the bathroom, off in search of Tom and one of the big, comfortable chairs for making out in. I stared into my own face in the mirror, flushed with the lipstick on my cheeks, and pulled my hair back behind my ears. For a moment, I tried to imagine a boy's face looking back at me.

When I found Sean standing around with the cottonwood trees, I led him off to a darker place along the privacy fence around the pool. We danced close all the way through "What Will My Mary Say?" and "Be My Baby." We kissed while we danced. When I felt sure of the lesson I'd learned, I shifted my thigh into place. Sean's breath rippled through his shoulders.

"Hmmm," he whispered in my ear, and pulled me as close as he could. "I didn't know you were that kind of girl."

"I'll be whatever kind of girl I want," I said.

There were a couple of problems at that party, things we hadn't counted on and couldn't control. But brave and unchaperoned, we managed, I guess.

The two Toms started poking at each other from opposite sides of the pool with those long aluminum rods you scrape the bottom with, and one of them fell in with his clothes on. We thought it was funny—*splish, splash, he was taking a bath*—but then Tom came back up again, sputtering water, and mad. He thought the other Tom had done it on purpose, and was ready to punch him, but Sean broke it up and made them shake hands. You know how boys are: two of them do something to each other, and then they shake hands, as if everything were just fine, because they don't want you to think they're bad sports. You can tell they'd just as soon kill each other.

And at one point, Bonnie and Bob had some kind of fight. He was a little runt, but he had a bad temper and sometimes flew out of control. Bob kept telling Bonnie to stop whining at him, and when she wouldn't he hauled off and hit her in the face with the back of his hand. He was all over her apologizing, but she started to howl anyway, and when she started to howl, the dogs in the kennels around the pool started to bark, and the noise got all mixed up with "The Monster Mash," spinning loud on the record player. I thought that would bring Lee's mom out for sure. She was crazy about those dogs.

But she never did show up, as Lee had predicted. Usually, a mother wants to get a look at her kid's friends, checking to see that they don't have cigarettes rolled up in their T-shirt sleeves, or making mental notes about what they're wearing so she can complain to her friends on the phone the next day about what the other mothers sent their kids out in. Maybe Mrs. Snavely didn't have friends to complain to, living way out there in the country. She didn't look us over once.

"You'd think she would have at least been worried that Tom's parents might sue," Lee said after everybody else had gone home. Their boy might have hurt himself falling into that pool.

We wandered around the swimming pool, wadding up soggy crepe paper and throwing away paper plates. All of a sudden I understood why the only flurry of maternal activity I ever witnessed in Mrs. Snavely was the time Blusie, one of their German shepherds, not a breeder but a house pet, took a bite out of me and my favorite pair of wool bermudas. Mrs. Snavely, all nervous fuss and bother, rushed me to the emergency room for a tetanus shot and paid for everything.

"You mean,'' I said, "if I'd asked she would have bought me a new pair of shorts?''

"You could have made money on the deal,'' Lee said.

From the driveway my mother, come to take me home, tooted the horn. I shot one more bedraggled decoration in the trash, and scooted off for the car.

"Two points,'' Lee called out after me.

"See you Monday,'' I called back.

My mother was full of questions about the party. What did you do? Who did you dance with? What did she fix to eat? Some questions I didn't particularly want to answer, and I struggled against the pressure coming from behind the steering wheel.

"Come on, Mom,'' I said finally. "It was a party. You know.''

She let it go at that. She wasn't after the details. When she came to the point she was driving at, I heard immediately the shift in her voice.

"How did you like Lee's mom?'' she asked.

In conversations with my mother, I had learned to listen closely. A little test edged into her voice, and under the circumstances, a lie was out of the question.

"She wasn't around much,'' I said.

My mother figured it out before her phone started buzzing the next morning. Some of the other mothers gathered force over the wires that very night, even before some of us arrived home. The next time Lee tried to plan a party, it never got off the ground. None of our mothers would let us go.

A few weeks later, Lee asked me to sleep over on Saturday, and I told her sure before I asked my mom, who reminded me that I'd have church the next morning.

"Ask your father,'' she said.

I knew what that meant. He would say, Ask your mother, and I'd run back and forth from the kitchen to the living room until I got smart and figured out the answer was no.

"We'll see," my mother mused, and we both knew that meant no, too.

From years of practice, we were good at beating around the bush. My parents didn't raise their voices with me because they didn't have to. They let the words *lean* one way or another. Under the pressure of their subtle weight, I didn't act, I adjusted. To move too quickly, to breathe too heavily, to speak too loudly might bring the house of cards tumbling down around us all.

I tried a different tack, to shift in the prevailing wind.

"I already told her okay," I said.

It was a mild threat, and I thought it might work.

"Why don't you have Lee to our house," my mother suggested.

She needed to keep an eye on me. I loved my fun with Lee, and wanted to protect it. But I had to protect my mother, too, who worried about my wandering too far out of range, where something bad might happen to both of us. To have it both ways, my fun and my mother too, sometimes I had to lie.

"Some other time," I said, with hardly a wince in my heart. "It doesn't matter."

After that, I stopped talking about Lee at home, and I tried to see her whenever I could at school.

Mostly it was in the afternoons, when I found her in the middle of a bunch of girls from her English class, clustered around the frosted window in the girls' bathroom. She was taking bets on the teacher's bra.

That bra was a distraction and an opportunity. At the beginning of every class, the strap started slipping out from under her sleeve, down over her wobbly, old-lady arm. And before class started every day, Lee met up with a group of girls from the class, each of them taking a guess at the statistics. How far would that strap get before the teacher felt the thin satin line against her skin? At what precise moment would she find an excuse to write on the blackboard, as if seized by the beauty of grammar, when really she was trying to jiggle her bra strap back up under her sleeve? Sometimes, she reached right into the front of her blouse and jerked the strap into place. Lee watched the clock all period, and then threw a paper wad at the girl whose guess came closest. Otherwise, she said, English class was boring.

Lee managed to avoid trouble for it herself. Donna, on the receiving end of some of those spitballs, got in trouble instead. At the parent-teacher meetings that winter, Donna's mother learned that her daughter was developing an "attitude," it interfered with her schoolwork, it kept her off the cheerleading squad, and the teacher suggested that the girl be encouraged to find other friends.

I couldn't have gotten away with it in my English class, even if I'd wanted to, even if Miss Gelvin hadn't been such an elegant lady, always meticulously dressed. At the first hint of an idle moment, Miss Gelvin had us all copy out our homework, the major spelling rules, or a poem by Robert Frost, or long lists of prepositions, on yellow tablet paper, marking across the top in big letters, CIM: "Copy in Ink and Memorize." Then we sat there, our hands cupped around our eyes (for the focus, she said), until somebody could stand up and repeat the whole page by heart. I had the most practiced memory in the class, and I might have to know someday why *preferred* has two r's and *offered* only one. There was no clock-watching or spitballing in Miss Gelvin's class. She kept us in line with a ruler.

I inherited memory from my father. Late Saturday nights or early Sunday mornings, my father's voice came to my bedroom, from behind the study door across the hall or up from the kitchen. I didn't hear the words distinctly, only the sounds—the rise of a question, the slight pause after one of his little jokes, the rhythm of a phrase repeated when clarity most mattered. In the course of the week, he had written his sermon, an elaborate structure of ideas and illustrations, and the night or the morning before, when I was in bed, he rehearsed his words, making sure he had them all by heart. When he stood in the pulpit, my father delivered that whole sermon, and he never used notes.

Words of one syllable, or more than one syllable accented on the last, ending in a final consonant preceded by a single vowel, double the final consonant when adding a suffix beginning with a vowel. I believed in spelling, and remembering was in my genes.

From *her* dad, Lee inherited science.

One day at school, she met me at my locker first thing, all excited.

"Did you bring your lunch today?" she asked.

"Of course I did."

"I've found a great place where you can eat it," she said.

When the lunch period came, Lee took me back to the alley behind the school building. All the hoods went back there to smoke cigarettes before school, and any other chance they got. Lee wasn't interested in smoking yet. She wanted to show me the biology shed.

They didn't teach biology to eighth or ninth graders, but the junior high used to be the high school. When the janitors moved the biology lab out to the new high-school building on the north edge of town, they'd left behind a bunch of stuff in a little shed in the alley. For Lee, it was a find.

"Look at all this," she said, when she took me in.

All over the shelves I saw scrunched-up dead things in big glass jars, brains and frogs and foetal pigs, creatures taken from their mothers' bellies at different stages in their development.

"Who killed all those babies?" I wanted to know.

"They were dead before they were born," Lee said.

"That's sad," I said.

"That's science," Lee said. "Won't it be neat in biology, cutting up frogs?"

I was unconvinced.

A person who wants to go to medical school has to get used to that kind of thing, Lee said, cutting up frogs and looking at dead babies while she is eating her lunch. Lee walked around the shed, her tuna salad sandwich in hand, peered into each jar, traced a shape in the glass.

"Look at that," she said. "That's a brain."

I said wouldn't it be fun if she could take over Dr. Howell's general practice someday.

"And spend the rest of my life poking Popsicle sticks down kids' throats?" she said. "Not on your life. I'm going to be a pathologist like my dad."

I didn't know what pathologists did. Lee said they looked at blood and stuff under microscopes and most of their patients were dead.

"It's in the interest of science," Lee said, "and disease control."

"I still think plain ordinary babies aren't so bad," I said. "Practically everybody has babies."

"Yeah," Lee said. "But absolutely everybody dies."

I couldn't argue with that.

"I hate babies," Lee said. "Babies are soft in the brain."

I shook my head, without meaning to, and looked at her worried. Maybe I hadn't heard her right. She'd been a baby herself once. All of us had.

My mother didn't let me spend the night at Lee's much anymore, but sometimes she relented about Saturday afternoons. I didn't get it. It seemed to me that a person could run into as much trouble in the daytime as after dark, especially at Lee's.

When I went to Lee's house on Saturday afternoons, we usually played out in the barn. It was a big empty shell of a building, with wooden ladders for climbing on and lofts for dangling your feet over. Barrels squatted here and there, old tools hung on the walls. All the animals had been sold off some time before, and a few others had invaded. Occasionally we saw a field mouse dart under a pile of old hay, and once a possum ambled lazily out from under a floorboard, in broad daylight, like she owned the place. Isn't that just like a mother, Lee said. That possum had a nest of babies under there.

The barn was full of lessons. In that barn, I found out about autopsies, and discovered a very disturbing fact about the dog food we fed our Misty at home. What did I think was in the can, Lee said, when the label just said "meat."

Most of Lee's father's patients, she told me, were dead *people*, but once, in the interests of science, he did an autopsy on a horse.

Right out here in the barn. You can still see the stains on the cement floor, Lee said.

The horse had been something like a pet; all the kids were learning to ride on it. But then one day it fell over dead, with a thud, just like that, without any apparent reason. That made Dr. Snavely mad. He cut the dead horse open in the middle, and spilled its insides out on the floor in the barn. He was out here poking around for hours, Lee said, trying to find out what killed that horse.

I had seen my father gut fish we ate for dinner sometimes in the summer, and I imagined this picture on a much larger scale, in a phylum more like my own. The toe of a heavy rubber boot prodded the dark red kidney, pushed against the liver, dusty brown and spongy. The lungs, flat and pink on the outside, fibrous and tough inside. Yards of intestine, complicated, milky, warm still toward the center. Inadequate instruments, undersized and blunt, did their work.

"What did kill it?" I asked.

"It had a bad heart from the very beginning," Lee shrugged. "It was just waiting to pop."

There wasn't a thing he could do about it, the heart, engorged and on fire, pumping its way toward explosion. I squinted my eyes shut with the picture of it. Afterwards, Lee said, her father fed the horsemeat to his favorite dogs.

Birds chattered in the rafters above us, and swooped around in the dusty air, unable to find their way outside again, even though the door stood wide open and the windows had no glass. I yelled at them, and waved my arms, *there, there, the window's over there*, and Lee laughed at me, because the birds didn't pay any attention. They fluttered and swooped and chattered in the frenzied air, and then one smashed into the wall by the door. It fell with a soft noise to the cement below, its feathers ruffled into a necklace along the line where the tiny bones had broken.

Lee and I were best friends for what seemed like a long time, most of seventh and all of eighth grade, first in the open and then in secret. We did all the things together that best friends are supposed to do. But then all of a sudden, for no apparent reason, she acted like she didn't want to see me anymore. In fact, she sort of disappeared. I didn't see her in the halls much, or in the girls' bathroom between classes, and she never called.

"I don't understand it," I said to my mother. "I don't think we had a fight."

"You've been spending a lot of time together," my mother said. "Maybe you have cabin fever."

My mother said it was a Navy term. Sailors got to feeling they were too big for the space they were in, stranded in the ocean in a boat. All they could think of was getting out, and they turned frantic about it.

"Is that why sailors have such a bad reputation? Like in *Mr. Roberts*?"

"They do have a wild time," my mother said, "when they're on liberty."

I wondered if it would ever come back to normal.

"It will be good for both of you," my mother said, "to take a rest from each other. Like shore leave."

She sounded relieved, and I tuned myself to her mood. I settled into her conviction. Lee and I had cabin fever, and needed a vacation from each other. Spring vacation, I thought, ought to do the trick.

It didn't. When you're twelve or thirteen and take a vacation from your best friend, the circle closes in to cover over the empty space. It has to be that way, because when you're twelve or thirteen, you can't go it alone. And maybe my mother knew that all along.

Eventually, I drifted back to my old gang, all of them cheerleaders, all of them daughters of my mother's friends. Once I'd learned from Lee Snavely that different people were meant for different things, Maggie didn't have so much power over me, and all the way through high school we were best friends again. I could sleep over at her house whenever I wanted.

I last saw Lee Snavely several years later, in 1971, on the other side of high school. We passed each other going opposite directions on Wooster Street, right next to the junior high where Lee and I had been best friends. She waved cheerfully, and called out to me from across the street.

"Is that *Lee*?" I shouted back.

I waited at the corner for the light to change, bouncing my eager heel against the curb. From across the street, I felt happy to see her thick, dark hair. Once I got closer, I changed my mind.

We exchanged facts for a few minutes on the corner. I was home from college for the summer. She was on her lunch hour from work at the drugstore on the east side of town. I shifted my weight, stared at my sandal, then found an excuse to make my way farther down Wooster Street.

"Let's get together before you go back to school," Lee said. "Eric would love to see you."

"Sounds great," I said.

For a moment it seemed that we were two old friends, two married ladies trying to arrange a white wine lunch at the Pheasant Room, as our mothers might have. I meant what I said, that I'd like to see them, spend an evening with Lee and her husband Eric, whom I'd known in high school, but I didn't make good on the promise.

I carried with me when I left a picture of what Lee was wearing, a blue knit miniskirt, and a white, sleeveless T-shirt, a more grown-up version of what she'd had on at the fair, that day nearly ten years before. One look at her outfit marked it in my memory. At her thighs, her upper arms, her shoulders, her collarbone, huge purple bruises ran to gaudy yellow, like jewelry dropping from her neck. We didn't share a circle anymore, but in a small town, talk doesn't respect a circle. I had heard at Christmas parties and backyard barbecues that Eric was hard on her. And seeing it for myself, I thought when I left her that day on the street that we weren't like two old friends at all. By that time, I had learned my lessons well. In her place, I would have worn long pants, long sleeves.

The Printer
Melanie Kaye/Kantrowitz

He lived upstairs—I meant to say, he worked upstairs, on the third floor, that's where his printing shop was, and I said "he lived" because we lived downstairs on the second floor in an office; but semisecretly. No one was supposed to know. I was scraping by as a free-lance proofreader, she did a multitude of odd jobs, none of which required her to leave the office for more than a couple of hours at a time. So we were always there with two dogs; then she left and I was always there with one dog. Occasional smells of food seeped out into the hall, though we rarely cooked: there was only a single hot plate and no refrigerator. Besides, she craved the soothing atmosphere of restaurants, where someone else does the cooking.

The printer must have known we lived there because he was around nearly as much as we were, but he at least went home, nine, ten, eleven at night, to show up again early the next morning. Sometimes we chatted on the stairs. Our car had New Mexico plates and his daughter lived in Arizona. He and his wife had visited years before and were planning another visit that summer. He loved to discuss the southwest with us, to contrast it with mid-coast Maine.

"The sky's a different color blue out there, did you notice that?" he'd ask, and when one of us would nod, he'd warm to his subject. "You can see for miles, like your head was a top, spinning. You can see in every direction."

Once, after days of soggy April, we had a particularly animated exchange about the summer thunderstorms for which the southwest is famous, and the vast rainbow arcing the horizon as the skies clear.

Another time he mentioned that he always used to think domes were ugly—domes are common hippie houses in Maine—but he said, "If the sky out there doesn't look like the inside of a huge dome, I don't know what."

The printer was small, maybe five foot five, and he looked remarkably like a mouse, a grey mouse with glasses, somewhat bald, and slightly pouchy around the mouth and jaw. He always wore a hat—not a cap—when he went out, and a coat, not a jacket. He must have been in his sixties. His eyes behind the glasses were grey too, but piercing, eyes that had paid a great deal of attention to detail. But why am I telling you about the printer?

Mid-coast Maine is where we lived/worked in an old office building with pressed tin ceilings and a fourth floor, now gutted, with splintery rotting floors. Once it was a dance hall, like the uppermost level of every single building on both sides of Main Street, when Glen Hill was a granite boom town and there was work and money and good times. Now there were empty offices and storefronts up and down Main Street and not even one bar (a blessing, considering the propensity of the town's young male population to drink).

We moved into the office in September. Lest you feel sorry for us, let me say it had three rooms, radiator heat, and a toilet, with (cold) running water, plus sidewalks shoveled and sanded, courtesy of the city, using the term loosely. The tin ceilings, originally designed to imitate molded decorative plaster, sported peaches, melons, and bunches of grapes, and the black and white linoleum squares covering the floors, though faded to charcoal and beige, were still elegant. All this for $150 a month; high living after a two-room log cabin with wood heat, no water, no

electricity, no insulation, an often impassable road in winter, and
mosquitos whining through the chinks in summer.

I am avoiding the point. The point is this: when we moved
into the office we had been lovers for nearly five years, through
most of which we fought bitterly, desperately—howling, screaming, sometimes throwing one another around, more often satisfying ourselves with intense audio effects. Most of the time we'd
lived together out in the country with no close neighbors, and
you can see what a blessing that was.

Here are our fights: her characteristic gambit was historical,
the dredging up of everything I'd ever done wrong, the same
poor little cluster of misdeeds which I would, clearly, never ex-
piate, so why it took me all those years to recognize atonement
was not in sight I don't know. My characteristic move was (and
by chance it slant-rhymes) hysterical; the injustice of her litany
never failed to unleash in me torrents of helpless rage so intense
I am surprised I didn't kill her or myself. What finally pushed
me to learn control was the night I put my hand through the
office window. Blood streamed down my arm, biting wind
rushed in through the broken glass, and I had to face the dangerous water I was trying to walk on—though, to tell the truth,
the cuts were superficial, and the icy wind blew only in my
fantasy, since behind the jagged window sat an intact pane of
storm glass.

But the next time I felt that killing rage rise up in me—she
had locked me out so that I was stuck on the narrow landing
outside the office door. It was a harsh wet night. The upper
portion of the office door was glass. . . . Guess what I wanted
to do more than anything in the world? But I thought. I thought
of consequences: of cutting myself, of needing to replace the
glass; the expense, the embarrassment. Iron-willed, I cooled myself out. Then I tricked her into thinking I'd left and when she
opened the door, I boldly pushed my way in.

But before that, while I was locked out sobbing on the landing,
the printer came by from upstairs. The walls and ceilings of this
building, while old and solid, were not soundproof. We could
hear his printing press, the phone, conversations with customers.

So we knew he heard our fights, vicious uncontrolled fights, fights between two women who were lovers in small-town Maine, a Jew and an Italian, neither with a lick of verbal restraint.

The printer came by from upstairs. "Hello," he said, "nasty weather we're having." I murmured agreement. "Doesn't it make you miss Arizona—I mean New Mexico, that's right. The dry air and the sun, how it comes out and dries every speck of dampness. My daughter says it doesn't even matter if you put laundry away damp." And then he passed along downstairs, restraining himself, I could tell, from reaching further into his favorite pocket of southwestern observations which he obviously did not get to trot out nearly often enough. His vague but flawless tact awed me, and it was possible to hate myself less because a perfectly decent, reasonable and, above all, calm human being treated me as another being like himself.

The printer was always up there in his shop, even though we knew by the footsteps on the staircase how few customers bothered to climb the two long flights. I heard from my friend Sylvia, a bookkeeper who knew the dirt on just about everyone in town, that he'd been considered an excellent and reliable craftsman and had once done a thriving business. But now there were three other printers in Glen Hill, all with state-of-the-art equipment; one had even moved up from Boston to specialize in arty press work. Glen Hill was about to grow, and by the time I left, Main Street would be showing definite signs of invasion from hanging ferns and primary-color salad spinners.

But the town was growing in services, restaurants, tourist shops; not industry and not business. We used to wonder what the printer found to do up there all the time. His southwest stories suggested a deep fondness for his wife that precluded any suspicion that he was trying to keep away from her. We decided finally that the explanation was simple. He loved to print. He loved his equipment, however outmoded. He loved solitude. I used to envy his calm up there, the sanctuary of it, high above Main Street with only the ghosts of turn-of-the-century Glen Hill dancing above his head, executing who knew what intricate capers to who knew what high-stepping music.

And envied it more and more, as the velocity of discord increased between us, the fights, me hurling the beautiful wooden-with-leather-seat desk chair against the wall, denting the wall and smashing the chair arm; the screaming, the sobbing. The printer was the one who heard, even more than several waitresses in various local restaurants where we compulsively spent money we could not afford on the one somewhat reliable pleasure we could come up with. Unfortunately, we often ruined this extravagance by fighting, and once we were crying so hard we had to walk out on an expensive dinner in one of the tourist restaurants that had just reopened after its seven-month winter break. I wanted to ask the waitress if we could take the dinner home, but I was ashamed to be caring about food at a time like that. It was a full year before I'd walk into that restaurant again, and then it was with Sylvia and her lover Florence, taking me out to dinner the night before I left Maine.

The waitresses by and large were kind, but they didn't have to listen to it day after day like the printer did. It was getting more intense. She wanted to leave. I was stricken though secretly relieved, my ambivalence—and hers—reflected in the trading off we did for the next few months: I'd beg her to stay and she'd relent just as I grew resolute; then she'd cajole me into softening just as she was making plans to go. We finally agreed to call it a trial separation, knowing this was a lie, and at last I set a date: "You have to be gone by June 1st," I said. And she was.

What did they think, all over Main Street—the stores we frequented, the restaurants; one day we were almost always together, then I was almost always alone. She had vanished. I might have committed murder for all anyone knew. Aside from friends—and there were not many, ours was not the sort of relationship people got close to—not one person asked where she was.

Except the printer. When I said she had gone back to New Mexico, he happily launched into reminiscence: "Remember all

the colors? I had no idea about the colors, all the things that live
in the desert. Did you ever see a yucca plant blooming?'' I nodded, remembering a huge, spiny half-globe with a stalk coming
out of the top. The blooms have the texture of tulips and hang
off the stalk like ivory bells edged with rose. ''I was just thinking
about those the other day,'' he added, without explaining why
the yucca had come to him from thousands of miles away.
''Around here, in the woods, even along the beach, there's so
much growing you take it for granted. Everything has it easy.''
I thought of the Maine winters, but I knew what he meant: he
meant water, lots of it. ''In the desert, every flower that blooms
is a tiny miracle, you know? Did you ever see the cholla blooming?'' He pronounced it correctly: choy-a. ''It shocked me the
first time, that color, just blooms out of nowhere. Magenta.''

Another time he stopped me on the stairs with a magazine
picture of desert paintbrush. ''Remember that one?'' he asked. I
did. Desert paintbrush is scarlet, you spot them a mile away.
''What do you think of the color, think they got it right?'' he
asked, professionally concerned.

''You should have been a botanist,'' I told him, ''you're really
into this.'' He smiled his self-deprecating mouse smile. ''Maybe
I'll do that next. Yup, maybe I'll be a botanist,'' sounding the
word like it was slightly unfamiliar.

It wasn't too long after that I heard the landlord had cancer,
inoperable, probably dying, and sure enough the building went
up for sale. Just a little more than a year after I'd moved in and
now there were no vacant offices on the whole street. Downtown
revival is what they called it here, as in scores of other American
cities where it was or wasn't working. I was scared my rent
would skyrocket, not to mention that a new landlord not sick
with cancer might pay more mind to the tenant whose business
was obscure, who no matter what hour of the day or night always
seemed to be at work with her dog along, and who—when the
realtor knocked at the door to show prospective buyers—would
spend a good five minutes running back and forth before she'd

open the door. (I was of course picking up or covering over signs of domesticity, which were many, including the new office-sized refrigerator and spice shelf.)

Around the same time I ran into the printer, on the stairs as usual, and he was nervous too. He'd been paying, he told me, the same rent for the last fifteen years, $50 a month. He figured anyone who bought the building would raise his rent to the going rate. He didn't spell out the implications, but we both knew there was no way he could afford to maintain his print shop with a higher rent.

It was a youngish couple investing cleverly in real estate who bought the building. They raised my rent a little, asked me to pay a reasonable share of the heating bill; and they chose, for the time being, to ignore my obvious domestic installation. But when I ran into the printer on the corner, one of our very few conversations not on the stairs, he told me his new rent was beyond his means. He said this matter-of-factly, and the details were filled in later by Sylvia the bookkeeper. Not only could he not keep the shop, he couldn't even sell his printing press, old and huge as it was. No one would pay to move it. Nor could he afford to move it himself, even if he had someplace to move it to, which he didn't.

So at the age of sixty-something the printer closed his shop. I saw him the day the moving men came to haul out such shelving and small equipment as he had been able to sell. "Are you feeling bad about this?" I dared to ask a Mainer, a man to boot.

"Well, it'll take some getting used to," he said. "The wife and I are driving out to Arizona, see the daughter. Then," he shook his head, "it'll take some getting used to, all right."

A couple of evenings later he knocked on my door and asked if I wanted any paper. "What?" I said, startled. "I'm closing the shop, you know, and there's a few boxes of good paper, no point in letting the trashman take it." I am a sucker for paper anyway, so I went upstairs with him, and not only were there stacks of decent white paper, there were smooth, sturdy gold-colored cardboards, rough-textured purple vellum, long strips of posterboard in rose and yellow and ivory. There were onion skins and cream-colored heavy stock bordered with red so dark it was almost black. I collected what seemed to me a huge quantity of paper. "Take more, I'm sure you can use it," he urged, piling my stack higher and higher until I had more than I could use in a million years.

Then he was gone from the building. He got a job working for one of the other printers in town, a much younger man, nasty sonofabitch named Wayne who took no pride in his craft and made everyone who worked for him tense and miserable. My friend Dora, who set type there and got paid exactly one-third of what Wayne charged his customers for her work, said Wayne was vicious to the older printer.

I saw him a few times when I'd stop by to talk to Dora. He always smiled like nothing was wrong, and we'd say hello and ask each other how it was going. But he'd be bustling from one end of the print shop to the other, carrying a stack of paper, a can of ink. There was no way or time to talk about our common ground, the building—my home and his old shop—or the soft air and flat light of the southwest, where scarlet paintbrush, ivory yucca and flaming magenta cholla blossoms somehow find water.

Crystal Ball
Lu Vickers

Mama mama mama could read mine and Bernard's and James's and Maisey's minds. She would tell Daddy what we were thinking, planning, or plotting and most amazingly of all she could predict the future, like the time she told Bernard he was going to have a boring life all because he wouldn't drink the eggnog she made, all because she spiked it with a little bourbon, and she was right. Bernard did not have fun, because he was working two jobs to get himself out of the house and out on his own.

When Mama got really drunk, sometimes, she'd just come out and tell us what we thought or felt, Y'all don't love me. Y'all wish I was dead. Y'all can't wait to leave me. And we tried to convince her that what she said wasn't true, but sometimes it was hard, because she was right.

Sunday afternoon. Me and Daddy and James are not watching golf on television. We are dozing. The announcer speaks in a hushed voice, almost a whisper, *we are at the ninth hole*, like he doesn't want anyone to really hear him and it's such a sleepy day. Later, Godzilla will come on and I will fall asleep to the tinny soundtrack. But we don't make it to Godzilla. Mama arrives home from work with a pint of Jack Daniels hidden in her purse, and I guess the sight of all us laying around the house,

the dishes undone, newspapers everywhere drives her to it;
something drives her to it. She changes clothes and comes into
the dining room gripping the bottle like a gun and holds it up
to her mouth pouring. Look at me, look at me, and we do, but
we are moving in slow motion. You don't want Mama to drink
because when she drinks, she becomes someone else, her eyes
blacken and I mean off one drink, all those years of Darvon, it's
like pouring ink into water.

She's done before we can react, done, and out the door, already wobbling a bit, but intent, intent on leaving the house in
broad daylight. This is a first, it's like she's got it all backward—you get drunk out and come in, but today she is getting
drunk in and going out. The front door slams and Daddy sits up
and looks at me and says, we got to go get her.

I don't want to go get her, I don't want to go near her right
now, but she's out there and we have to pull her back in. Not
like it used to be. The day Mama and I were sitting at the red
light uptown and when she gave the old Plymouth gas, we didn't
move; the engine revved but we didn't move and it was because
the transmission broke right there. Mama put the car in reverse
and stepped on the gas slowly and the car moved and it was
funny, the car wouldn't go forward only backward, so she said
I guess that's that, I'll have to drive it on back to the house and
she threw her arm over the seat and started backing to the house,
backing and we laughed the whole way. She didn't even get mad
and I loved her for that because our stuff was always breaking
but she laughed and said, how'd you like to drive to Cincinnati
like this, and people drove up behind us, our cars eye to eye,
and we waved at them like we were in a parade or something,
driving along in one of those trick cars.

Daddy and I leave James on the couch and walk outside and
Mama is gone, nowhere to be seen. We get into the Plymouth
and head uptown. Heat rises off the pavement in dizzy waves.
We spot her on Main street; she's already made it to the Baptist
church, swinging her arms like a monkey, leaning forward like
she's walking into a strong wind. We cruise up beside her and
I roll the window down and say Mama, come on, let's go home,

and she won't look at me, she'd lose her balance if she looked at me, but I say it again, Mama come home, it's too hot to walk, and she says, Y'all don't love me, and I'm leaving, and I look at Daddy and he nods ahead toward the next block. We could cut her off and get her into the car. He pulls around the corner and Mama keeps walking, she just goes on around us. Daddy coasts the car onto the side of the road and puts it in park. He leaves the engine running and gets out walking behind her. He looks goofy wearing Bermuda shorts and black wingtips. Elaine, come on. Stop this. He talks to the back of her head. She keeps walking. Every now and then she bumps into one of the azaleas planted next to the sidewalk. Daddy comes back to the car and we start following her again. I feel like we are in a big boat, floating up the street. We should have a net; that would do the job. A couple of cars pass us. Heads turn. We are going so slow we can hear the electric whine of crickets. Hot air washes into the car. Mama isn't slowing down at all though. I think Daddy and I both want to stop her before she gets uptown. Nobody is really out, just people doing their Sunday drives, but who wants to be seen dragging their mama into a car. I'm going to get her on the next block, Daddy says and he means it. We go on ahead of Mama and turn right onto the next street. He parks in the grass in front of Mr. Varnadore's house, old Mr. Varnadore who was born with two club feet. Mr. Varnadore waves at us from his porch. Daddy waves back and tells me to open the back door. We are going to shove Mama into the car. He goes toward her and grabs her arm. She jerks around and screams goddammit let me go, but he doesn't and she digs her heels in like a little kid and he pulls her along screaming, her mouth wide open and he keeps pulling, his lips tight, his face so serious and somehow he gets her into the backseat and pushes me in beside her and says hold her and he jumps into the driver's seat and off we go. Mama gets the door open and tries to jump out but I pull her back and realize she is serious, she wants out and I am going to have to really get a grip on her so I get behind her somehow and wrap my arms around her body. She kicks at the back of Daddy's seat. I'm surprised at how scrawny her shoulders are; she's wiry as a

cat but I'm stronger. She screams in my ear, let me go, let me
go, let me go and I hold her tighter and she screams even louder
let me go, you goddam queer, you goddam queer and I am so
amazed. My own mama knows the word queer and she thinks I
am one, and it's strange hearing my own mama call me something I hadn't even really thought of being yet. How did she
think she knew so much about who her children were? I hold her
tighter and tighter and daddy drives us home, Mama screaming the
whole way, I don't know how I ended up with a queer for a daughter; I don't know how I ended up with a goddam queer.

I saw Cat Reeves riding by the high school one day right after
the last period bell, really slinking by in her jacked-up bug with
those gangster whitewalls, the engine purring like a tiger, one of
those naked ladies flying off the hood. Cat wore a big fluffy
Afro and dark glasses, like she was one of the Jackson 5 or
something. She carried herself like one too, cruising by the high
school looking at all the kids, really, letting them look at her,
and I looked and so did Brenda, my best friend. Brenda told me
that Cat had almost got arrested one time for going in the ladies
restroom at a Sneads football game. Some old redneck woman
thought she was a boy, Brenda said, probably because she didn't
have a beehive hairdo and nine-inch nails. Anyway somebody
ran and got the cops and they went right in and dragged Cat out.
She was screaming the whole way, I'm a woman you stupid
motherfuckers, well she probably didn't call them motherfuckers
but you know that's what she was thinking. Anyway, she ended
up just ripping her shirt off and showing her titties and they
apologized.

I started seeing Cat everywhere after I noticed her the first
time; she'd appear out at the lake when Maisey and Brenda and
I went swimming; once she walked out on the dock with her
friend, a guy she called Mr. Dog. She wore low-slung blue jeans,
and when she bent over to sit down I could see the rim of her
underwear. I couldn't believe it; she wore B.V.D.s. Why on earth
are you wearing boys' underwear, I asked, and she smiled and
said lasts longer. I was fascinated.

She smelled like pine and she had muscles as big and hard as a man's from working pulpwood; she'd push up her shirtsleeves and flex her arms for me and Brenda, grinning slyly; sometimes, she'd raise her shirt and let us look at the hard ripples on her belly. She told us where she lived, drew us a map, and whenever we could get away we'd drive down the orange dirt roads to get to her house and she'd buy us quarts of beer and we'd sit on her porch and get drunk.

One day, Sue Baxter, who sat next to me in band, told me that Cat was queer. No she is not, I said. I knew what queer was. When I was about nine I was reading Ann Landers and saw a letter about homosexuals and I looked the word up in the dictionary. Someone who is attracted to the same sex, it said. She likes girls, Sue said. Everybody likes girls I said, and Sue said no, she likes them a lot; you better stop hanging around her, or people will think you're queer too.

I don't know any queers, I said.

After our washing machine broke down, I volunteered to go to the laundromat. I moved like lightning, shoved the clothes in a machine, dumped the detergent in and hauled ass over to Sneads, to Cat's house. I couldn't have explained my desire to see her. Once when I went over, we drank a couple of beers and she whispered in my ear, let me kiss you, and her face was so soft and so close, but I said no, and she leaned even closer and said, let me kiss you once and I closed my eyes and turned to her and she kissed me, just like that, she touched her lips to mine, none of that tongue-shoving, lip-grinding stuff I'd experienced with boys. I was hooked; I would drive over to her house just to kiss her and drive home again.

Sometimes after school Maisey and I walk up to the mental hospital to watch movies. Chattahoochee's own theater closed down a long time ago; I barely remember going into it. Maybe two frames from two movies stick in my mind. The Son of Flubber floating over a football field, and a Lassie lookalike running across a field. And I remember Maisey loose in the aisle, tooting on her empty Milk Duds box, Daddy sending Bernard to catch her.

The hospital auditorium is dark, except for when someone comes in the door, then late afternoon light shoots across the room. My friends and I sit in wooden auditorium chairs, looking toward the screen over a scattering of grey and bald heads waiting for the movie to begin. Our being here is a secret; not many kids know about this. The movie isn't for us; it's for the patients, but we come along to watch. John Wayne, Jerry Lewis; we don't care what is playing, the object is to sit in the dark. There is no concession stand; we don't eat popcorn or Jujubes or Jr. Mints or Milk Duds or drink Cokes; we laugh and talk with the boys and finally when the movie flickers onto the screen, we grow silent.

We've been in this auditorium, many times. Usually as the entertainment.

Christmas 1965. I am seven years old and part of a group of Sunday-school children who have come to sing to the patients. We sing "Silent Night" in high-pitched voices but the night is not silent. The patients want to sing along, and some do, jumping on the words, like they are jumping on a merry-go-round already moving. Others sort of hum or yowl along like dogs whimpering at a painful sound. I'm singing along too but I can't hear the words; I'm all eyes, transfixed by the people before us. They are crazy. They are wearing their nightgowns, their hair uncombed. They are sitting in wheelchairs or on fold-up chairs. Some are smiling, some are blank-faced, droopmouthed; some rock back and forth. A solitary old woman rises to her feet in the back of the room and begins dancing, twirling slowly, her pale blue nightgown trailing behind her. She is smiling.

Later, when the hospital staff serves us refreshments, I go near the old woman. She smells faintly of urine. The skin on her hands and arms is etched with tiny white stars.

We come to this dark room to let the boys kiss us; they are all lips and tongue and hands. All breath and damp skin. Licked

lips and loud juicy smacks. My boy has recently started shaving
and the bristle on his upper lip hurts my mouth, feels like wet
sandpaper. He stabs his tongue into my mouth and I open my
eyes and watch as cowboys and their horses gallop across the
screen behind this boy's head, yellow dust rising in the air
around them. I think of Cat's mouth, soft as velvet against mine,
her tongue luscious as chocolate.

I am supposed to be camping out at Lake Seminole with my
girlfriends (the boys will arrive after dark, undercover), but instead, I steal away from the bunch, say I'm going after more
beer, and thunk across Victory Bridge in my daddy's yellow
Plymouth to see Cat. I turn down her orange dirt road and drive
carefully past the Blue Wave, turn again, then creep in moonlight
up her road.

I'm sort of embarrassed, don't know what I want from her.
I'd seen her several times since she'd kissed me; once out at the
lake again. She'd walked up to the car with me, kicked the tires,
called them maypops. Whatcha' doin' ridin' around on those
maypops, girl, you ain't gonna make it home on those tires; they
thin as balloons. She smiled devilishly at me.

I saw her again at the bait shop; I was with Mama, and Cat
just sat in her bug and watched me walk in the store and then
out with a box of crickets in my hand, her dark brown eyes all
over me, sticky as mayflies. She didn't say a word.

Now, driving out to her house, I wonder what I'll say to her.
Hi, I just came to see you. Hi, thought I'd drop in.

When I get to her house, I pull up in her yard. It doesn't look
like anyone is home. I get out, close the door quietly and go
right up to her porch. The front steps are gone, so I swing myself
up and to the door, knocking softly. I wait. Turn around, watch
the lightning bugs blink green paths across the road.

The door opens. Cat stands there rubbing her eyes. She's
wearing the kind of white sleeveless T-shirt my grandfather
wore. What in the hell are you doing out here so late, she asks.

Came to see you, I say.

She steps outside on the porch next to me. Looks at me. Rubs

her eyes some more. Stretches. Doesn't say anything. I tell her
I'm supposed to be camping out, can't stay long, and I ask her
if she wants a beer, but she doesn't move, just watches me, the
way she watched me that day she saw me and my mama down
at the bait shop.

Uhh, she says. Uh huh. Just came to see me, she says. Here
I am; look at me.

I feel stupid now, ready to jump off the porch and get back
to the boys; they've probably got a fire going, are probably wondering where I am. Before I can make a move, Cat sits on the
edge of the porch, dangling her legs, motions for me to sit next
to her. She smiles. I sit down beside her, not too close, but close
enough that I can smell the sweet cologne she has on. After we
kissed that time, she'd given me a small bag of wooden beads
with that same smell. Later, I held them in my hands, rubbed
the soft wood against my cheek, inhaled their sweet scent.

Cat put her arm around me, pulled me to her. Whispered
mmmmm in my ear. I'm glad to see you, she said.

I feel too stupid to talk; I wish she'd put her other arm around
me and pull me in tight. That's what I came for; she knows it
and I know it, but neither of us will ever say it. I keep thinking
about the rules, what girls can and can't do, how boys are supposed to be the ones to call or to kiss or to hold your hand and
I know she's not a boy but I feel like a girl around her, and I
don't know how this is supposed to work. I'm a girl and she's
a boy but she's not and that's why I like her so much, the way
she's not a boy. But I don't know what to do with her.

Cat nuzzles her lips against my cheek, not kissing me and I
can't help it. I break the rules. I turn to her and say kiss me and
she does. We lay back on the wooden floor of the porch and she
moves on top of me, kissing me deeply, her body moving in
waves over mine. I like it.

Convoy
Sheila Ortiz Taylor

My mother is sitting on the couch examining a dust mop. Across from her sits the Fuller Brush Man. I sit on the Corn Goddess rug between them, playing with a vegetable brush. The Fuller Brush Man's black case is open on the floor. He holds shiny books on his knees. My mother keeps adjusting the neck of her housedress, which inclines to fall open just below the lace of her slip. The Fuller Brush Man, with his twice-a-year visits, always surprises her. She is often not quite dressed. She must throw a housedress on, appear, as she puts it, "without her face."

But this purchasing of brushes is serious. It requires black cases, shiny books, forms that must be checked off, signed, torn along perforations. These are supplies that must be had. Like the sailors in newsreels, we need things that must be brought to us, against great odds. Like them, we are at sea.

My mother does not drive. My father says it is not necessary. Twice a week my mother pulls me in the Radio Flyer to the Mixville Market. Otherwise, supplies are brought in. On Mondays and Wednesdays the Helms Bakery Man comes in his yellow and blue truck. We climb inside while he pulls out large, fragrant drawers of baked goods. He lifts cookies, coffee cakes, cupcakes, brownies in squares of waxed paper, and places everything carefully in white bags. He keeps his change in a machine on his belt. He flips the lever with his thumb and dimes fall into his palm. We run into the house with our white parcels, laughing, smelling of bread.

Every other Thursday the Date Man comes. He rocks along the dirt road in his Model A truck, dust clouds streaming behind, scale clanking, isinglass windows winking in the California sunshine. We crowd around, fingering plums, dates, grapes. His scale is a miracle of tin, chain, arrow and dial. My mother lifts a cluster of dates, slides them into the brown bag he holds. His dry neck rises out of a high collar. He must be a hundred years old. Old as raisins.

The Fuller Brush Man is younger. His hair is thick and blond. A thick flax-colored mustache covers his lip. From the presence of brushes he has begun to sprout them. He tells jokes, asks my mother if he can take off his coat. It's that warm.

She opens the French doors. I think of the joke my father tells, the one I don't understand, where he lifts me up in his arms, strokes my blond hair, says to my mother, "Must have been the Fuller Brush Man."

And the Skies Are Not
Sheila Ortiz Taylor

I am standing before an easel, wearing one of my father's soft and sweet-smelling dress shirts backwards. I dip my fat brush into a can of blue calcimine paint and streak it across the top of my rippling paper.

At last I am in school. Allesandro Street School, the only school in the city named for an Indian. I have waited five years for this day, the day when I would walk to school with my sister along the winding streets, down the steep concrete steps, across the red car tracks, across this territory that the Mexican government granted my great grandfather, Miguel Ortiz, for an obscure favor performed long ago, land subsequently lost to the family out of a certain characteristic vagueness about property and ownership.

I breathe in the warm chaos of Mrs. Gordon's kindergarten class. Behind me children build rooms out of giant wood blocks, others sing, others recite their alphabet. I paint, streaking my sky, this picture shaping itself from top to bottom.

What are you doing? asks the girl next to me in a tone I have never heard before but will in time become familiar with. "Skies aren't stuck up at the top. They come all the way down to here." She bends over, indicating to me the tops of her ruffled socks.

I stop my work, looking from the girl's socks to the top of my picture.

"Does not," says the girl on my other side. I look over gratefully. She has deep dark eyes, straight black hair. Her eyes say it has cost her something to contradict this girl who knows everything. Her name is Hazel Medina. I fall in love with her then and there. Hazel Medina.

"And skin color," says the first girl. "This is skin color for when you make people." She moves a can of calcimine from her easel to mine. I look into the can. The paint is the color of pale seafood sauce. I decide never to paint people. Oceans, maybe. Or deserts.

"Time for music," calls Mrs. Gordon. "Bring your chairs into a circle, here, around the piano." I stand with my brush poised. Hazel Medina shows me how to set the brushes into jars of water. We take off our fathers' shirts and pull chairs up near the piano. Then the first girl pulls her chair up on my other side. She is wearing a new plaid school dress that has a little white apron attached. She smooths it carefully. A large white bow holds her hair in place. The teacher keeps calling her Eleanor dear.

We are halfway through "Little Wind Blow on the Hilltop," when my vaccination starts itching. I look up high on my left arm where a scab has formed. Now that I have looked at it, thinking of anything else becomes impossible.

It looks like a dormant volcano; black, ashen, and very very dangerous. Eleanor dear looks also. She gives a little shudder of disgust, turns back, straightens the little white apron. Red Buster Brown sandals form a grid over her ruffled socks. I examine these socks once more to see if blue sky comes all the way down. Then I check Eleanor dear's arm for a vaccination. Nothing. Then I look out the window.

When we finish "Little Wind Blow on the Hilltop," Mrs. Gordon tells us we have a treat because Eleanor Manning plays the violin. She gestures with her hand and says Eleanor dear as if it were an invitation. Eleanor Manning gets up, smooths her

white apron, and accepts an enormous violin case from Mrs.
Gordon. This violin case looks like my Uncle Jake's coffin, even
to the pale blue velvet inside. I see my Aunt Thelma reaching
inside to pick up Uncle Jake's pale, slender hand to pat it in
consolation. Eleanor Manning reaches inside and extracts a
gleaming violin and a tiny velvet pillow. She puts the tiny pillow
under her chin and nestles the violin on top of it. Eleanor Manning draws her bow across the violin and adjusts the tuning. I
feel a tiny pain in a back tooth each time Eleanor Manning
moves the bow.

The itching in my vaccination becomes more intense. I look
over at Hazel Medina, who is staring out the window thinking
of home. I glance around the room for evidence this violin playing has set off an itching in everybody's vaccinations. Nobody
could come to school without these vaccinations, my mother has
said, and yet no one else seems to be driven half crazy like me.

Eleanor Manning plays "Twinkle, Twinkle Little Star"
through twice, then puts away her violin and then the tiny pillow
and hands the case back to Mrs. Gordon. She returns to the chair
next to mine, arranges her white apron. Mrs. Gordon says,
"Thank you, Eleanor. Wasn't that just wonderful, people?"

At last I scratch this left arm of mine, defying my father's
express command: I might scar myself for life if I scratch. Nevertheless, I scratch. Relief and well-being suffuse me. When Mrs.
Gordon passes around the triangles, sandpaper blocks, maracas,
and tambourines I reach happily for a beautiful polished block
with a padded drumstick. I touch the block softly with the stick
in my left hand and send out into the air a melodious tree sound;
this is the meaning of the word *forest*. I glance sideways at
Eleanor Manning, violinist. Then I see it: right in the middle of
Eleanor Manning's immaculately aproned lap, the guilty cinder
of my vaccination. I stop breathing.

The others are all singing "Home, Home on the Range" and
hitting wood blocks and triangles. Eleanor Manning sings, her
head lightly tilted back, her eyes half closed. I close my own,
and join my voice with hers and with Hazel Medina's. We sing
through to the end, joy and confusion bubbling inside me, until

Mrs. Gordon collects the rhythm instruments and tells us the first day of school is over.

We jump up, run outside. My mother stands in the schoolyard waiting under a eucalyptus tree, the bright California sky floating over her head like a blue banner.

blueberry

Clover L. Cannady

she said, "blueberries," lettin' it just roll around in her mouth like it was too good to let go, but she had to so i could hear.

she said, "you mean you ain't never thrown blueberries at nobody." i shook my head, a despondent no.

she said, "here i thought you knew somethin'," lookin' at me, hard, like she was tryin' to x-ray my brain, see what else i didn't know. i just tried to think of all the things i did know so she'd see that instead.

she said, "my mama loves blueberries," takin' her eyes off me ta gaze off into her thoughts, "that's what she said, said i looked like a ripe little blueberry she plucked right out her womb, all sweet an' round, said she could have eaten me up right there. come on." then she ran, flat out, as if something big and ugly with tentacles and scars and one eye with brown ooze coming out of it and green ooze in the other and his big toe sticking up out of his left sneaker, or a man, or her mother with the switch, was chasing her never lookin' back, her skirt sailing out behind her, runnin', like she knew i'd follow, and i did, fast following her sailing skirt, lookin' like the flags of the yearly festival flappin' in the wind, i watched her. she said she loved to run, said she loved the way her heart sounded like many,

wished she could run off the earth, said she'd wait for me there,
playin' a guitar / sometimes / the earth spun around her / she
said spirits wouldn't reveal themselves to you if you were afraid
and lions never ruled the jungle / sometimes / i'd blow bubbles
in the dirt for her / sometimes / even before she asked / she said
/ i was beautiful / like hawaii

she fell into the startled green green grass, breathing hard and
laughing, then tried to trip me when i caught up, i tickled her /
she threw grass in my hair grabbing my hands to make me stop.

"my brother first showed me about blueberries," she started
whittling a little song with the grass. "threw a heap of 'em at
me, felt somethin' like erasers, not hard like peas. i got him on
his nose."

i blew the parachuting seeds of a dandelion, conjuring mist /
sometimes i wanted to hold her / sometimes i did / sometimes /
i had to

she said we had to go to new york city because then we could
be public lovers and sometimes not be treated so cruel / just like
hold hands / and walk / she said don't want to shuffle 'round,
actin' like you ain't mine / she told me / my skirts were / cap-
tivating / not the skirts themselves / but the me in them / she
said i made them sound like dew and honey. i told her / you
shake the moon. she took the stem of the dandelion / stripping
it into several strings / and worked it into her song / sometimes
she'd run into herself on the street and be silent for hours afterwards / sometimes / she'd cry / sometimes / i could hold her i
tickled her and she said, "come on, got to get you some blueberries," and she picked up and ran leaving a bracelet of green
with one yellow flower in the grass

she said the ocean was deep, but people were deeper and i
knew she was right because she was wide like the river we
couldn't cross and deep like the sky. she said we'd go to africa
and make love under that african sun, said maybe then i'd see,
said she'd cover me with beads and love me all day and then
take me out and show me, me in the fish and stars and trees, she
said maybe she'd do it in new york, but not here.

we ran / lettin' sunlight tangle our hair / laughter trip our toes / panting breaths that slowly erased us / she said / you are the sky.

and i fashioned some meager existence somewhere between me them you us / somewhere not breathing / lurking / under trees

we used to play along the river wading in and out / trying not to get our skirts wet / or / letting them get real wet / all wet / and then shivering in the sun i would frequent dark underpasses shadowed day under day / lurking past myself / on sunken reefs / i would stumble in half step time to foreign urgings / i would imagine foamy water / and you and i / us / on the shore / laughing / eating us / running / standing / us / sitting / us / tiny waves / swirling water / tickling our toes / then ankles / then legs / the embrace of water like your arms / as you pull me in / your startled scream / when i dunk you under / us / upon the shore / us / spread before us / us / infinite / reaching / us

she said each blade of grass had to stand on its own / and i hunkered down expecting a breeze / expecting a tiny green wind of pecan and willow / expecting oceans and rivers to lurch up and tease the sun / expecting tiny little half currents of solar time to register my brain / like your arms and hips and elbows / fleshing out my brain / fleshing out each electrically charged microscopic cell / so i could be more

and i couldn't see how beautiful her nails were or our tree house we had behind a bush

she said / you are my sky

Why I'm Here
Lucy Jane Bledsoe

When Diane called me from Little Rock, she claimed she wanted only to talk, to hear how I was doing. But then she told me how the anti-choice folks were swarming around her women's health clinic like ants to honey. I could hear the fear in her voice, though she wouldn't admit to it.

"You need protection," I announced. "I'm coming down there." I taught school and had the summer off. I loved the idea of protecting Diane from the clinic blockaders. Besides, Mama had died the year before and I craved revenge. A good fight. Something to plug that aching hole in my gut.

"Hold on, Boo Boo," Diane said, using Mama's pet name for me. "I don't think that's a good idea. This isn't California, you know." Meaning, I—the drama-queen California dyke—wouldn't know how to act in Little Rock. Oh, ever-cautious Diane.

She called back a couple days later and asked, "Don't you have a cousin down here?"

"Yeah, why?"

"She has your same name, right?"

"Yeah, why?"

"What's she look like?"

"I haven't seen her since I was twelve, the last summer we spent together on Grandma's farm down there."

"Is she sort of angular, high cheekbones, long dark-blond hair?"

"Sounds right."

"She's in charge of the blockaders."

I was shocked for a moment. Then I thought, *figured.* Cousin Marylou had been my lifelong opponent. During those three summers we spent together on Grandma's farm outside of Little Rock, when we were ten, eleven, and twelve years old, I'd exulted in competing with her, and winning, over and over again. In horse-racing, in one-on-one basketball, in getting Grandma's love. Somehow, whether in the flesh or just in spirit, Marylou had been on the other side of every fight I'd ever fought.

I felt the adrenaline surge down my arms and legs. "Next flight out," I told Diane. "I'll be there."

"No," Diane ordered. "Stay where you are."

"I want to help defend your clinic. And you shouldn't be staying alone. They've *killed* a couple doctors, Diane. Your being Black and lesbian doesn't exactly help." I heard her groan and knew I was starting to win. I added, "Besides, I feel responsible. That's my *cousin* messing with you."

"Stay in California." Diane's voice trembled. She knew I was coming. And I knew there was a part of her that wanted me to come. Why else would she have called?

Diane and I met back when we were the only two scholarship students on the Oregon State basketball team. The first time she ever talked to me about anything other than basketball was that night I decked a girl in our dorm for calling Coach a dyke. "You better check that temper," Diane told me. "You're wild, girl." I lay in bed that night going over and over her advice, thinking that her rare smile was the first thing I'd ever encountered that was more interesting than my anger. A few weeks later, Diane discovered that my people, like hers, were from Arkansas. Then she took me on like a project. She was still working on me, twenty years later.

"I'll call you back with my flight number," I told her, and

she hung up. She didn't say "good-bye" but she didn't say
"don't come" again, either.

On the airplane, I wondered what Mama would think of what
I was doing. She'd probably think it was funny. Mama loved
irony. Then again, maybe she wouldn't think it so funny, after
all. I'd be digging around in her most painful wound, her es-
trangement from her older sister whom she'd loved so much as
a child. In the same year Mama, who never married, had gotten
pregnant, Aunt Jo married a fundamentalist Baptist. And deserted her sister.

It'd been Grandma's idea to have me and Marylou spend those
summers with her. I think she hoped that Marylou and I would
become fast friends and help mend the animosity between our
mothers. We did have a lot of fun those summers, but Cousin
Marylou loved to lord over me all the things that made her le-
gitimate: a father, the girl-scout troop, grace before dinner, the
hundred brush strokes she gave her hair each night. Though
Marylou and I were the exact same age, and though I was always
a good foot taller, Aunt Jo sent me Marylou's hand-me-downs
all the way through high school. I used to beg Mama to throw
the boxes from Arkansas away, unopened, but she got some
strange satisfaction from opening them, snorting at the used contents, then dumping them in the trash. She always laughed too
hard at Marylou's old clothes, the only gifts she ever received
from her sister.

I relished the idea of opposing Marylou. And getting a few
weeks of Diane in the bargain. As the airplane bounced down
in Little Rock, I clapped my hands and belted out a staccato
laugh in anticipation. I must have frightened the passenger next
to me because he lurched up, even as the flight attendant told us
to remain seated, and opened the overhead compartment for his
briefcase.

I'm used to people overreacting to me. Besides being six foot
one, my hair is white-blond, and I'm always too loud. Diane said
I reminded her of a prize farm animal, a beautiful specimen in
a county fair setting but a little frightening in the everyday world.

Diane, on the other hand, looked as ordinary as oats. She straightened her shoulder-length hair and wore it parted in the middle, layered and fluffy. She'd had the same style of wire-rimmed glasses for twenty years. Still, there was something about her ordinariness that I found powerfully attractive. I just knew that if I found the right place to touch, all that propriety would explode like fireworks.

I deboarded the plane and walked down to baggage claim, looking for her the whole way. As my suitcase came around on the carousel, I started to get nervous. Diane was never late. Then I heard her familiar voice. "Hey, girl."

"Wow!" I whooped. "Look at you!" In the two years since I'd seen her, Diane had cut her hair into a short Afro and gotten contact lenses. She'd gained a little weight, too, and looked more comfortable in her body. "You look gorgeous," I said way too loud for Diane. Her big copper earrings tinkled when I grabbed her to me. "My God, look at the color of your eyes. I could never see them before. They're almost orange."

"Okay," she said prying my arms off her. "My eyes aren't orange. And this isn't California anymore." She eyed my haircut.

"They don't hug in the South?" I teased.

She ignored my question. I kissed her cheek and told her I loved her. She smiled, just a little, and said, "You look good, too. In spite of the haircut."

"Thanks," I said. Then, "So where're those right-wing crackers. Let me at 'em."

"I hope this wasn't a mistake."

"What? Me coming?"

"Yeah."

"No problem, sister. They won't know what hit them. We got this one licked."

She gave me that look that said, *down girl*, like I was a big puppy, cute but too exuberant, then repeated, "I hope this wasn't a mistake. What'd you do to your hair?"

I reached up and felt the shaved bottom half of my haircut.

The top was all one length, parted in the middle, and hung to an even ledge halfway down my head.

I said, "I'll grow it out."

It was very late, so Diane and I went right to bed, in our separate rooms, and didn't talk that night. The next morning, we got up at six, made sandwiches for lunch, and drove to the clinic. Diane told me that a woman named Betty organized the clinic protectors. They showed up every morning around eight. The blockaders arrived any time during the day. Diane and Betty never knew what to expect. I felt proud being the personal escort of the clinic's doctor.

Diane pulled into her parking space at seven and said, "Fuck."

"What?" I asked. Then I saw that someone had thrown a bucket of thick, sticky red paint on the front door, steps, and sidewalk of the clinic. We got out of the car and approached the mess. I touched the glossy red film forming on top of the congealing paint.

I'd never seen Diane's face look so hard and brittle.

"I'll take care of the paint," I told her. "You go on in the side door and get ready for work."

Diane threw back her head and looked at the pale hot sky, breathed in the already sweltering air. I put a hand on her back. "Really," I said. "Don't give it another thought."

Diane nodded and went around to the side door.

I used a shovel for the globs. Then I started scrubbing with a metal-bristled brush and paint thinner. At eight o'clock Betty and two other clinic protectors showed up. Betty looked like a sitcom housewife, Vera was an old-school bulldyke if I'd ever seen one, and Roger was a handsome young man who wore a ponytail and spoke like a New Englander.

After scrubbing the pavement for another hour in the sizzling heat, while Betty, Vera, and Roger escorted patients from their cars into the clinic's side door, I realized the paint wasn't coming up. You couldn't have a bright red stain on the entrance to a health clinic, so I borrowed Diane's car and headed to the hardware store.

At noon, Diane stepped outside. The second I saw her face, I knew I'd made my first mistake.

"Lavender?" Her voice faltered. She leaned against the building.

"I thought it'd be nice." I'd already painted the steps and half the walkway.

The New Englander grinned. The bulldyke paced importantly. Betty piped up, "I told her to check with you first, but she—"

"I thought you'd like it." I'd charged the paint on my own credit card. I wanted her to know she could trust me to handle any crisis.

Just then a maroon Dodge caravan pulled up to the curb.

"Get back inside," Vera ordered and Diane did.

The blockaders, about eight of them, piled out of the van. They gathered for a moment in the street, heads together, praying. Betty, who'd already pegged me as a hothead, scurried to my side and said, "Doctor's orders. Absolutely no contact. We conduct ourselves with dignity. We just do our job. Escort women into the clinic."

"Sure," I said and examined the face of each blockader until I found her. She emerged from the prayer huddle and walked right toward me.

Maybe it was the wet heat, maybe just the sight of her rawboned features, but I was instantly transported. I was twelve years old riding bareback in the hills behind Grandma's house, Marylou yahooing on the horse behind me. Sweet watermelon juice sticky all over my face and the smell of horse sweat filling my nose. I could feel the horse's muscles contract between my legs, hear Marylou calling my name, the same as her own.

Without thinking, I left my post in the clinic yard and started down the short embankment toward her. Family can be like that. A mirage that, in spite of everything you know, keeps you lunging for it.

Then she saw me.

"Marylou?" she whispered when I stopped ten feet from her. "Is that you?"

A thin man with black hair, a sharp jawline, and bright, hungry eyes came up and handed her a sign. She hoisted it, still staring at me. "Love your baby, don't kill him," it said.

She looked up at the sign as if she didn't know what to do with it, let it fall back on her shoulder, and approached me. I didn't know if I was supposed to touch her or not. "How's your mother?" I asked foolishly.

"Oh, she's okay." Marylou looked at her feet. "I was sorry to hear about yours."

I looked away briefly, then waited.

Marylou's face was open. Perhaps she'd not quite registered that we were enemies on this clinic battleground. She asked, "But why are you here?"

"I'm defending my friend's clinic." My voice shook and I tried to toughen it as I added, "And women's rights to make decisions about their own bodies."

A stocky woman came up and took Marylou's arm. "What's going on?"

"This is my cousin!" Marylou cried, as if she hadn't heard me. "Her name's Marylou, too. We're both named for Grandma."

Her enthusiasm brought on another rush of memories: trolling for catfish in the stream and building a fire of willow switches. Eating the catfish with its charcoal crust between pieces of the corn bread Grandma had packed for us.

"Wow," the stocky woman said, flashing a genuine smile.

"This is Janetta," Marylou said touching her friend.

By now Betty, Vera, and Roger had come to stand behind me. The thin dark man stood with Marylou and Janetta. I reached out to touch my cousin's shoulder just as the thin man with black hair shouted, "Don't do it!"

I jerked back my hand but then realized he wasn't talking to me. A teenage girl had just gotten out of a station wagon and began walking up to the clinic. The anti-choice folks surrounded her, defying a court order that restricted them to the sidewalk and street.

Vera grabbed the thin man by the arm, twisted it behind his back, and "escorted" him back to the sidewalk, while Roger rescued the teenage girl and led her inside.

Marylou hoisted her sign again, but before she turned away from me, she said, "Maybe—"

That night, after a big show of sighing and headshaking, Diane allowed that a lavender walkway and porch wouldn't hurt anything. We'd finally settled into reminiscing about old times when, at ten-thirty, the phone rang.

I leapt up and grabbed it as Diane yelled, "Wait!"

"You just relax," I told her and answered, "hello?"

The caller hesitated, apparently surprised to hear someone new answer the phone, then said in a dry, flat voice, "Baby killer. A murderer lives at 426 Elm Street."

I carefully set the phone receiver back in its cradle and looked at Diane slumped in her overstuffed chair.

"Nice fellow asking if you wanted to subscribe to the evening paper," I tried.

"I'm afraid," Diane sighed, "that when they find out you're here, which they just did, they're gonna start dyke-baiting me, too."

"Oh, yeah, like that dyke Vera isn't going to tip them off."

"She's not staying with me."

I reached up and felt the shaved lower half of my haircut. "I said I'll grow my hair."

Diane sat up in her chair and looked at me hard with those copper eyes that, without her old glasses, looked too bright against her dark skin. I thought she was angry, but she said, "I'm sorry. I'm just so goddamned tired. Every single day I think about closing the clinic. Open up a family practice in some nice neighborhood. Make some money. I got Daddy to look after. I don't need those goons shooting me."

"You could do that, hon," I said, moving over to sit on the

arm of her chair. I dared to rub her neck a little. "You don't have to sacrifice so much. You've run the clinic for ten years. Someone else can do it."

Diane leaned into me. "Do you know how it would feel to let them know they broke me?"

I shook my head both yes and no.

She sagged against my leg and shut her eyes. I thought for a second she was going to sleep right then. But she sat up again and said, "Doctor in Alabama had his mother in the hospital. The anti-choice maniacs broke into her hospital room, stood around her bed chanting, 'Your son kills babies.' So help me God, if they ever start in on Daddy, I'll kill the first one I see."

"You need a break," I persisted. "You've been working so hard, you haven't even dated anyone in, how many years?" Of course working hard wasn't all that prevented her from dating, but I made it my business to occasionally remind Diane of her lack of a social life.

Diane moved away from me, tucked her head down on the other arm of the chair, and curled her feet under her. In a second, the scowl on her face unfurled and I knew she was sleeping. I found a blanket in her bedroom and covered her. "Diane," I whispered and kissed the peak of her hairline.

Marylou and the blockaders didn't show up the next day and I was annoyed with myself for being disappointed. Diane had dinner with her father that night. I waited up for her, hoping for more talk, but she came in saying she was exhausted and went straight to bed.

I took a tall glass of sweet, strong ice tea out on the porch and sat in the rocker. I ached with longing. A great huge general longing that sucked at me from the thick air. I wanted to feel the cool crunchy grass under my bare feet as I darted after fireflies. Marylou and I used to catch whole bunches of them in glass jars, then take our firefly lanterns on explorations out past the barn to the pond. The truth was, I'd loved those summers on Grandma's farm.

I went into the house to look for something to put in my ice tea, like Southern Comfort, but Diane didn't have a drop of liquor in the house. Figured. As I padded back out to the porch, the phone rang. I let the answering machine pick up, but I stood holding the screen door open with my hip and listened. "Baby killer," the voice said. "You and your family will pay for each baby you kill."

Driving to the clinic the next morning, Diane said, "Betty told me you were talking with the blockaders."

The accusation in her voice took me off guard. "Well, Marylou is my cousin. You know that. Was I supposed to pretend I didn't know her?"

Diane pulled into her parking space without answering. She got out and checked the mailbox, then ruffled through the bushes in front of the building. Each morning so far, she'd refused to let me get into the car until she started it. She wouldn't talk about it, but I knew she was thinking of bombs.

I got the lawn mower out of the car trunk and watched Diane unlock the clinic door. Before going in, she said, "Be careful."

"You know I'd never do anything to compromise our friendship. Or the clinic. Don't you?" I asked.

Diane looked tired, and a little sad, like she didn't know, but she said, "Yeah," and went inside. I mowed the lawn and sheared the shrubbery way back, so Diane didn't have to root around in it every morning. At eight o'clock, Betty, Vera, and Roger arrived. Five minutes later, the van of blockaders parked across the street.

Marylou stood at the back of the van, handing out signs. When her team was squared away, she looked up the hill at me and waved, hesitantly. Her friend, Janetta, grinned at me like we were old friends.

I went inside and got ice teas for my team. Then, at the last second, I poured about five more glasses and put them all on a tray. Vera scowled as I walked down the grass embankment to offer the fundies ice teas. She needn't have worried. Not one of them, not even Marylou or Janetta, took a glass off my tray.

"Doctor's orders," Betty told me as I climbed back up to the porch. "Absolutely no contact with the blockaders."

I nodded and drained two of the ice teas.

On Friday night at ten, I stood on the corner by the Chevron station, a couple blocks from Diane's house, thinking I must be out of my mind. Family is like a drug. You know it's going to kill you and want that fix anyway.

Diane wasn't speaking to me. She understood the part about my wanting to see the place I'd spent three summers and where Mama spent the first twenty years of her life. But she didn't understand why I had to see it with Marylou.

A red '75 Mustang pulled up. My cousin leaned out the driver's window. She didn't smile. I folded myself into the back seat, said, "Hi. Great car."

Janetta, sitting in the passenger seat, turned around and grinned at me. The two women wore their hair in identical long shags sprayed into place. They also wore matching make-up, light-blue eye shadow and rusty lip gloss, which looked sort of okay on Janetta who was blond and pink-skinned, but all wrong on Marylou with her tawny coloring.

This whole thing had been arranged in about five seconds earlier in the afternoon. It was my turn to walk down to the cafe and pick up sandwiches for the clinic protectors. Betty, Vera, and Roger all walked a big circle around the blockaders when it was their turn, but that seemed silly to me. I loped down the embankment and started to walk right through them. Janetta piped up with, "Marylou says you play basketball, too."

"Yeah," I said.

"You should come shoot hoops with us sometime."

I glanced at Marylou who gave Janetta a dull look, which inspired me to say, "I'd like that."

Janetta beamed.

Then I blurted, "You know what I'd really like. I'd like to go out and see the old farm."

Marylou said that'd be trespassing, but Janetta jumped all over the idea. I told them to pick me up that night at the Chevron station, so Diane didn't have to deal with them, and late, so the current farm owners would be asleep. My cousin didn't answer, but I could tell that although Marylou was in charge of the blockaders, Janetta was in charge of Marylou, and Janetta said they'd be there.

Marylou and Janetta played in a city basketball league, so we chatted mostly about hoops as we drove out to the farm.

"Must be some genetic thing," Janetta commented. "All that you two have in common. Your names, basketball, how you both teach high school."

"And both unmarried," I added. "Some think that's a genetic thing."

Janetta giggled, but Marylou didn't. It was hard admitting to myself that a fundamentalist Christian was cute, but Janetta was. Her personality was like her body: big, round, blond, and compact. I got the sense there was a lot of compressed humor in her, waiting to be released.

At eleven o'clock, Marylou turned off the Mustang's headlights as she drove up the dirt road to the barn. Once there, she turned the car around, for a fast getaway if necessary, and parked.

"Look." I grabbed my cousin's arm and pointed. A bent and rusted basketball rim hung off the side of the wooden barn. We'd spent hours under that rim, running homemade drills, perfecting our behind-the-back passes and trying for slam dunks. Grandma used to drive out with a big jar of ice tea and egg-salad sandwiches, saying, "I know you girls won't come home for lunch." Once we talked her into letting us teach her how to shoot a lay-up.

Marylou shut her car door quietly, then stood with her hands dangling at her sides, looking at the barn.

"Remember?" I asked, elbowing her gently, wishing we had a ball with us. For a moment, it seemed like it would be so easy to recapture that sweaty farm-girl feeling, maybe even mend something.

Marylou pressed her lips together and nodded.

Janetta darted to the other side of the barn, and I went to touch the rotting siding under the basketball hoop. I knocked gently on the old wood. This used to be a sturdy barn, but no one had kept it up. Marylou followed me, burrs gathering on our jeans as we walked through the thick grasses to the front. The barn doors were gone, leaving a big gaping opening which sucked me right in. A flurry of swallows clouded above our heads for a moment, then settled back into the dark recesses. The place smelled of aged manure and mildewed straw. Hardly sweet-smelling, yet still intoxicating for me.

"Our mothers grew up in this barn," I tried.

"Yeah," she said. "They were close, then."

So she did feel it, the pain of their separation.

Marylou and I walked deeper into the barn. Much of the roof had fallen in and I could see the sky and stars through the openings. Then Janetta burst into the barn interior, laughing, calling out for us.

"Back here," I called to her, and Marylou said, "Shh."

Janetta's eyes adjusted and she found us standing in a pile of old hay. All of a sudden she twisted my arm behind my back and gently kicked the backs of my knees. I collapsed into the stinky hay and she straddled me, laughing.

For an alarmed second I couldn't respond. What was she doing? Then I got it. This was a jock thing. I pretended I'd been bluffing for a second, then threw her on her back so fast she expelled all the air from her lungs in a big grunt. She laughed hard and grabbed my upper arms, trying to roll me off her. I let her because I liked the feel of tangling with her. But then I remembered my cousin and stopped. Marylou stood off to the side, looking out the opening of the barn, not watching us.

Janetta panted, "You're strong!"

"I want to see the pond," I said, sensing my cousin's impatience. "Then we can go."

"That's too far," Marylou objected.

"A pond!" Janetta cried. "Can we swim? I'm hot."

The pond was a hundred yards from the barn and the car. I stripped and tossed my shorts and T-shirt under the big willow.

"Whatchya lookin' at?" I teased the two fully dressed women

staring at me. I could almost hear my body sizzle as I slipped
into the cool muddy water, loving the caress of the pond. I ran
my hands over my arms, legs, and belly, rinsing off the sweat,
the heat. Then I swam out a few strokes, turned, and looked
back at the shore. Janetta had gotten all her clothes off except
her underpants and tried to kick out of them while running to
the pond's edge. Her toe caught in the leg opening of the underpants and she fell onto her hands and knees.

"Smooth, Jan," Marylou said and went to help her up.

"Come on in," I called to Marylou.

"Shh," she said.

"My knee is bleeding," Janetta said as she waded into the
water. She had big round breasts, not pendulous but full like
perfect half-spheres. Her nipples were pink and as big as silver
dollars. She splashed in toward me.

I hoped she didn't want to water wrestle.

As if Marylou had had the same thought, about not wanting
me and Janetta to wrestle, she undressed quickly and joined us.
She was gangly with hollow places everywhere, like inside her
hipbones and on either side of her collarbone. Her nipples were
hard little raisins.

We all swam out to the middle of the pond, then dog-paddled
in a circle, Marylou's face shadowed with anxiety, me and Janetta grinning at one another. I asked, "So how come you girls
don't have dates on a Friday night?"

"Dates?" Janetta laughed. "Golly, you get to our age, and
well, you know."

Actually, I didn't. But I laughed with her and said, "What
about you, cuz?"

Marylou shrugged. "I've been seeing this guy who lives up
in Chester County. But that's a ways away. We don't see each
other too often."

"How far away?"

"Half an hour."

"Oh," I said.

"Janetta's engaged," Marylou added, as if engagement were
a minor detail in this discussion.

"Not exactly, Marylou," Janetta said. "Matthew and I have an understanding."

"That you'll get married."

"Not exactly," Janetta said again. "I'm not sure." She paddled closer to me and changed the subject. "What about you? You have a boyfriend out in California?"

"No," I said. "I had a girlfriend until recently, though."

Blank stares. The water began to feel very uncomfortable, like a lot of icy fingers pinching me.

"Do you mean that—" Janetta stopped and searched for the right words. I let her think. "You're homosexual?"

"Jan," Marylou warned.

"Yes," I said.

"I don't want to talk about this," Marylou said. She had that righteous look of hers, which made me want to give an explicit accounting of lesbian sex.

Instead, I said, "Hey, I don't know many straight women our age who still play ball. You must play lesbian teams all the time."

"Oh, sure," Janetta said. She hesitated, glanced at Marylou, then added, "We pray for them."

I snorted, thinking about that wrestling. "I bet you do," I said. "Fervently."

Anger seized Marylou's face. Her voice trembled when she accused, "You've always just taken what you wanted, haven't you?"

"Excuse me?" I said.

"Whatever you want, you take it." Marylou turned and swam toward shore.

I looked at Janetta and raised my eyebrows.

Janetta watched her friend climb out of the pond and said, "It's not up to us to judge. But we don't believe in that."

"Well," I said, "it's not really a matter of belief or disbelief. My body loves women. It's just a fact." Then I followed Marylou to shore.

Marylou grabbed her clothes and dressed as she stumbled back to the Mustang. I used my T-shirt to dry off and watched Ja-

netta's dark figure still dog-paddling in the middle of the pond.
Then she too swam back. She crawled out of the water like an
amphibian, on all fours, then stood up. Evolution in one emer-
gence. I wished.

I climbed into the backseat of the Mustang and didn't speak
until Janetta got in, too. Then I announced I wanted to sleep on
the ride home. They kept quiet, but I didn't sleep. My skin felt
brittle.

About fifteen minutes outside of Little Rock, Janetta broke the
silence. "What's that like . . . making love with a woman?"

Marylou's neck nearly snapped as she whipped around to look
at her friend.

Janetta had tried for a conversational tone, as if she were ad-
dressing "an issue," being fair. But she couldn't hide the wist-
fulness riding her words like an undercurrent. The way she'd
wrestled told me a lot about how she'd make love. Back there
in the barn straw I could have put my hands over her full buttocks and drawn her into me hard and she wouldn't have resisted.
Not before she'd absorbed the heat and feel of my body for a
moment.

Still, I didn't answer Janetta's question. I wasn't going to let
her be both a fundamentalist and a voyeur. She'd have to choose.
A thickness, like humidity, held our silence. I knew that Marylou
was embarrassed, even mortified. I couldn't tell what Janetta was
feeling.

At one in the morning, as they let me off at the Chevron
station, I stuck my head back in the Mustang and said, "Let
your imaginations go wild. Then you'll know what it's like making love with a woman."

Diane spent all day Saturday with her father. When she got
home around nine o'clock, I was just stepping out of the bathtub.
She wouldn't even say hello.

Wrapping my terry-cloth robe around me, I said, "Diane,
maybe my talking with my cousin and her friend will help.
Maybe I can bridge some sort of chasm."

Diane took a long, deep breath and looked at me like I had

an IQ of 50. "Do you know how long the Christians have been dominating western civilization with their small-minded hatred? Do you really believe you could have a profound effect? Think again, sister."

"I'd never do anything that would hurt you or the clinic. Why don't you trust my judgment?"

"I know how thick blood can be."

I dropped onto the couch, heavy with the sudden realization that she was right. I thought I hated my cousin. And I thought I loved Diane. Still, I went with Marylou against Diane's wishes. I'd made a choice. Thick blood.

Just then the plate-glass window in Diane's front room shattered. A stone the size of a grapefruit rolled to a stop in front of the couch. Diane wailed softly and passed a hand over her face. Then she kicked the overstuffed chair with all her might and screamed, "Shit."

I picked up the rock and unwrapped the twine that secured a piece of paper to the rock.

"Give it to me," Diane said and I did. She read the note, wadded it up, and threw it in the fireplace.

I couldn't make my voice any bigger than a whisper as I offered, "I saw some plywood in the garage. You go to bed. I'll take care of the window."

"Why are you here?" Diane demanded.

"I'm here to be with you," I still whispered.

"No," Diane said. "You're here to make some perverse connection with your family. And to get me killed in the bargain. Fuck you."

On Sunday I cleaned the house, weeded the flower bed, bought groceries, and cooked a fine dinner. Diane spoke to me, but ultra politely, like I were a new foreign-exchange student staying with her. I couldn't find any words to express my regret, nor any to convince her of my loyalty. By Monday morning I felt so tightly coiled I could have hurled the whole Dodge caravan across town. The fundies rolled up at exactly seven, just as Diane and I arrived and before the clinic protectors. I jumped out of Diane's car and strode down the grass embankment, stretching myself so that they got the full effect of my six foot one inches.

"Wait, Boo," Diane shouted after me, but I ignored her.

Marylou was just stepping out of the van. She held a styrofoam cup of steaming coffee which I knocked out of her hand. The coffee splashed all over the hot pavement. Droplets flew onto the white shirt of the thin, dark-haired man standing next to her. Janetta jumped out of the van and grabbed my arm. I couldn't tell if she was defending me or my cousin. Marylou gave her a sharp and confused look. Janetta let go of me.

"You call yourself Christian," I said. "What kind of Christian throws rocks through good people's windows?"

Marylou raised her chin a half inch and glared at me. Her two cheekbones, high and bony, rode her face like righteous little pulpits. "What?" she asked.

The dark-haired man said, "What's she talking about?"

"What do you think Grandma is thinking about you now? I'll tell you what. She's thinking shame."

Marylou spoke in a calm voice. "You're as hot-headed as your mother."

"Don't you talk about my mother."

"Grow up, Marylou. You *are* just like her. Take, take, take. Me, me, me."

I laughed. "What am I taking from you now?" I asked and looked at Janetta. She looked back at me with what could only be read as hope.

"Get back in the van," Marylou ordered her cohorts.

"Janetta," I said, not so much out of goodwill but to provoke Marylou. "Your body is your own. You have choices."

Marylou stepped so close to me I could smell her coffee breath. "Do you know what would have happened if your unmarried mother had had a choice? The only reason you're here right now is because she didn't."

I felt as if the atoms that made up my body suddenly dispersed. Like I became instantly nothing.

"Your mother would have aborted you." Marylou spoke

softly. "But she didn't have a choice. That's why you're here."

"Come on, Boo Boo." It was Diane's voice in my ear, gentle, and her hands on both my shoulders. "Let's go."

"She's your *cousin*," Janetta was saying to her friend. "Marylou, get a grip on yourself."

Janetta reached out and touched my shoulder. "She didn't mean that."

I couldn't help the tears. I wanted to lunge at Marylou. I wanted to beat her into a paste. But Diane's hands, Janetta's touch, dissolved my fury.

"Go home," I told Marylou in my tear-thickened voice. "Leave me alone. Leave Diane alone. If you're my cousin. If your mama is my mama's sister, then go home." I doubled over crying and Diane held me from behind. Janetta squatted in front of me and brushed back my hair, repeating, "She didn't mean that. She really didn't."

After getting control of myself, I straightened up again and faced Marylou for the last time. Her face spasmed briefly, like a twitch of pain, maybe even a hint of the shift, an urge toward resolution, that our family so badly needed. "I didn't mean that," she said flatly. "I'm sorry."

Life is so crazy. If I'd punched out Marylou like I had wanted to, Diane would've put me on the first California-bound plane out of Little Rock. Instead, by breaking down like that I finally got her attention. After she took me back up the hill and put me into a bed at the clinic, she said, "I've been waiting twenty years for you to let yourself feel the pain."

"Oh, wise one," I cracked at her through my tears. "My guru."

"Be quiet and lie still for a while."

That night, after we got home from the clinic and had dinner, I followed Diane to bed. She didn't stop me. I crawled under the sheets and curled up next to her. "What are you doing?" she mumbled. I reached around and touched the top of her spine, then ran my finger down to its base. She didn't even wince at my touch. "I was all wrong about you," I told her. "You know how I always give you a hard time about being cautious? How could I call anyone cautious who lets me in her life?"

Diane laughed. "I heard that."

"It would be too corny to tell you how courageous I think you are."

She was quiet as I knew she would be.

I ran my finger back up her spine and asked, "You want to know why I'm really here?"

"Yeah," she answered. "I do."

I cupped my hand around the back of her neck and touched my lips to hers. She sucked my lower lip gently for a second, then sank into the long kiss.

Later, when I pulled away, just briefly, I couldn't resist saying, "Ah, I've been waiting twenty years for you to let yourself feel the joy."

Diane drove me to the airport a week later. School started on Tuesday. She still had moments of anger.

"Your methods—" she started in all over again as we waited for me to board my plane.

"Let's talk about my results," I suggested. "Is your clinic still being blockaded?"

"No."

"Have the calls stopped?"

"For now."

"Has the vandalism stopped?"

She sighed, then tried to kill her smile. And failed.

"You call me," I said. "I'll come back whenever you need me."

"It's not like they've stopped blockading clinics," Diane rallied. "They've just stopped blockading mine."

I raised my eyebrows to say, what, not good enough?

When the airline attendant called for rows twenty through thirty to board, Diane grabbed me. "Damn you, Boo Boo," she said. We clung to each other as the airline attendant boarded rows ten through twenty, then everyone else.

Finally, the waiting area was empty except for us. Diane reached up and brushed my grown-out blond hair from my eyes. "You get a haircut soon as you get back to California, hear? A real wild one."

"I love you," I said.

"I love you, too," she admitted. She gave me one of her exceptional smiles. "You make my life interesting."

"Oh, I could make it a lot more interesting than this," I promised, running my hands down her hips. "If only you'd let me."

"Some day," she said carefully. Oh, always careful. "Some day I just might."

Phase Two

Catherine Lewis

"Pull up your pant legs and let me see your sox." Waxler shines his flashlight on my ankles and the glare of white greets him. "Un-fucking-believable."

I've just earned a 1 on appearance, the lowest possible score. It doesn't matter that my shoes shine, my leather gleams, my uniform is crisp.

Waxler tells me to get in the car but as I open the driver's door he pushes it shut. He reaches through the open window and grabs the steering wheel. "This is *my* car."

"10-4," I say, walking to the passenger side. Perhaps I should turn my back while he lifts his leg and pees.

Still hollering about regulation dress, he drives across the parking lot. He slaps his hand on the steering wheel making the horn toot toot toot as he pulls up to the gas pumps. Imagine if he knew I was wearing a John Coltrane T-shirt beneath my vest. He'd lapse into agonal breathing.

"I don't care what kind of grades you made from Jonah. Phase Two rookies don't know shit. One month under your belt and you think you know it all. All you know how to do is check the oil and fill the gas." He waits for me to get out of the car. "You do know how to pump gas, don't you?"

10-4.

"Then what the hell are you waiting for?"
I can see the bulge in his larynx bobbing, waiting to explode.
Nothing. I step out of the car.

The first call of the evening Waxler drives 10-18, lights and
sirens. One hand is on the wheel, the other on his weapon like
he's preparing to draw. What's he thinking? We're going to an
auto accident, not a shootout at the OK Corral.

The weight of my utility belt shifts as I step out of the car.
Lightning-quick pain shoots through my right flank. Sometimes
I think my body will never heal, never bring me pleasure the
way it once did with Makayla. It's been three weeks since our
argument. The slight advantage of working midnight shift is the
unlikelihood of running into her.

I ask Waxler to direct traffic so I can work the accident. He's
indignant, saying through clenched teeth that he's my trainer.
"10-4," I say, shutting the door. Before I can call Joyce, I hear
her on the radio saying she's on the way. Waxler sits with his
clipboard making notes as I shine my light onto the cars. It's a
T-bone accident, the front of one car into the side of another.
One driver is injured. He's holding his license in his hand and
hyperventilating. There's a spiderweb crack on the windshield
made with his forehead. It tells me he wasn't wearing a seat belt.
"It's my fault, I know it," he says. "I couldn't stop at the
light."

"Relax. We won't worry about that right now. Do you hurt
anywhere?"

"Just my head," he says.

I slide my hand into his, counting pulse and respirations
undetected.

"Whatta ya got, Fitz?" I turn around. Clay, one of my old
paramedic partners, is staring at me with partial expression.
Shrapnel from Vietnam severed his left-side facial muscles.

"Frontal lobe hematoma," I say.

Clay's an excellent paramedic, but on the wild side. Disappearing for days at a time, drinking Jack Daniels and hunting
quail on plantations up in Thomasville and Valdosta.

"You spent too much time with that patient," Waxler says. "That's a medic's job. You're not a medic anymore, you're a police officer. Your job is to take control of the scene and you should have done it sooner." 10-4.

Clay loads his patient, shuts the ambulance door. He shakes his head at Waxler. "You want me to shoot him, Abby? End your misery?"

I tell Clay it's not worth the paperwork.

Waxler tosses his clipboard on the dash and starts screaming as he drives toward the hospital. "Why the hell didn't you issue him a citation right there? You should be halfway through your report." He picks up the clipboard and circles a 1 under "Uses Time Wisely." The pen shakes in his hand.

At the Hogg, Waxler buys a white-bread sandwich filled with processed meat. I lean against the trunk and finish the accident report as Joyce drives up with her new Field Training Officer. Rid of Waxler, I expect her to be elated but she seems sober, preoccupied. Her mascara and hair bun are holding up, but something's not quite right. "Free at last," I say to her.

She looks at Waxler through the store glass. He's stuffing the sandwich in his cheeks like a hamster and browsing through an *Enquirer*.

"I hate him," she says, her face ashen. She squeezes the night stick on her belt until her knuckles turn a gray white beneath the neon. "Just be careful, Fitz. He's gotten worse since the shooting."

I wonder if he's second-guessing his actions, having nightmares like me, but Joyce is evasive when I ask her what she means. I think about his reckless driving earlier this evening, but before I can get anything out of her, Waxler walks toward the car.

9 p.m. check-on the next night, I sit downstairs at the station with the other rookies and our trainers. We are waiting for Sergeant Bolero, who is standing at the podium, to finish reading

the last bulletin. I copy down information on a kidnapping, a four-year-old boy abducted from his front yard this morning, the tag number of two stolen vehicles, a rape and robbery suspect . . .

Cuidado! Arrive alive. Sergeant Bolero stops pulling on his moustache long enough to toss keys. Each shift, officers are assigned different cars, the vehicle numbers recorded on the sergeant's administrative sheet. No keys fly my way because Waxler has a take-home car, a privilege of seniority, or sometimes just favoritism. I sit and wait as the other rookies are out gassing up their cars. When he's good and ready, Waxler unsnaps the keys on his belt and tosses them in my direction. Gas it up.

The toss is about five feet short. I have to pick the keys up off the floor. In about ten minutes he'll stroll out to the parking lot and yell at me for being slow. All the other rookies are 10-51, en route to their zones. *You're still stroking the dipstick,* he'll say.

Warm wind fans my face as I drop the hood. The winds of hell, ten hours in a car with Waxler. I check the tires, turn signals, headlights, blue lights, sirens. I inspect the exterior and undercarriage for damage. I inventory the trunk: flares, fire extinguisher, first-aid kit, spare tire, jack. I disengage the backseat and search for contraband. It's important to do this search at the beginning of each shift and in between prisoner transports. Unless you search the car before and after sticking a prisoner back there, contraband or concealed weapons charges will get tossed. Any mediocre attorney can make the argument and win.

It happens instantly. I cut the headlights and drive around the back of Gold Key Storage. Out walks a guy carrying a 13-inch TV. *Hey, you.* He drops the TV and sprints off like a jackrabbit through the woods. *Police. Stop.* A second guy bolts from the storage space, and I take off after him. We're running through the woods. I'm so close that branches are flying back in my face, and then my foot catches a tree root and I fall forward full force.

He's climbing over a retaining wall when I catch up to him. I grab his ankle and yank like I've just snagged a hearty grouper. Falling back on my ass, I reel in a size nine Nike.

My pants are torn at the knee. I scrape out the tiny blood-soaked pebbles, move unsteadily back down the path. Then the real pain hits me. I don't have ribs anymore, just splinters. I lean against a tree, calm myself.

At the edge of the pavement leading to the woods, I see Waxler, standing there holding his gun. He reholsters when he sees me carrying evidence by a string.

"You were close enough to get his shoe and you let him get away. Un-fucking-believable."

I limp back to the car. "Amazing, isn't it, considering all the help I had."

"You don't know shit," he says. "Someone had to stay and protect the crime scene."

"Yeah, right." *Protect the crime scene.*

"You think I'm scared, don't you. Don't you?"

I get my clipboard out of the car, begin to inventory the stash of merchandise outside the warehouse when I hear something like a bug zapper. Waxler is watching the electricity jump back and forth in his stun gun. "I'm not scared of anything," he says. He takes the gun and stabs it into the back of his thigh. His knee buckles as 150,000 volts discharge through it. Two more times he jolts himself, then points to the blue and white medal on his chest he got for shooting the kid. "This says it all. So don't go copping a nigger attitude with me. You don't know shit, you hear me. You hear me? I'll wash your sorry ass out of the program."

I keep writing on my aluminum clipboard.

At the Hogg, I lock the bathroom door behind me, drop my jump bag on the floor. It's getting easier to fight back tears. None want to come out. I splash cold water on my face, hold my breath until my leg is propped on the sink. On my knee I pour peroxide, watch it bubble, turn white as it burns.

Joyce is standing by the *Democrat* news box, munching on a

Snickers. "Hey," I say, fastening the leather keepers that hold up my utility belt. "I know what you mean about Waxler."

Joyce's eyes glaze over. She looks at my torn pants. "You didn't do it, did you, Fitz? You stood up to him, didn't you?"

What? She's making no sense. What the hell is she talking about.

Joyce realizes we're on different wavelengths. "Nothing," she says. She pushes the final bite into her mouth, crinkles the wrapper.

The next night I drag myself in to work, resisting the urge to call in sick. After check-on, Waxler takes his sweet time giving me the car keys, making me late, which gives him another opportunity to yell.

I hustle out to the station parking lot. There's a line of patrol cars gassing up so I check the engine, tires, turn signals. I inventory the trunk contents. Behind the backseat I find a stub nose .38. It's Waxler's backup gun. He pressures me into going faster, hoping I'll cut corners, then he plants this gun. Asshole. I pop the thumb latch, drop six rounds into my pocket.

I pump the gas, watch fumes bend in the air until there's a click. Gas burps up on my hand.

"Nice move, Fitzpatrick." Camp's biceps bulge beneath his short sleeves but they're less toned than usual. Six weeks on the road and already I can see a ripple around his waistline. Camp's shift ended thirty minutes ago but he hangs around to brown-nose his sergeant, the watch commander, even the janitor who has keys to the supply closet.

"You heard Dingerson washed?" Camp's smile tightens around the wad in his lower lip. That makes five.

I could care less about Dingerson right now. I've got my own problems just trying to survive, but I'm not about to let Camp see me sweat. I lock the nozzle back into the pump. "I thought Dingerson was your buddy."

"Sorry bastard couldn't cut the mustard after all. His FTO locked him in the backseat with the window up. Turned his gear in the same day."

I screw the cap back on the gas tank, unclasp the keys from my belt. Camp follows me around the car as I slide into the driver's seat. It's one of the few times I'm allowed behind the wheel.

"Odds say another rookie will wash soon." He leans down, looks in the window. "Waxler says you're looking peaked, Fitzpatrick."

I slide the gearshift into drive. Go to hell.

It's two o'clock in the morning and quiet. We haven't had a call in over an hour. I see a dead animal alongside the curb. Waxler says, forget it. When I shine the spotlight on it, a blue tag reflects in the light. I can tell it's a cat. I park the car and walk over with a plastic bag. I slip off the collar. The tag gives the name of a woman who lives three streets over. I kick Budweiser cans out of the way, slide the limp feline into the bag and tie it shut. When I was ten, I found my dog dead alongside the road. Ants were crawling out her nose.

"You should be looking for that rape suspect on the BOLO, not carting dead carnage. Un-fucking-believable," he says, as I lay the bag inside the trunk and slam the lid. "Your priorities are fucked-up, Fitzpatrick."

Waxler's ferocious pen scratches across the page as I drive to the address on the tag. All the lights are off as I step out of the car and open the trunk. I set the bag on the doorstep and take out one of my cards. I write: *I'm sorry for your loss.* I hang the collar on the doorknob.

At the Hogg, Waxler munches on another mystery meat sandwich. I walk past him, toward the cooler, inhaling the glue-like smell of white bread. Jonah is leaning against the counter, swapping stories with Mavis as she cuts biscuits for the morning rush. Waxler interrupts to tell them the cat story. Apparently it's become humorous. Mavis and Jonah don't respond, but Waxler keeps talking and chewing. Nothing like a fresh road kill to stir the appetite. Waxler walks outside.

I pay for a pint of milk, watch Jonah chew on that tiny bone
in the isosceles part of the wing as I tell him about the gun
Waxler planted in the backseat. He stops chewing, his look in-
credulous. "You're sure it was loaded?" he asks. I take the
impound sheet out of my front pocket and start to unfold it.
Jonah says, "Some FTO's toss a squirt gun or rubber knife if
they've got a lazy rookie and are trying to make a point, but a
loaded weapon?"

I hand Jonah the impound sheet. *Item 2, Quantity 6, Bullets:
.38 hollow points, silver tip.*

"This ain't right, Fitz." For a moment I think he means I
shouldn't have impounded the weapon, that I should have
handed it back to Waxler. Laughed it off. I take a big gulp of
my milk, pushing the carton up too quickly. "This ain't right,
Fitz," he says again. "What?" I say, wiping a white moustache
off with my fingers. "Waxler's been on my back for weeks."

Jonah looks at me. "What you did was fine. Just like the
policy manual says. But a loaded weapon just ain't right." He
points the chicken bone to the incident number on the paper. "I
never heard you radio for a case number."

"I used the phone in the downstairs lobby to call dispatch.
Waxler figured I'd use the radio, and that if he heard me call
for a found-property case number, he would cancel the request."
Rookies are all the time screwing up radio transmissions for case
numbers. It wouldn't seem unusual.

Jonah hands me the paper back. "As far as Waxler knows,
the gun is still in the backseat?"

I nod yes. We haven't had a prisoner yet. I think he's waiting
for me to get one so he can burn me on the spot. I'd be out for
sure, putting a prisoner in the backseat with a loaded weapon at
his disposal.

Jonah points the chicken bone at me like the familiar tooth-
pick. "Be-care-ful."

I finish the carton, fold it over into a square the way I used
to do when concealing beets from Sister Patricia, the garbage
monitor.

"It won't look good for him. Waxler'll have a hard time explaining to Bolero how his backup weapon ended up in impound. It could get pretty sticky, Fitz."

"It already is," I say.

"That why you drinking so much milk lately? Wasn't nothing but Cokes when you rode with me."

Nosy cop.

I pop the hood, check the brake fluid, oil, coolant. Hell just got hotter these last four days since Waxler found out I impounded his .38. I check the lights, turn signals, sirens. My life is reduced to a circle of 1's and it's very possible I'll be kept back, terminated if he has anything to do with it. I inventory the trunk: flares, fire extinguisher, first-aid kit. With performance scores so low, perhaps I should take up golfing. I disengage the backseat. Nothing. I don't care. I did what I could live with.

Waxler screams at me as we pull out of the station. He's been razzed about his rookie pulling a one-up on him and he doesn't like it. "UN-FUCKING-BELIEVABLE. You missed the turn."

10-4. Of course it's believable, I think. How can I learn this zone when half the time he won't let me drive. Waxler's louder than the sirens. I turn around and pick up the missed street. Dispatch says the 911 call was phoned in by a ten year old. Off the asphalt, I veer up a dirt road that snakes past a sprinkling of off-grade houses. Beneath a streetlight I see a cluster of little black children swaying back and forth like minnows. One breaks away, runs up to our car. "He inside." She points to a house with missing shutter slats.

Thanks, Sugar.

From an angle, I move along the bushes and up the side of the front porch. The blue light of the television flickers through the open screen door onto the front porch. Quick peek through the window: TV, couch, La-Z-Boy with a throw. No one in sight. Waxler and I stand each to a side of the door, weapons drawn. My knuckles thud against the wood. No answer. *Police*, I say. *Open up.* A last look inside before I pull the screen handle.

I search the living room, then move to the kitchen. There's a skillet of Beeny-Weenies on the stove. In the hallway are three doors, two of them are open. I enter the first door: bunk beds and a brown dresser. In the closet are kids' sneakers, clothes, a baseball. I'm leaving the room when I hear a low whimper. Maybe not. Maybe it's just a floorboard. Across the hall I enter the bathroom, yank back the shower curtain. Shit. A shotgun. There's a boy curled up in the empty tub, arms wrapped around his knees, crying. "What happened," I say, picking up the double barrel by its metal neck. He tries to talk but sobs instead, burying his head in his knees. "I'll be back in a minute."

In the hallway I stand to the side of the closed door, reach across to turn the knob and push the door open. The room is washed in red. Pieces of gray matter cling to the ceiling, the walls, the dresser mirror. Near the double bed I see tiny legs clad in jeans and Reeboks. I walk across the room to the other side of the bed and find most of the kid's face gone except for an ear, nostril and a couple of teeth. *Downgrade the ambulance*, I radio Dispatch. *It's a Signal 7.* No sense in racing to a dead body. I reholster my weapon. On the wall is a black velvet painting of Martin Luther King, the cocoa skin of his forehead impaled by a flying piece of bone. I need a sergeant en route, also a crime-scene technician. I walk out of the room. Waxler stays to gawk a while longer.

In the bathroom I sit on the edge of the tub and lightly place my hand on the back of the boy's neck. He's still sobbing. I wait for him to gain a moment of control. "You need to tell me what happened," I whisper. He gasps for air, then out it gushes: I didn't know it was loaded. He leans his head against my thigh, his shoulders heaving. I pull him out of the tub and put him on my lap. He buries his face in my shoulder and cries like there's no tomorrow. There's nothing to say. I rock him. Listen to the splat of tears on my badge.

Finally Waxler closes the bedroom door. His boots, sharp

against the wooden hallway floors, scrape to a halt. "How quaint," he says.

I give him the finger.

On the way to the Hogg I'm waiting for Waxler to blast me into a new universe, but his uncanny silence makes my neck itch.

He buys a bag of Cheetos, gets back in the car as I'm paying for a carton of milk. Neither of us speaks for a mile or so and Waxler starts whistling, a vintage Billy Joel melody from *Stranger*. When he hits one of the high notes, I realize where we're going. He pulls up the curb onto a dirt trail leading to the holding pond. I know the place. Jonah and I used to cruise it, looking for perverts and teenage drinkers. He cuts the lights, circling the pond in total blackness. Branches scrape against the car as we bounce back and forth, each wheel on a separate plane. Slowing to a stop, he reverses, backs into an alcove facing the pond and cuts the ignition.

Waxler opens the Cheetos and sets the sack between his legs. His crunch is loud like the bullfrogs. "All those 1's, Fitzpatrick, it's a shame. I'm washing you out, you know." He leans his head back and chews, staring at the ceiling upholstery.

I slap a mosquito on my neck.

"Yes sir," he says, reaching for another handful, "and then there's that little matter of flipping me off. Disrespect. Insubordination. Conduct unbecoming of a trainee. Sounds like your career is in steady decline, Fitzpatrick."

"What's your point," I ask. He smiles, his shaved head like waxy cabbage in the moonlight.

"The point is," he says looking over at me, "things can change. Take Joyce, for example. A little cooperation on her part and she managed to pass first phase."

I slap another mosquito off my forehead, play over Joyce's conversation in my head. Now I understand.

Waxler licks each of his orange fingers, starting with his thumb. I think of crushed fireflies. When he's eaten all he wants, he tosses the bag out the window, lifts the armrest between us. Only then do I see his bulging crotch. "I seem to be having a problem," he says, "but then I hear you lesbians give the best head."

"Don't do this," I say.

"Do what? I'm only asking for a little cooperation. You do know how to cooperate, don't you," he says, unzipping his pants.

10-4.

"Good." He breathes in through clenched teeth, then extracts his penis. "Blow me."

"You wouldn't like it," I say.

"Just do it." He grips the steering wheel, knuckles white in anticipation. My holster snaps and it's all over. He moves. "Hands back on the steering wheel, NOW." I shove the cold barrel of my 9mm into his penis.

"You're crazy," he says.

"You're just now figuring that out? You want a blow job— prepare yourself."

"This is un-fucking-believable. You're a goner, Fitzpatrick."

Now it's my turn to smile. "What makes you think you'll live to tell about it?"

"You don't have the balls."

"In about three seconds neither will you, and you know, I'm really going to enjoy it. How many other women, Waxler, tell me. After I shoot you, Joyce and every other female officer whose face you've raped will be right behind me, nailing your coffin shut."

I see his left hand start to loosen. I shove the barrel hard into his scrotum until he groans. "Don't even think about it," I say.

Sweat drips off his nose as he leans forward, resting his forehead on the steering column. "Don't," he says. "Please don't."

"Why shouldn't I? Is there even one reason why I shouldn't —because I sure as hell can't think of one."

"It'll stay on your conscience."

"Maybe I don't have a conscience."

For seconds, neither of us speaks. Bullfrogs croak in the pond, mosquitoes suck away on my arm, Waxler's limp penis hangs on my gun. Life is absurd.

Finally I say: "You're going to promote me this phase, not because of tonight, but because of every night for the past month that I've shown you I can do the job. And if you even think about trying this again, I promise you whatever short supply of conscience I've got will have long since run out. Like you've said, my priorities are fucked-up."

Slowly I ease my gun away and lean back to my side of the car. "Zip your pants and let's get out of here. The mosquitoes are terrible."

Leap of Faith

Hilary Mullins

I have been thinking it over, turning it around and around in my head, while up above me the hay elevator is gnashing, bales shuttering up in line one after another, big bulky blocks rising up and along in jerks. At the edge of the steel belt each one juts out like a huge tongue, hangs suspended for a moment in midair, then nose dives down to the floor of the loft below. That's what I'm thinking about doing too—taking a plunge, but me, I want to fall further, just keep going forever, not like these big chunks of hay that bounce down ten feet to Dad. He scoops up each bale, turns and hurls it all in one graceful swing that lands it at my feet. He's small and sturdy, stronger than he looks, and those bales really fly. I kind of look like him—both me and Warren do, with our square faces. But neither one of us can throw a bale as far as Walker Hammond can.

It is hot up here, so hot. A swarthy haze of sun blazes through the hay doors high up, and the whole loft shimmers with the July heat. My eyes are stinging with the sweat dribbling down from my forehead. But I don't care. I don't care about anything anymore, and Dad, he doesn't even know, he's pitching bale after bale to me, and I'm bending down for them, lifting and turning to shove them into the growing stack. It's stupid. You know? I just want to die all the time, but the hay still has to go

in. So I try to let my mind go blank, and just watch as the next
bale flies through the air and clumps down in front of me. Bend,
lift, turn and push. And again. Working helps, I guess. You don't
talk, you just swing and stack, swing and stack. The rhythm is
its own language. Keeps me from crying anyway.

When the elevator cuts out and I lift the day's last bale into
place, Dad pauses for a moment, propping the brim of his Blue
Seal cap up to wipe the sweat off his broad forehead with his
old red handkerchief. I walk toward him, and he looks up, nods
my way. Good work, that's what my dad likes. I follow him
down the whitewashed ladder.

Out front Warren and Lucas are standing off to the side of the
hay wagon and tractor, standing in the shade the barn throws,
gripping bottles of Coke. Joking about something. The ice chest
sits next to them. I walk over, grab the opener off the faded
orange top and reach in, grab a bottle and crack the cap off with
one wrench. Tip it and my head back, let the cold kick swirl
down my throat, washing out the grit. I don't know where Dad
went, he's still back in the barn, fiddling with something in the
milk house maybe.

The sun is pounding out here, and I take another long swig,
see my old very ex-friend Lucas eyeing me from where he stands
leaning against the barn, the bottom of one thick boot cocked up
against the side so that his leg crooks out and back at an angle.
He has one big mitt of a hand roped around his soda, the other
at his hip with a finger jammed through a belt loop. Shirtless,
his chest sprouts thick dark hair that wasn't there three years
ago. He's lanky but graceful too, has tanned arms that thicken
going up and a square jaw. Nice body, if that's what you go for.
Lots of girls at school do. I tried, but it didn't work, and he took
it personal. These days he talks to me like he never used to, with
this edge in his voice that cheapens everything, snotty and crude
all at once. It wouldn't be so bad if we hadn't been best friends
growing up. But that's all over now. Now it's my big brother
Warren he comes over to see, Warren he'll do anything for. He's
even helping Warren out with the chores this weekend while me

and Dad and Mom drive to Pennsylvania for the Hammond Family Reunion.

Being around Luke these days is so friggin' impossible. Makes me want to cry again. I'm not going to though. Lucas doesn't want to hear about it; he made that clear enough. I nurse my Coke, and then see my father come out the front door of the barn. He walks over to us, grabs his own self a soda.

"Hay came in pretty dry, huh Dad?" Warren says. He's so godammed eager around Dad sometimes it makes me sick. Ever since he graduated two years ago and started working as a real partner with him on the farm. Lucky shit. Nobody ever gives the farm to the girl in the family.

Our father pauses a moment before he answers. "Pretty dry, yeah."

"Good thing," says Lucas. He looks at Warren and then at my dad and then back to Warren. He's going to ignore me now. But at least that way I don't have to worry about him hassling me. It's one or the other. The talk turns to tractors—hydraulic shafts and PTO's. I don't know what I'm standing here for. There's nothing left for me to do, and none of them even look at me. I drain the last swallow of Coke and jam the bottle back in the pack with the other empties.

"See you guys later," I say, voice low as I turn. Don't want to interrupt anything. I don't look back, but as I cross the road I can feel Lucas's eyes on me all the same. He'd turn them into welding torches if he could, burn a hole under my left shoulder blade and right through my heart. Weld it to his with all that love and piss and anger. I just keep walking.

A couple of barn swallows swoop out the wide doorway when I step into the garage, skirting the Ford. My dirt bike is propped against the far wall, faded green with its tattered black seat. I grab the handlebars and arc it around fast, roll it out into the hazy sunshine. I have to get the hell out of here before I lose my shit. I turn the key up and grip the bars again, breaking into a jagged run, pushing the heavy thing alongside of me until I have enough speed and swing over on the seat, kicking the shifter up into second and feeling the engine catch and jump into action. I throttle her and peel out of the driveway, without even a glance toward the barn. Up the dirt road I go, heading for the back roads on Gates Hill.

I ride, clipping along, and after a mile south and two miles east, I'm coming up on that old abandoned house on Gates, beautiful old thing with porches and big windows and gray weather-beaten sides. I want to live there. Not alone either. But that will never happen. I rev my bike as I pass the front of it. The yard is tall with grass going to seed, but I don't really look as I aim my bike hurtling toward that big bump in the road. The front wheel points up, and then I'm airborne, flying a few blurred feet and coming back with a whump to the ground. Even when I'm feeling this bad, it's one thing that still feels good. Flying. I know every rock, every crest, every place where the road gives me a place to jump off of. Out another mile and down past that washboard hill where the lake road starts there's one slope of rock that angles up enough for me to really get going. Today I go there, launch myself and my bike up it again and again, five times, ten, fifteen times, until I am nothing but that moment of hanging weightlessness, everything in me suspended while the bike screams and the trees flash by in streaks of green.

That fixes me for now. Finally I turn the bike around and head back the way I came. But right before the old gray house I find myself turning off the road and up the tractor path that rolls up the hill behind it. Lower down somebody hays this huge field, but as you go farther up, the grass gets long and wild, clotted in places with thickets of berry bushes.

At the top, I switch my bike off, leaning it against an old gnarled apple tree. Walk forward in the waist-high grass. That's when I start thinking of Louise. Washes over me. Nothing you can do. This is not ever going to work. I make a kind of dive forward, plunging down into the deep grass, throwing my arms out to break the fall. But there's no way to break the falling inside now that I am out here, this free-falling through space, everything solid unraveling in me. Louise, Louise, Louise. I'm just lying to myself when I say I don't love her anymore. I twist my hands around bunches of grass, trying to hang on. Louise, Louise. The earth gives way under me as the sobs come in scalding bursts, and then I am nothing but waves of it, seized and thrown up one crest and then the next and the next. On and on it goes, a kind of vomiting up of my guts, all my terrible twisted feeling spewing out.

I hate it. I hate crying. I will stop thinking about her in a minute and then maybe it will get better. But it's not ever going to get better for real. There's too much other shit on top of it. I mean, here I have been riding out the summer, moving from chores to haying to any kind of work I can find, but this storm keeps brewing anyway. I'm gay and it's wrecking my life. I can't tell anybody. When I told Luke, that's when he started hating me. I wouldn't even try telling Mom and Dad. They would never forgive me. If they didn't kill me first.

Just thinking about that wrenches another spasm through me, sets me writhing in the grass on my side, these choked cries that don't even sound like me blatting out of my mouth. I can't stop them. Pretty soon it's going to be taking over altogether. But I know how to get out of all this.

That thought backs off the sobs enough for me to gasp a few breaths. It's the only thing that makes it all bearable. I lie face down for a minute longer, snuffling the moist smell of dirt and gathering myself together. Turn on my back, scrunching a hollow for myself in the earth. Eyes start to clear, but all I can see from down here is the brushlike tips of grass waving slightly, stretching up over my head like trees. And beyond that, one piece of sky, blue and empty.

Only one more month 'til school. If I think it's bad now! The way Louise is going to be walking by me in the halls pretending I'm not there. And then what if Luke sounds off? He's pissed enough to broadcast it to the whole school—Karla Hammond is a lezzie. Little Miss Sally Guidance Counselor Michaels won't think I'm such a neat kid then. All her big plans for me. "Now Karla, I think you should apply to the University of Vermont. With that pitching arm of yours, you really might have a

chance.'' But school is hell, Miss Michaels. The way you always
have to put on an act, pretend you're just like the rest of the
kids. Why in the world would I sign up for four more years of
that?

'Cause I'm not like the rest of the kids. And there I thought
Louise was like me, and I just couldn't stop myself from leaning
over and kissing her after practice last spring. But she's not like
me. Not when her face looked the way it did after—the disgust
in her eyes. So much disgust.

And I'm not like Luke either. He's normal. And now he thinks
I'm a cold bitch, came on to him just so I could get him going
and then jerk back to leave him hanging, all open and wanting,
haw haw.

But that's not what I meant. I just made a mistake. A bad
mistake. After Louise I sort of got desperate. I mean, it made
me think what kind of life am I going to have if the people I
love think my love is disgusting. Shit for a life, that's what. I
had to try it the normal way.

So. I already knew Luke was in love with me. It's been a
couple of years now. So I kissed him up in the loft one night
when we were up there checking out the new kittens. And he
wasn't disgusted, no way. Surprised at first, but then he got right
into it, didn't yank into reverse after a couple of minutes like
Louise. I knew that was a good sign, but my little experiment
wasn't working out as good for me as it was for him. It just
didn't feel right—nothing like those first moments with Louise
when she was kissing me back and the fire blazed down my
backbone and into my crotch. Sitting there with Luke all I could
feel was a piece of hay that was scratching my back under my
shirt. His thick fumbling tongue against mine. I just started feeling so hollow and false that I had to stop. So I pulled my head
back, told him I couldn't do it. At first he didn't believe that I
meant it, but when he did, he sort of started crying. And that
made my heart bust clean open, hearing his voice crack like that.
My friend Lucas, my silly old boy pal, my best friend in the
world!

So I told him the truth. And that's when he got pissed. Got

up, shaking his head. Hard. "What they say at school is right, Karla. You just want to be a guy." He spit the words out. And went clomping down the ladder. I tried talking to him the next day, but he wouldn't even listen, and he's been a shithead to me ever since.

See, that's the kind of crap that happens when you're gay. And it's just going to get worse. Because there's no place for somebody like me here. No place. That's why I want to do it. Do it now before it gets really bad.

Do it now. I jump to my feet and go right for my bike. Swing it around facing back down the path, climb on, let the rolling gather its own momentum, me just bumping on its back, along for the ride. By the time I kick the shifter into gear, I'm going fast enough so that the bike seems to lurch back with the momentary slowing. The engine kicks in and I head down the hill, turn right at the bottom, back the way I came from, not toward home. Bounce back down the washboard hill, go right again and hurtle up over the jumping rock one more time, keep going, out the old lake road, all rutted and grown up in the middle with grass, down across the field with the done-over barn where somebody lives now, down into the cedar woods, and back out into the bottom field. Here the trail runs along the cliff, and from the corner of my eye, I can see the lake stretching out a good hundred feet below, deep blue glints winking at me. I wind the bike way up, tearing faster and faster along the grassy edge, wind pushing all the air out of my lungs, scoring my insides clean of everything.

Everything but this one thing, this movie I watched once when I was little. On Walt Disney. It was about this Indian boy on a reservation. He didn't have any friends at all. But there was this eagle his tribe kept, and it was tied to a big post out in the middle of this square, and the boy was friends with the eagle. In the movie all the other kids on the reservation teased this boy about being weird, but he didn't try to change himself into something he wasn't. Then one day he decided to free the eagle, but just as he started to untie the rope that held her to the post, all the other kids came running to stop him. But the boy was very quick

and he grabbed the huge bird and started running, the whole pack
of kids pouring after him, like they were going to kill him and
the eagle both. And he ran and ran and ran, lit up this big hill,
and then the camera making the movie pulled back and you
could see the hill from far off, and you could see the boy and
the bird and the horde of other kids screaming for his blood, and
you could see out past that where he was running to—this huge
high cliff that just dropped off far far down. And the boy was
pelting toward it, still hauling that bird and when he got close
to the edge, he threw the bird out, and there was a dead moment,
and then she was stretching out her wide wings and taking flight.
And the other kids were almost on the boy, but he just kept
running, running right out over the edge, and there was another
dead pause, some kind of blur on the screen, and then you could
see the boy had turned into an eagle himself, and he was sailing
up after the other bird, and they were keening out to each other
flying off, winging away into the sky.

I cried for a long time after that show. A long time. And I've
always remembered it. But now it's ten years later, and I'm
careening along the brink myself, done with the tears. Done with
them for good. I want to do it now. Soar out over this edge and
keep going. Who can stop me? Luke? Louise? Not hardly. I
wrench the throttle back as far as she'll go, everything quick-
ening. Up ahead I can see where the tractor trail bends to the
right, cutting back out into the field and toward the woods where
it runs down toward the lake past falling-down summer places.
Before the bend, there's this one last part along the cliff that
kind of crops out, even lifts a little up and toward the lake.
Perfect. I aim the wheel. I got to do it now. There are people
farther down. Just a few. Up for family outings. Faster, faster
and the bike shrieks, winding out. Maybe one of them will find
me. Maybe someone up for the weekend with her kids and her
whole extended family. Maybe someone up for a family reunion.

Family reunions. Ours this weekend—Mom, Dad, all those
cousins, and the old aunts. Christ, you can't kill yourself the
Friday before all that. I let off the throttle so suddenly that the
bike kind of coughs, catching, and I have to hang on to keep

myself from pitching forward over the handlebars. Pulling back
up straight, I let the gas off all together and the motor stalls.
Silence swoops down. Grass waves on either side of me, fills
open space for a second, but then everything smashes down once
more. I shake my head, the green world blurring, the ugly sobs
starting again. I cry and cry, sit there slumped on the seat, helpless while the bawling splits me open. I can't believe I'm still
here, that I have to go through this anymore. I can't believe it.
I am supposed to be gone, vanished, dead to all this. But here I
still sit, howling like a dog with its guts coming out.

For crying out loud. Why didn't I just do it? I suck in a ragged
breath, wiping my eyes. I still could. I could run over there now
and jump. Get it over with. But something about this very big
deal of a family reunion is sticking in my throat. Something
about how my going is the least I could do for them before I
make this big mess in their lives. I slip off the bike to my feet
and grab it by the bars. Walk it to the edge of the field, listening
to the slight clicking it makes in neutral. When the trail starts
its gradual slope down into the woods, I lope alongside it, swing
back on and jump her back to life, heading down for the lake
and the long hill back up that will bring me home.

My mother is at the kitchen sink when I walk in the back
door, her back to me. I try to slip my shoes off as quietly as I
can, but she hears me anyway.

"Karla, where have you been? Get on in here and help your
mother."

Some part inside still not sewn back together wants to blurt
out, "Gee Mom, I just about drove my motorcycle off a cliff
and that's all you have to say?"

But I don't. I tell her that I have to go wash up first, and tread
up the back stairs in my socks. It's really strange, but somehow
everything looks different, changed, charged. Maybe this is the
way ghosts feel when they come back to their old life, everything
crammed with substance but them. I slip up the stairs, marveling
at the old boots and sneakers lining the wall going up either side.
Cracks in my brother's old leather boots, mud caking up the

sides of my softball cleats. There's so much detail! Even my
room seems brighter and bigger, like something out of a movie.
Weird. I shake my head and go into the bathroom, splash water
on my face. In my eyes. Pee. Sit there, get lost. Blue sky. Louise's face. The smell of hay.

"Karla!! Have you fallen in up there?" My mother's voice
makes me jump. I can picture her at the bottom of the front
stairs, leaning forward to throw her voice up toward me, her
apron draping around the bottom post of the banister. Gray hair
pulled neatly back and up off her ruddy face.

"Coming!" Christ if she only knew.

Warren is walking through the side screen door when I get
down to the kitchen. He swings the icebox open, pulls out the
pitcher of iced tea, his fingers making drooling prints on the
foggy surface. He breaks ice cubes into a glass. He's already
done with milking. Damn, I was out a lot longer than I thought.

"Karla, I've got to go do my chores. Use the rest of the ro-
maine to make a salad. And don't forget to use that tomato on
the sill there." Our mother unties her apron, carefully hooking
it up on its nail in the doorway of the pantry, heading for the
back hall and her barn boots. "Check the meatloaf in a half
hour," she says from the other side of the screen door. I watch
for a moment, turning around so I can still see her as she walks
with that sure step of hers toward the milk house.

When I turn back, Warren is already gone. I hear the TV in
the living room switch on, the twang of the announcer starting
up, rattling off sports scores. Warren never has anything to say.
He won't even know the difference when I'm gone. From the
refrigerator, I haul out broccoli, green pepper, spinach, an old
box of raisins. Maybe none of them will. I stand at the counter
slicing, cover the cutting board in a heap of furious green slivers.

"Which one are you again, dear?" Mabel, sitting with her
crocheted shawl draped around her legs, squints up at me. We're
sitting on the porch at Hammond Hollow, my great-grandfather's
place. I look down at Mabel from where I'm perched on the
railing. I can't remember exactly who she is either, not more

than her name anyway, but I think she must be a hundred years old, her glasses braced in the loose folds of her face.

"I'm Karla Hammond," I say loudly. "Walker Hammond's daughter."

"Oh you're Walker's girl. That Walker. Takes right after his daddy. They're good workers, those boys."

I nod. I don't want to be here. I mean, here we are on a farm, what used to be a farm anyway, but me and mom and dad are the only farmers left of the bunch. All my cousins are kids from the suburbs, with their slick-looking shorts and T-shirts. I see two of them, Liz and Shelly, walking by toward the picnic table. Makeup and perfect blow-dried hair, shaved legs gleaming. Then I realize Mabel is saying something to me. I excuse myself; she repeats her question.

"Are you a farmer too, dear?" she asks.

"They don't let girls be farmers," I say, looking toward the road, hearing in my voice how pissed I sound. "Just farmers' wives."

"Hogwash," says Mabel matter-of-factly. "You do exactly what you want, never mind the rest of them."

I look back down at her again. Maybe I should be paying more attention here. She looks back, and for the first time I see her pale blue eyes behind the dark framed glasses. Then she's looking away, shifting in her high-backed wooden chair, re-tucking the shawl under her old pink and green dress.

"Did you do what you wanted?" I turn to face her directly, part of me afraid I'm being rude.

"Of course not. That's why I'm telling you." She talks awfully brisklike for such an old woman. "But now I do whatever I please."

"What did you do?"

"I was a telephone operator for forty-seven years, can you believe it? Now my husband Silas, he was your great-uncle, he wanted this farm, but he ended up running the feed store in town instead. Nobody in this family ever did what they wanted to do. We didn't think that way back then. You just went into something." She's looking back at me again, blinking a little, as if the glare of the hazy day is bothering her eyes. "Your generation is lucky, everybody running off to find themselves. We could have used more of that in our time."

I slip from the railing and perch on the end of the fold-up chair next to her, thinking to myself how the family hasn't really changed at all—even if the times have.

"So why didn't Silas get the farm?" I ask her.

"He didn't have the heart to fight for it," she says, "not after we lost Daniel. He didn't have heart for anything much for a long time after that." She pauses, looking across the road, up toward the hollow. I can't tell what she's looking at. Probably nothing that's here now. "I didn't have heart for much myself."

Sitting next to her silence, I don't know what to say. I bend down, fiddle with one of my shoelaces, wondering why I have never heard of this Daniel person. It must be bad, whatever happened. Mabel keeps gazing off into a lot of space. Finally I just ask, kind of blurting it out.

"Who was Daniel?"

Mabel seems to catch herself, fixes her shawl again. When she starts to answer, she's still not looking at me. "Oh, Daniel, he was a sweet boy, such a sweet boy. It's a shame no one's even told you about him." She shakes her head. For a second I think maybe I shouldn't have asked, but she goes on. "Daniel was Silas's brother, your great-grandfather Warren's brother too. He was the baby of the family. You could tell they had all doted on him, because he was so charming. He couldn't have been any older than you are now when Silas and I first started courting. I enjoyed that Daniel so much. But once he started getting into his twenties, well, he grew unhappy. Oh, he'd always flash that grin, and he didn't slack off around the farm, but I could tell something was eating him. I'd get after Silas to talk to him, but I don't believe he ever did. He thought it was girl trouble."

Mabel stops, turns a little toward me, sizing me up, or so it seems to me. Waiting.

I take my cue. "Was it? Girl trouble, I mean?" I ask.

I think she likes that I asked, because she moves toward me a little, lowering her voice in this close way.

"No. No, it wasn't. Of course nobody did ever admit it. But I thought so all along." The pale blue eyes fix on mine, and I understand somehow that I must not look away.

"Daniel was, well, different. He wasn't the marrying sort, if you know what I mean. He never told me so, but I had a friend who knew about him and this other boy. Evidently they were involved in some way. I didn't tell Silas of course. It would have upset him so. And Warren too. And then their folks! They were very serious church-going people. I believe they would have turned him right out."

I am sitting bolt upright next to this old great-aunt of mine, hardly daring to breathe, sure my face in hers is giving me away. Her eyes come very close into mine, and then she sighs, a long deep sigh, and turns to point across the road.

"He went up that way one morning. Very early. Before chores. Nobody else was up yet. The oil wells they had up in the hollow were still working then." My mind's eye flashes across some of the oil pumps we saw yesterday along the road, just small ones, their strange up and down jerking like ostriches going in and out of sand with long stiff necks. "The hollow's grown over now, but back then in the thirties, it was all open. And up at the top, there was a big cement platform about six feet high with a tank for the oil down in it."

She stops again. The horror is icing my veins. I want her to stop. I want her to tell me everything.

"That poor desperate boy, he climbed up the side, pried the big manhole cover up and lay down. And the fumes from the oil killed him, just like that. He knew they would." Mabel sighs, the air going out making her shoulders sag. "Well, it took them all day to find him, and what a terrible day that was, the waiting and wondering. When Warren and Silas came slogging down the field that evening carrying his body slung between them like a deer, I could barely look. Some things are almost too hard to see."

Sitting there, looking out across the road with her, it's like I see it too—Silas and Warren with rolled-up sleeves and suspenders, bearing that terrible load between them.

"Of course, he'd be just another old geezer now—'senior citizens,' that's what they call us." I glance sideways to see if I'm imagining the mocking in her words. I'm not. But then her voice goes soft again.

"I always wondered, as the years went by and we all got older, what Daniel would have been doing. Say at thirty, and then forty. It would have been such a pleasure to watch him build his life." She shifts suddenly in her chair to face me. "You don't mind hearing an old woman's babblings?"

"No ma'am. Not at all. I don't think you're babbling," I say, my insides squeezing, hoping she knows I mean it.

"You're a good girl Karla. Why, you look a little like Daniel yourself—must be those pretty gray eyes of yours. I'll tell you, I've often wondered if there wasn't something more I could have done for that boy. I've wished a million times that I could have told him not to care a whit about what anybody said. That he was just fine the way God made him, and if people here were too small-minded to appreciate that, well, there were places in the world where other people would. Of course, I was a little small-minded myself back in those days. But not after that. No, not after they brought him down from the hill that evening, the life passed out of him. All that beauty gone. And for what? That's what put the smallness in me right to shame. Those preachers love to rant about sins, but the real sin was we let it happen. It's the beauty in a person—that's the only sacred thing. Never forget that, Karla."

And with the mention of my name, it's like she remembers herself, and draws back. "But now I really am babbling, aren't I? You're such a dear to let me go on and on. You must be getting hungry. I see your daddy over by the food now. Why don't you run along and eat with him, I'm sure that would make him happy."

What's happened? Why is she trying to get rid of me? I scan her face, suddenly seeing how handsome she is, the deep lines etched in around her clear eyes. How could anyone not see the beauty there? But she is nodding me over toward my father, and I follow her gesture, getting up, thanking her the best I can, and walking slow down the steps in the direction of the picnic table. At first I mean to grab a paper plate at the end, but the next thing I know I'm cutting out of the line of cousins, crossing over the lawn and ducking under the tall pine to cross the road. No one seems to notice—no calls float after me. I walk fast, wonder if Mabel is watching me go around the old gray barn until I disappear behind it. Here the grass gets high, the small field humming with little creatures under the midday sun. I follow the old tractor trail along across it until the woods start, the trail petering out in the first ten feet of trees. I cut left, heading up one side of the hill. Water trickles somewhere up ahead, but the brush is thick, and I can't see very far. I wind back and forth in my new white pants, the sweat starting to break out on my forehead. I'm going to look like a hick when I get back. But I don't care, push on up through the thicket of new growth toward the stream. I can almost see that boy trudging along ahead of me, and my throat is closing in from wanting to call out his name. Crazy, I know, but I don't care about that either. I have to find that place, find him somehow and then, I don't know what, I'll figure it out when I get there.

I pick up speed, scrambling along the slope, the water babbling to my right. Over a rise and then through the trees, I see the hollow, this crease in the hill, the stream slicing down its spine, banks rising up in a slant on either side. My shirt is starting to stick to my back. I half slide, half run down to the stream, fall once on my butt, jump up and keep going, heading up again, wending my way along the water, imagining the trees and prickly ash gone and the hillside open, birds warbling their dawn songs. And up ahead of me, Daniel wading heavily through the knee-high grass, determined to make the pain stop. I know the way his chest feels, all tight, and how he sees faces in his head—parents, brothers, lover. Did he love that other boy? And hate himself for it? The way I hate myself?

And then it's Louise's face that floats up to me, the way she looked out back behind the town hall that time after practice, the softness there in her, the sharpness of her mouth between the first kiss and the second when she leaned back into me for it.

Her face didn't lie then. I was right all along. It was some other part of her that lied later, saying she didn't feel that way. I see her again, those wide-set eyes, the way they took all of me in, entire worlds spinning inside the light hazel. And those same eyes again later, gone flat and shuttered, casting away toward the wall, the ground, anywhere but at me. Climbing faster and faster up this hill behind Daniel, his footsteps all grown in with twigs and brush, I finally understand how many ways there are to die.

That's when I start crying again, tears streaming down my cheeks and dashing off on my plaid shirt. But this time I don't mind; it's just another kind of water running in these woods. I open my mouth to shout and then shut it. Then open it again. Let out all the crying—crying out his name, crying out hers. Telling them that they are beautiful and I love them and that they don't have to die. The trees blur through the wall of water and I stumble around rocks and saplings, sobbing their names.

That's when I see it—the flat concrete bunker built into the hill, a dark iron ladder scaling its side. I stop, staring at the blankness of it. Catch my breath and walk forward. The thing isn't even the six feet high Mabel said, probably about five instead. I could get up by climbing the bank around to the low side in back, but I grab the bottom rung of the ladder and swing on up the front.

At the top, I haul myself up, step out on the flat surface, looking around. The woods ring with the silence Daniel fell into some fifty years ago. Is he here now? Lying at my feet? Or did he get sucked down that manhole over there, shut tight? How many more are down there with him, buried or drowned? All that beauty lost.

I walk right over to that cover then, hook my fingers under and yank it up. It clatters onto the cement, the hole gaping open like a mouth at my feet. No poison fumes vaporing out now, just darkness I peer down into, whispering Daniel's name louder and louder until I am just talking to him, telling him that Mabel still misses him, and that I do too, even though I never got to meet him. Telling him that fifty years later I don't have to jump in after him, that I'm going to hold on through one more year and find me somewhere I can stretch my wings. Because if Mabel understands, maybe someday my family and Luke will understand too. But that even if they don't, here's one bit of beauty that's going to fly out into the world.

When I get up to go, I leave the thick iron top open to let the light and air in. I'm still kind of crying, as I walk back over to the edge of the platform, but it's OK. Everything is OK. It ain't so far down this time. Taking a leap, I fly out, arms outstretched. Land with both feet solid on the ground.

The Gift
of Wholeness

Rebecca Brown

Mrs. Lindstrom lived in a house in a different part of town than most of the people I worked with. I took the bus there. It was a neighborhood of nice small houses with yards. There were dogs and bikes and trikes and American cars in people's driveways. Mrs. Lindstrom's mailbox was painted red to look like a barn. The windows of her house had tied-back frilly curtains.

When I knocked on the door she answered immediately. She'd been waiting for me. I was glad I was exactly on time. She opened the door and said, "Hello! Come in!" and put out her hand for me to shake. She ushered me in and said did I want coffee or tea. She didn't say it like it was a yes-or-no question but an either-or.

I said, "Coffee, please," and she motioned for me to follow her into the kitchen. Her clothes were loose. She had curly white hair. She walked with a cane but steadily.

She told me to have a seat at the kitchen table so I did but she didn't. She leaned against the counter, her hands on either side to steady her. She put one hand over her chest like she was saying the pledge. She was breathing hard.

I got up. "So, is the coffee in the canister?"

There was a set of matching canisters on the counter.

"I'll get it," she said breathlessly.

I hadn't meant to rush her but I didn't want her waiting on us. I sat back down. There were two matching cups and saucers out on the counter.

She gripped the edge of the counter and took deep breaths.

I looked around the kitchen. "You have a lovely house," I said.

"Thank you," she wheezed.

She asked me if I'd had breakfast, which was what I usually asked them. I told her I had, and before I could say anything else, she said she had too but maybe I was hungry after the bus ride. "You did take the bus, didn't you?" she said.

She was still trying to catch her breath, so I said yes, then told her a very long, detailed story about how I could have taken the 10 or the 43, or even the 7, to downtown, and how I got the 43, and where I got it, and where I got off downtown to change, and where I caught the 6, and about asking the bus driver for her street, etc., etc. I stretched the story out until she was breathing evenly. I finished by saying what a nice neighborhood she lived in.

"Thank you," she said. "I've lived here my whole life."

She turned around to get the coffee and tea. The coffee was a jar of instant. I wished I'd asked for tea.

Margaret had told me Mrs. Lindstrom's kids had tried to get her to move in with them, and that her son had said he'd move back home with her, but she wouldn't have either. She would let her kids do medical things like take her to appointments and medicine errands, and she let the nurse come see her at home, but she wouldn't let her kids take care of her body, like feeding and bathing, or of her house, like cleaning. But when it got to where she really couldn't cope at home alone if she didn't get some help, she finally gave in. I was her first home-care aide.

She got the tea out. I heard her lift the lid from the canister and pull out a tea bag. She unscrewed the lid of the coffee jar and clicked the spoon in and put it into the cup. It took her a long time to do everything.

She started talking. She asked me where I lived in town, in a house or an apartment, if I had pets and so on, all nice polite questions someone that age would ask. She pulled a plate of cookies from the cupboard and took the plastic wrap off and put them on the table. When she sat down she was breathing hard again.

She said the cookies were homemade, her own recipe, but by her daughter Ingrid. She said to help myself to a cookie. I took one and said, "Thank you." She didn't take one. Then we didn't say anything. I heard myself chewing.

When the water boiled she got up for it. Her hand looked tight on the kettle, her veins were sticking up. She was working hard to lift it. I wanted to offer to help but I knew not to yet. She wanted to feed me.

She poured water into our cups and took the kettle back to the stove.

When she sat down again we stirred our coffee and tea for a few seconds. Then I said, "Well, Mrs. Lindstrom, what can I help you with today?"

She looked down at her lap, "Oh. Yes. Well. Let's see." She looked out the kitchen window. "What would you like to do?"

No one had ever asked me what I'd "like" to do before.

"Well . . ." I said, "do you have some laundry?"

"Oh, don't trouble with that," she said.

"It's no trouble," I said. "I like to do laundry."

She put her hands around the edge of her saucer and said, "Well, maybe I can find some laundry for you."

I asked her where the machine was. She made me finish my coffee and eat another cookie and told me she kept the hamper in the bathroom and the soap and bleach and machines were in the basement. She said she'd go down and show me, but I told her I could find them myself and if I had any questions I'd ask her.

Then I said, "Maybe I can clean the kitchen while the laundry's in."

"Oh, that's all right, you don't have to." She looked around and said, embarrassed, "Do you think it needs it?"

I didn't want to make her feel bad by saying that her kitchen did need work, but it did. There weren't dirty dishes in the sink, or open cans of food around, but the counters and floors looked coated.

"I'll just tidy up a bit while the laundry's in," I said.

"Well . . . all right," she said, "if you're sure it's no trouble."

"It's no trouble at all, Mrs. Lindstrom," I said.

She mumbled something about not cooking much lately, not being in the kitchen much. Then she said stiffly, "Well, I guess I'll get out of your way," and got up to go. She set her hands on the edge of the table and took a deep breath and pushed herself up. I stood and started to take her arm, but she waved me away.

She went into the living room and I took the laundry down to the basement. On my way back to the kitchen I looked in the living room. She had the "Today" show on and was sitting in one of the two big overstuffed armchairs. She had her knitting stuff in her lap, but her eyes were closed.

When she heard me going by she looked over at me. "Are you finding everything you need?" she asked.

"Yes, ma'am," I said.

"There's not much in the fridge, but please help yourself to anything. There's all those cookies."

"Thanks," I said.

The kitchen was full of cooking things, but nothing was being used. In the fridge were a couple of dried-out casseroles in dishes that didn't match hers, a bunch of wrinkled fruit and vegetables, lots of yogurts way past their sell-by date, and a case of Ensure hi-cal protein drink.

I went there in the mornings three days a week and stayed till noon. Sometimes I was there when the nurse arrived, but I tried to be gone before he did. Mrs. Lindstrom didn't feel comfortable around the nurse and me together. The nurse was there for medical reasons, there was no getting around that. But sometimes it could seem like I was just there to help around the house, like a companion or a maid or even a neighbor who drops by when you have the flu. But it couldn't seem like that when the nurse was there too.

There's something about no one else knowing someone is taking care of you. When UCS, Urban Community Services, started and people were afraid their neighbors would panic if they knew they had AIDS, you weren't supposed to tell anyone exactly what you were doing. You'd say, "I'm a friend." But when I saw the nurse or he saw me, Mrs. Lindstrom couldn't have the illusion that no one knew she was being taken care of because she was sick.

The first weeks I was there I cleaned most of her house, except her bedroom, which she felt very private about, and ran errands and went grocery shopping and cooked things she said she used to like and sat down with her when she ate and that's when we talked. She asked me where I'd gone to college and what my interests were and about my family and hobbies and pets. She told me about her family, her three kids, Diane and Ingrid and Joe. Joe, her youngest, was just two years older than me. There were four grandkids and a fifth on the way. She had pictures of all of them plus of Miss Kitty, who'd moved in with Joe and Tony when Mrs. Lindstrom got sick. Mrs. Lindstrom said she truly missed Miss Kitty, and laughed that she'd only really gotten serious about knitting when Miss Kitty adopted her so Miss Kitty would have something to play with. Miss Kitty came along after John, Mrs. Lindstrom's husband, passed away. She said that when John died she was devastated, like she'd lost her whole life. They'd been sweethearts at the local high school and had lived with each other their whole lives. But then after he died she made herself do things, like the Animal Shelter and the Literacy Program and the Neighborhood Block Association. She started spending tons of time with Ingrid's twins. "I missed him so much," she told me. "I didn't know how I would survive when he died, but I did."

After she told me all that she told me to call her Connie instead of Mrs. Lindstrom. That took me a while to get used to, but I did.

Then after I'd called her Connie for a while, she said would

I help her with her bath. That was the last thing she'd kept doing herself. I said, "Sure."

I ran the water in the tub and put in some bath oil. I kept the door closed so the bathroom was warm. I went to get her when everything was ready. We walked down the hall together. I carried her clean clothes. She held her cane in one hand and kept her other hand on my arm.

We got in the bathroom and closed the door. She sat on the toilet seat. I helped her undress. She hadn't let me dress or undress her before.

When she opened her blouse I couldn't help the look on my face.

"You don't have to help me with this," she said.

There was a big flat dent on half her chest, and a long white scar where they'd cut it off. The scar wasn't shiny, but it was old. They'd cut it off before they tested the blood supplies.

"You don't have to help," she said again. "I bathed myself alone when I had my mastectomy."

They'd cut it off before there was Urban Community Services. She didn't get help recovering. But even if she had had her surgery when there was UCS, she wouldn't have gotten our help because it couldn't be a mastectomy or only cancer or something else, it had to be AIDS. I felt ashamed.

"I can do this alone," she said again.

I hadn't moved since I saw it, but when she said that, I said, "I can help," and she let me.

I helped her off with the rest of her clothes. Her other breast was shriveled and small. I tried not to look when I covered her with a towel.

She didn't look right without her clothes. Her body wasn't whole.

I put my hand in the tub. I touched the water to the inside of my elbow to test the temperature the way you do when you wash a baby.

I helped her to stand and walk to the edge of the tub. We dropped the towel. I lifted her arm and put it around my neck.

She held on to me tight, and we sat her on the edge of the tub.

"Are you all right?" I asked.

"Yes," she said.

I held her there a few seconds, then lifted her body and slid her onto the bath seat. She gripped the handles on both sides of the seat. The veins in her hands stood out. She was holding her breath and her shoulders were tight. I lifted her legs and put them in the water.

After a while she let out her breath and her shoulders relaxed and she said, "Oh, this water feels nice."

I soaped the sponge and washed her arms. I washed her neck and back and stomach. When I got to her ribs I hesitated. I was afraid about the scar.

"It doesn't hurt anymore," she said.

Then I could wash the place around the scar.

When she was clean I helped her out of the tub and patted her dry and got her into her nightie. We walked her to her room. She pulled my arm around her waist and leaned on me to walk.

She sat on the bed and gripped the edge. She was breathing hard. I lifted her feet and helped her lie down. I held the back of her neck and laid her against the pillow and pulled the covers up. I tucked the covers around her close, the way my mother did when I was young.

Sign

Linda Smukler

I forgot to tell you about the red sheets my sister bought for us that were incredibly cheap on sale and that we couldn't replace with the blue sheets we wanted because the blue sheets were now full price I forgot to tell you about the reason I wanted to make love last night and instead we had a fight I forgot to tell you that I came out in sign class a class of twenty or so under thirty women and one man all from the teaching professions all straight from E. Greenbush I forgot to tell you that the week before the teacher asked me do you have children and I snapped my fingers together to say no and slapped my hip to say I had a dog she made me finger spell our dog's name and then the teacher said bring pictures of your family next week I forgot to tell you that this week I brought pictures of you and our dog I showed them to the class and when asked I slapped my hip and gave the sign for dog and pointed to the picture of you and made the sign for love and person which is the sign for love person or lover and some of the students looked at me and were very polite some even smiled it was so easy to say husband and children and all I wanted to say was lover and dog so I wondered why after all these years I still had to blush

I Wanted to Add

Linda Smukler

2:00 pm 12 hours since I hung up with you last night and I don't
see you and have to resort to loving you over the phone lines
I have been out to breakfast done house chores had a meeting
with a real estate broker caught up on some calls none of my
own work and I am not angry at you this morning you had to
hang up just as I was saying that I woke up feeling out of control it was not a good place to hang up there was so much more
to say I wanted to add a life I wanted to add talking you
through until your voice was sober and not so separate and suspicious of every inflection in my own I wanted to add the light
of you I wanted to add walks I wanted to add patience I
wanted to add heaven I wanted to add your dog's tiny kisses
and my dog's heavy feet I wanted to add how much I wanted
to make you come to live sometime in 2058 when it would be
nothing to travel from here to there and back in a matter of
seconds because if I could have I would have thrown the fucking
phone out the window and transported myself to stand you up
in an alleyway I wanted to add muscle and bone mass I wanted
to add a room and two writing studios I wanted to add every
challenge you will ever give me I wanted to add that I brought
myself off with a vibrator when I finally got into bed too tired
for anything else I wanted to add the warmth of this room and

the rain outside and the soft flannel of your pajamas I wanted
to add your eyes wandering but not too far I wanted to add
concerts and museums and ancient towns and more history of
my family and childhood and that I burnt myself this morning
putting wood into the stove and that my lover has always yelled
at me for not using gloves I wanted to add that I went out to
breakfast and my friend said I looked different red and burnt
and in love I wanted to add a peculiar plagiarism words of
power without translation cock and cunt and queer I wanted
to add that you are a whore who takes very good care of me
that someday you will wear a black dress and black stockings
for me and someday I will turn you over and take your stock-
inged legs and force them apart I wanted to add that I will
watch your ass wanting in that black dress and I will take you
from behind and I will tear you apart and make you whole I
wanted to add that I simply wanted to add that you have my
heart my fist my left nostril my eyelashes my lips my teeth you
have my desire to run and sometimes you have my fear you
also have my faith my belief and that I take none of this lightly
I wanted to add that there are no coincidences that someday
you will choose to see how human you are that there is no right
or wrong I wanted to add come close I want to smell you to
breathe your air to take you with me stomping through the
forest

Garden Blues
Sarah Lane

Buddy Guy growled, I pity the fool. Petra was standing in front
of the tape deck watching the heads spin, watching the tape pull
taut like dental floss between teeth and then relax back around
the head again, flashing metallic for a second in the light from
the garden. A flash like Mud's smile. Smile sharp like glass.
Like the glass Petra broke yesterday trying to pour some water.
It had crouched into deadly little gems. She had been afraid the
dog would imbed them in his paws and bleed.

But the glass had been swept up. That danger was over. Now
Bessie Smith. St. Louis Blues. Petra thought about St. Louis.
She had never been there but in her mind it was full of black
iron scaffolding and broken bottles. Green and brown ones. Lots
of places down by the river where people hung out to smoke.
No trees. In her mind it was a good place for the blues. The
blues had no shade.

The metallic cassette tape caught the light again. Petra's eye
turned down. In the tape-deck window, she could see a miniature
color reflection of the garden. The catmint lounging over the
redwood edging. The delphinium fragile, blank-minded. The aster still green and unblossomed. It was September and not a
bloom. And right beside the aster that big brown spot where the

coreopsis had died. Something had to go there. But for now it was just space.

Mud had left the day before for school. Twice a year, she'd go off for about ten days, clear across the country to Vermont. They called it a low-residency program. Every time Petra heard that she couldn't help but jump in thought right over to low-impact aerobics and wonder if this program was designed to go easy on the bones. But it didn't seem too easy on Mud. She'd come back all furrowed and hunch over her little desk, books cascading over the sides, paper pooling at her feet.

In between Mud's trips to school, they'd talk for hours at their scratched-up table to go over the issues of being a writer again and again. Petra would read Mud's stories and Mud would read her poems. They'd talk until the second-hand wood would cut into her shoulder blades and she'd bring a leg up under her ass to balance better. Mud would get them more peach tea. Petra would ask, Is that a cliché? Is that what I'm really trying to say? She would riffle her hair and push her brows. Will I ever be any good or am I just a mediocre editor full of big ideas? Mud would put her feet on the table, the toes of her big wool socks stretched out, flopping over. Rabbit ears. Mud wondered, Is what I'm writing even true? Mud would wave Petra's poems over the candles and say, "You're hiding. If you don't deal with this, your poem isn't going anywhere." Once a poem had even caught fire that way.

When Mud would go off to school, Petra couldn't bear to write. The clock in the kitchen bellowed like a bodiless heart. The water in the bathroom dropped flat and hollow in the sink. The dog followed her from room to room, ears scattered like an interrupted card game. There could be no poetry in that house when Mud was gone. Petra would think about the plum tree in the front—the one that never gave any plums.

So Petra would garden. For ten days, Petra and the dog would wake at seven and then creak and limp to the kitchen where the dog would get noodles and liver and she would get toasted sesame-seed bread, buttered. The dog would wait on the green

bath mat while she showered. They'd return to the bedroom and
Petra would put on her muddy stretched-out Gap shorts and
a white T-shirt. Then they'd head out the patio door to the
garden.

Always when they gardened there would be music. And always when Mud was gone it would be the Blues. Robert Johnson, Blind Lemon Jefferson, Sippie Wallace, Memphis Minnie,
Leadbelly, Ma Rainey, Blind Willie Johnson, Alberta Hunter.
Country blues, Chicago blues, Memphis blues. Guitar, honky-
tonk piano, banjo, washboard, Jew's harp, spoons, sax. Sometimes Petra would make up her own words, borrowing from
whomever was singing at the moment.

> Sitting here in my garden
> Trying to make something grow
> Sitting here in this old garden
> Wondering why she had to go

For hours, she and the dog would garden. The dog on
his back, tongue stuck between his teeth. Or on his belly,
gnawing on a stick Petra found in the tomatoes. Petra
yanking weeds, deadheading the plants, digging a new bed for
more lettuce. Tossing an occasional slug over the fence into the
neighbors' yard. She transplanted the catmint because she was
afraid neighborhood cats would trample her garden. She scattered some sweet basil, seeds the size of fleas, into a pot of
manure and then shook out a layer of potting soil on top.
Put the pot on a jar lid in a basket. Found a sunny spot in the
kitchen.

The sun would saunter toward the Olympic Mountains. Petra
and the dog still gardening until dark.

Mud called. From a booth in the lounge of the dorm. On a
tiny swivel chair. Mud said the booth smelled of cigarettes and
patchouli oil. Petra tried to smell that from their wood-paneled
living room. She thought of linoleum-tiled floors and metal window frames. Chairs with aluminum legs, seats covered in plastic.
A phone booth, made of pressboard, initials doodled into the

walls with ballpoint. She thought maybe she could see the booth, but she couldn't smell it.

On this call, Mud's voice moved forward like a ship with no water beneath it. It just glided on air. A ghost ship. Mud said, I've been hanging out with one of my instructors. She's a writer.

Petra said, Maria Guzman.

Mud wanted to know how she knew. The name had just appeared in Petra's head like an unpaid bill. She knew that Maria was an instructor at the school but she didn't know anything about her except what you learn by reading a person's writing. Petra told Mud that she had read one of Maria's books about six months ago.

Mud kept going. Anyway, she's been really encouraging about my writing. Even though I'm a student, she keeps seeking me out. We've had some incredibly intense conversations. She's brilliant. Did you like her book?

Petra had read it through in an evening. She could still see one of the characters, an Indian woman, kneeling on red dirt, ten miles outside of town, setting herself on fire. It was evening and the novel's townspeople had thought the distant orange flames were the sun's fingers clinging onto the canyon before tumbling off into the night.

They talked some more. Petra told her about the dog's fleas and about the garden. Mud said, I feel so torn up. I need to see you soon.

That night, the rain padded on the leaves of the Madrona tree outside the window. Petra turned on the light. She scratched the dog's ears. She flipped through some old catalogues. There was a silverware drawer organizer they might want from Lillian Vernon. She turned on the Hitachi Magic Wand, but it sounded like a lawn mower or maybe just an angry bug. She turned it off. Her mind stayed on.

Petra tapped along the bookshelf to find her way into the dining room. She lit the candle on the table and then carried it over to the record cabinet. She picked out Alberta Hunter. Her eyes had adjusted and now she could make out the shape of the turntable.

I might be as brown as a berry
But that's only secondary
You can't tell the difference after dark

She grabbed the blanket off the couch and opened the door to
the patio. There was no moon. There were no stars. A misty rain
pelted the fiberglass patio roof. Petra sat on the rocking chair
and the dog groaned into a ball on the cement.

For two hours she and the dog sat there.

Mud. Mud's black hair. Mud's lips on her head. Mud's voice,
Everything's going to be alright, baby. Mud reading every line
of her poems, telling her something about each one, looking into
her brain like the poem was a map. Mud's hands on Petra's belly,
her nose on her ear.

Six months before, when Petra read Maria Guzman's book
she had the sensation of having read it before. She had known
the Indian woman was going to burn when she first appeared in
Chapter One. Petra knew Maria's eyes and her wide mouth from
the book jacket as if she were a neighbor or worked at the Safe-
way. She imagined Maria as the burning woman on the edge of
town.

In her mind she saw Mud and Maria laughing. She saw it
once and then she went inside to get a sweatshirt. She grabbed
a flashlight and headed back out.

In the blue night, across the lawn from the house, Bessie
Smith's voice drooped like a staircase in a gutted mansion. Nobody knows you when you're down and out. In my pocket not
one penny. And my friends I haven't any. Sippie Wallace
whined, Baby, I can't use you no more. Daddy, daddy, Momma
don't want you no more. Ma Rainey hollered, I went down to
the river each and every day.

While those women tinned across the garden, Petra gathered
stones in her hands. Stones from the loam bed. With her flashlight, she found stones beneath the blackberry bushes. Stones in
the birdbath. She found stones piled up beside the house and
stones next to the compost. She took all the stones to the garden

and, studying how the drizzle sloped across the flower bed, she
built channels to direct the water to and away from each plant.
She directed the water through the brown spot. When she ran
out of stones, she went looking into the corners of the yard for
more. The dog gave up following her and retreated to the cover
of the patio where he watched, his brows wrenched together.

She worked like that until the birds yawned and stretched.
Until the sun spread out over Seattle toward her island. Then she
went inside to shower.

Clean, hair wet, barefoot, she returned to the garden drying in
the sun. Every day Petra checked on the garden, as if it were a
litter of kittens. She followed up on the stories already started.
The spider who webbed between the purple leaves of the lysi-
machia. The butterfly who preferred the crayon-blue delphinium.
The lavender heads that bowed when they needed more water.
The stubborn grass that kept pushing through from sneaky sub-
terranean roots to peek out of the brown spot, reaching for some
light.

Mid-morning, Petra went to the nursery, the dog in the back
of the car, his nose reading the woods as they drove past. She
wandered the aisles, looking over petunia, impatiens, geranium,
begonia. She looked at the cedar flower boxes, the red ceramic
planters, the arboretum with potted Douglas Fir, plum, apple,
and pear trees. Five-pound bags of cedar chips. Peat moss. Manure. She smelled warm dirt. Perfumy lavender. Onion.

At the end of the aisle, atop the pine potting bench, a small
sunflower. Its petals the red of lipstick. The orange of glowing
coals. A man in a green apron cut off half a paper bag to sheath
the bottom of the pot so it wouldn't soil her car. She showed
the plant to the dog. This is the one we were looking for. He
shoved his wet nose into the pot.

At home, Petra changed into her gardening shorts and the
white, now stained, T-shirt. She filled the dog's bowl with water.
She put on her Bull's cap backwards and slid a record onto the
turntable. Billie & Dee Dee Pierce. She turned the volume to
eight.

Careless love oh careless love
Careless love ooh love careless love
Well it caused me to weep
And it caused me to moan
And it caused me to leave my happy home

Don't never drive no stranger from your door
Don't never drive no stranger from your door
Cause you may not know who it may be
It may come to be the best friend of you
Don't never drive no stranger from your door

Why those two verses were in the same song had never yet made sense to Petra.

The sun looked like a pat of butter overhead—a square, pale heart. Petra eased the sunflower from its plastic pot. She tucked its roots into the spongy mud of the garden's gaping spot. And she began to understand.

That was the thing about the blues—they brought the news without shade.

That was the thing about a garden—once you did what you could do, it was out of your hands. But you had to welcome the chance.

The Vanish

Mary Beth Caschetta

for Jon

Jason lives and is getting ready to die in a six-story walk-up on
First Avenue and First Street. The doorways on his block and
beyond (from Third to B) look so much alike that often I worry
about the junkies and the 5 A.M. drunks finding their way home.
So much life crowded together makes a soul weary, and after a
while everything—even the blunt distinctions—get lost. A clutter of architecture and graffiti, a blur of noise and flesh, there's
only so much a person can take.

"*Kak tibya zavoot?*"

It is the Russian, who stands outside the shoe repair on Jason's
block, asking my name in the familiar. Swaying in the breeze,
he smiles at me.

"What's it to you?" I reply, meanly.

I have been mistaken for a Jew, a boy, a criminal, a prostitute,
some lost child's mother, and now a Russian maiden. The
grocery-checkers call me "sir." But nobody mistakes me for
who I am: "What are you, some kind of fool?" Or now that it's
chic to be gay, "Aren't you one of those lesbians?" But
identity—mistaken or not—doesn't rankle far enough to touch
me.

I've noticed, too, that nobody ever mistakes me for you. Nobody rushes up behind me, calling your name, grasping my hand, pushing their fingers through my hair. I have forgotten exactly the shape of your face, the shade of your eyes, or taste of your skin, otherwise I would transform myself into you with a renewed hope for recognition.

But how likely is that? Since I stopped returning your calls, I've taken to insulting old men with the ripe indifference of a fourteen-year-old girl. Since shirking your life of daylight and work, I've led my own in wandering.

The thought of running into you makes me avoid corners and motors me forward at a fast clip. After work, I have no choice but to cross town in daylight. I am furtive, clocking my route as follows: My apartment on the west side to the pharmacy for Jason's seconal takes thirty-five minutes. The grocery where I pick up a few things for his dinner adds fifteen, more if the aisles are crowded with homeless exchanging their empties for a dollar. Another step or two around the corner brings me to the shelter of Jason's doorway. His is easy to keep track of amidst the clutter and undistinguished architecture because it is posted on either side by dull pink columns of stone. They blend vaguely with the faded brick of his building, but once you see them, they are like signposts in the night's monotony.

There are few other distinguishing features on these streets save for the pigeons, remarkable in number and sheer audacity. The shopkeepers along Jason's block seem particularly generous with bread crumbs or somehow interested in goodwill and aviaries.

Pigeons are calm at sunset, fervent at midnight. In the mornings, they whine like insistent tender alarm clocks.

"How are you today Jason?"

His apartment feels damp. A wall of cool bricks painted white at the far end keeps the heat down. On a good day, he will get on his knees and scrub the kitchen tiles. "Does it smell like I'm dying in here?" he asks, especially after someone has come for a visit, an old boyfriend or the delivery man. I shake my head, a lie.

Today's question is the same as yesterday's, is the same as always.

"How are you today Jason?"

"Visionless," he says. He hasn't seen angels all week.

Jason is famous for his spiritual transformation, an ascent to the rafters that happened unexpectedly after a bout of shingles. At that time he was a teacher and a waiter with nothing remotely godlike up his sleeve. Now like an uncalled-for miracle his bed is surrounded by votive candles and the Tao Ching. He's not exactly famous, despite the sermons, the harmonic convergence, and the public television appearances. His world, after all, is precarious, a universe jury-rigged by disease. But his name has a kind of currency in the new economy of HIV, and the story of his redemption is passed from person to person like a collection plate.

"They don't get it," Jason says lamenting his comrades, the street activists, as he sulks over a bowl of chicken broth.

I, too, have come to eat only what his stomach can tolerate.

"Get what?" I say, watching my own soup grow cold.

"Spiritual salvation," he answers. "They need to make everything ugly. They need an enemy so bad that they turn on their own bodies. Then they turn on each other."

I imagine the virus a disgusting infestation of killer flying bees or a filthy invasion of microscopic creatures that nest just under the skin. Guilty, I try to change my thoughts to something else, hoping he hasn't taken to reading minds.

Jason's eyes catch the last of the day's light—blue, when he is feeling well. I'm not sure I understand, but, as with all his lessons, I am patient.

"Well, not everyone can be a believer," I say, wiping my mouth. "Not everyone is a savior."

It's a stab in the dark, really, and I watch to see how close I've come.

"Wrong!" Jason barks, happily. "But exactly my point. Don't you see how they stomp around? Do you look in their eyes? They believe just precisely *that* with all their hearts. They *are* the new salvation. *Anyone* can be Jesus."

He leans back on his pillow, exhausted from dinner and his outburst. His index finger is still extended toward the ceiling.

I stare at him blankly.

"Don't you see?" he says, quietly, trying again. "We have to be the ones to do what Jesus couldn't."

"What's that?" I say, an ex-Catholic, still availed to blind faith and easy alarm. "What couldn't Jesus do? He raised the dead and loved his enemy. For God's sake, he delivered us from evil."

"Piece of cake," Jason says, starting to sparkle again. "The hard part came when he was hanging there on the cross. He couldn't save himself, could he? He didn't even want to."

How long has it been? It was the week before Christmas when I stopped returning your phone calls. Somewhere near the first snow, I began the final preparations of the Vanish. I was pleased with myself, because it was a trick I stole from you—this particular kind of disappearing. You used to tell me stories in bed about the lives you left behind in other women's apartments—stereo disc players, closets of clothes, tax records dating back from 1972. In an attic somewhere in Toledo sits an abandoned bed frame you once crafted by hand. In Orange County, it was every last piece of your Polish grandmother's china left carelessly to the only man who loved you. All of this was before you were a lesbian, before you were a prostitute, before you were a politician. In Duluth, you unloaded a love seat and matching sofa while your unsuspecting sweetheart slept off a hangover during the first beams of morning. That time you slipped a note—crisp like a traffic ticket—under her windshield. The garbage men waved you good-bye.

Those early escapes you count among your first attempts at the art. You were youngish then, a fugitive from nothing in particular, still imperfect at the Vanish. The older you got, the less likely you were to leave fingerprints. But you were always more fond of the mistakes than your moments of genius. You handled them lovingly like simple-minded children: the times you almost got caught, the near-death escapes. You used to sit in dark rooms turning each horrible detail over in your mind, polishing it smooth until you transformed it from an irritating piece of sand to a pearl. You made strings of them for me to wear around my neck, and I did so willingly.

This year the street activists are slightly hung over and bloated from the long winter. They are young men in white socks and black boots with full red lips that glisten when they speak of health. They are Jason's followers, ever on the prowl for a glimmer of hope. Despite their often unspoken status, they sport slim, tight bodies, more beautiful than any single woman I have ever laid hands on. They come to see for themselves how Jason has learned to outlive—through meditation and prayer—every bacteria and cancer, nearly without symptom. They recline by his side, captivated by Jason's luck, which they call his will.

I have seen it for myself. Jason's body does not respond as expected, and he seems to be a self-healer. Even the most vile drug infused through yellow tubing causes him only a week or two of napping, some minor difficulty with his longer errands or trips out of town. Each time, it is as if he has risen from the dead practically unscathed.

"Immune tolerance," he announces one day after a quick struggle with mild PCP. He plops a textbook for medical students on the table in a diner across from his apartment where I am sitting. He orders a turkey dinner with cranberry sauce as if it is Thanksgiving and he has received the gift of his appetite again.

"What?" I say, shifting in my booth, a place where I spend considerable hours trying to heal myself from the raw effects of obsessive love. I order mint tea as if I am the one who's been ill.

"It's the perpetual ability of a body to regain stasis and live no matter what has happened, is happening, or will happen to it," he reports.

"It is not just a philosophy, but a little-known immunological fact," he adds to prove his point.

I imagine the scientists passing this theory around laboratories and cocktail parties, hoping such blasphemy won't spoil the chance to name an important disease molecule after themselves.

"The theory itself is older than medicine, proven by history and public health," Jason continues. "Living things change to accommodate life. If they are unable to, then they die. It's as simple as that."

"How long does it take?" I ask, vaguely calling up my memory from high-school biology.

Jason shrugs, uninterested in mundane chronology.

But in my heart I know the answer: It takes a lot of time, a long time, more time than even Jason's got.

By spring, the activists begin to turn like spoiled milk. They pass Jason's words around like rude, passionless kisses. They report on his immune tolerance, although they don't call it that. The ones who are less invested in cures, respond with increasing ridicule. These are a small crowd of jaded young men and a handful of soap-scrubbed dykes. They run the general activist meetings every Monday night like clockwork. They facilitate each topic with a microphone and an amp, moving the conversation along like Nazis. When the discussion includes espionage, they worship the virus like a twelve-step obsession.

Others, unable to afford the cost of such cynicism, are more cautious.

"Jason Silverman outlived microsporidiosis by eating sushi and spending time with the gurus," one positive gay man says to the next.

"Pass it on."

The summer of Jason's inevitable dying is when they all admit that thirteen years later—an unlucky and not insignificant amount of time—nobody knows a thing about anything. Not the scientists, not the politicians, not even the enemies.

"Finally," Jason says, approving of the surrender because he knows his own is near.

For the most part, though, the whole crowd is growing restless, beginning now to see that power is cheap and nothing is as it appears. For instance, the FBI isn't interested in phone-tapping anymore, and no one's being saved. The activists suddenly have little to do, now that there's no real direction, now that lying down in the street is passé. The money is running out. The young men are dying as fast as ever, added to the ranks of the others: the women; the junkies; the poor sex-working lesbians; the incarcerated; the grandmothers; the shop owners. It is a whole city of AIDS.

Before long, no one seems to have the heart to recline by Jason's side. The activists see him around, though not at their meetings. Jason doesn't mind or even notice. He's moved on. He spends time at an ashram upstate, and organizes on a completely different level.

"We are equals," you said the first time we met. "You'll be more dangerous than me by the time we're through."

You put it to me so simply, complete with a finite ending and a goal. It was difficult to resist. You seemed so sure of yourself, so sure of me. I had to know if I could do it, if I could be involved in love without leaving marks—no scratches or cuts. If I could want without needing. Somehow I thought I was ready for the challenge.

"You belong to me," you whispered in autumn.

Then to my surprise I found myself waiting for your Vanish. It occurred to me at the strangest times—in the shower or while brushing my teeth. Countless nights, I hoped to step out into the living room, dripping wet from the shower or ready for bed, to find you gone. But you were always there. We watched CNN in front of the TV you insisted on buying and keeping (still yours, of course) in my apartment. We tuned you in, interviewed on the late-night news. We applauded your brilliant political career and admired the Sony entertainment center for its electronic complexity. Meanwhile, I held my breath, braced for your inevitable and cruel exit. By the time December rolled around, I was beginning to catch on. This was not as you promised.

How many times had you recounted in great detail that very first time you had flung yourself airborne? I can still tell it by heart: a mere ringletted girl, you were barely thirteen, wrenching yourself free from a disappointing mother and her coterie of odd boyfriends, who wanted to touch you when no one was looking. The mere act of catapulting is what thrilled you. You were never so unafraid in your life, although eventually you would land somewhere in West Virginia only to become a slave, a prostitute, and a hippie in the foster-care system. It was worth it, you said, all worth the freedom of flight. Nevertheless, as more snow fell, you lay in my arms and seemed forgetful of flying.

The pigeons coo dreamily inside Jason's wall. They nest there and flap with an intrigue and reason all their own, inhabitants of a whole separate world. At first I don't notice them.

"Maybe tomorrow they'll come," I say, meaning the angels. But Jason is growing doubtful.

"I'm losing this battle to pigeons," he says.

He is the one who points them out first. How they live their swollen lives tucked away behind the fridge and the stove. How they squeeze between the buildings to nap and preen. There are dozens of them. Each one is singular in its markings. Each one is crafty and suffering like a sly murderess.

He stands momentarily at the window on his way back from the bathroom. Hands on his hips, he exposes the blades of his shoulders, a few of his razor-sharp ribs, the surprising full moon of a hard white belly. He begins suspecting that pigeons will be the death of him, having had his worst luck yet with this recent onset of cryptococcal meningitis. Cryptococcus is a disease of the brain that is, in fact, unearthed from moldy pigeon droppings, deadly to the immune-impaired who inhale. In a city with such a graceless presence of birds, it is nearly impossible to avoid exposure.

At night, Jason finally rests after a few spoons of dinner. The headaches have passed, the medicine infused, and he dreams uneasily through a fever. A washcloth on his chest holds in the life-heat his body might otherwise expel.

"I've had a vision," he says between dozes.

"A vision of what?" I ask.

Our bodies are nearly touching in bed. He doesn't answer right away.

"There isn't an enemy . . ." His voice trails off in a whisper.
". . . Not even in dying."
He rolls away on his side, away from me. It is late. His mood
is unpredictable. The last word is his.

When he finally sleeps, I am roused by a thunderous flapping
of wings. I sit for a while and listen to the ruffling like music.
When I step out of bed, I am careful not to wake him. I feel my
way in the dark across the apartment to the stove, cautious not
to knock over the rows of Jason's medicine, vials and bottles
lined up on every surface. Behind the opaque glass of the window they watch me, dozens of button-sized yellow and black
eyes, peering steadily. When I flip on the bathroom light, they
rush the window like giant moths.

"Stop," I whisper, tapping at the pane. "Go away."
They continue to butt at the glass, their tiny heads the size of
subway tokens. I pull up the window to shoo them off, throw
my hands through the air. They take to me like crazed martyrs,
impaling themselves on my fingers, scratching with orange toes.
Some of them wear an iridescent shawl of green and purple
feathers, others are remarkably white, bloated and sick with begging. A wind shaft rushes them in all directions through the small
crevice between Jason's building and the one next door. They
mate for life, pigeons, and travel in extended families.

"Stupids," I seethe, attacking them now with a damp dish-
towel.

Finally, as if a message has been sent electronically from one
to the next, they ascend like a blanket into the sky. I take it as
a sign myself and make my way silently down the five flights
and out through the pink marble doorway. Unsteadied, I press
my eyes to rub away their image. I step through the breezes like
a sleepwalker shaking off a bad dream, pretending to myself not
to be searching for you, the one, in the midst of losing so many,
I willingly set free.

I loosen my joints, feeling connected to everything: the street
lights, the liquor stores, the Chinese laundry. The men in un-
dershirts sit on their stoops, staring at yesterday's paper like a

movie. You'd never guess it was almost daybreak. The grates
on the stores are locked tight against intruders. The fire hydrants
let loose, spout water from the O's of their mouths. The calm
blue glow of late night TV escapes through various windows,
and I am anything but lonely. All of this serves to remind me
that in a city of eight million people, only one of them is you.
The thought is both comforting and horrible.

What was there left for me to do that Christmas except prepare
myself for flight? Reluctant to prove you right, I did it anyway.
The Vanish this time was mine. It was easy, really: a simple
change of apartments. My lease was up anyway. I left a for-
warding address should you want to pursue it. You didn't. You
had moved on, it seemed, to another lover even before I'd decided to go. I ought to have recognized the signs of the affair—
the sudden lapsed hours, the smell of a new soap, the way you
perched night after night on my Navajo pillows like the empty
shell of an insect long gone that leaves the hollow image to fool
enemies, to throw me off track. But now, in the middle of a New
York night, even that seems irrelevant.

I have made my way clear across town and am heading up
the street you live on between the Chelsea Hotel and the Associated Blind. I am standing next to your door, when I spot you
stepping out of a taxi. I want to turn around and say it's all a
mistake, a 5 A.M. insomniac miscalculation, an error in naviga-
tion that anyone could make. But you are flush in the face and
dressed from some gala event.

Perhaps you are running for office.

"How are you?" I say.

You don't seem surprised at all. You pay the taxi with a
twenty that you take from the smallest black-pearled evening bag
I've ever seen. It fits charmingly in the palm of your hand.

"I didn't exactly file a missing person's report on you, but I
called a few times," you say.

It's an apology of sorts, as much as you ever muster.

"How's Betsy?" I say, inquiring after your latest lover, someone I used to know before she dyed her hair jet black and changed her name to something more dangerous.

"It's Bess," you correct. Your ire rises and falls like mercury. We stand close under a street lamp.

"You know what it's like," you continue, intimately. "We never exactly plan to see each other again, but we always somehow do."

These lies are predictable, since you use people to fend off loneliness the way the rest of us use gravity to walk around the block. The grapevine is select in details: You're paying for a trip for two to Cozumel. Betsy/Bess, in the meantime, has taken to the streets like a bully, plans on graduate school at your expense, and likes to press finger-size bruises into your arms like the fertile seeds of small budding flowers.

"Well," I say, a cue to move along.

"Well," you jump in like a matter-of-fact sales clerk. "You're awfully quick to forget what a good thing we had. You used to say we had a great love."

I shrug, unable to move anything but my shoulders, which have come unhinged. I am still slightly buzzed by the realization that you make yourself up from scratch each day—a loner, a cowgirl, a spy. The look you give me lifts my sex and innocence impossibly like Lazarus. Then, coyly, you pull me close and put your mouth on mine. Long, slow, and hard, you draw me out. Time merges like rush-hour traffic, and suddenly I am traveling through you. As if in a movie, I remember why it is my character fell in love with yours in the first scene. It gave me a purpose better than salvation; it secured my survival as the hero. Besides, no more or less than anyone else, I love a good enemy. It is, after all, the essence of self-definition.

I pull away and stare at my feet, toying with the idea of dropping to my hands and rubbing my face against the sidewalk. Perhaps it's only true love when you leave a small mark on someone's tender flesh. Perhaps it ought to be my own small mark on my own tender flesh. A kind of sign that I remember love at all.

"We could have it again," you say, always one to hedge a bet, to trade a something for a nothing.

Only you would be glib in the language of loss.

Why do we never cherish innocence? You'll never know how brief mine was, what a flash of light, irrevocable as a birth, a gift, a slamming door. Sometimes I still long for the days when I ignored pigeons, worshipped at the temple of danger, and drank you in like a salt-water lake. Now I have soothed the dying, and there is no way back. Now I have held the weight of a lie and the truth in my arms, and I cannot tell them apart. And what does it matter, anyhow, since soon they both collapse into dust and feathers.

When I look up you are gone, but your memory has diminished to a human proportion, and I begin to wind my way back to Jason's. Usually I find him half-awake, restless and miserable. Then there is nothing to do but rub his spine, purple and bruised by the needles.

"Help me," he whines in a voice I barely recognize.

I rush to the corner, hoping he'll be awake when I get there so I can tell him this final story of you. But standing with my key in the door of his building, I hesitate. I let them drift by, the small parade of lost souls, angry activists, vanished loves. Ghost-like and silent, they skulk by like the ones who did us wrong or the ones we destroyed. Jason is different—I think to myself, wishing them away from his door—his ending will be neither ugly nor misunderstood. He did not count on enemies to find his way, although it is hard to imagine who could have guided him more easily than they. In the end, they are the ones who suffered, the missing persons, the East Village dwellers, the hollowed-out shells of activists. I stand in the door to wish them well.

When I enter Jason's apartment, it is drafty. The ceiling fan is not running, but the window is spinning out dirty breezes. I shut it quietly and follow a faint trail of soot to the edge of Jason's bed where I see everything so clearly. The distinctions, all together in a blur, snap temporarily into focus.

No signs of life except pigeon feathers, hundreds of them everywhere.

"They have come," I whisper, as if I have known all along the filthy city creatures were Jason's angels.

The frothy scent of redemption is rising.

"And who was saved?"

I hear him, ever the teacher, in the back of my mind.

"The ones who suffered," I say, since I have known them well.

"And who are they?" he asks to make sure I understand the question.

It occurs to me to close his eyelids, to pick up his hand and hold it in mine.

"Us," I say, though I wonder now if there's any such thing.

To Be Like That

Leslie Pietrzyk

Louise slides her legs to a cool part of the sheets. Jillnoon still sleeps; Louise touches her bare shoulder, but she doesn't move. If Louise forgets to call later from the office, Jillnoon will sleep until one or two in the afternoon.

She spends a moment easing the confusion out of her mind. Some kind of dream about seashells, something unconnected. An unfinished fragment of someone else's dream maybe; maybe Jillnoon is dreaming about those same shells now.

Louise gets out of bed. On her way to the bathroom she loops Jillnoon's terrycloth robe around herself. The curtains dangle open because after Louise goes to bed, Jillnoon "lets in the night" so she can write. Jillnoon is a young poet. Her name used to be Jill Masters, but she changed it to Jillnoon Lasky. Her first book of poems, *Spike and Heart*, is scheduled to appear in the fall, issued by a small press in Wisconsin. The title poem is Louise's favorite—a poem about building the transcontinental railroad. It's the idea of spanning the country that Louise likes, making the edges accessible to those living in the middle. The poem is dedicated to her, but that was done even before she said how much she liked it.

Louise was born in the middle, in this city, and she stays. Her daughter Bridget lives with her ex-husband Marty in one of the

northern suburbs by the lake. Marty's new wife, Anne, picked
the house because she liked the garden of Grecian statues in the
backyard, Bridget reported. Louise wonders whether it was the
statues' elegance or their tawdriness that seduced Anne.

She turns on the hot water in the shower. She and Jillnoon
share the kind of apartment where, as Jillnoon says, "Hot water
is an untested theory." Sunlight randomly roams the apartment's
odd nooks; Louise likes those nooks and the way they fill with
scattered sun. The day she and Jillnoon moved in, before un-
packing the boxes that crowded the floor, Louise tapped her
knuckles along the walls, listening for the hollow spots that
might mark secret cubbyholes. "Nancy Drew would have found
an abandoned cache of emeralds or a mysterious leatherbound
diary," Louise explained. Jillnoon said, "All you did was give
headaches to a few roaches." They laughed, and together they
emptied box after box, combining their belongings as dorm
roommates would. Jillnoon bunched the sunny corners with stat-
uesque plants; Louise lined the walls with her black and white
photographs of the steel mills in Gary, Indiana. The prints are
deliberately grainy, pressing more grit into the twists of smoke
pumping from each thin column, the orderly sprawl of metal-
gray buildings, the unsmiling faces trying to hide under hard
hats.

Louise has converted the walk-in closet in the second bedroom
to a darkroom; she prefers it to the modern, spacious room she
had in the house where she and Marty and Bridget once lived.
It seems long ago. Back then she spent her free time photograph-
ing leaves floating in ponds, waves washing away sand. Old
women waiting like props on park benches, resting their feet.

Louise pokes her wrist into the stream of water. Still cold so
she brushes her teeth at the sink, keeping her movements slow
as if polishing diamonds in an heirloom setting. She likes to
brush her teeth, likes the way toothpaste bubbles up along her
tongue. No one she knows enjoys brushing their teeth—not even
Marty, who's an oral surgeon. Their first conversation revolved
around teeth. "My front teeth are so big that in sixth grade four
others were pulled to make room for them," she told him. "I

insisted that my mother save the teeth in a plastic box. I thought I might want them back some day.'' Marty had laughed and inspected her mouth. Then he kissed her.

Bridget has the same large teeth. "Gross," Bridget would say to the suggestion of saving teeth in a box.

Louise rinses her mouth with water, then spits into the sink. Jillnoon leaves behind toothpaste dribbles at the bottom, near the drain. "They're so easy to rinse away," she reminds Jillnoon many times, "really."

Jillnoon has never been married. Louise thinks that might change. Jillnoon's still young and likes children, so she might want to marry one day. Certain things about Jillnoon seem ephemeral. Signing the lease in pencil. "I wasn't thinking," she'd said with a loose shrug. "I write poems with pencil." Louise shrugged. So she'll break the lease and I'll be alone. She's my lover, not my life.

Today Louise is meeting Marty for lunch. He was vague when he called yesterday—he plans things far in advance and maintains a coded organizational system of books and calendars, so there must be something major about this unplanned meeting. Something about Bridget because there's nothing else in common now.

She was married to him for thirteen years, ten of them could be called happy. Divorced two years ago.

Rather than one big bang break-up, theirs was a slow dissolution. She thinks of a photograph soaking, the first patch of gray slowly emerging. Only moments later the whole picture appears, obvious and uncompromising. Respective partners are superimposed images added later, giving dimension like clouds in a previously blank sky.

The water is finally warmish and, shedding the robe, Louise steps into the shower, pulling the curtain shut behind her.

The choice to move away from Bridget and Marty wasn't easy. But to stay would have been to deny the vastness of her unhappiness. Louise's un-suburban actions scared away her old acquaintances long ago; her new acquaintances, friends of Jillnoon's, claim to be shockproof. Both groups seem happy to have arrived at their agreed-upon codes of behavior.

When Louise first moved in with Jillnoon, Marty tried to keep Bridget away from her. Now Louise is allowed to see Bridget on Wednesday nights and Saturdays. They go to galleries where Louise hopes to show her photographs someday or to ethnic neighborhoods overflowing with exotic smells and foods, or sometimes they go to parts of Gary, Indiana, to take pictures. Bridget uses one of Louise's old cameras; Louise plans to give her a camera for her birthday in June.

Bridget likes Gary, and Louise is happy to know that. "It's a real city," Bridget says. "A real failure," Louise says. "Like a dinosaur. Don't romanticize the truth out of it. You've got to recognize what it is." Bridget says she'll live there some day, and Louise doesn't tell her she won't. Bridget also tells her that Anne thinks Gary is dangerous. Louise laughs when Bridget says: "I guess she thinks honesty is dangerous."

Jillnoon and Bridget have met many times and are friends. For Career Day at her school, Bridget invited Jillnoon to speak to the sixth graders about being a poet. Louise knows that Anne thinks Jillnoon is more dangerous than the city of Gary. Anne thinks Bridget shouldn't be exposed to that sort of thing. While Marty is not happy with Louise's present life, he has accepted it. "Anne will never accept it," he tells Louise over and over, though she believed him right away the first time he said so. Anne refuses to meet Jillnoon.

Louise is glad to be a mother and not a stepmother; a lover, not a spouse.

What she thinks of now when she thinks of marriage is a recurring nightmare she used to have. It took place in the shower: As the water sprayed onto her body, she scrubbed herself with a loofah. Though she could see her skin flake off as the sponge passed over her body, she scraped harder and harder because she couldn't stop. She'd finally wake up, hands rubbing the sheet along her legs. Louise has not had this dream since moving away.

She quickly rinses the conditioner from her hair and turns off the water. She stands in the shower for a moment, letting dribbles of water trickle the length of her body. Then she steps out, reaching for a towel.

"How about a promotional celebrating our millionth resume?" the advertising manager of Louise's print-shop chain asks. "A sign like McDonald's: 'Over 1 million printed'?"

"I don't know," Louise says. "Have we done a million? If we have then I'm sure plenty of other places must have."

"Does it matter? We'll be the first to make a big deal out of it. It'll really go over big. We'll start a trend."

"I don't know," Louise says. The manager, just out of college, impatient to "start a trend," is marking time before heading to Madison Avenue. Why do they all expect to start a trend out of college? "Write up the details in a memo. I'll see."

"Great!"

"But no flashing neon. Something subtle."

"It'll be on your desk by the end of the day." She leaves Louise's office.

Marty bought a print shop for Louise when they were married, but she's since paid him back and expanded the first store into five. Marty wouldn't accept the interest due on the loan though she insisted. Finally, she added it to Bridget's savings account.

Jillnoon used to work as a typesetter at one of Louise's shops, and before they became involved, Louise almost fired her for working on her own poems instead of Harold Straub's rush-job resume.

The photographs of machinery on Louise's office wall were taken by Bridget. "The blurriness makes them more interesting," Bridget explained. "So they look less like regular machines and more like how you want them to look."

Time to meet Marty. Louise pulls on her trench coat. She'll take a cab downtown. Marty works in a hospital by the lake. His whole life seems to be engulfed by water. He met Anne on a chartered flight to an island Club Med.

Driving is slow because her cabby is a novice, unaccustomed to mowing through lines of pedestrians, continually surprised by intruding vehicles. He moves like a slug down his lane, frequently glancing back as if expecting to see a trail of slime.

He leaves her at the restaurant's door and she tips him more than he deserves. He blinks quickly, then eases the cab into the traffic, turning the wrong way onto Clark. At one time she would have immediately thought to work this into an amusing story for Marty.

The restaurant, Marty's favorite, overflows with businessmen and their billowing conversations. Its reputation rests on inexpensive, authentic German food. The waiters are curt. Louise wouldn't choose to come here herself, but Marty always asks to meet here. "It's convenient," he explains.

"Louise." Marty, suddenly behind her, pokes his finger into her spine. "How are you?"

"Good," she replies. "Yourself?" This restaurant, with its solemn entrees and walls loaded with ornate beer steins and carved cuckoo clocks, makes her economical with her words.

"Great." He offers a brief, stiff smile. "I have a table. Over here," and he leads her to a place by the window. He's already eaten one piece of bread—she knows the basket always, always contains five slices, and theirs has only four. He helps her take off her coat, which she slings over a chair. "You look good."

"Thank you." She opens the menu. This restaurant claims to have invented the sauerbraten sandwich; it is a permanent lunch special.

"New dress?"

"Not really."

"I've never seen it."

She murmurs a nothing-word. Her new clothing continues to surprise him. As if he thinks she timelessly languishes on a shelf between their meetings.

A waiter, barely civil, takes their order.

"Well," Marty says, jabbing his finger into his glass of water, a habit he's always had.

"How's Anne?" she asks.

"Oh, good. Her firm has a big case. The Thompson thing. Maybe you read about it in the paper."

"Sure. And Bridget?"

"She's trying to decide on a project to enter in the Science Fair."

"I thought she was building a volcano."

"Half the sixth grade is building a volcano."

"Too bad," Louise says. "She was excited at the prospect of all that erupting mud."

"Boy, what a mess." Marty reaches for a piece of bread. No wonder he's gaining weight, she thinks.

"I don't know how to say this," he says. Then he stops and looks at her.

Louise watches as he butters his bread. The butter is in a bowl of ice so it's hard, and Marty ends up with crumbles. "Well?" she says.

"Well. Bridget invited her friend over, the one with the red hair. . . ."

"Andrea."

"Andrea, right, invited her to stay overnight Saturday. No problem there. They watched TV for a few hours, giggling like maniacs. Then they went up to Bridget's room, still giggling. The usual. You know how girls are."

"Yes."

"So we think everything's fine until Anne pokes her head in the bedroom to tell them there's popcorn downstairs. We were watching a video, and she made a big batch, way too much for the two of us."

"Yes."

"Both Anne and I thought you should know."

"Know what?"

"So Anne pokes her head in the door and sees the two of them sitting on the bed kissing each other. Bridget's got her arms wrapped around Andrea's neck; Andrea's grabbing all over Bridget. Anne couldn't believe it. I couldn't believe it when she told me."

"What did they do when they saw Anne?"

"They were embarrassed. They stopped. Of course."

The waiter brings them pea soup, pulling spoons from his apron pocket. Marty seems relieved at the interruption and does not speak.

Louise sips her soup, warm as the water from her hot-water faucet, and wonders what she is supposed to think, supposed to say. She never read Doctor Spock's book. She knows Marty wants to see her looking guilty, claim the blame. He finishes his soup quickly, tilting the bowl to fill his spoon with the last dribbles.

Finally he says, "Well?"

"What did you say to Bridget?" she asks.

"Anne was so shocked she couldn't say anything, just told them about the popcorn. Acted like she didn't see."

"It's a normal phase for girls," Louise says. "Really. It is."

"When I talked to her later, Bridget told me they were practicing kissing. For when they start going out with boys."

"See," Louise says. "I wouldn't worry. It's no big deal."

In passing, the waiter grabs the soup bowls off the table, and they grind in his hands.

"Anne thinks Bridget shouldn't see you anymore. That you encourage her to be like that."

"That's ridiculous. That's utterly ridiculous."

"Is it?"

"I'm her mother." Louise's napkin falls to the floor. She does not pick it up.

"Would the courts think it's ridiculous?"

"I don't believe this," Louise says. "A simple kiss between two sixth-grade girls. If she were kissing a boy, no one would be concerned. I wouldn't have been summoned like this." She pauses. "I want to talk to Bridget."

"I think you should. Anne and I are very upset about the whole thing."

"I don't believe this," Louise says again, and she sets aside Marty's outburst of directives: Tell her this, explain that, make sure she knows. . . .

It probably is a phase, Louise thinks, like triple-pierced ears. And even if it isn't. Even if it isn't, who's to say what's right —not Anne, not Marty. If it's so bad, what does that mean about me? But it's a phase, nothing more. And if it isn't? "Excuse me," she says to Marty, standing, interrupting him. Her mind is caught on a cubist canvas—all angles at once and none clear to her.

She walks downstairs to the telephones and calls Bridget's school, leaving a message for Bridget to meet her on the school steps at 3:00.

On the way back upstairs, she overhears someone call, "Shelly!" and that makes her remember a patch of her dream this morning. Stacks of seashells along the high-tide mark in the sand. Stacks and stacks, in neat piles, and it was her job to photograph each individual shell from every angle. But she only had a wide-angle lens.

It's a phase, she reminds herself.

When she returns to the table something immersed in drippy gravy has been deposited at her place at the table. "I guess I'm not hungry," she says, and she and Marty talk of the weather and the impending baseball season and somehow fill up the rest of their time together.

Before leaving to meet Bridget, Louise telephones Jillnoon, punching the buttons of her own phone number as if they're a secret code. The phone rings and rings; she has the feeling someone is hearing but not answering, and just as she is about to hang up, Jillnoon says, "Hello?" Her voice is skimpy, something the wind could shake loose. "Louise?"

"How'd you know it was me?" Louise asks, curious though not surprised.

"I was just coming in, and I heard the phone through the door while I was looking for my keys. Who else would keep a phone going for eighteen rings?"

"You counted?" Louise says, imagining Jillnoon standing outside the door, her bright lips moving as she counts, becoming

so linked with the sound of the phone that she forgets to dig through her purse for the ring of keys.

"More or less."

Now that she has Jillnoon's attention, she doesn't know what to say. There are rehearsed explanations, pleas for advice, but those words are too sharply in focus; they don't interest her now that she's talking to Jillnoon. She thinks of Jillnoon's face, of how her nose crinkles at the top when Louise says something funny.

"What do you do when you know you're right and the rest of the world thinks you're wrong?" she asks.

"Shout it from the rooftops," Jillnoon says without a pause for thought.

Two thumps come across the phone line, and Louise sees Jillnoon pulling off her boots, letting them drop to the wooden floor, settling herself into the rocking chair in the corner next to the phone. Jillnoon does not know what it is like to not have an answer. Louise cannot be so bold. Such a quality could carry a person in unexpected directions. Surely that's not all bad?

"What if you're not sure that you're right?" Louise asks.

"How could you not be sure?" and it seems to Louise that Jillnoon understands what she's asking. "All you need to do is look at what's right in front of you." Despite Jillnoon's wispy voice—or perhaps because of it—the words become something solid, something to hold onto.

Louise thinks of what seems long ago, Bridget was six, maybe seven, and Marty took them to the top of the lighthouse in Evanston. The tour guide—"chipped teeth," Marty whispered—droned like a revolving fan, fact after fact. How many hundred stairs. How many hundred feet. How many hundred ships. The blue in the sky was wide and long, distracting. Then Bridget begged to jump into the pile of crackling brown leaves far below. She waved to the man who was raking; maybe he'd beckoned? Marty touched her shoulder—"too far down," he told her, calm, "look"—and Bridget cried. Cried and cried until Louise wished

the lighthouse were not so many hundred feet. She couldn't think of how to explain so many hundred feet to Bridget.

"We're going to Evanston," Louise tells Bridget and the cab driver. "To that lighthouse." Bridget, who has informed Louise that she is missing a mandatory after-school play practice, shrugs. The cab driver turns around.

"I never heard of no lighthouse in Evanston," he says.

"On Sheridan Road," Louise says.

The cabby drives fast, passing car after car. Louise rolls down the window. Loose newspapers on the floor flutter, and Bridget holds them down with her feet. The cab curves into and along the road.

"Does Anne know not to pick me up?" Bridget asks. "She was going to get me after rehearsal."

"She knows," Louise says. "Your father told her." If he remembered.

"We're in Evanston," the cab driver says. "I don't see any lighthouse."

"Keep going," Louise says.

They wait at a red light, and Louise admires the college students passing before her. The jumble of brightly colored sweaters spilling across the street reminds her of stones on a beach. She has read that this school is known for its academic programs. Her advertising manager attended this school. Marty already talks about where Bridget will go to college. "This will be the back-up school," he says, "in case she doesn't get into Princeton or Harvard." Can Bridget feel the weight of these expectations?

"Andrea's sister goes to school here," Bridget says. "She's in a sorority, and she showed us the secret handshake. We promised not to tell because it's a secret, and she could get kicked out of the sorority for telling."

The cab driver says, "I bet for a million dollars you'd tell me pretty fast."

"Show me the money first," Bridget says. The driver laughs.

"Smart kid," he says.

The light is green, but they wait for one straggling student to cross the street before pulling forward.

Bridget seems the same, and Louise wonders what drastic changes she's looking for.

"Quit staring at me, Mom, you're giving me the creeps."

At the next traffic light the cabby asks, "What's at this lighthouse? Why're you going?"

Does he ask all his passengers why they choose their destinations? Because my ex-husband's new wife thinks I'm turning my daughter into a lesbian and I want to know if she's right.

"We need to get off the ground for a while."

"Yeah, getting some perspective," he says as they continue north, "I can relate, you know. But my fares are on the cement."

"How will I get home?" Bridget asks.

"Don't worry," Louise says to Bridget. "I haven't ever left you stranded, have I?" Then, "Turn right here."

"Oh, *this* lighthouse." The cab driver pulls into the gravel parking lot. "Yeah. I've been here."

Louise hands him money. "See you later," she says, guiding Bridget out of the cab.

"Sure," and he's off, his cab skimming along the surface of the road.

The Association of University Wives, Louise, and Bridget stand on the catwalk at the top of the lighthouse. The guide explains how important the lighthouse was, how the ships depended on seeing its light. Then she talks about how the lamp worked, how the keeper had to climb the 206 steps carrying two buckets of kerosene. "That would keep you careful not to spill," says one of the women. The guide seems miffed, as if her best line has been stolen.

The air is chilly. Louise scans the lake, searching for something to indicate that the dream this morning was really hers. She doesn't know what she wants to say to her daughter. Bridget knows the facts, is forming the opinions.

"I wish the lake was as blue as the sky, don't you, Mom?" Bridget says. "Wouldn't that be cool?"

Louise nods. The University Wives call down to a gardener on the ground who does not hear them. A gull drops into the shimmering lake.

"Look," Bridget says, "that's Gary." She points to a small, unfocused shadow to the south. "You need your camera."

"I've never seen Gary from so far away," Louise says. "It looks like nothing."

"Clear today, isn't it?" The guide moves next to them. "It's not often this blue." She stands, smiling proudly, then her loud voice begins to gather everyone together for the descent. "Come along, there's another group waiting to go up."

Before Louise speaks she wonders, What will Bridget think of me? How will I change in her eyes and how permanently? and she instantly sees her selfishness. I'm Anne and Marty, posed like Greek statues, looking for things that Bridget only sees in her out-of-focus way. Gary and Jillnoon. Bridget will choose neither. She speaks quickly, "You shouldn't be kissing your friends that way."

"What?"

"Nothing," Louise says. "See how the sky and water mingle along the edge. I want us always to be like that."

Vera

Minnie Bruce Pratt

Toward the end I go to the hospital every day and rub her feet
with rose oil and lavender salve. Her big feet, size 12 at least,
loom in my hands, with pale sole and arch, darker instep and
ankle. Her skin, dry from months of chemotherapy, crumbles
under my touch like dead leaves. She is sore everywhere, the
wound in her belly is blood rose-red against her dark skin. I rub
her back which hurts all the time. I rub her feet until my hands
can recreate every crease, every line of the flat contours of feet
that have borne her stone weight and presence through a short
lifetime of hard work. Toward the end I can do nothing but rub
her feet and listen as she tells me about being alone in the labor
room of the hospital in Florida, fourteen years old, and the white
doctor who slammed his fist into her face because she was
screaming with pain, how she went home with a baby boy and
a black eye. She tells me about sitting in the Job Corps dorm in
Oklahoma as the trainees from New York City came in off the
bus, her eyes lighting on the femmes and the butches flaunting
their style. Later, on the way to her first date with a woman, she
remembered them, bought a painter's cap, put on jeans and an
oxford shirt, rolled up her sleeves and stuck her Luckies in.
She'd watched the other dykes, she knew better than to carry the
purse on her date that she took to her day job at the garment

factory. She tells me about trying to take care of her woman and her son, the construction jobs she worked as the only woman, the only African-American woman at every site. The bosses told her she did her work better than any of the men. She built prefab trailers, she insulated houses, going up into attics in the summer to spray asbestos in suffocating heat, no protection except a flimsy face mask from a glassy dust finer than pollen. We both know the work she had to do to feed herself and her family had ended up killing her, and what else could she have done? One day, on morphine, she tells me how she fantasizes escape from the hospital to go shopping. "What would you buy?" I ask, and she says, grinning lasciviously, "The first thing I'd get—something sexy for Cathy—a black see-through lace nightgown." And for herself? "Some purple Birkenstock sandals, very comfortable for my feet." In her closet she has some red leather hightop Nikes sent by her dyke sister, for the day she walks out of her sterile isolated room. Meanwhile, in its cool dark we pretend we're strolling through the mall into a Cineplex Odeon. I go past the nurses' station down the hall and heat popcorn in the microwave. We eat it and watch an old movie about Josephine Baker on the rented TV. The day before she dies I bathe her all over, her big strong body shrunken in on itself but still beautiful in shades of darkness and rose. With water I freshen the aureoles of her nipples, her tender labia, the crease of her ass, the pink and brown creases of her feet. I complete the ritual of wash with not much soap a little bit of skin with the rest covered by sheet, rinse, pat dry, then another leaf of skin revealed, then the painful lifting and heaving to get to her back, to change her diaper, the special soap to guard against bedsores, the vaseline and cornstarch. Last I wash and dry her feet, and sit at the end of the bed with them in my hands, rubbing in the sweet salve. The next morning when I come with Cathy to stand by her cold and stiffening body she is already encased in her plastic coffin bag. I can only rest my hand on the outline of her toes. Later, at their apartment, Cathy pulls clothes out of the closet to send home to Florida with her body. She says, "We talked about the funeral, and she wanted her good black pants, and this purple oxford shirt. I'm not sending anything else down to them. She made me promise not to let them bury her in a dress. I'll send those clothes down, with her black penny loafers she kept shined up so nice.'' In my hands the shoes are brittle and empty as broken husks, as shed skin, their only liveliness the bright pennies that still wink in their sockets, as we refuse to weight her eyelids down in final oblivion.

There's a Window

Sapphire

"Is this just something to do till you get out? Till you get back to your old man?" she sneered.

I didn't answer her. I just kept pushing her blue denim smock further up her hips. The dress was up to her waist now. I wanted to get one of her watermelon-size breasts in my mouth, I was having trouble with her bra.

"Take off your bra."

"Oh, you givin' orders now," she said amused. Her short spiked crew cut and pug nose made her look like a bulldog. Her breath smelled like cigarettes, millions of 'em.

"Yeah," I asserted, "I'm giving orders. Take that mutherfuckin' harness off."

She laughed tough but brittle. The tough didn't scare me, the brittleness did. She nuzzled my ear with her nose, her hot, moist lips on my neck, "Call me Daddy," she whispered.

Oh no, I groaned. She stuck her tongue under my chin. It was like a snake on fire—fuck it, I'd call her anything.

"OK Daddy," I sneered, "take off your bra." Something went out of her. I felt ashamed. "I'm sorry," I whispered trying to put it back. I had the dress up over her waist now.

"Take it off," I whispered.

"My blues!" she protested referring to the denim prison smock.

"Yeah, I don't wanna fuck no piece of denim. Take off that ugly ass dress." I was eating up her ear now. My tongue carousing behind her ear and down her neck that smelled like Ivory Soap and cigarette smoke. I was sitting on top of her belly pumping my thighs together sending blood to my clitoris as I pulled the dress over the top of her head. I was riding, like the Lone Ranger on top of Silver, no, take that back; Annie Oakley, I was riding like Annie Oakley. Actually I should take that back too but I can't think of any Black cowgirls right off hand. Looking down at her face I wanted to turn away from it, keep my eyes focused on the treasure behind the white cotton harness. Hawk-eyed, crew-cut butch, she was old compared to me. How the fuck did she keep her underwear so clean in this dingy hole I marveled. They acted like showers and changes of clothes was privilege. I leaned down stuck my tongue in her mouth realized in a flash the Ivory Soap, clean bra and perspiration breaking out on her forehead was all for me.

She was trying. Trying hard. Probably being flat on her back with me on top of her was one of the hardest things she'd ever done. I admired her for a moment. Shit, she was beautiful! Laying up under me 50 years old, crew cut silver. I'd told her in the day room when she slammed on me, "Hey baby I don't want no one putting no bag over my head pulling no train on *me*. Shit baby, if we get together it's got to be me doing the wild thing too!"

She'd said, "Anything you want Momi."

And I wanted her to take that fucking bra off.

I slid down in the brown country of her body following blue veins like rivers; my tongue a snake crawling through dark canyons, over strange hills, slowing down at weird markings and moles. I was lost in a world, brown, round, smelling like cigarette smoke, pussy and Ivory Soap. My hands were on her ass pulling her cunt closer to my mouth.

"Here," she said pushing something thin slippery and cool into my hand. I recognized the feel of latex.

"Just to be on the safe side," she said.

My heart swole up big time inside my chest. Here we was in
death's asshole, two bitches behind bars, hard as nails and twice
as ugly—caring. She *cared* about me, she cared about herself. I
stretched the latex carefully over her wet opening. "Hold it," I
instructed while I pulled her ass down to my mouth. I started to
suck; fuck that latex, it might keep me from tasting but it
couldn't keep me from feeling. And I was a river now, overflowing its banks, rushing all over the brown mountains. I was
a Black cowgirl, my tongue was a six-shooter and my fingers
were guns. I was headed for the canyon, nobody could catch me.
I was wild. I was bad.

"Oh Momi," she screamed.

Um huh, that's me, keep calling my name. I felt like lightning
cutting through the sky. She pulled me up beside her. I stuck
my thigh between her legs and we rode till the cold cement walls
turned to the midnight sky and stars glowing like the eyes of
Isis. The hooves of our horses sped across the desert sand, rat-
tlesnakes took wings and flew by our side. The moon bent down
and whispered, "Call me Magdelina, Momi. Magdelina is my
name."

Our tongues locked up inside themselves like bitches who
were doin' life. No one existed but us. But the whispering moon
was a memory that threatened to kill me. She slid down grabbing
my thighs with her big calloused hands.

"Yeah, yeah, yeah," the words jumped out my throat like
little rabbits, "go down on me go down on me." Her tongue
was in my navel. "Use dat latex shit," I told her.

"Do I have to Momacita?"

"Yeah," I said, "I like the feel of it," I lied. My heart got
big size again. They didn't *give* nothin' away in this muther-
fucker! How many candy bars or cigarettes had she traded for
those little sheets of plastic.

"Ow!" Shit, it felt good her tongue jamming against my clitoris. Oh please woman don't stop I begged but at the same time
in the middle of my crazy good feeling something was creeping.

I tried to ignore it and concentrate on the rivers of pleasure she was sending through my body and the pain good feel of her fingers in latex gloves up my asshole. But the feeling was creeping in my throat threatening to choke me; nasty and ugly it moved up to my eyes and I started to cry. She looked at me concerned and amazed, "Mira Momi did I do something wrong?" She glanced around, then at herself as if to assess where evil could have come from. "Not this damn thing?" she says incredulously. Her eyes gleam with the hope of alleviating my pain as she hastily unhooks her bra. I shake my head no no but she has her head down, her hands behind her back pulling the white whale off her brown body.

"I . . . I don' know, you know I have this *thing* about being totally nekkid—*here* you know. I ain been naked in front of nobody since I been here, cept you know doctors and showers and shit," she laughed in her glass voice. "It jus aint that kind of place Momacita. You know you snatch a piece here, there; push somebody's panties to the side in the john so you can finger fuck five minutes before a big voice comes shouting, "What's takin' you so long in there!" Least that's what it's been like for me. 7 years," she said, the glass broke in her throat, "7 years."

Her words overwhelmed me. I felt small and ashamed with my pain. But this thing in my throat had snatched my wings. I knew I had to speak my heart even though it felt juvenile and weak, speak or forever be tied up to the ground.

"I ain seen the moon or the stars in 6 months," I felt shamed 6 months nex to 7 years on the edge of nothing. Silly shit to be tear jerking about. I started to cry. I had 7 years to do yet. She'd be gone by the time I turned around twice. She looked at me thoughtfully, her gray crew cut seemed like a luminous crown on top a forehead creased with lines. "Listen," she said quietly, "in six months or so you'll go from days in the laundry to the midnight to 8 A.M. kitchen shift if your behavior is good. Volunteer to peel the potatoes. There's a window over where they peel the vegetables. You can see the moon from that window."

I felt the nipples of her huge breasts hardening in my fingers.

We retrieved two more precious pieces of latex, fitted ourselves
in a mean 69 and sucked each other back to the beginning of
time. I was a cave girl riding a dinosaur across the steamy pa-
leolithic terrain snatching trees with my teeth, shaking down the
moon with my tongue.

The Faintest of Rumbles
Cynthia Lollar

Most women with a butt as big as Marva's tuck into themselves, but Marva just pitches through town like she's riding ocean swells, her huge hips the ballast for a cargo of gold. The first time I saw her, little bubbles broke out in my mind like newly opened soda and the air took on this clarity like right before a rainstorm, all iron-sharp and clean. I was riding my bike on the way to the library, a twenty-three-year-old woman trying with one hand to let a little air in under her sweat-soaked bra. My deliveries were done for the day and it was time to sit back in some free air-conditioning and catch up on the news. Of all the big-city newspapers kept at the library, my favorite, just for the name, is the *New Orleans Times-Picayune*. It sounds so Walt Disney: *Times-Picayune*. Like little dwarves lay the thing out and talking dogs write the headlines. The *Queen's Peak Sentinel* I deliver isn't nearly so much fun.

When I saw her, Marva was sailing up Magnolia Avenue where it runs past the library at the intersection with Beech. "Look at her," I thought. "That's a woman." I don't mean I was surprised by this; she was every inch identifiable as a woman. Light brown hair streaming back from her head like a banner, breasts round and bunched as pillows, and of course all those hips. But she commanded the sidewalk, not apologizing for the space she took up like some of us women do. She walked like trees grow, like rivers run. As steady as the turning earth itself.

When she reached the library she mounted the steps and pushed through the doors. I locked my bike in the rack next to the bayberry bushes out front and ducked inside myself. But she was gone. I roamed the downstairs stacks for a bit, thinking any minute I'd come upon her mighty figure squeezed between the rows, a copy of *O Pioneer!* in her hands. No go. I climbed the narrow spiral staircase to the library's second floor and took a look around there, too. Biography? No. Regional history? No. My heart fluttered. Human sexuality? But no.

It was a real mystery, and that evening I told my girlfriend all about it. Rachel works as a secretary in the chemistry department at the college. She was born and raised in a little place down river from Queen's Peak called Clapper Falls, but she doesn't talk about the Falls much and I don't push her. We were sitting on the white wooden steps that climb up to our apartment on the second floor of an old Victorian house near campus, eating baked beans and wieners in the day's dying light. It was warm and leaves pirouetted through the air.

"I looked everywhere, even under the stalls in the women's rest room, but she'd disappeared," I said.

"That must have endeared you to the library's other patrons." Rachel favors the precise word. Endeared. Patrons. My heart always pangs when she does that.

"Oh, hell," I said, swatting at a fly. "If any of them noticed I'm sure it was the biggest thrill of their day. A peeping Tom-ette, right here in Queen's Peak."

Rachel speared a wiener with the fork in her left hand, cut it in two with her knife and shifted the fork to her right hand before eating. The flies didn't seem to be bothering her.

"What did you learn at school today, dear?" I said. It was one of our little lines.

"Reactions that are catalyzed by sound," she said. She tossed back her shoulder-length hair and adjusted the strap on her sundress. Rachel liked to eavesdrop on the teachers and students in the hall outside her office. "It seems that chemical reactions can be speeded up with ultrasonic waves. You know, sound we can't hear?" I nodded, admiring the way Rachel could hold this stuff in her head without screaming. Me, I never set foot on campus except to deliver pizzas to the dorms. The day I graduated from high school was the day I first tasted freedom, and I hadn't had an appetite for anything else since.

"The sound waves generate tiny bubbles," Rachel continued, "and when they collapse, they send out shock waves that create heat and pressure. Boom. Catalysis."

"Sort of like the opera singer shattering the wine glass," I said.

"A singer you can't hear," she said. "A dumb diva."

"Hey, who you calling dumb?" I launched into the only operatic lyrics I knew. I'd heard them once on a Bugs Bunny cartoon. "Figaro, Figaro, Fig-a-ro!" I stood now, arms flung wide, trying to approximate with my wiry figure someone more of Marva's stature, complete with horned helmet and breastplates. Rachel just looked up at me from her seat on the steps.

"I trust our child will be able to find appropriate musical influences outside the home," she said.

I shut up then and sat back down, pushing aside my half-eaten supper. "There you go. Another reason to reconsider. Bosco shouldn't be burdened with a tone-deaf coparent."

Rachel looked at me and said nothing. She hated the name I'd given her wished-for child, said it best suited a bulldog and showed only my stubbornness. She was right, of course. That's one of the reasons I fell in love with her, back when her knowing me so well was a comfort. I stuck a wiener on the tines of my fork and catapulted it into the yard for the squirrels. At one time Rachel would have cut me a look with her eyes to say how exasperating yet cute I was. Now she merely gathered up her plate and cup and disappeared behind me into the kitchen.

"Honestly, El," was all she said.

The next day on my routes I kept an eye out for Marva. From eleven until three I delivered pizza to office workers, stay-at-homes and college students, crisscrossing town on my sturdy 15-speed Trek with the pies strapped tight on the rack behind my seat. After that it was the afternoon delivery of *The Queen's Peak Sentinel.* A car would have been easier but we didn't own one, and I'd convinced my employers that bicycle delivery would lend to their businesses a charming antiquity sure to be appreciated by the town's many longtime residents. That was Rachel's line. Charming antiquity.

But I didn't see Marva. Who could she be? A visiting professor, perhaps, down from the state university? I stood up on the pedals to scale Mulligan Street where it climbs alongside the Casper River. No, something more. A private eye over from Raleigh, on the trail of an elusive serial killer. Pump, pump. My muscles burned. Sweat dripped between my breasts. I know. She's the bastard daughter of the town's balding mayor, born of a clandestine tryst with a harlot down in Charleston, now rising up to assert her hereditary rights. My lungs strained for air. I crested the hill with one final wish: Marva, down from New York City to conduct research for those lesbian history archives I'd read about once in the *New York Times.* Surely she'd want to talk to me.

By five I was done. As I rode up to the library, I saw Marva's remarkable bottom going through the doors like the eight ball down a pocket. This time I didn't bother to lock my bike. Running up the steps I got inside just in time to see Marva sign in at the front desk and enter a back room unlocked for her by Fayla Cooper, the research librarian. I must have looked a little wild-eyed. "What's the matter, Ellie," said Fayla, returning to her post at the desk. "Mr. Cotteridge's dog been chasing you again?"

"Yeah," I said, trying to regulate my breathing, "I'm just lucky he's as old as Mr. Cotteridge." I leaned an elbow near the sign-in pad, glancing at the most recent ink-heavy scrawl: Marva Rinkle. "Say, what's back there, anyway?"

"The archives. Official city documents dating back to the town's incorporation in 1823, geological surveys of the area, old newspaper clippings, that sort of thing."

"What's that woman looking for?"

"Now, Ellie, that's privileged information. You wouldn't want me revealing your seemingly endless appetite for urban crime articles, now would you?" Fayla looked at me, her dark face stern.

"Just curious, Fayla," I said, backing off with my hands raised. "You know how nosy I am."

"Well, you can nose around the archives yourself any time you like," she said. "You just need to sign in."

That was a thought. I headed toward my favorite chair in the current periodicals section. I'd need a cover, though, something to explain my presence in the back room to Marva. I picked up the *Times-Picayune,* dated last Friday because it took a couple days to get here, and flipped through the front section. MAN KILLS WIFE, THREE CHILDREN. I shook my head. Reading newspapers was like going to a human zoo and standing safely outside the cages. Below the fold on the third page a photograph showed a man holding a gun to the head of a convenience-store clerk. Neither man looked scared or angry or even emotional. It was always that way in these photos. Like their lives having gone horribly awry was something that could have happened to anyone, anywhere.

Which gave me an idea. I put the paper down. I had my cover, and it was time to go home to Rachel.

It was last spring when she first mentioned it. I was kneeling under the bathroom sink while Rachel stood in the bathtub, both of us scrubbing away a year's worth of mold from the tiles. Rachel was naked. She'd scrub a four-tile patch of blackish grout with a hard-bristled brush, then turn on the showerhead to clean it off before moving to another square on what was clearly a vividly imagined grid. My technique was less thorough though no less strategic, and involved making broad circular swipes at the wall in a way that brought me closer and closer to Rachel's glistening skin. I had my eye on a spot just under her right breast, where the flesh drooped in a full gentle curve before lifting up and away to form a warm hollow for my lips. I swiped at the

wall with my cloth and peered up past the metal underside of
the sink. The edge of the sink and the side of the bathtub framed
Rachel so that I could see only her sleek torso, wet with sweat
and water. She said, "Ellie, have you ever thought about us
having a baby?"

I poked my head out from under the sink and smiled at her.
"Sorry, can't hear very well under there. Could have sworn you
said 'baby.' "

"I did. I did say baby." Rachel's cheeks flushed and she dug
deeper at the grout.

The smile on my face remained as my emotions worked fran-
tically to rearrange themselves. "Gee, Rachel, can't say that I
have," I said carefully. "It's not as if we have all the necessary
ingredients, if you know what I mean."

"The sperm would be the least of our problems. There are
sperm banks now. And there's your friend Al. I wonder if he
might be willing to help us. He's a sweet and intelligent man."

Things were moving way too fast. Al was another carrier at
the newspaper, a single, part-time plumber who'd come over a
few times for hamburgers and beers. He'd gotten the picture
about Rachel and me early and would ask about her while we
rubber-banded the newspapers each afternoon, like you do about
somebody's spouse. I could just see his face, though. Oh, and
when you get done with your route today, Al, would you mind
filling this little cup?

"For crying out loud, Rachel," I said. "I'm only twenty-
three."

"And I'm twenty-five. My mother had four children by the
time she was as old as I am." Rachel's voice quavered and she
slipped a little in the wet tub as she spun to face me. "I've just
always wanted to give a child some of the things I didn't have.
I've just always wanted. . . ."

The space under the sink suddenly felt too small. I waddled
backward and pushed myself to my feet, the air around my body
squeezing me in its fist.

"Look, can we talk about this later? I think I need to go for
a ride."

Rachel's lips became a dark underline and she turned back toward the wall. "Oh, by all means. Flee to your bicycle. I'll just stay here holding things together until you get back, and when life gets real again, I'll stay here and you'll go for another ride. Really. You go on. I'll just stay here. You can count on me."

Each time she said "I'll stay here," Rachel swept her brush up the tiles with such force it seemed her arm would break through the ceiling and roof and into the sky, like some sort of human eruption.

"Rachel?" Her fury rooted me to the floor even as my feet yearned for the door. "I had no idea a baby was so important to you."

"It's not the baby."

"What then?"

But that's all she would say. Rachel didn't talk about the baby much after that but I could feel it blowing cool between us. At some point I started referring to the baby as Bosco and it doesn't make me proud to say I enjoyed the annoyance that name brought to Rachel's face.

That's why I don't blame Rachel for what she did later. She wasn't trying to get me fired. And she didn't mean to humiliate me (I think she used the word "chasten"). In the end what I learned was that freedom needs something unfree beneath it, holding steady. That love flies highest on a string.

After cleaning out the bean pot and stowing away the weiners Rachel and I puttered silently about the apartment, practically tripping over all the things we weren't saying. Eventually we got tired and went to bed, but I couldn't sleep. Rachel lay with her back to me as I slipped from bed and headed out to my bike.

The hills of Queen's Peak never failed to calm my mind. Something about the shifting gears and my muscles' slow, burning victory over any steepness, every turn, pumped hope back into my lungs and a kind of wild freedom into my soul. I rode hard away from the apartment, up and down the streets of Queen's Peak, past the dark clapboard houses with their neat geranium borders and deep porches, jumping curbs and zigzagging around garbage cans left out for the collectors at dawn. When I reached the bottom of Tank Hill, I leaned my bike against the fence and climbed over. A full moon threw bright beams through the hemlocks, poplars and pines. Frogs chirped and belched, leading me to the river's edge. The running water sounded like muffled hooves. I wanted to jump in and ride away. A baby.

I sat down on a rock and thought back to the first time I'd seen Rachel. I was a waitress then at the diner near campus. She came over occasionally for lunch, always the same thing: tuna salad on toasted whole wheat with tomato, no lettuce, no mayo. I liked the way she arranged herself in the booth. She'd adjust her skirt underneath her, then reach up and pull the utensils toward her a little more, getting them just the right distance from the edge. Then she'd slide the napkin out from under the fork and carefully flatten it out big and white on her lap, like it was a road map she'd need to refer to as she ate. She wasn't stiff exactly, just poised, which intrigued me. Everything in my life was jumpier than grease on a hot skillet. I'd pretty much been on my own since my folks dumped me at Grandma Skimmer's when I was fourteen; they'd come home early from the movies one night and found me and my best friend Alma necking on their bed. Grandma didn't care but she died when I was seventeen. So I came to Queen's Peak looking for joy where I could find it. I'd had a girlfriend here and there, but nobody that grabbed me like Rachel Starch.

I started messing up her order so I'd have an excuse to go by her table more often. One day a slathering of mayonnaise. Another day lettuce, but no tomato. She'd smile at me sweetly when I'd come to take the sandwich back. At the time I thought she was just remarkably patient but later she told me she'd tumbled to my game early and was stringing me along until she could figure out how to see me outside the diner.

One day I delivered her sandwich on toast so black it looked cremated. I'd only meant to scorch it a little but I got to daydreaming over the toaster until the smoke woke me up. I dropped the plate off hurriedly, like I was preoccupied with all my customers and hadn't a moment to notice the charred remains of her food. Rachel grabbed my wrist before I could get away. The coolness of her touch drove all the blood to my face.

"Excuse me," she said. "I know you're awfully busy. But is that your bicycle outside?" She was thinking about buying a new one herself and would appreciate any thoughts I had on the matter. Would I mind? She got off work at 4:30. . . .

We moved in together three months later. Peanut-butter sandwiches were practically the only thing I ate, so Rachel showed me how to shop and cook a little. I got her to sleep in on Saturdays instead of popping up at seven and starting in on housework. Some weekends we'd lie in bed until noon, tangled in the sheets and each other's arms while I taught her all the dirty limericks I knew and she searched my skin for signs of sun damage.

At first she enjoyed the fact that I delivered pizza and newspapers for a living, said it reflected an iconoclastic spirit, but after a couple of years together she started asking me what else I might want to do with my life and had I thought about taking classes at the college. She didn't do this in a mean way and she still smiled at the stories I'd tell about the people along my routes, but all the same I felt uncomfortable. After a while when I looked at her—stooping over the skillet to taste a forkful of dinner, propping her head on her hand as she lay on the couch to read, bowing down to wipe polish on the toes and heels of her shoes—some element in her posture struck me as sad. No, not sad exactly. Motionless. As if she were suspended, waiting for something. And I didn't know for what.

The thought that it might be a baby caused me to rise from where I was sitting by the riverbank and kick at the leaves. That's when I saw her across the water, changing shape and color in the quilted moonlit night. She was a boulder's hulking shadow, now a tree stump, now a bush. Marva.

She picked her way across the steep embankment, pausing every now and then to brush away leaves and sticks and examine the ground with the help of a powerful flashlight. Twice she stopped to look up and down the slope and along the river, as if gauging the spot relative to other objects in the area. I watched her until she moved out of sight around the bend. Just as she disappeared the breeze shifted and the heady fragrance of honeysuckle filled my nostrils. I couldn't tell where the scent was coming from but I believed in the sweetness it brought.

Later, after I'd ridden home and crawled back in bed, Rachel turned toward me with closed eyes and mumbled, "El, I don't want to fight about us."

I just stroked her hand where it rested on my pillow and pulled the covers up tight around us both. I could afford to be nice. I wasn't thinking about us anymore.

The next afternoon I arrived early at the *Sentinel* drop-off, both to avoid seeing Al, whose crotch now loomed annoyingly in my mind, and to get through my route in time to arrive at the library before Marva.

The pace was brutal but I made it. At quarter to five Fayla led me into the archives and flipped on the light. "Let me know if you need anything," she said, shutting the door behind her. The room was windowless and rectangular, about twelve by sixteen feet, with shelves of boxes lining the walls and a long table and several chairs set in the middle. I walked around the room, reading the labels on the boxes, and pulled one out marked "Queen's Peak Sentinel: 1923." I chose papers at random and skimmed their pages. The summer months were filled with exciting news of the upcoming centennial celebration in October. However, I wasn't looking for happy events.

Suddenly the door swung open. "Hi, I'm Marva Rinkle," she said, sweeping into the room and reaching out a hand. "Fayla said I had company today."

I grasped her hand and felt faint. Up close she was even more powerful than I'd imagined. Her grip was firm and I could feel the weight of her arm as we shook hands, like an old-fashioned pump drawing water. She was wearing hiking boots, chinos and a loose-fitting floral shirt that draped over her waist. Her hair hung down almost to the middle of her back, framing a round, broad-cheeked face with large blue eyes. I realized I was staring at Marva's breasts. Prodigious, I thought, then cringed to catch myself relying on Rachel's vocabulary at a time like this.

"Ellie Skimmer," I said.

"A pleasure," said Marva. I couldn't place her accent. Southern and honey rich, but not from around here. Marva set a sheaf of papers and a pencil down on the table and turned around to pull a box from the shelf behind her. Let's see, I thought, replaying my tour of the room. Those would be the geological surveys.

We worked in silence for a while. I leafed through the newspapers, trying to think of a way to ask her what she was doing with the maps. Then a headline under the *Sentinel* banner dated July 24, 1923, caught my eye: WOMAN, TWO CHILDREN KILLED IN FLOOD. I scanned the story. "Hmmm," I said as thoughtfully as I could.

Marva looked up from her maps. "Find something interesting?" she asked. I nodded. My cover was going to hold after all.

"I work for the newspaper here in town," I said, trying not to look like I was fudging. "There's been all this talk in the national press about the rise in urban crime, and I just thought I'd do a little research into what kind of trouble Queen's Peak has experienced over the years."

"Seems a pretty peaceful place to me," said Marva.

"Yeah, it is," I said. "But here's a story about a woman down river from here who fell into the river with her two babies back in 1923. There was a flood going on, and she had climbed the rocks around the falls to get away from it." I scanned more of the story. "Folks who saw her up there said one minute she was sitting on a ledge, a baby in each arm, and the next thing they knew, she was gone. One guy says she might have jumped. Now why would she do that?"

"That's terrible." Marva had laid down her pen and was concentrating on me. "You never know what really moves a person, do you."

I nodded and we fell silent again. I couldn't think of anything to do except stare at the article in the paper. After a while, fearing that my inactivity would raise questions in Marva's mind, I stood to go. Marva raised her head from her work. "See you tomorrow?"

"Sure. Well. Maybe. I'll . . . uh . . . have to talk to my editor."

"It was nice with you here," said Marva, smiling. "It's kind of lonely working alone." Her blue eyes shone at me and I felt the way you do when you're fishing and the bobber dips suddenly below the surface.

Now that I'd found her, I kept running into Marva all over town. Tuesday is pizza day for the nurses at the Main Street clinic, but this time from their stoop I watched across the way as Marva left Mel's Hardware with a new shovel, popped into the bakery next door for a frosted cinnamon bun and took off down the street in a beat-up black Jeep. On Wednesday I spied her through Suds and Duds' steamy picture window, and stopped to add my own foggy breath to the window's other side. She was shoving muddy jeans and sweatshirts into a washer. Her hair hung in a braided velvety rope down her back and her arms pumped like pistons over the open mouth of the machine. On Thursday Marva's Jeep sped through an intersection I was nearing on my newspaper route by the river. I pedaled furiously to the corner but by then only a faint trace of exhaust lingered to mark her passing. I breathed deeply anyway and it was as if the aroma carbonated my blood, I felt that dizzy.

Of course, I described all this to Rachel. That may seem odd, but it's just our way. She tells me about the things she learns at work and I tell her about the people I run into during my day. I admit I get a little carried away sometimes but Rachel never gets jealous. She hears me out, even asks me questions like, "Exactly what does one of Mrs. Strumley's prize tulips look like flattened under the Sunday paper?" which shows me she really cares.

So it surprised me when in the midst of one of my Marva tales Rachel blurted out, "Just what do you see in this woman?"

We were sitting side by side on the couch watching television, some crisis-of-the-week movie about a couple of middle-class parents whose All-American son turns out to be a serial killer with a penchant for dead prostitutes. It seemed to me a good example of the unnecessary risk of procreation but I didn't say so and instead concentrated on amusing Rachel with my adventures. Her question brought me up short.

"See in her? I don't know. I wonder what she's up to, is all." As I spoke, Rachel worked at a needlepoint project, punching the needle in and out of a bright red rose caught tight in a circular vise.

"You're mooning over her. Honestly, peeping through windows."

"You call that mooning? What about the time I rode the Tilt-a-Whirl twenty-six times at the state fair just so I could see that cute ticket taker up close. I puked corn dogs and blue cotton candy for a week. Now that's mooning!" Something felt wrong about this line of defense but I didn't have time to worry about it. Rachel's eyes welled with tears.

"Come on, Rache," I begged, stroking her arm. She stiffened at my touch and raised her chin as if to tip the tears back inside her eyes. "You know if you had reason to be jealous I wouldn't be telling you any of this."

Her eyes gauged me from a distance I'd never seen in them before. The air felt suddenly cold and I clutched her hand. After a moment, she squeezed me back.

"What would I do without you?" I said, relieved. "You're the ground I walk on."

"That's just it, isn't it," she said, picking up her needlepoint again.

I didn't know what to say. "You want me to forget about Marva?"

Rachel hunted through her needlepoint bag and picked out a bright spool of violet thread, which she began to stitch into the rose's stem and leaves. The pattern there clearly called for green. Rachel never deviated from the pattern, but it didn't seem the time to point out her mistake.

"Oh, I don't know what I want," she said. More tears slid

from her eyes. "The thought of you domesticated makes me feel
even worse." I moved closer to her on the couch and leaned
into her ear.

"Moo," I whispered.

One corner of her mouth lifted. I helped the other corner up
with my tongue. And when I'd gotten through purring and barking and oinking every friendly animal sound I knew, I took her
to bed with a promise in my heart not to hurt her with my mean-
derings again.

But it was as if Marva wanted me to follow her.

At least that's what I told myself on Friday when, on a pizza
run to the dorms, I saw Marva's battered Jeep parked outside
one of the big limestone buildings at the center of campus. I left
my bike in the rack outside and entered the foyer as if hypno-
tized. Animal skulls, rock specimens and tinker-toy molecules
filled the glass display cases sunk into the walls on either side.
The stairway ahead offered two choices: up or down. I chose up
on the completely senseless theory that Marva was not the kind
of person to hide in the bowels of buildings.

Upstairs, there was no sight of her in the hallway to the right
of the stairwell, only door after door behind which I could hear
the murmur of voices or the punctuated bark of a teacher trying
to penetrate the coma students like me always fall into the moment we plunk our butts in a classroom. Past the sixth or seventh
door there was a sharp chemical smell I couldn't identify. It
reminded me of the morning I'd tripped in the kitchen while
carrying a spoonful of clog-busting drain crystals toward the
sink. A bunch of the crystals flew into the pan of sizzling bacon
on the stove and the resulting mess—Draino flambé, Rachel
called it—stank up the apartment for days. I could feel my stomach rolling over so I turned around and headed back toward the
stairwell and the rooms on the other side. Just as I reached the
head of the stairs, doors flew open as if pulled by a common
string and students filled the hallway. I caught snatches of conversation as I edged my way along one wall, feeling like a trout
fighting its way upstream. ". . . cafeteria again, but I'm starving

and I've got another class at 12:30 . . ." ". . . boring as hell but at least he's nice to look at . . ." ". . . anion, ion—who can keep them straight . . . ?"

I saw Marva come around the corner ahead of me just as Rachel stepped out from behind a door marked "Office."

"Ellie?" Rachel said, her eyebrows arching like furry frowns. She held some papers and a pen in her hands. "What are you doing here?"

"Um . . . ah . . ."

Twenty feet away and closing, Marva looked like a giant boulder in a spring creek of students. Only this time, the boulder was moving with a kind of immutable force all its own. Fifteen feet, fourteen. . . . Who would have guessed that Fate wore extra-large chinos stained with mud, a canvas bag with a strap slung over her shoulder, and a green baseball cap that read "Dig It" over the brim? Or that at ten paces she would stop to stare and announce in a voice suitable for long-distance calls without a telephone, "Ellie! Just the woman I wanted to see!"

I closed my eyes and wondered if it was possible to will an out-of-body experience, or perhaps accomplish it the old-fashioned way, by dying. When I opened my eyes Marva and Rachel stood before me like a double monument to my stupidity. There seemed only one thing to say.

"Marva, this is Rachel, the woman I live with," I said. "Rachel, this is Marva."

The two of them shook hands. "Nice to meet you, Rachel," said Marva. "Ellie and I ran into each other at the library recently while she was researching a story for the newspaper. It must be fun living with a reporter, getting all the hottest news first."

"A reporter, yes," Rachel said, smiling as if she were having her photograph taken. "Fun."

Marva turned back to me. Standing next to her was like standing before the old copper beech tree in the park on Main Street, roots twenty feet down and a three-hundred-year-old trunk. I wanted to climb up and away from all this. "Ellie, I've got something I want to discuss with you," Marva said, patting her canvas bag. "Something I think would make a good story and be a public service, too. Can we go somewhere and talk?"

"Well, you see, my editor has, uh, reassigned me and . . ."

"Why don't you come for supper tonight," interrupted Rachel. She jotted something on a corner of the paper she carried, ripped it off and handed it to Marva. "Here's our address. It's a blue Victorian house with white shutters. We're on the second floor. I get off work at four-thirty. How about six?"

"That would be great," said Marva, tucking the paper into her shirt pocket, which lay nearly flat on the great expanse of her bosom. "Gotta run now or they'll arrest my Jeep for vagrancy." She shook my hand without seeming to notice it had all the warmth of a dead fish. "Don't get scooped, now."

"I won't," I said, looking at Rachel. I already had been.

"More potato salad?" Rachel inquired.

Marva nodded, her mouth still busy with a recent bite of barbecued chicken. Rachel spooned potatoes onto Marva's plate and wordlessly passed the bowl to me. It was an automatic gesture because I hadn't touched the food that already filled my plate to the rim. Marva's canvas bag lay on the picnic bench beside her. My eyes kept jumping between the bag and Rachel's face as she engaged Marva in a conversation about the finer aspects of rocks.

"Most are aggregates of several minerals," said Marva. "The minerals and what they look like tell you a lot about where the rock came from."

"Igneous," said Rachel. "That's a kind of volcanic rock, isn't it?"

"Right," said Marva, her broad cheeks creased in a smile. Within ten minutes of Marva's arrival Rachel had established that Marva was a geologist down from the University of Tennessee in Knoxville, that she was an expert on southeastern mountain ranges, and that she was looking into the geology of Queen's Peak for a regional research project. If Marva wondered why Rachel was peppering her with questions while the "real" reporter exuded all the verve of a lobotomized cow, she didn't let on.

"It's funny," said Rachel as she helped herself to some more baked beans. "You don't normally think of rocks as deserving scholarly attention. You chuck them into ponds, pull them out of the garden, climb them for a good view, all without being particularly conscious of them. Rocks are just rocks."

"Oh, but rocks are words the Earth uses to record its own history," said Marva, her blue eyes brightening. "They tell a four-and-a-half-billion-year-old story. In poetry, no less." She paused to clean her hands on a napkin. "Sometimes when I'm having a hard time falling asleep or if I'm anxious about something, I'll repeat the names to myself because they're so beautiful. Olivine. Dolerite. Gabbro. Travertine."

Marva herself was beautiful as she crooned the names of the rocks she loved. I realized as I watched her that it was her passion more than her size that made her seem so robust and strong. It animated every word and gesture, and made anxiety sound like an impossible emotion for Marva to have.

"Ellie, don't you have some questions you want to ask?"

Rachel smiled as she spoke, but I knew she'd caught me staring at Marva. Marva looked at me expectantly.

"Well, I've been wondering," I said, falling back in desperation on the truth. "What have you been up to this week? I've seen you all over town and one night I even saw you poking around the riverbank."

"A good reporter never sleeps, eh?" Marva laughed. She reached for the canvas bag and pulled from it a stack of paper. From the pile she took out a large square sheet with what looked like a giant fingerprint on it. She pointed to a section near the bottom left-hand corner.

"These are geological surveys of the region around Queen's Peak," she said. "And this is the area to the west of downtown, near the river. See how close the topographical lines are? That means it's quite hilly."

I nodded. The slopes of those hills were in every muscle I had. Marva then laid a thin piece of tracing paper over the map. Jagged lines penciled on the paper intersected the map's topographic circles like so many varicose veins. "Well, those hills

lie along a series of small cracks in the Earth's crust. I've placed
a number of tiltmeters there in the last couple of days because
I'm working on a hunch that the cracks are going to act up
sometime in the near future.''

"What are you saying," I said, staring. "An earthquake?"

"Probably only a small one." Marva tapped her finger on the
map. The tracing paper made a dry, crinkling sound. "The cracks
don't constitute a major fault. They're just in a weak part of the
crust. The meters I put out will pick up changes in the slope as
small as one ten-thousandth of a degree, and if that occurs rapidly, you're looking at an earthquake about to happen."

I didn't know what to say. The squiggly lines on the
map seemed to shimmer under Marva's hand. Somewhere over
those lines ran streets I knew, Cherry and Gordimer and
steep River Bend. I rode them nearly every day and they'd always felt solid under my wheels, reliable as gravity, structural
as bone. Now I knew different. Somewhere far below, bones
lay broken and strain accumulated. At least, there would be a
warning.

"Of course, often there's no tilt at all beforehand," said
Marva. "The earthquake just comes." She shuffled the maps
back into her bag. "I've been a geologist for twenty years and
it always impresses me how little we can predict. Fortifies my
faith in Mother Nature, you know what I mean?" She looked at
me, her blue eyes kind and deep as lakes. They didn't comfort
me at all.

"That was fun," said Rachel.

"Fun usually implies laughter," I said, pointing to my
clenched jaw. "I'm not laughing."

"Oh, loosen up." Rachel placed another washed plate into the
rack. Steam rose from the sink to add a touch of rose to her
cheeks. Or was it from excitement? The thought, for some reason, terrified me.

"Rachel, this could get me fired."

"Just pass along the tip to the editor. He'll be so happy to

get a big story like this he won't even remember you imperson-
ated a reporter. Really, that was very clever of you.''

I narrowed my eyes, feeling more witless by the moment.
Everything seemed as if it were tipping away toward some cock-
eyed horizon that had sprung up out of nowhere, challenging the
sky and redefining my vision. I reached for a dishcloth but
Rachel airily waved me away. "Oh, don't bother. They'll dry in
the rack overnight.''

At this I panicked. "Okay, what's going on," I said, slamming
the towel across the counter. "You always insist we dry the
dishes at night. Water droplets breed bacteria, remember?''

"I know," she said, patting my arm. "But it's time for me
to take a few chances in life, don't you think?''

"Don't pat my arm," I hissed. I had just flashed back to a
moment earlier in the evening, after we had walked Marva down
to her Jeep to say good-bye.

"I wouldn't want people to overreact," Marva had said.
"That's why I've been doing a lot of my work at night, to avoid
raising anyone's suspicions. The newspaper story should put
things into perspective. All that's likely to happen is a little
rumbling.''

My brow must have furrowed because she reached over to pat
my arm. "Really, it's a good thing," she said. "Earthquakes
make the mountains grow.''

Now Rachel reached over to flip off the kitchen light. The
apartment's only illumination, a soft rich yellow, came from the
lamp in our bedroom down the hall. She stretched out a hand
and I let her pull me close.

"Ellie, I don't know precisely what I'm asking," she said.
Her breath warmed my neck. "I don't really know what I need.
But I'm always here for you when you come back from one of
your flights of fancy. Can't you be here for me?''

We went to bed after that but I slept fitfully. Sometime near
dawn I gave up and went to my bike. The streets were empty
and awash in that silvery gray that heralds the coming of light.
I kept looking at the pavement, alert for any signs of rifts or

fracture. Unfortunately, the signs were many. Street repair wasn't high on the list of the town's budgetary musts. Every crack, every depression kicked an extra beat into my already struggling heart.

Finally at the bottom of Tank Hill I pulled over by a tall burr oak whose whispering crown seemed to disappear above me into the dim but brightening sky. I can't live like this, I thought, my breath hoarse and ragged. I have to believe there's something solid under me or I'll go crazy. That's when I thought of Rachel and noticed how my breath slowly steadied. I thought of Rachel, and of a day in spring when she had stood alone and naked in a slippery bathtub, an arm flung skyward in defiance. I thought of all this, and I got back on my bike to finish what I had started.

Up Dale, down onto Park. A left at Fuller where sometimes Mr. Cotteridge lets his terrier off the chain for a run. Fuller rises to meet Grant, which stretches out along the ridge for a good three blocks, at the end of which Rachel slept, dreaming of a child whose name, I now knew, was not Bosco. The ridge looks flat when I ride on it, but an imperceptible gradient always speeds my journey home. By the end I was coasting, pedals still, legs at rest. And the faintest of rumbles drifted up from my wheels, spinning faster and faster on the ground.

A Kosher Megila

Lexa Roséan

On Purim one is supposed to get so drunk as to not know the difference between Haman and Mordechai or shall I say Hitler and Schindler. It is a once-a-year release equivalent perhaps to Halloween as the reading of the *Megila*[1] of Esther is followed by a masquerade. My sister and I went as Buffalo "Yankel" Bill and "Chana" Oakely. I fashioned a mustache, goatee and chest hair out of fur clippings from our Old English sheepdog. The poor bitch had a few bald patches for several months. I sprayed my hair white and tied it back under a Stetson except for my long curly forelocks which I let hang down Chasid style. I had on a little western shirt, gaucho pants, cowboy boots, *tzitzis*,[2] a holster, cap guns, and a long lasso. My sister wore a suede fringed skirt with cowboy boots, a dress shirt, ponyskin vest, a holster loaded with two small freshly baked *challahs* and a Dolly Parton wig underneath her Stetson. It is the tradition to make up *spiels* or little plays to entertain each other.

My sister sang "I Want To Be a Cowboy's Sweetheart" with a Purim twist: *"I want to be a Chasid's sweetheart. I want to*

---

[1] Story.
[2] Fringed undergarment worn by Jewish men. It symbolizes the 613 commandments or *Mitzvot*.

*learn to bake a kugel. I want to cross the Red Sea and the desert
to the land of the great Western Wall. I want to hear the Chasids
prayin', while the sun sinks in the west. I want to be a Chasid's
sweetheart, that's the life that I love best. L'chiam. Mazel Tov!''*

As she sang each verse I would lasso in a different girl, wrap
her tight around my hard body, and like the world-famous poster
heralding the arrival of Buffalo Bill, I would shout *"Je vien"*
"I'm coming!" It was a night to be remembered, perhaps the
happiest most carefree night of my life. A night when innocence
and sensuality still held hands. A night without *Havdalah*.[3] Without separation. A night when our enemies and our heroes became
one. Each girl stood in line waiting for a turn to be lassoed by
the Great Buffalo Yankel. Finally at the end of the line I saw
my beloved Bible teacher, adorned as a Catholic nun. As I pulled
her close to me she tugged playfully at the pair of socks stuffed
in my crotch. She smiled and kissed me. Full on the lips. The
kiss of a woman. All the girls gasped and stood back awed in
the circle. I shot my cap pistols in the air and shouted *"Je vien"!*
I felt like a cowboy riding a bucking bronco in the Cheyenne
Frontier Days. All the sweet ladies smilin' and gigglin' behind
their fans titillated by my prowess. I felt like the Red Sea about
to part. Miracles all around me. I *was* the Burning Bush. My
lips, both sets were vibrating. I was ridin' high in the saddle. I
was the closest thing to a guy in the place. The next thing I
knew I was thrown; laying face down in the dirt. Rabbis Flower
and Stern had entered the saloon. The Sheriff and the Deputy
comin' after the outlaw. Showdown at the *Chaf K* Corral. I
reached for my pistols. They were capless. When time's running
out, close yer eyes, pick another time. Pick another place. Pick
another outlaw . . .

The chagrin of old Pharaoh when the Wonder Jew boys
crashed his party and pulled out their rods—old Pharaoh and his
mages pulled out their rods. Everybody turned their sticks into

---

[3] Prayer said at the conclusion of the Sabbath, to separate the holy from the
secular or profane.

writhing snakes. Easy trick. Then Moses and Aaron broke out
in stuttering song: *mmmy GGGod's bbbetter than your gggod
mmmy GGGod's bbbetter than yourn. MMMy GGGod's bbbetter
cuz He's gggot a chchchosen nation, mmmy GGGod's bbbetter
than yourn.*

"Sagacious fucks," thought Pharaoh, "what do they think the
Egyptians are, chopped liver?"

The biblical brothers tap danced to the tune of their Lord and
their snakes ate ole' Pharaoh's snakes. Swallowed them up in
front of all his court . . .

You don't crash somebody's party and show them up too.
Especially with a choreographed miracle. It's a sure way to
harden their heart. I hung my head in resignation as Rabbi
Flower proclaimed that the party was over. Miss Kossack removed her hands from my cock I mean sock, smoothed her habit
and turned her gaze downward. Rabbi Flower eyed her suspiciously. I pawed my boots dejectedly in the dirt. No one noticed.
The attention and the focus was now all placed on the men.
Rabbi Stern insisted that he was a *Mezuzah* for Purim. He attached himself to the doorpost and insisted all the girls kiss him
upon exiting. He was obviously fulfilling the *Mitzvah* of Purim,
having had enough alcohol in him to not know the difference
between a *mezuzah* and the Pope's ring. Rabbi Flower eyed him
suspiciously or perhaps jealously and Stern released my sister
who had been cornered in the doorway. Released her after kissing her full on the lips and inserting his tongue in her mouth. It
was in that moment that I saw him break all his precious rules
of *Nige'ah.*[4] It was in that moment that I believe my sister re-
solved to one day marry a Rabbi. It was in that moment I understood the heart of Pharaoh. Learned it in a way no Bible class
could ever have made clear. I watched all the girls form a circle
around the Rabbis and listen ardently to the closing words of
wisdom they offered. They told the story of Queen Vashti and

[4] Ethical code of behavioral conduct between men and women. Touching any
woman over the age of menstruation besides one's wife is not permissible.

how she had refused to dance for the king's court. And how the King had cut off her head for her insolence. Ever reminding us to be women of valor they sent us home.

That night I dreamt of three women. Woman *A* had huge nipples with an infant hanging on each one. She had the face of a heifer and wore a disheveled wig. She was serving a large platter of meat to a well-groomed man. He sat at a long table with a white linen cloth. There were Sabbath candles lit in sterling-silver candelabras. The light reflected off his face. Her face was hidden in the shadows. She placed the platter of meat on the table and backed away into the darkness. His face became very bright and he said, "It is good. *Tov.*" Woman *B* was dancing naked under neon lights. Her breasts were pierced with golden rings. The hands of men grabbed the rings, pulled them; the men shouted "you're good baby, you're sooo good." Woman *C* was a headless whirling dervish. Her body was covered with colorful veils and from the top of her neck a fountain of blood spewed forth. She held a sword upraised in her right hand. On the sword was her severed head. The mouth was open but produced no sound. Then I was in a ballot booth with three levers marked *A*, *B*, and *C*. A sign said "Select *one.*"

I AM THE L-RD THY G-D. THOU SHALT HAVE NO OTHER GODS BEFORE ME. Sometimes I used to wish G-d would just lighten up. He is like a jealous incensed lover. Too monotheistic for His own good. It is my belief that a healthy but moderate amount of flirtatious idol worship can only enhance the primary relationship. One god cannot be all gods to every person.

Miss Kossack had become the dark goddess. The cruel and punishing goddess. The *Shekina* hidden in a cloud. Her grace turned away from the nation of Israel. After the Purim incident she refrained from all physical contact. Instead of those precious and exhilarating slaps and ear tugs she would just order me into the trailer. The dreaded trailer. The offices of Stern and Flower. The out-of-place addition to the warm brick-red schoolhouse. The place of fear. She would stand at the foot of her desk and point a huge finger at me across the room. Sometimes not even a word. Just a huge finger of banishment. Let the Rabbis deal with me. I would plead with her with my eyes. But her eyes dared me to indulge in even the sense memory of her kiss. It was the period of prohibition. My cunt was dry. It was the darkest hour, but by dawn I would learn that every desert has its oasis. There were long hours spent waiting in the trailer. When the Rabbis were teaching they were not in their offices. I would spend time with their secretary. The good goddess. Lenore. Lenore was beautiful. Thin waist long lean legs and a huge bust. You could always see her hard nipples through her bra. She wore a blond wig although she wasn't married. It is customary for married women to cover their hair. I always wondered what color her hair really was. I thought it must be chestnut. To match her eyes. Whenever Lenore and I were alone in the office, she would put her work aside and read me poems by Lawrence Ferlinghetti and Alan Ginsberg. Poems about love and fucking. Lenore was not religious but very spiritual. I always wondered how she got the job. Stern and Flower were so meticulous about outside influences. We only had two. Lenore and Jose the Mexican janitor who was the designated Shabbos Goy. Employed to do the work forbidden to Jewish hands. Lenore used to tell me I was a lot like her. That I didn't really belong in this place. Whenever I asked her what she was doing here, she'd wink slyly and say: "just hiding out."

Facing the Rabbis became intolerable after a point. Always these long discussions about the minute details of why I had been sent in. Always lectures, stupid lectures. Then threats. It seemed like sometimes I just got sent in for looking the wrong way at Miss Kossack. I could no longer bear the look on their faces upon finding me waiting outside their offices.

I sought and found a haven. Whenever Miss K would send me down I'd give Lenore a kind of forlorn look and plead: "Just hiding out?" She'd smile and turn in her swivel chair allowing me to crawl in the space under her desk. She'd swivel back around and conceal me. Sometimes squeezing me between her legs. One day I fell asleep with my face right in her lap. Man I felt so close to something. I don't know what. Just so close. It got to the point where I would crave Lenore's legs and just do something purposefully antagonistic to get out of those Bible classes and into the safe haven between Lenore's long luxurious legs.

The Rabbis never saw me when they came back from their classes. No one even noticed my absence. Lenore's smile was always deeper when I hid out. People would come into the office and say so. I wasn't learning much Torah those weeks but I never wanted to leave the safe haven of Lenore. She would stay after school let out and everyone had gone. Then she would release me from my little cage. Sweetly kiss me good night. Only my sister and Jose would witness this. Everyone else was blind. Lenore Lenore Lenore. Sometimes I would pretend to fall asleep; curl my body in between her knees and rest my head on her lap. Her skirt would climb up allowing my face to rub against her thighs. Peeking under her skirt, I could see the black and gold garter fastened to scented stockings. The smell of Frangipani would make me dizzy. I would close my eyes, barely breathing, and imagine Lenore holding me in a headlock between those fabulous gams. I wished I could run my hands up and down her silken calves and thighs. I wanted her legs to dance around my head, to squeeze my neck, I wanted to feel her heels digging into my back. I thought of those beautiful sexy pictures of women I had seen in *Playboy* magazine. My father kept a stack of them in his underwear drawer. I used to sneak them out when I was home alone. First I would sit in a chair, cross my legs and squeeze them together tightly as I leafed through the magazines. Then when I found a woman I really liked, I would lay down on the bed on my stomach with her picture under my face. I would push my nose across the page inhaling the ink. Circling my nostrils around her nipples. Imagining what they would really feel like. Then I would press my lips to her lips. Careful not to open my mouth. Once I got so carried away that my tongue drooled all over the page, and where the model's breasts and mouth had been you could now read the print from the page behind it. Her breasts and mouth were completely worn off the page. I was terrified if I kept this up, my father would notice that someone was fucking with his magazine collection. So with

pursed lips and a pillow under my pelvis, I would rock my hips
and thrust my pounding clit. Run my engine and imagine driving
right into this beautiful bunny. Slam bam pow. Knock that bunny
right outta the road. Drive my throbbing clit right into her. This
masturbatory ritual would always end on the same note. I would
neatly fold and replace the magazines; smooth the sheets on the
bed; then kneel beside the bed, hands clasped, recite the *Havdalah* and pray for my father to change his evil ways and cancel
his subscription.

One afternoon—it was the day after *Simchat Torah*, that is
the day the Jews celebrate receiving the Torah from G-d at Mt.
Sinai—that afternoon, as I lay in her lap, I felt Lenore's hand
on the back of my head, stroking my hair.

I remembered the day before, I had felt a gentle hand on the
back of my head pushing me forward in the crowded synagogue,
pushing me toward the Torah. I felt the hand on the back of my
head as my lips moved forward to kiss the sacred scrolls as they
passed. Everyone dancing around them in a frenzy, lifting them
high above our heads, the scrolls out of the ark twirling, dressed
in their ornate jewels. I watched in awe as someone lifted the
jeweled cloth covering from the Torah. Up on the *Bima*, the
scroll was lifted and unrolled. Sounds of chanting, the reading
of the sacred passage, filled my ears. Moments later the scripture
was carried down from the pulpit into the crowd. Again a hand
on the back of my neck, pushing me up front. My lips pressed
forward touching the naked parchment, kissing words, my
tongue rolling across sacred letters.

Lenore lifted a leg, kicked off a shoe. Placed my hand on the
small bulge of her garter strap. We pressed it together and it
came undone. Slowly we rolled down the black silk stocking
exposing one glorious leg. It was like undressing the Torah. Lenore squeezed the biceps at the top of my left arm. "Sweetie,
would you massage my feet? I've been on them all day."

"Sure Lenore," I whispered beside myself. As she removed
the other stocking exposing a second glorious leg, I touched my
bicep where she had touched it. I began to wrap the first stocking
in a tight spiral seven times down my left arm. When Lenore

handed me the second stocking, I stretched it taut across my forehead, doubled it around and made a tight square knot right between yet slightly above my eyes. I felt faint. In the darkness of the crawl space under her desk, the holy words my tongue had touched danced before me; *Bind them as a sign upon your arm and let them be as frontlets between your eyes . . . Sanctify*[5]

Lenore speaks: *All things please the soul,*
Parts her legs, *but these please the soul well.*
I press my face into her lap as she instructs:
This is the female form, A divine nimbus exhales from it from head to foot . . .
She pushes a foot under each of my hands. I lift my head from her lap. Sejant before her, I am Lenore's own heraldic animal. My ears become erect at the sound of her voice, my nose lifts to catch her scent, my hands press into her arches.
Lenore sighs and continues to read:

> *It attracts with fierce undeniable attraction, I am drawn by its breath as if I were no more than a helpless vapor, all falls aside but myself and it . . .*

She is reading me a new poet. It is not Ginsberg. It is not Ferlinghetti. Kneeling between her legs I can see her panties. I can smell detergent underneath the Frangipani and something else. I circle my nose in the air trying to decipher the bottom note. It is Sheila. No, it is like Sheila only more musky. I think of where I had left off with Sheila. If only Sheila had let me smell her and not just the material that lay next to her. I feel myself dripping. The dry spell over I think of Miss Kossack. I see her finger wagging and pointing over scriptures. Lenore's voice shatters this image.

> *Books, art, religion, time, the visible and solid earth, and what was expected of heaven or fear'd of hell, are now consumed, Mad*

[5] Deuteronomy 6:8, Exodus 13:2.

filaments, ungovernable shoots play out of it, the response like-
wise ungovernable . . .

Lenore pauses and purrs. Her feet curl in my hands. As a sign
of encouragement she once again places her hand on the back
of my head stroking my hair. I want her to push my face forward,
past the endless thighs. I want my lips to graze against the pubic
hair peeking out from her panties. I want her to push my face
close enough to kiss the Torah. I want to bury my tongue in the
sacred letter *V*.

Hair, bosom, hips, bend of legs, negligent falling hands all
diffused, mine too diffused

My hands fumble. The left one, blood swelling, pulsing to the
beat of my heart, drops her foot and grasps her thigh. The right
one, becoming confident, follows suit. My hands knead like the
paws of a kitten burrowing into its mother's teat. I push my head
into her lap wanting to feel the soft milk pour over my tongue.
Craving the taste of her heavenly manna. The arches of my feet
begin to tingle. My clit goes hard. Begins to throb.

Ebb stung by the flow and flow stung by the ebb, love-flesh
swelling and deliciously aching,

Sounds in the darkness. Sex noises? They must be sex noises.
The noise of my sex or of her sex? An electric humm. Pit pat.
Pit pat. Thrump thrump thrump. A bell rings. Awestruck, I identify the sound. The distinct sound of a carriage return. How can
she type, recite poetry, and have her thighs massaged all at the
same time? Just as I think her talents and concentration have
reached their zenith, another bell sounds, sharper, several in suc-
cession. Lenore momentarily interrupts the poem to answer the
phone.

"Modest Daughters of Israel. May I help you? Friday at
4 P.M.? No that's *Erev Shabbos* we'll be closing early. No deliveries. Could you come on Monday? Yes, thank you for calling."

Lenore danced in my mind like one of those beautiful Indian goddesses with eight arms.

"Let's see now where was I?" asked Lenore hanging up the phone. "Lee do you remember where I was?"

"Deliciously aching," I moaned.

"Very good," she said continuing:

Limitless limpid jets of love hot and enormous, quivering jelly of love, white-blow and delirious juice . . .

My hands shook and sweated against her thighs. On my knees before her I felt my butt muscles begin to move involuntarily. My clit thrusting forward meeting the empty air. I closed my eyes and my shaking thighs tight. My whole body quivering I was—

Lost in the cleave of the clasping and sweet-flesh'd day.[6]

As Lenore delivered the last lines of the poem my knees spread out from under me and I sat right on her foot. I felt a hot squirt of cum escape from my vagina. I was mortified. I knew it had leaked through my panties and touched her bare foot. I sat frozen under the desk.

"Perhaps Whitman is too much for you," Lenore said knowingly, while slowly inching her foot out from under me.

I was trembling. Thinking of a way to save face. Trying to remember the name of the poem.

" 'I Sing The Body Electric'?" I asked.

"Yes, you certainly do," Lenore laughed and pushing her feet against the inside of the desk, she rolled back to look at me beneath her.

"What have you done with my stockings?" She gasped.

"I just, umm, I don't know. They reminded me of *T'fillin*," I said.

[6] Walt Whitman. "*Leaves of Grass*", from *Whitman Poetry and Prose*. NY: Library Classics of the United States Inc. 1982.

"You mean phylacteries?" Lenore laughed. "But why?"

"The poem seemed so holy. I wanted to remember it. The *T'fillin* are supposed to serve as reminders," I said.

"What would the Rabbis think?" Lenore shook her head.

"You won't tell them will you?" I said my eyes bulging.

"No, of course not. The same way you won't tell them about your nonapproved literature courses."

"It's a deal," I sighed in relief.

Lenore began to unravel her stocking from my arm. "You know you're a little kinky," she said.

"Kinky?" I asked while pulling the second stocking off my head. "Am I having a bad hair day?" I brushed my fingers through my scalp.

"No, kinky. It means perverse. Although I like to think of it as unconventional in a sophisticated way," she responded.

"Really. Do you think I'm sophisticated?" I asked as I clumsily handled her stocking putting a huge run in it.

"Actually no, I don't," she said eyeing the stocking. "But I believe one day you will be quite sophisticated in many ways."

"Do you really think so?" I asked while sheepishly handing her the torn stocking.

"Yes I really do," said Lenore and she bent over kissing the red mark on my forehead that had been made by the knot of her stocking.

Julie

Susan Fox Rogers

Julie Tullis and I were brought together our junior year of college because we had both been abandoned by our roommates of fall semester. Julie's roommate Katie had abruptly transferred to another school, and rumors had it Katie's parents had insisted on it. Julie and Katie were lovers, the most prominent lesbian couple on campus.

When Julie appeared at my door she didn't look like someone who had just lost a lover. There was a tautness in her cheekbones, but that only made her look older, more experienced than the rest of us. Otherwise, she looked like Julie had always looked, her eyes open and focused, curious about the world.

"I'm Julie," she said holding out her hand.

I knew who she was. Along with a dozen other girls I had had a crush on her for a good part of sophomore year. In those sexually confusing times, we all were drawn to Julie, because she was so definitely, so absolutely a lesbian. We were sure she was born knowing the language, walk, and talk. And, we all assumed, she also knew the sexual moves. Somehow, if we could touch or be touched by her it would resolve all of our questions.

During that year many did have their questions answered. But I was not a part of these sexual initiations into the world of women's lovemaking. It wasn't that I didn't want to be a part of Julie's harem, it was that I had unconsciously decided to explore the depths of longing. I now think of it as my year of the nun and it was my last attempt to find a life in a women's community before I fully succumbed to my lesbian desires.

"I'm Alexandra, Alex," I said.

She nodded and smiled, "I know." I remembered days of unwanted adrenaline rushes and weak knees, what it felt like to live with a crush on Julie.

We had been given the option of moving into either her room or mine and Julie had come over to assess the situation. She sat on my bed, and looked over at what would be her half of the cinderblock room: one set of drawers, one desk, one small twin bed. I lived in Livingston dorm, the newest building on campus, which promised constant hot water, a working heating system, and three phones per floor. But beyond that, the rooms were without character, didn't hint at the offbeat past this small, expensive liberal college had weathered.

"I think my room is nicer," Julie finally said.

Julie and my friends Sandra and Joan helped me move my stuff into Julie's room that afternoon. It was an airy room, with leaky picture windows that looked out onto a large field, covered with snow, and then beyond to the Catskill mountains on the other side of the Hudson River. The room consisted of an unworkable fireplace, one desk, and a king-sized bed with six white pillows.

"What's with the bed?" Sandra whispered to me.

I shrugged. Later, Julie offered to put the bed into storage and retrieve our assigned singles, but I sensed that she didn't want to relinquish her bed.

"It's okay," I said. "I'll stick to my half." Though I knew I wouldn't sleep well. The first night I lay tense on my side of the bed until the lights were out, and darkness had fully settled in. Then we began to talk. She told me about her family: her mother who had left, her spacey father, her twin sister Lisa and younger sister Danielle. The three sisters were all gay, she explained. I laughed as I considered the odds, and figured this was the one time a parent was allowed to ask: what did I do? As Julie talked

I felt as if I had entered another world of family life and relations so attractive yet remote from my nine-to-five, two-week-a-year-vacation family: my father the pharmacist, my mother the librarian, and my sister the straight A at Ohio State. Because I had gone east to college, had pierced my ears more than once, and could imagine beyond a four-by-four family life, I was the rebel in my family, but not in this school where everyone had their own shrink and history of family madness.

As I listened to Julie talk I wanted to be a part of her family or to have a family like hers that was full of emotions and opinions and real-life struggles.

Our talk trailed off around three that morning.

Julie and I became lovers two nights later. First our limbs entangled, then our lips, as if the whole thing happened by accident. For the first two weeks we pretended to each other and to the rest of the school that nothing had happened. But every night we crawled into bed and remained on our sides until darkness had completely settled in. And then we reached for each other, exhausted but excited. We never slept before three and often it was later. If it was near dawn we would get dressed and walk down to the river to watch the sun rise.

Julie taught me everything there was to know about young lesbian love: how to give massages, the joy of love notes found under the pillow or in the middle of my anthro notes, candles to make love by, and the importance of talking in bed. Once the lights were out, and only a candle was illuminating the room, a certain ease fell upon us. We called it the truth of the night, and it allowed us to feel safe to talk, to say what we felt, and wanted. I told her when my nipples ached for her mouth, and she told me when she wanted me deep inside of her.

And then one night Julie pulled out a silk tie and securely fastened my hands to her bedframe. To an inner music, she stood and danced for me, her hips moving with the help of her hand. And there in our tiny dorm room I thought I was at once participant and witness to the Perfect Orgasm.

From that point on, we joked that we were the women in search of the Perfect Orgasm, or the P.O., and she often asked

idly, while standing in the cafeteria line, if I had checked my
P.O. box that day. We thought we were hilarious, creative, the
discoverers or inventors of love and sex, and that we had invented it right.

That semester, I was awake to the world, and despite my sleep
deprivation my studying improved: I got an A on my anthro and
feminism midterm and aced my weekly French quizzes. I was
fully aware of the wonderfulness of that spring semester and also
fully aware it would never last.

I never dreamed Julie and I would stay together and we didn't.
But we were together long enough that she taught me how to
love being a dyke, long enough for me to meet, and fall in love
with her family. It was spring break and instead of going home
to Ohio as I had planned to do six loads of laundry, and let my
mother feed me, I accepted Julie's invitation to come to her
home in Westchester County. I wanted to meet this family that
I knew but couldn't imagine.

"I don't want you to meet my twin," Julie said one night as
we were lying in bed after making love.

"How's that?" I asked.

"Because I know you'll fall in love with her." She said it
matter-of-factly.

And I did fall in love with her. She looked exactly like Julie:
short brown hair, olive complexion, deep brown eyes and tall
and slender with no hips. But where Julie's energy was all directed outward, Lisa pulled you in. It was as if they had been
born opposite ends of a magnet, one positive, the other negative.
Julie was the seducer; Lisa the seduced.

"You know you'll break my heart if you sleep with her,"
Julie said.

It hadn't occurred to me that Julie's heart could be broken,
that she could love me enough to allow that to happen.

Most of the sexual energy in the house emanated from Danielle, who as babiest butch of the family, was trying to follow,
perhaps surpass, her sisters' seductive charms. When we played
games of O Hell and Hearts she rested a foot on mine under the
table. At meals she always served me before everyone else, and

she didn't seem to be able to change into the slim T-shirt she
wore to bed in her own room. The first night we were there, she
walked into the spacious room Julie and I were sharing, her top
half off, then stood, naked except for her black underwear, her
small brown nipples slowly becoming erect from the attention,
from the awareness that they were the focus of the room.

"Strip for someone else, sweetheart," Julie said.

I laughed.

"I came to ask if you guys want to go to Joan and John's on
Saturday. It's girl's dance night."

Julie shook her head. "I don't want to dance."

"Do you want to go, Alex?"

I loved to dance. "I'll see," I said.

Danielle and I did go dancing that Saturday night, with a
group of her friends. She introduced me to dozens of women
and we danced close for all of the slow dances.

"Do you like my sister?" she asked on the way home.

I nodded in the dark. I loved her one sister and was infatuated
with the other. But it was Danielle who was kissing me softly
in the car before returning to the house.

I pulled away. "No," I said.

"Did she make a pass at you?" Julie asked as I wrapped
myself in her sleepy arms.

"What do you think?"

"Brat," she called out. "Whore." It rang through our bedroom and rapped around the quiet of the house.

I wondered what Mr. Tullis, who I was to call Bob, thought
of this evening commotion.

"He's used to it," Julie said. "He gave birth to three butch
dykes, who have been bringing girlfriends home since they were
thirteen."

"Does he ever say anything?"

"He's cool."

I wondered if he might just be out of it, oblivious to his daughters and their ways. He was a gentle man, tall and long-limbed
like his daughters. He spent his days and evenings painting in a
large studio attached to the house. At first he tried to cook for

us, but after three dinners that were variations on eggs we took over.

It was clear that the parent who ruled the house was the absent mother, the mother who had left when Julie and Lisa were five and Danielle three. They called her Kris, not mom, and during my visit, she called twice from her home in New Mexico. Both times Julie refused to speak to her. It wasn't that she hated her mother, that was too strong a word. It was almost as if having a mother was optional, and Julie had simply opted out. From Julie's perspective, though, it was her mother who had opted out.

"She doesn't want to be my mother, she wants to be my friend. Or rather she wants to be me," Julie explained calmly. Yet I sensed a pain in her body, and I knew that Julie's calm was only temporary.

I smiled and hugged her, unable to really understand her pain. I did the only thing I knew to help relieve but not take it away: I made love to her there in her childhood bedroom.

I wrote to Julie over the summer and she called and wrote as well, more often than I expected because I knew she had fallen in love again. More than being jealous I was intrigued, curious, and told her not to worry: my heart wasn't broken, I loved her still, always would. My love for Julie was the most curious, unpossessive love.

Through senior year Julie told me of her seductions and I told her of my crushes. When we said good-bye at graduation in the spring of 1977, I thought it wouldn't be for long.

Julie moved to San Francisco to work in public television and I to New York City to work in book publishing. We called and wrote to each other and I also kept in touch with her family. Danielle wrote to me regularly, telling me about her landscaping business, her girlfriends, the restaurants she would take me to if I visited. And I wrote to Lisa, who had become a writer with a few published short stories, telling her to continue to write, to send me her manuscripts. And I told her of the restaurants I would take her to if she came to visit the city.

It was three years before I was able to fly to San Francisco for a week to see Julie. She showed me her favorite hangouts, bars that catered to gay men.

"Sometimes I need the energy here," she explained.

Julie and I slept in the same bed, stayed up all night talking. She told me about her last love affair, her lack of faith in relationships. And she talked about her family. The struggles between the three sisters were active, political, emotional, as if all of the nasty infighting within the lesbian community over style, ethics, class, and race were being waged in a distilled form. Lisa fought for the working class, and didn't want to discuss sex; Danielle had a lipstick girlfriend and was seriously bourgeois; Julie had been dating a Chicana woman and neither of her sisters, she was convinced, understood the importance of race. It didn't matter that they were all dykes, family was family, and being gay only seemed to make the issues more serious, more volatile.

The biggest war for the three sisters was over their mother. Their mother had just come out, had recently moved to San Francisco and was living not more than a mile from Julie.

"What are the chances?" I said with a quick laugh.

"But she's not a dyke," Julie said.

"How can you be sure?"

"It's something you know," Julie said. And it was true Julie did seem to know. All through college she had had an uncanny ability, not only to select who was who or what on campus, but to predict when, as she termed it, they would flower. Sometimes she was instrumental in that flowering, the Miracle-Gro of sexual discovery, but sometimes she simply watched at a distance as two nineteen year olds stumbled into love. She would smile and nod and say, "the world is a better place." Not so for her mother's coming out.

I knew Julie wanted a mother, just not the one she got. And it became clear that she had realized she couldn't simply opt out. She was beginning to wrestle with her mother.

Julie was single that trip to San Francisco, and I was going through a promiscuous stage. I was surprised, actually delighted in my sexual life and Julie was the only person I felt I could

talk freely with about this, the only person who would understand and not judge. So I told her of all my women, except one.

On my last night in San Francisco we made love. It felt wonderfully familiar. I remembered every part of her body, the soft
small roundness of her breasts, the smell of her body, musty
deep like olive oil. It was that smell that I wanted to mark my
body. The women in my life came to me in unexpected often
unwanted places through smells I associated with them. And I
wanted Julie to linger in my mind when I smelled that smell
walking the streets of the Lower East Side, or while eating a
plate of tomatoes with fresh mozzarella in Little Italy. I wanted
Julie to come to mind because Julie made me smile.

As Julie and I lay in each other's arms, watching the sun come
up, she said, "You know you are the only woman who ever left
me."

I pulled away to better look at her sleepy face, to see if her
eyes were laughing at me. But they were mostly closed, as if
maybe she had spoken from a dream.

"But I didn't."

"Of course you did," she said, her eyes still closed.

"Remember without editing," I said. It was my refrain those
days, a rule I handed out to friends, and the authors I was working with.

"Editor that you are," she smiled.

"No, I just believe in the truth."

"Then you left me."

"Summer vacation. What was her name. Exotic, beautiful,"
I hesitated. "Sonya," I remembered.

"That was a crush," she said. "You I loved. My whole family
loved you. Danielle tortured me all summer telling me she had
slept with you."

"She did," I said matter of factly.

"Brat," she yelled into the emptiness of her apartment. We
were silent a moment. "Why didn't you tell me?" she asked.

"I was too new at this game. Too embarrassed. Too in love
with you."

"But later?"

"It seemed beyond the point. I guess I should have. But honesty, responsibility, where does it begin and end?"

"Never ends with us. You have to tell me everything." She squeezed my hand, rolled over on her side, fully awake now. "I'll tell you anything, everything you want to know."

I smiled.

"Was it fun?" she asked.

"Please," I said.

"Truth of the night," she whispered.

"How could I say? It was in the front seat of your family's car. We'd been drinking rum and cokes, smoking cigarettes. It was too quick to be fun."

"Did you ever sleep with Lisa?"

"No," I shook my head to emphasize my innocence. Truth of the night. "I couldn't. You said it would break your heart."

"Looking out for my heart?"

"Yes," I said quickly, almost defensively. "Yes I am."

Julie kissed me. "I know you are. I'm sorry." She lay for a moment in silence. "I did," she said flatly. "Lisa was the first woman I slept with. I guess that's pretty normal with twins, but we didn't stop until we were sixteen." She hesitated. "I've never told anyone that."

It actually didn't surprise me. Nothing about the Tullis women surprised me anymore.

"Have you ever talked about it with her?"

She shook her head, "Why?"

"I know a few shrinks who would love to get their hands on you."

"You're the sick one," she said grabbing me, pinning me to the bed and then kissing me on the lips.

"Promise you'll always tell me everything," she said.

"Everything," I repeated, knowing I was already lying.

And then her tongue trailed to my ears, my neck, my breasts.

The years passed and Julie and I found less and less time to write, call, get together. But when we did talk it was as if we had just spoken the day before. And if I didn't hear news directly from Julie I heard it through her sisters or the lesbian grapevine. Mostly it was girlfriends lost and found and Julie's new sexual toys and tricks—nothing that surprised me. But the news I couldn't believe was when I heard she had settled down, bought a house, was contemplating having a baby. It didn't sound at all right, it didn't sound like Julie and so I had to go and see for myself.

I flew out to San Francisco and took a taxi from the airport to the bus station, and then north to the suburb where she had settled. I was prepared for almost anything, except for the sight of Julie. She had gained about one hundred pounds and I could barely wrap my arms around her to say hello.

"You haven't changed," she said to me, leaving me somewhat unfairly with nothing to say in response.

"I know I have," she said softly. "This is Sheila," she said, introducing me to her girlfriend. Sheila was small, compact as if she might have been a gymnast. She had black hair, black eyes set below dark eyebrows and she seemed to stare at me with a measure of hate in her eyes. I tried not to take it personally because there was no reason she should hate me. Maybe, I thought, she hated the world.

Sheila had made brownies for my arrival. She had us sit, brought us tea, and left us alone to catch up. I didn't know where to begin. Julie's new weight weighed on the room, was like a wall set up between us, though we sat side by side, often touching, and always looking each other straight in the eye. But for the first two days I felt like we were talking over or through that wall in secret code so that Sheila couldn't understand. The problem was, I couldn't understand either. I wondered how someone who had stood so tall, been so physically self-conscious could have changed so.

Julie didn't want to go out: moving was painful for her so we sat, and talked and ate when Sheila fed us. When Sheila wasn't hovering over us she was on the phone behind closed doors. Later, she would emerge glowing, flushed, to feed us more, to make Julie comfortable. Somehow everything Sheila did added to the electric paralyzing heaviness in the house. So I was more than relieved when Sheila announced she was going to visit a friend in the city for the weekend.

"She's good to me," Julie said once Sheila was gone.

"She does take care of you," was all I could respond.

"No one ever took care of me. I always wanted my mother to take care of me, make a peanut-butter sandwich, even once. But she always wanted to be my friend, maybe even my lover. Who knows how twisted she is."

I found myself thinking that Julie's mother had finally caught up with her, taken her over.

"Does she still live out here?"

"About six blocks away."

"What is she doing, following you?"

"Sheila runs into her at the bakery, the Shop Rite. She's beautiful, Sheila says. Has four earrings in each ear." She laughed to herself.

"Have you ever talked to her?" I asked.

"Why bother? What would I say, 'you can't live in this neighborhood,' or 'you can't be a dyke.' "

"You could say 'leave me alone, lead your own life.' "

"She does. I never see her. I never even talk to her. She never asks me for anything. The only way I know what she's up to is through Lisa and Danielle. They talk to her. They even like her. They tell me I'm just paranoid."

"That's helpful," I said.

"You see I'm being the mean one, the awful one."

"Right," I said. But suddenly I wondered if maybe Julie didn't half believe them.

As I crawled into bed that night and that now-familiar suffocating air weighed down on me I felt wound up. I had an urge to leap out of bed, drive down to Kris's house and yell, "Leave Julie alone, leave your daughter alone." Instead I got up and walked across the hall to Julie's room. The door was ajar and I pushed my way in, letting in a ray of light. She didn't seem surprised to see me. She simply parted the covers and slid over to give me room to lie down beside her. It felt warm, comfortable to be in the same bed with Julie. Lying next to her, my head resting on her shoulder, her physical size seemed unimportant. It was the familiar smell that I wanted to inhale, the texture of her skin that I wanted to feel.

"Thanks for talking," she said. "Sheila won't let me talk about my mother. She says I get too wound up. I'll have a heart attack." She laughed. "I suppose I could."

"You're not going to have a heart attack talking about your mother. You might if you don't, though," I said.

"Umm," Julie said. "What to do?" I could tell she was much nearer sleep than I was. We lay silent for a moment, and I felt more calm.

"Do you think Sheila would mind that I'm in bed with you?"

"No, she'd love it. Then she wouldn't feel so guilty."

"About?"

"Her girlfriend, of course. Isn't it obvious she's fucking around? I think she might be the phone sex queen of the valley."

I laughed, relieved that Julie wasn't oblivious to her life, to her girlfriend's activities.

"I'm the wife. I stay at home." She hesitated a moment. "You know, I never saw myself as a wife."

"Does that bother you?"

"What? The wife or the fooling around? I've become the master masturbator. I think I have ten dildos, every color, size, and shape."

I laughed again. If Julie were no longer seeking the perfect orgasm then I would worry about her.

"It's weird, after all those years of sleeping around I'm now lying in bed, watching everyone else do it: my lover, Danielle, you, God, even my mother." She pulled away from me. "Did you ever meet Kris?" she asked the question as if she were surprised she didn't know, or that she had never asked.

Truth of the night, I thought. "Yes," I said.

"Where?" Julie asked. "Out here?" She asked it innocently but I could feel her body begin to tense.

"In New York. In a bar."

Julie sat up, and looked across the room, out the door. I could hear her breathing heavily. "She slept with you." She said it slowly, softly.

I didn't say anything.

She threw back the covers and got out of bed, moving faster than I had seen her move all week. She pulled on her overalls, and put on her large flattened tennis shoes.

I didn't get out of bed, only watched her energy build. I knew I couldn't stop her. I knew what she was going to do and I didn't want to stop her.

"Let me explain. Let me tell you," I offered.

"I don't care," she said. "I'll be back." I heard the screen door slam behind her.

It was two in the morning when she returned. During those three hours I tried to read, tried to watch television. But all I could do was replay my affair with Julie's mother. It had all happened quite by accident on my part, and it was only later I realized it had been perfectly planned on hers. For several week-ends running she had appeared at my favorite local bar, Cousin Sallie's. She just watched me in an obvious way, from a distance. Besides the burn of her gaze, I was drawn to look at her because she was quite stunning. Had I looked more closely I might have seen Julie, thirty-five years older: tall, slim, with creases of wis-dom around her eyes and thin lips, and graying hair that gave her a dignity, a sophistication I liked, was attracted to. But even once I offered to buy her a scotch on the rocks and asked her her name I didn't put it together. There are plenty of Krises in the world.

We talked that first night, and exchanged phone numbers. As part of my aggressive dating campaign, I called her on Tuesday and set a date for Friday. She talked about her pottery work, her trips to an ashram in Massachusetts. She seemed uniquely with-out family ties. And then she asked me about myself: a hundred questions as if I might have the most fascinating life. She asked me home and I accepted.

Her apartment on the Upper West Side was spacious and un-derfurnished except for a king-size bed: the Tullis trademark, I later thought. It was a gentle, exciting night with only the usual awkwardness of first encounters, and we set a date for the next weekend. The apartment was more furnished six days later. Photos were on the wall and a table had been added to the living room. While she was in the kitchen preparing drinks for us I looked at the photos. My heart raced madly as I stared at one that was too familiar: Julie and Lisa hand in hand in their front yard, age four. Julie carried the same photo in her wallet.

I had my coat on when Kris returned with my glass of wine. "I can't stay," I said.

She looked at me without expression. "Is it the photo?" she asked.

"You knew?"

She was silent. "Do you want to talk?"

"No," I said. It felt completely perverse, all wrong that this had happened. There was no way to make it right. As I walked home, I realized she had come to find me, to sleep with me, to seduce the woman all three of her daughters, but especially Julie, were connected to.

Julie's eyes were glowing when she walked through the door, bringing in a gust of cool night air. Julie didn't look angry, rather she looked like someone who had just run a marathon: exhausted but elated, victorious really. She went straight to her bedroom and lay down on her bed.

"She listened to me. I think she listened to me." She sat up. "Help me," she said lifting her arms above her head. I slipped her T-shirt over her head, then I helped her pull her pants off. She crawled under the covers.

I crawled in next to her, wrapped my arms around her.

"Tell me," I said. I rubbed her back.

"Tomorrow," she said. She lay still for a while and then I sensed that, exhausted, she had dropped off to sleep. I soon followed her.

Early that morning, before the sun was up, Julie rolled over and I felt her body push against my left arm. I reached for her, kissed her without being fully aware who I was kissing.

"How nice," she said kissing me on the forehead. "You awake?"

"A little," I said.

"Will you go on a walk with me?"

"Sure," I said. "I'd love to."

She began to move, to get up.

"You mean now?" I asked. "It's five-thirty in the morning."

"What's happened to your sense of adventure? I want to watch the sun come up."

"You're serious," I said.

We were dressed and out of the house, heading for a hill a mile away that would give us a view of the world, Julie promised. We didn't talk much on the walk, only tasted deeply of the fresh morning air. Everything was green and wet and I understood how people could love this country. The sun was slowly lighting the sky when we reached the top of the hill. She sat for a moment, breathing heavily, staring down onto the green field below her and, in the distance, the Pacific Ocean. I stood next to her, quiet, listening to the silence, to Julie's deep breathing. Then she rolled onto her side and began to tumble down the hill, rolling, laughing in the high green grass. I could hear her laughter rising from the earth as she came to rest. I stooped down and tumbled after her, laughing as I came to rest beside her. Then I moved so I was lying on top of her looking into her eyes, both of us breathing each other's breathless breath.

"The only woman who ever left me," she said. I started to protest, but she continued. "Sheila might too, but maybe she'll never be brave enough. She pities me too much."

"That's awful. I've never even thought of pitying you. And I never left you either. We've been through this before." I tried to sit up but she wrapped her arms around me, held me close.

"You're the one who got the apartment off campus senior year," she said.

"Remember your girlfriend that summer, and the half dozen fall semester?" I hesitated. "I can't believe we're going over this again."

"It's the facts game," she laughed.

"But it's true. I didn't leave you."

"Maybe true in detail, but not true in feeling. I've begun to

separate the two. You let go of me the end of junior year. I went
because that was the mode I was in: seduction campaign 100.''

"Or 101,'' I added.

"In therapy last year I realized I didn't want us to separate. I
was still in love with you.''

I was almost holding my breath.

"Maybe I have always been in love with you.''

I held her closer. "Jesus, Julie,'' I said softly.

"Kiss me,'' she said.

I kissed her lightly on the lips.

"No, really kiss me.''

I hesitated. "I can't.'' We lay staring at each other in the early
light. Our bodies felt warm together though it was still cool out
and our bodies were wet from rolling down the hill. "I'm looking after your heart,'' I said. We lay in silence for a while.

"Thanks,'' she finally said. "Thank you.''

I smiled, then let my body slip down next to hers, worried
that I might be crushing her.

"No, stay,'' she said. "This feels good.''

A Room, in a
Stone House, in Spain

Jenifer Levin

When she winked I followed her into a laundry near the Patis-
serie de Tunis. Crazy clothes spilled from her panier into the
machine basin: dyed purples, beige faded to grayish yellow
stained with mustard and red wine. She held up a tiny green
shirt.

"My son."

It was half proud, half apologetic. I asked how old but kept
smiling, and she seemed to relax then, told me four years last
month.

"Nice birthday party?"

She grinned; I spoke French terribly. It seemed a wise
expression on her, not cutting at all, white teeth glowing
suddenly against the background of smooth light-brown skin,
full lips tinted red. Our hair was the same color, almost
black; mine was short, though, hers past her shoulders, and
I wondered for a minute, disturbed, whether it was the simi-
larity or the difference that had led me thoughtlessly this
close.

"Pardon. It's your first time here."

I nodded.

"France pleases you?"

"No."

I left it at that. Why bother? What I'd come here exiled from, Israel, the army, grape harvesting and machine shops and bullets and fatigues, another life I'd torn myself out of—it all seemed like old news, like something lost quite long ago.

"You're Spanish? Italian?"

"I'm a Jew."

Ah, she said, as if that explained something quite puzzling. Then, with a mixture of discomfort and relief: "You know, so am I."

She shook some faintly blue detergent into the stew of clothes. Soon the washer rattled away, cloth spun wetly, momentarily meshed together, made vibrating rainbow streaks against the round little window. She had sad dark eyes that I wanted to kiss shut. I wanted to kiss her neck.

"Matches?"

I didn't smoke but found some anyway in a pocket, lit her Gauloise nonfilter and waited almost breathlessly until she puffed out the first heavy cloud and cocked her head at me, shrewdly evaluating, then nodded once, accepting my homage as her rightful due. I leaned against another machine. Felt something changeless in me spin through the dissipating smoke over washers and dryers, rise feather-light to peer coolly, painlessly down on the wintry damp streets of this shabby arrondissement, and on her, and me.

Somewhere a machine creaked open. Steam poured out, with a smell of sodden cloth. Then doubt cleared from her face and she smiled back at me, softly teasing, puffing doughnut-shaped clouds, until I blushed and looked away. In the too-large woolen sweater and sagging denims, American style, she seemed terribly small for a moment, and frail, never mind the tough filterless hanging from her lips. I noticed that her boots were worn at the toe, but a good black leather; that the scarf she'd arranged around her neck was bright multicolored silk. There was pride in that —there was vanity. Somehow, too, there was danger. I got a burst of courage then. The changeless thing inside that made me different, strange, like some creature out of place and time, nodded, and moved me a little closer.

Her apartment was small, very shadowy and old, in a shabby building just a few streets away and a few flights up, so it made perfect sense to help her carry things there. Inside it smelled of ginger and other things. She turned lamps on, drew curtains, shutting out the night. Then it made sense for me to light her another Gauloise, and for her to serve me tea. I watched the bright tips of scarf disappear into some small vestige of kitchen where she ran faucets, clattered with pots and silverware, and I settled back in a worn old sofa and looked and sniffed around. Not just ginger, I smelled, but the yellow paste of turmeric, ripe raisins, crushed almonds, salty oiled olive skin mixed with the scent of sweat and powder, of damp city streets. I thought immediately of flat bread and grape leaves. Then imagined going into the kitchen and walking up behind her, reaching gently around to hold her breasts. The room and the smells made me terribly homesick, although for what place, in what time, I didn't even know, but tears abruptly filled my eyes. She came in holding a big tray full of cups and saucers, and I had to brush them away—the tears, I mean—they couldn't have been explained; at least, not in words. Then, a purely physical fear pounded me back and forth: she probably wanted someone more refined on the outside, a lot tougher on the inside, more worldly, someone free and careless and pretty. I was tired, probably inattentive and numb from all the traveling; my touch might disappoint her.

"Sugar?"

"Thanks."

On one shelf was a tarnished old menorah, base crusted with white wax. Bound bunches of dried wild flowers. Over the traces of an ancient arch, now filled in by wall and poorly plastered, Jesus hung from his cross, rough-cut wooden feminine form twisted in a distinctly Spanish agony: ribs protruding, slender muscles and internal organs striated clearly against the dark-brown skin, face framed by black hair, blood streaming over the closed, anguished eyes. So clearly out of place and time here, in cuisine-conscious, style-conscious France; I stared at it a long time, then back at her, full of questions and surprise.

She sipped her tea, amused. I suddenly understood.

"Your people—Marranos?"

She nodded, at me, at Jesus. "Yes, sure, long ago. They brought him with them from Spain."

"Your parents were born here?"

"No. Morocco, Algeria, everywhere."

That was all she knew, she told me. Anyway, the past was the past. It hardly mattered. Her family did not speak of it much.

Ah, I said, as if I knew the story. I didn't, really; I barely knew my own. From Spain some had managed to make it to Turkey, Moldavia, Romania, had met and mixed with Russian and German and Polish blood; how much by consent, how much by duress, no one alive would know. And few were still alive.

"Would you like to see my son?"

"No."

"Why not?"

My French was too poor to explain. I barely knew why not myself—and how to say, anyway, that I wanted to know her only as a woman, not a mother; that I wanted just certain pieces of her, now, nothing more, for reasons and terrors of my own. She seemed momentarily disappointed, then just shrugged and sat.

She began folding clothes, plucking baby socks from the overflowing panier and rolling them into tiny white pairs. It occurred to me that she was right; the past might not matter at all—at least to us here, in this room, this life, in the flesh; and wasn't it, after all, her flesh that mattered to me really, right now, and her eyes and breasts and lips—that mattered much, much more than any status of motherhood, or peoplehood, any gaping erasure of history?

I put my tea down unfinished and stood and went around behind the sofa, ran unsure hands through her hair, bent to press a cheek against it, began massaging her shoulders.

That's sweet, she said, just like that. That's nice and strong and sweet.

Later we were both standing somewhere else on a worn old rug, halfway between the menorah and Jesus, facing each other, very close. She seemed much easier with it all, much more relaxed than I, telling me just when to kiss her, how much and how deep, and how good it felt, sometimes sighing to close her eyes. When they opened I'd examine them—looking for something, I thought, some sign of love or fear or memory—and I noticed they were green-brown with flecks of orange and gray in them, like mine.

"Would you like to come to bed with me?"

Her hands fluttered very softly along my hips, persuading. What about your son? I asked, and she said, simply, It's late, he's asleep. Then her hands became bold and pulled me right against her, rocking us both back and forth, so that after a while she began to breathe very quickly, I no longer felt tentative, or worried about being too gentle or too rough, and the whole standing, rocking motion we made together developed a kind of urgency and recklessness, I could feel the control of things shifting to me, and the momentary sweet anonymous helplessness of her need—as if there was something that could burst right out of me, through my skin, my clothes, through hers, and reach deep to touch some hungry wanting thing inside her.

Down a hall with an old tiled floor, in a closet-sized bedroom, in the mess of sheets and a warm tired colorless quilt that smelled like her, between lamplight and cheap shades and curtains that kept out the cool damp breeze of night, she took off her own clothes and I began to strip too, then stopped, the dark cold strange little thing inside, that could deform me sometimes and save me at other times, begging me, now, to go only so far. Seeing this, she smiled. It was a gentle smile, utterly soft and knowing and female. She opened a drawer and took things out. In the dull light I watched, surprised and almost amused, smelled leather, aluminum buckles, rubber or silicone forms of different sizes and colors. She brushed past me naked and I smelled her hair and flesh. She lit her own cigarette.

Okay, she said, you choose.

Then she sat on the bed and watched, smoking. Remnants of her smile remained.

I was afraid but intrigued. And admired her for doing this: here, by asking me to choose what I'd fuck her with, she'd force me to reveal at least a little of myself, too. How did I want to represent myself, to her, tonight? Big and hard and dangerous, too much to take? Small, playful, energetic, inventive? Or something in between? Knowing that, this first time, I'd choose only what I could handle. In the end I chose but undressed only partially, strapping the harness around my naked waist. It had been years since I'd used one of these. Something hot and stinging blurred my eyes. But I remembered without fumbling. The trick was in the tightness. Everything else instinct, just a motion that fits.

We pressed together in a fleshy textured place you had to close your eyes to see, and feel: dark red behind tight-shut lids, brown nipples, musky sea smell when I kissed the insides of her thighs, understanding all over again why in Spanish and Ladino the word for conch shell is the same as the word for cunt; just momentarily, as ever, that customary twinge of shame stopping me—that I could desire without love, could feel myself utterly carried off by the feel and sight and smell of her, drifting willingly in and out of control, and all this without knowing her; I barely knew her first name. It was supposed to be different. Love and desire were supposed to be the same for us. To feel any other way was to feel as a man; was, almost, to be a man.

Still, here I was. Here we both were.

I made love to her, pressing inside when she was ready with the toy that wasn't really a toy, just a tool I'd chosen that might hurt her sometimes, or sometimes give her pleasure. But I was more enchanted than I knew. Causing pain was the furthest thing from my mind—though I did want to hear her cries and, when I did, felt myself melting and almost lost control. Cars sloshed through puddles on the city streets. Far-off sirens wailed from a Premier Secour ambulance, passing by into silence. She was covered with sweat and a soft, soft relief, opening my shirt, kissing

in a straight line down along my body. No, I told her, no, there's
more isn't there? and pulled her back underneath between damp
flesh and sheets and pushed simply, easily back inside her. All
in the motion and, this time, I had the rhythm and the old, old
feeling back again. I half-crouched over her and could smell
olive oil somewhere, held her feet on my shoulders, whispered
ungrammatically in several languages that here we were, in a
little room somewhere in a little country, she wanted something
she'd seen in me and so I was fucking her, once, twice, and it
felt oh so good, didn't it, to be so deep inside her, what a miracle.
On the bed I could feel her shudder, tense, swell. This time she
moaned long and hard, a sound beyond relief or pleasure, like
aching, or crying.

Later I let her fuss with all the buckles and straps herself. She
shoved them unceremoniously off the side of the bed. The little
harsh cold shadow of me gave off warning signals the closer she
got to belly and cunt. I held her head in both hands, guiding,
forbidding, encouraging, as if I really could control her and myself. I spread her hair out right, left, to cover each thigh, until
the hair was a cape safely swaddling me, and I stroked her head
and watched until my eyes flicked shut and I couldn't watch
anymore.

She slept, off and on, and until two-thirty a.m. I held her.
Then I got restless and she must have sensed it, sitting against
pillows soaked with the smell of us both, searching along the
nightside table for a cigarette. I reached across her for matches.
Struck one alive in the dark, perfectly, dutifully. In the sudden
light, like a firefly tail, thought I saw tortured brown Jesus on
the wall, watching. The Gauloise tip glowed orange ash. In
stilted French we talked some, then—she about her job, and old
girlfriends and boyfriends; and I told her a little about America,
Israel, the army—but what we said, really, I wouldn't quite remember. In the dark her eyes looked large, glittered with a kind
of humor; and every once in a while, between thick musky puffs
of smoke, she'd run a finger along my lips and pout, and giggle.
When she finished the cigarette we started to kiss again. I

glanced sideways, once, to a cluttered nightside table, an alarm clock, an ashtray, a last fading ember, imagined it a prowling glowing eye riding weightless over the bed, urging us on. She slid underneath very easily and naturally, as if we'd been doing this every night for years, and pulled my head down until her mouth was right up against my ear. "Will you? Try to put your hand inside me?" Oh, I said, can I, may I please?

Afterward I slept, and had a dream: of me and her long ago, on a pallet, on a floor, in some hot and foreign climate. The air smelled of firewood and smoke, dried fruit, livestock, hot baked stone. A single blast of conch shell reverberated, through the dust of a sun-seared afternoon, called the faithful to prayer. She was then as she was now, but I was different—physically, maybe, or in some other way; and, whether male or female, I could not tell. There was the sense of life being difficult but often satisfying. Bitter. Frightening. Treacherous and mystifying. Yet expansive somehow, full of sun and air, curiosity, occasional laughter, love. We had a child, a dark little toothless laughing boy. On the bed, in the afternoon heat trapped by stone floor and walls, echoing with the last almost-musical blast of conch shell, air filled with a smell of almonds and of raisins, animal hides, a child's dusty pounding bare feet. Cattle moaned. Outside, people rolled in pits of crushed dark grape, making love, intoxicated, clothes drenched as if with blood.

I woke and wanted to tell her. She was sleeping, though. The tiniest hint of sunrise had seeped through curtains now. I slid out of bed feeling tired and anxious, as if I'd lost something important, and would never get it back.

Still, I had to pause and admire the way she breathed so fluidly, delicately, thin shoulders sighing in untouched perfect rhythm. I noticed, in gray light mixing now with the closed dark fleshiness of the room, that there were faint stretch marks along the sides of her breasts, across the slender belly. She was a mother, irrevocably. It seemed to me utterly regrettable, yet somehow magnificent.

I was still glad, though, that I'd refused to see her child;

this—a pretty woman, naked in bed and peacefully asleep after
lovemaking, skin faintly marked by life and other women and
by a few men and even children—this was the way I wanted to
remember her some day; and I certainly didn't mean to get into
it any deeper. Kids were a hook—you could ignore them, and
thus stop things between you and another woman dead in their
tracks; or you could set an endless roller coaster of emotion
going by opening your arms to them; but, in either case, once
the designation Mother got tossed into the pot, the relationship
stew would never be the same. On the one hand, I had been
traveling too long and was exhausted; it would be nice to know
her name, and, if she agreed, to spend a few harmless days with
her here in Paris. But on the other hand there was the problem
of the kid; and, after all, I told myself, I had had enough of
mothers. Now, thankfully, love was not involved. I could simply
avoid that kind of trouble, could quietly move on.

We always like to believe we are in control.

I stepped into the hallway, upper arm rubbing along the wall
for direction. In the boxlike bathroom with a big colonial tub
taking up most of the space I found and pulled a dangling string
until a single dull light bulb switched on, glittering against a
water-speckled mirror that I avoided. My own reflection was the
last thing I wanted to see. I did check her little cabinet, though,
for drugs. Sleeping pills, tranquilizers, these things were as easy
to get in Paris as crocque-monsieurs. After months and years of
the peculiarly volatile hyperconsciousness required for Middle
Eastern survival, this kind of readily obtainable oblivion was like
candy to me and, ever since arriving in France, I'd turned to it
often. Not even for sleep, really, but for a pleasurable, hazy
tranquility to blur the edges of each moment. Predictably, she
had several bottles of prescription things in very low dosages,
and I took one of each. Then perched on the bathtub ledge, let
my shirt fall off, and ran hot water first. The building's pipes
started grinding bitterly behind old walls. I glanced up at the
light bulb, lost track of time, slowly cranked on the cold water
too and then, after eternity, eased down sliding and almost
drowning into the steamy enveloping bath. I rested my head

against a faucet. Remembered the dream. Something about it was
disturbing, had made me want to cry—I remembered, now: the
smell of raisins and of almonds, of hot baked stone and a woman
and a child and a southern climate that was mine, all mine.

Let me stay here with you, I breathed into the steam. Let me
stay here with you like I did in that past life, in your house that
smells of ginger and turmeric and raisins and almonds, grape
leaves, flat bread, a child, our people. Don't make me leave.
Don't send me away again. This is my skin, my climate. Hold
my head between your breasts. Let me find that place once more.

The urge to cry dissipated, drifted. A serene drowsiness crept,
seeping, from my toes up, spun me in a web of tranquil sleepless
relief.

Was it real or hallucination, the brown sleepy-eyed boy standing between toilet and doorway, yawning, asking in a barely
comprehensible baby French, Was I one of Mommy's friends?
I heard myself tell him: Sure I am. Fumbled for the plug. Listened to the water start draining away in sorry sucking noises.
He rubbed his lumpy brown belly button. Stuck a thumb between
his lips, watching me calmly.

"Mommy's asleep?"

"Yes."

"Why?"

She's tired, I told him, sometimes big people get tired.

All the water drained and suddenly I didn't feel serene any
more, just small and beaten, shivering naked without the shield
of steam and heat around me.

He was a pretty little boy, her coloring, her eyes. There was
something familiar about him. Then I knew: I had seen him
before, both recently, and long ago: He was the child of my
dream. Of course. Utterly familiar, though I had tried not to
know him; probably unavoidable—in fact, inescapable—no matter how much I tried to evade him, or her, or whatever fully
fleshed present-day life we might enjoy, together, between the
shards of past and future.

I'd taken too many pills and my eyelids were starting to roll,
down, down. Before they shut completely I heard her voice in

the background—sternly questioning, in French I could not quite
understand, a mother's tone—and I ran cold water suddenly,
splashed myself awake, stood unsteadily until I was more than
twice his size, standing there, naked and dripping, a fumbling
foreign woman. Tranquility washed me again, along with a
dimly felt exhaustion. Panic withered away inside. Then I was
rooted to the colonial bathtub, the French ceramic spot, smiling;
trapped by serenity drugs, and myself, and by a woman and a
child. Her voice came closer. I could leave soon, yes. But it
would be nice to know her name.

I reached for a half-clean towel. The boy blinked and yawned.
When I wrapped it all around I noticed that his little dick was
pointing straight out at me while he yawned, like an invitation,
or a warning.

What We Do in Bed

Lydia Swartz

My lover has AIDS. We're lesbians. You either ask what we do in bed or wish you had the audacity to ask. This is what we do in bed:

I pull two latex gloves out of the box on the headboard—one for her and one for me. She holds up her good hand (the left) and I smear KY jelly on her fingers, then help her into the glove. She bites my neck (carefully) and nips and sucks my breasts while I gel my hands and fumble into my own gloves. She lies on her partially paralyzed right side, propping herself with pillows so that she's not increasing the pain in a damaged nerve, and so she can touch me with her good left side.

It's 11 P.M. on Thursday night. She tries to tell me something about her complex relationship with Judaism, which is her mother's cultural and religious heritage. I rest my head on her numb right arm and she gestures with her left. She elucidates the tenets of Judaism as they relate to lesbianism and socialism. She talks about her mother and her mother's mother, and cries. I don't intend to, but I fall into an exhausted slumber while she is still talking.

She wraps a black T-shirt around my head, blindfolding me. I can hear her walking around the bed. She teases me by speculating on which toy she should use on me and how soon the first one will strike me and how hard. She puts her hand between my legs and feels the wetness through my panties before she's touched me with any of the toys. I'm drenched already, which makes her chuckle evilly. I hear something whistle down and thunk next to me on the bed. The martinet? The whip? I tense in fear and anticipation.

We argue about her ex. We argue about my ex. We argue about arguing about our exes.

I pull her down on her knees and lean her over (or she pulls me down and leans me over) my lap (her lap). Then I slap her (she slaps my) buttocks, spanking hard, soft, and in between, until both sides of her (my) ass are warm and red. No matter how cold the bedroom is. I pick up her (she picks up my) pleasure through her (my) cheek on my (her) thigh, where she is (I am) crying out as the spanking grows more intense. She manipulates (I manipulate) my (her) clit through my (her) panties. I pretend (she pretends) not to notice even though my (her) clit is sticking out a mile, not to mention how wet it is. Then I sharply push (she pushes) her (my) hand from between my (her) thighs and say(s) "NO!"—and increase(s) the force of the spanking.

She reads a draft of the story I'm working on while I curl by her side, pretending to be half asleep. She laughs heartily. I forget to pretend I'm sleeping and ask her, "What part? What part?"

She is on her back, leaning on a pile of pillows. She is moaning. Her legs are parted. Her hips toss and thrust so vigorously that I can barely keep my thumb on her clit and my fingers inside her, and keep my other hand pushing the dildo into her. She yelps and gasps, "Harder! Ouch . . . O yes!" My own cunt is streaming and I'm leaning into her, pushing against her thighs while I fuck her. She's so hot and wet I get that sensation that panicked me when it first happened: I can feel her so well, it feels like the gloves are missing, maybe torn, maybe pulled off. I can feel her skin, her moisture. The gel inside the gloves stings small cuts on my hands; it feels like her own moisture on my skin, in my skin. I'm so aroused and sensitive I can feel each of her individual pubic hairs—through the gloves. The smell of her cunt, my cunt, the warm latex is making me so hot it almost feels like the dildo is inside my own cunt.

She coughs and coughs until she gags. I think about having to get up in five hours and face a day of meetings with young MBAs who dream only of their next car, boat, house—my clients. I cradle her breast and feel disloyal. I see her scowling at the dark. Then her eyes close. She dozes. Her right arm twitches. Her right foot jerks, kicking me. It's involuntary; she doesn't feel it or wake up. My hysterectomy scar hurts. I can't sleep. I want to ask her to go sleep downstairs. I feel disloyal.

I tell her a story about a bad girl (her) who is forced by her mistress (me) to walk out in the almost-cold autumn woods and choose her own birch switch. She claims she doesn't like stories. She claims they don't turn her on and they just make her uncomfortable. So I have handcuffed her to the bedposts. I tell her about the girl being roughly pushed over a mossy fallen log and sternly told not to move or it will go more badly for her. Especially considering how wicked she's already been. She squirms. I tell her about the caning the bad girl gets from her mistress. I tell her about the girl begging and tingling. I add details. She likes this story. I punish her for liking it. She likes that. I like the story, the punishment. I like her liking it.

She's downstairs—asleep, I hope, but more likely spending another hyperactive, sleepless, nausea-plagued night listening to short-wave radio and corresponding with people via computer BBS. I've come upstairs to sleep. I finish reading the last chapter of the novel and lie bleakly staring at the ceiling. I don't know I've fallen asleep until I dream that she has died and has come back to visit me, standing at the foot of the bed and looking at me with love and longing. She is whole, healthy, smiling. Slender, like she was before she got sick. Aggressive. Hungry. I want her, too. I wake up crying.

She likes it rough. I like to give it to her rough. I paddle her bottom until it's red with white bumps. Until I can feel the heat standing a foot away. I keep it warm and glowing and whack her across both buttocks when she's least expecting it. I move around her, move from side to side. She thrashes and moans. I check in with her. Her eyes are huge and soft. I snatch at her ear with my teeth. She nips at me—not even close to giving up. I start on her back with the martinet, first through her shirt. Soft. Brushing her almost . . . just . . . not quite. Then one, two sharp ones, muffled by the shirt. She's too hot for much of that. Her back humps toward me. Greedy bitch. I push her shirt up, bunching it around her shoulders to keep it out of the way and to protect the area where she doesn't like to be struck. I inspect the skin, put tape over a couple of small lesions. I whisper to her and she whispers back. Something around her kidneys? OK. I get the magic marker. I poke gently with one finger in a concentric pattern on her side and she says "OW!" or "OK" at each touch. When I have the shape of the sore spot, I draw an oblong around it to remind me where to avoid. Today she wants the martinet, and I give it to her until her back is striped from the lengths of it, speckled from the tips of it. I feel her crotch just to be sure. Soaked. I'm dripping down the inside of my legs, too. I sit down on the edge of the bed, pull her forward onto my lap and let her nudge into my crotch while I finish her off with the belt. (Two days later, the resident in the emergency room glances up at me when she notices the odd, rather pretty little violet bruises on my beloved's back, and the magic marker circle on her side. I stare back fiercely, challenging the doc to ask. She looks away quickly and says nothing.)

I'm furious with my lover for some reason neither of us understands. I'm yelling at her. I want her arms around me so badly I ache all over. When she reaches out to touch me, I slap her hand away.

It is so long since we have made love. Her pain has been devastating. The bruises on her buttocks are not pretty; they come from shots of Demerol, not from my sweet belt strokes. When she can sleep, when the medication lets her dream, she has vivid images of us together, of her loving me with both arms and with all her strength, of doing everything we want to do for, to, and with each other. I dream too—of being more playful, less careful, of pushing her and letting her push me. I wrestle with her phantom self. My phantom self rolls in sweaty abandon with her. One night late, I am holding her (real her) and patiently explaining once again that everybody in the room except her and me is a hallucination. She can't get over it. But wasn't there a man here asking . . . ? So I explain again. She nods off for a few minutes. Then her eyes pop open, startled, dark. She asks if I want to make love. I am horrified and ashamed of being horrified. What if this is our last chance? What if she notices I am horrified? I cannot touch her. And I want her, and I'm afraid she's gone forever.

Our wet thighs and bellies are pressed together. My cunt remembers her hand. My hand remembers her cunt. Her breasts are smashed against mine. She is gripping me with her good arm, I am holding her so tightly our hearts touch. I have my face in her neck, her hair. And hers is in mine. I want her for 20 years. I suckle on her earlobe. With any luck, she won't notice I'm crying. I love you I love you I love you.

The Vale of Cashmere

Gerry Gomez Pearlberg

I. Three Seasons

Wintertime is suspension—snowflakes dangling like bad decisions in the air, her breath hanging like a veil about her, her eyes continually averted from the disinterested sun, body lumbering through its nights and days as if in exile. Then comes springtime and the renewal of Wanting—new blooms froth on their branches, slow-digging insects make their way back to the surface of the soil, birds sail between the trees like vivid ships in the hesitant unmooring of dawn.

But summertime is a whole other story. Fast and furious, she smokes again, drinks again, writes poems and stories and diaries again. She unearths the mirror and likes what she sees, rises early to wander the summer-empty streets with her dog, and sleeps beside him on the cool linoleum floor in the midday heat. She takes long, cold showers at dusk and rubs herself down with oil, slaps cologne on her cheeks, buttons her white sailor pants and wanders onto the ancient streets of her boiling metropolis in search of adventure, or failing that, love. She's attracted to the naked arms of the other women and men who roam there, the loiterers and meat packers and bookworms and stoop-sitters who seem to come out of the woodwork with the nearing of the sun, its perpetual attentions. It's summer and everyone is searching for something—the touch of flesh, a glance prolonged, a priceless moment spent in that elusive dangling between the Wanting and the Getting and the Having Had.

In the summer, cigarettes embody all of this and more. She worships them, though she knows it's wrong. It feels good to worship something so wrong. To revere an unpopular goddess feels strangely pure, and the more her friends complain about the smell infiltrating their clothes, the sexier that burning becomes, the more she searches for traces of it in the sheets, on her person, and on the lips of those she desires. She never pays for cigarettes—she always steals or borrows or barters for them. And she never ever pays for kisses. Or returns them once given.

On summer nights her room is permeated with the smell of smoldering matches, flowering trees, mango slices on Fiestaware, and pornography folded under the bed in wings of sheet. In this room reside all the moments between her own particular Wantings and Gettings and Having Hads. The room is crowded with them, moments that stand around dumbly staring, aching and remembering, picking lint off their suits, and endlessly bumming cigarettes from one another, cigarettes they'll never smoke, for these moments have no matches.

II. Statuaries

Alone on the balcony on cool summer nights, after brief but tumultuous showers, she'd watch the newly transgendered wandering arm in arm in the rose gardens below, dancing like scissors in a darkness peppered with white and yellow blooms. Their silvery dresses seeming to absorb the moon's luminescent puddles of forlorn cologne. Their arms shimmering like blackberry branches, white gardenias, alabaster, amber. Sometimes they'd pull their capes over their heads and twirl in place, their queer oscillations igniting the leaves and branches in a thrilling artificial light. And she desired these transsexuals she was not supposed to want, with their hormones and their surgeries and their scars, with their litanies of sorrow like anyone else's sorrowful litany, anyone else's hormones, surgeries, scars. She envied their transcendence of the most seemingly final of destinies. That transcendence was something she wanted to put her hands on, to French-kiss in the dark.

Sometimes, before going to bed, she smoked alone in that garden. Cool nights, after summer showers. Leaning bare back into the shivering trees, she'd watch the fountain's serpents and dolphins spouting stars from lips of mossy stone. The lighting of a match exciting the undersides of the leaves and branches above her, thrilling them to spurts of green and brown in the pitch-black dark. The air seemed so much more fragrant in the darkness, as if the flowers—the lilacs and the lilies—expanded and became more porous in the privacy of nighttime, allowing themselves to be lifted, released, and absorbed by the atmosphere with an abandon barely imaginable in the light of day.

It was in this darkness of spurting color and scent that desire would course through her, a sea monster slithering wildly through the canals of yet another summer where things happened too fast—where lovers came and went and transmuted into enemies or acquaintances, where friends grew thin and prepared to die, and where exquisite summer days were passed in air-conditioned hospital rooms easing ice chips between cracking lips.

In those days the streets were anything but a way of getting home. They were a way of life, a canine territory, an arena for cruising ungendered strangers. The streets had a mind of their own, a dangerous, hidden personality that only the ones who were looking could detect—the ones with night vision, the ones with perspectives altered by the inhospitable lights of too many hospital hallways, by endless processions to the tombs of heroes, by the perpetual passages of friends and lovers into strangers, enemies, the dead. For those so attuned, all streets led to that most dire of all possible worlds: the perilous statuaries, playgrounds, and gardens that women were not supposed to even know about, let alone speak of, dream of, approach.

III. Outskirts

On the night he died, a giant lemon-yellow moon overtook the whole corner, stunning me with its bright and lonely face, moving me to wander the streets like a hound in search of a stranger who would touch my body, who would see me through. I headed east toward the river, to the narrow park along the sparkling shoreline where women are forbidden to go at night. To the playground, the abandoned jungle gym. The moon cast shadows there as sharp and certain as compass needles pointing to indelible new worlds.

She came out of nowhere. She rode around me on a blue bicycle. Around and around and around in a circle, radiant and magnetic, beautiful and absurd. It was she who said, "Will you fuck me, or shall we call it 'making love'?"

She jumped off the bike and it clattered to the ground. She stood before me, a planet on display. I watched her pull her dress halfway up so it covered her face. Her jockstrap shone like a moonbeam. She groped for me blindly, pulled me to her, and kissed me through the veil of the dress. Stepping out of the underwear, she pushed me down before her, and, defying gravity, poured my fist up into her like a hot ore, a semiprecious metal. Lips perched on the top of my head like a tiny hat. A hot black moth alighted between my shoulderblades, clasping and unclasping its wings. "That's your dead friend," she declared *en Español*, but I had already brushed him away in fear. An air-raid siren moaning, a sloshing whirlpool tightening around my hand. My arm strained in its socket, but without pain. The *shush* of the river made me think of a secret my blood had once told me and that secret made me weep. What was it she poured over me as I cried? Kisses? Sequins? Granules of sand? Or the compound eyes and antennae of some phantom insect whose signals I couldn't begin to comprehend?

"Your friends, the dead are everywhere," she cried, and her grip on me loosened with a sudden force. When I pulled out of her, a confetti froth of multicolored moths followed my fingers from her cocoon as if they'd been waiting there, held in limbo all her life. Together we arranged the dress back around her waist, the insects fluttering beneath its pleats like Chinese fireflies trapped inside a paper lantern, pressing their dusty rouge upon the soft cheek of a night of Losing Everything, the weathered cage of the Getting and the Having Had.

IV. Nothing More Than Sex

If someone, the New One, leans up against you, holds you from behind, lays her cheek on your left shoulder, does that mean she wants you? With her, courtship consisted of birding adventures —a snowy owl on a rowboat, a screech owl diving for mice on the Brooklyn-Queens Expressway, peregrines nesting in the Chrysler Building, and the tight-lipped flight of a barred owl above pine stumps the color of iodine.

The New One doesn't know that I learned everything about sex from bird-watching in the Vale of Cashmere at dusk. Dark, heavily wooded and secreted away from the major walking paths of Prospect Park, the Vale provided a welcoming environment for migrating, nesting, and queer birds alike. Oh, the amazing things I saw there, the illegal lewd caresses of beautiful men who turned my head, putting their mouths on each other in the underbrush, laying their hands upon each others' stiffening wings. Those handsome hawks, sharp-eyed birds of prey who never laid a finger on me, snapped open my young imagination, broke inhibition's scrawny neck, and fed on that sweet, wet meat in the high, luxurious branches. My body, watching theirs, became a kind of phantom, lonelier and freer than it had ever been before.

It was hot the night I met Ungendered Stranger there. She climbed on top of me and took me from behind, holding my head down, crewcut clenched in her fist, calling me "boy." In a sailor suit, bloody white. In a motorcycle jacket, deep-sea blue. In the safest of places, where women are forbidden and girls are a language against the law.

How I loved the Vale of Cashmere, how I longed to take the

New One there. Not to watch the birds, but to set her falcons free. Blindfold, head mask, jess strap, talons. Fresh meat on a gloved finger, whistles signaling something special coming on in the oncoming dusk. And a hovering in the air, a suspension, a sharp cry penetrating the ozone, causing the leaves to turn on their hinges, the heart to shift on its axis.

Take a risk, the New One seems to say, and once this would have moved you. But you've taken plenty of risks already and these days risk seems so much riskier, so much harder to take. Perhaps all those hospitals have taught you nothing.

You'd just turned nineteen when your college English teacher described you as "happy-go-lucky." That might've been a put-down, but he said it with such gentle envy that you knew it must be a precious thing, and you began to treasure that image of yourself, to build your city of life around the notion that you *were* happy, that you *were* lucky. Then came a plague that turned even your most intimate histories into relics of the distant past, things to be memorized or looked at in books, visions viewed through a sandstorm. And that's how you learned there was no such animal as luck, that luck was not a mammal, and that happiness was a cold-blooded thing in a hell of a hurry. Sweet bird of youth, bluebird of happiness, stammering owl of all that remains.

Take a risk, she whispers, and you do.

The New One doesn't know that your Last Lover wanted you to be her knight in shining armor, her conquering hero, her cowpoke, her rescuing prince, her unforgiving, voluptuous, hot-water-bottle Dad. She was always so in control. It took you years to realize that her reserve, her self-containment, were trace elements of terror. Years and a half-million miles deep into the site of the disaster.

The New One doesn't know that sometimes you wondered if the things you and the Last Lover were doing in bed had anything to do with the incest. That you worried the games might do more harm than good, but that you kept on going because the sex was so compelling. You didn't want it to stop—you liked it. It made you feel powerful to have someone fetishize your every move. To be able to break down her cool facade with friction and tension and heat and taboo.

But you couldn't help wondering about the stone's throw of a difference between a game someone forces—really forces—you to play, and a game you were brainwashed as a child into wanting.

There was something so disarming about the way she'd kneel to let you fuck her. Wasn't that what sex was supposed to be all about—a dissolving of the self? A kind of evolutionary "stepping back" into a more authentic place, a land beyond the land of thought and repression, politics and conscience? And wasn't the exploration of that soft sexual underbelly the cultural imperative of a marginal tribe striving to reappropriate the margins?

The New One knows none of this. She doesn't know that it was like the sexual end of the world when the Last Lover said: *You remind me of my father. What you and I have done was never making love. It was sex and nothing more.*

The New One doesn't know that you're afraid of your desire now. That you don't trust it, don't want to be in the same room with it, won't let it anywhere near your wallet. That fear has snuck up behind your back and changed your secret recipe. And you want it back, that cake called desire that used to taste so good, that sacred uncooked meat. You want it back as it was before, your particular amalgam of tastes and textures, unmolested. And though you hope someday you'll find it again, you know there's no such thing, really, as "again," that you'll never have it back intact, that at best you'll retrieve some version of it, and even if it's all okay someday, it'll always be a little less okay, 'cause now there's Caution. Now there's Fear. Now Shame is a neighbor, Shame's moved in across the street, and it's jerking off in the window across the alley and staring you down like it's coming for you, and it's there when you lie down in bed, suspended in the amber resin of your eyelid, a great horned insect stubbing itself out in the ashtray of your brain, a photophobic insect rife with poison, a hawk-eyed insect without wings.

V. Mariposa Nocturna

Richard took Páramo home from the hospital to die. "I want to say goodbye to my plants," said Páramo, "And then, before you know it, I'll be gone with a capital G."

Páramo died on the last night of the blizzard. The next day, his family arrived from Mexico City. We all sat together in the living room, drinking tequila and reminiscing about his two lives, in Mexico and in America. It was the first and last time I spoke Spanish all night long. Shortly after midnight, a tremendous black moth appeared on the ceiling, wings open, still as a stain. It clung there, a midwinter anomaly, throughout the night, its presence at once disturbing and reassuring. We all saw it, but none of us acknowledged it directly, not then and not since. By morning, it was gone.

VI. The Meat Rack

The New One takes me to the Isle of Flame and wines and dines me on the beach. Sweet pickles, smoked meats, and bread of sudden seeds. Cookies she kisses me with, nuzzling me blue, a Cookie Monster seductress.

Later, we wander through the Meat Rack, an area stubbled with blueberry bushes and scrubby pines repressed by salted wind. Huge wooden telephone poles tower there like driftwood storks, frozen in position, gazing up at the redemptive sky. Rufous-sided towhees, chickadees, and mourning doves land on the wires, looking out past the dunes toward the sea, calling to one another over the distant groan of ocean, seeming to sway to its rhythmic gravity.

Here, among the blueberries and low-lying firs, the men wander in search of sex. The Last Lover and I came here a year ago looking for the same. On the periphery we found a patch of sand secreted away by a mesh of fallen trees: the kind of place a deer might sleep the day away. And we made love there, precariously, in spite of a rib I didn't know was broken—knew only that it hurt to breathe, to sleep, to stand, to sit, to laugh, to come. And to be touched.

Afterward, the Last Lover and I lay beside one another in that nest of brambles and sand. The sex had hurt me, had stabbed and stabbed my heart. It was hard to breathe, impossible to speak. There was nothing left to say; it was over between us.

Birds cried out all around us, although the air was hot, the sky brilliant as a salt lick. I was watching the story of my body like a newsreel, my rib detaching from its rib cage, rising toward the surface like driftwood, piercing the threshold of my skin, and resting there like a bone cradle or a scroll. When the sand crane landed beside me, I remained immobile. It lowered its yellow beak and gently lifted the bone from my breast. I watched, quieted and amazed, as it carried the rib upward on huge and silent wings that scattered thin layers of sand upon me until I felt like an artifact, a sad memento of my own unmemorable life. The crane's silhouette, distorted and unfamiliar in the stretchmarked oceanic light, became smaller and stranger with every flap of its prehistoric wings.

It was only then that I began to miss the part of me it had ferried away.

The New One and I have come here to walk the sandy trails that slip like sidewinders between bushes, telephone poles, and broken pines. We crouch down, out of the wind's reach, to share a cigarette and watch the birds. Her hand is on my knee. Lone men wander past, disappointed by our presence. I do not tell the New One about what happened here last year. There is much the New One and I do not talk about, and much that we already know. We discuss the birds, their migrations and nesting patterns, the regional dialects of songs we strain to memorize. I tell her about a species that spends its entire life span on the ocean, never setting foot on land. I think to myself, *This is all she needs to know about what has become of me.* We extinguish the cigarette in the soft sand and carry it away with us, a burnt and dangerous souvenir. On the way out, I stop to pee near the place where Last Lover and I lay together. I am not sure whether I mean to defile or consecrate it. I am not even certain I am stand-

ing in the same place. This terrain is repetitive and offers few
clues.

VII. Wanting, Getting, Having Had

Ending that affair was like withdrawing from the most viciously
delicious drug I've ever known.

Once, early on, when we were making love, these words came
into my mind, not through my brain but through my body, my
bloodstream and bones assembling them: *I belong to you.* In
some profound way, I felt myself given to her. Who gave me to
her? Did I give myself away? Or did she take me, steal me in
the night when my guard was down? In any case, she had me
for a long, long time.

I did not call her, though I wanted to so badly. My body called
her. Did she hear it calling, through the gag of pride that kept
me alive? Can she hear me calling now, from the pay phone of
my heart, the filthy, ancient pay phone on that bone-bleached
Edward Hopper corner, longing to be sanctified by a blinding,
driving rain?

What would I say if she could hear me? *I want to be your
raptor again, the architect of your desires, the girl you dream
of when you can't remember your dreams, the one who holds
the clock face to her breast until time forgives everything, until
the hours and the minutes and the seconds drop their weapons
and throw their hands into the air. I want to be your kingdom
come again, your stud, your supernova, lord and master of your
sheath of sleep. In every sense, I belong to you. In every sense,
I am yours.*

VIII. Pathetic Fallacies

The New One and I are walking along the ocean, smoking cigarettes that it takes forever and a half million matches to light
in the wind. It is dusk, and darkness is rapidly settling in, turning
the ocean foam from white to bluish white, the sand to a wet
gray shale, the sky and water to black sparklers, hard diamond

and charcoal. We stop to watch this changing of the guards, the keepers of day passing their instruments, their hours and their minutes, to the shimmering custodians of dusk.

And with the turning over of the light, as if on command, everything has changed. The ocean's sound is suddenly more visceral, the crashing water splicing the dark air around us, so that we must now raise our voices to be heard. Everything—body, breath and touch—is compressed and reopened anew by the repeated slashing of the waves against the sand, their churning return to the frothy white marrow of the next unfurling tusk of wave.

"Listen," I say. "The ocean's so much louder in the dark."

"Your senses are compensating for the reduction of vision," she says.

"Maybe that's why people close their eyes to kiss."

"No," she replies, "that's not the reason people close their eyes."

Later, we will make love on that beach for the very first time. She will climb on top of me. I will tell her to do it. Over her right shoulder I will watch the huge red moon ascend the vocal ocean of the sky. I will hear her movements in the sand chafing against those of the water. And when she kisses me, when she puts her fingers inside me, watching my face for signs, I will look right back at her. I am going into this thing with my eyes wide open.

IX. Fathoms, Phantoms

"After my swim, I am coming for you," she tells me. I watch her paddle out like a yellow bear. The moonbeams on the water are clinical white, shivering like bones disgorged from a still-beating breast. It is a lonely sight, but the bear is brave and swims back to me with the rib, huge and brilliant, between her teeth. Or it becomes the boat she returns to me in; an owl's wing is its sail.

The bear emerges from the water, shimmering with salt and light and spray. She flops down breathlessly beside me, her long yellow hair separated into dripping strands, her body shining like a serpent of ore. *Sea monster*, I think to myself, and something tightens, incrementally, around my heart.

She takes cookies from a paper sack, one by one, chewing them slowly and deliberately, her eyes fixed on the glittering sea. Her expression is vacant, like a contented mutt. She transmutes from creature to creature before my eyes. And when she climbs on top of me and kisses me with cookie kisses, sweet and powdery, I think: *Cookie monster, sea monster, topiary of the heart.* Her fingers spread inside my rivulet playgrounds and I remember the woman with her lantern of moths. Her lips tap my nipple like a moth cupping its listening wings to the wintery ceiling of night and oh Páramo, it's your breath I hear. She pours sand on my belly and I think of this new nocturnal geography, where birds live out their lives on unmapped oceans, where boys locate their passions just before leaving us, and where bones are our notebooks, our cages, our clarifying hatchets of light. She murmurs in my ear and I am a cashmere veil laid softly upon everything I must listen to and remember: every promise, every myth, every story foreshortened. And I watch her transfigurations in the dark: night hawk, sphinx moth, serpent, bear, and so many other creatures—cold- and warm-blooded—I cannot classify, fathom or define. This is why, when she kisses me, I never look away. I do not want to miss a thing.

Lines in the Sand, Cries of Desire
Riki Anne Wilchins

"We are the women who like to come, and come hard."
Amber Hollibaugh

We spoke last week: just your average phone call. And then, just as we're getting off, you suggest I might want to write about the boundaries where my different selves meet: the complexity of this place, its borders and contours. And your suggestion leaves my face burning with shame and anger as if I had been struck: who has ever wanted to hear such things, and where on earth is the boundary where a lesbian, a preoperative transsexual with a cock, a woman, a femme, an addict, an incest survivor, and a postoperative transsexual with a cunt intersect? Upon what map is it drawn, and upon what states does it border?

I have spent my life exploring the geography of this place, mastering unfamiliar terrain and alien customs, wandering regions as fresh, as uncharted, as inexplicable to me as private visions; surveyed its pathways as ignorant and blind as any first-time explorer, and finally discovered myself at day's end: lost, alone, bewildered and afraid. With time, my tracks have intersected and converged, crisscrossed again and again, until at last they have woven their own pattern: my life itself has become the place where these different selves meet, my skin the boundary which contains them, and the women in my life the states upon which it borders.

Now you say you want to hear about this place, its complexities and desires, its contours and terrain. It is 1:00 Saturday night, and at the moment I am more involved with the contours and terrain of the cock dangling about 2 inches before my face. I am 42, and I have been coming to this mostly straight, couples-only sex club in mid-Manhattan for almost a year now, working my way through acts successively more challenging and frightening for me, pushing back the boundaries of what I can do or imagine, practicing with newfound skill staying present and connected during sex, exorcising demons and ghosts by now so familiar I know their names and faces within an environment so anonymous I often don't know those of my partner. A place where straightforward sex is the commodity, physical beauty the currency, and lust the only coin. This is the ground I have chosen to confront my deep fear of butch or masculine sexuality, of possession and surrender, power and vulnerability, where I can finally recover the much, the many, the myriad ways and fragments of my life lost to incest, transsexuality, shame and self-hate. I am trying to reclaim myself and I want my body back.

I want my body back.

I want my clit, my scrotum, my vagina, my cock, my beard. My buttocks, my thighs, my bush, my asshole, my urethra, my semen. My lips, my tongue, my wetness and my saliva. I want my breasts back, the ones I watched go through a second complete puberty at 29. I want my nipples back, with the scars just beneath my pink areolae where the implants went in, the left incision making the nipple over my heart mostly numb to touch or tongue. I want the scar on my throat, the one people notice and ask about thyroid conditions, the one opened to shave my Adam's apple down. And I want the scars you can't see, on the inside of my labia; the ones you get by doing the stitching from the inside, so they don't show. The ones which ache when I'm getting ill and itch strangely when I'm getting exhausted.

I want my body back.

I want the clear ejaculate which still trickles from my urethra when I come hard and fast. I want my clit back, the one the super-surgeons, who can make almost anything into almost any-thing else, made by transplanting the very head, the glans, of my beautiful, long, ivory pink and blue-veined penis right between my labia and then waiting three months for it to heal and the blood supply to stabilize, and then in a second operation, carved down to the little clit-like apparatus I have now, which is some-how still so sensitive it makes me tense and shiver as his wife uses her left hand to open my lips and her right to rub it in-quiringly, watching my face closely for any reaction and then smiling in satisfaction when my eyes unfocus, my stomach muscles harden and my thighs spread a little of their own accord.

Into my mouth goes his prick, tasting first of latex and then nonoxidyl-9, which makes my lips and tongue go ugly bitter and numb. A little gag starting and then he is in my mouth and firming up nicely, the glans beginning to extend itself along my tongue and pushing up against the roof of my palate. An exciting and strange experience this, but stranger still is having had a cock and having had women go down on it, I'm unwillingly, suddenly, almost shockingly aware of how each movement of my lips and tongue must feel to him. Strange too, is that nerve endings which once made their home in my cock, and which now nestle in my cunt, are starting to remember too, and they're getting hot, turgid, and wet and for several transcendent moments I cannot distinguish if I'm giving head to him or to me.

He is fully erect now, much like my dildo except the skin of his penis is very smooth and gripping it with both hands, I feel an unexpected softness around a firm core. After a moment I begin turning on my hands and knees, moving around on the mattress to face his wife as we begin to kiss. Her black hair is loose and shoulder length, her mouth is soft and wet and opens to hard little biting edges which nip at my mouth, tongue and neck. I notice the small, downy hairs on her forearm glistening in the damp overhead light: its muscles work as she reaches for my cunt again, turning the hair blond as it catches the light.

Exorcising demons and ghosts: I told my closest friend I was 41 and knew nothing about men and didn't want to wake up at 51 and still know nothing, but the truth is much closer to the bone. The truth is that unable to outrun or contain the contradictions of my life, I had been celibate for the past five years. And with celibacy I had dead-ended into every cold and silent secret I had trailed behind me into a dozen monogamous relationships and scores of one-night stands but never once confronted, till at last it dawned on me, laying in a bed I had entered only hours ago and would never see again, my chin cradled in my hand as I idly watched the sun slowly traversing the coverlet, that all my adult life I had successfully avoided anyone butch enough to turn me on or top me.

And your question brings me back here, to things I dream of alone at night, to desires I acknowledge in the dark, to exposed edges and hot, melting shame. To the things about which I neither speak nor write, to only the things about which I truly care and therefore make a career of avoiding. "Your writing is very direct," you said, "you're very in-your-face." Well I haven't had much choice; as far back as I can remember, my life has been a puzzle with missing pieces.

I hadn't even known the word "transsexual," nor that it was a word meant for me. In fact, I hadn't even known if transsexuals really existed, until at 28 I read Christine Jorgenson's book and finally admitted to being one. A year later, strung out, a suicide note wound in the typewriter and the garden hose snaked out to my shit-green Volkswagen, I knew I would have surgery or have an end to it. I remember thinking I could always return to this place, but it would be a shame indeed if a livable life was waiting on the other side of surgery with a patient, indulgent smile and I had not lived to see it. So I hauled my weary white ass into the Cleveland Clinic Hospital's Gender Identity Program. But transsexual women were supposed to be straight, and

I had never looked twice at a man, nor felt any erotic heat in their presence.

Determined to be a "successful" transsexual, I worked earnestly at being straight, at developing the proper attraction to men. I examined their firm little butts, learning to decipher which were cute and which not. I cruised the hair on their chests, their beards, clothing and stance, the width of their shoulders and the bulge of their cocks, judging its length and thickness by the way it deformed the smooth, muscular profile of whichever jean-clad thigh it was worn on. I faithfully reported each foray into heterosexuality to the hospital's noncommittal therapist, desperate to be the good patient upon whom she would confer surgery when my waiting time was up.

I finally informed her that I could not be straight, that I was, in fact, a complete bust with men, that the only thing which still gave me my somewhat limp, estrogen-impaired erections were other women. I knew then, suicidal as I was and living day to day only awaiting surgery, that when they threw me out I might make that trek out to the Volkswagen after all. "Oh yes," she said, as she peered up from my manila-foldered chart, "we had one of those last year." And she went back to writing case notes in my chart about my "illness," and I went back to breathing.

This was pretty amazing stuff at the time. The head of the only other gender program in town had solemnly informed me I could not be a lesbian. "All transsexual women," he declared, "want to be penetrated." Well, yes. But I thought maybe he knew even less about woman-to-woman sex than I did, and fearing his primitive sexual cosmology was accepted as revealed truth within the profession I hoped would save my life, I determined to keep my attraction to women as secret as my own pulse.

So I learned that I could be a transsexual, as well as attracted to women. But could I be a lesbian? Certainly the lesbianism into which I came out in the 70's said I could not. It told me then, as it often does, that I was a surgically altered male, a man invading "women's" space, my trespass tolerable to the precise extent I displayed the very oppressive, stereotypically feminine behaviors from which many of my lesbian friends were in the most earnest flight. As for what lesbians did in bed, the women's community into which I emerged reversed the statement of the doctors: "No lesbian," it solemnly intoned, "wants to be penetrated." Penetration, I learned later, was for straight girls.

A transsexual she-male freak and a lesbian slut turned on by penetration in an orifice still under construction was bad enough, but even worse, I found out that the type of lesbian I wanted meant I was into "roles." And I learned from all quarters that "roles" were dead. Interred with them went the best of my desires: those strong, femmy butches who strode arrogantly across my dreams and scared me half to death with their power and my need.

Perhaps roles *were* dead, for in truth I saw neither femmes nor their butches at the few women's bars or functions I was allowed to attend. Even lesbians who professed support for "roles" were roundly ignored or actively reproached. The lesbianism into which I came out was dry and pale and bordered by bowl haircuts, no makeup, torn jeans, half-buttoned ubiquitous flannel shirts and humorless, hurting women whose sexuality was firmly suppressed, politically obedient, and completely foreign to my own erotic tides.

I didn't know butches and femmes still existed, or even if they ought to, until you started telling me about them. You taught me the theory, and even more you taught me respect, resuscitating the femme parts of me with words like "complex," "courageous," "many-layered," and "specifically lesbian." "For many years now," you wrote, "I have been trying to figure how to explain the special nature of butch-femme relationships to feminists and lesbian-feminists who consider butch-femme a reproduction of heterosexual models, and therefore dismiss lesbian communities of the past and of the present that assert this style."

It was not until sometime later that you taught me the practice as well, and moreover that the women I craved still existed, that it was okay for me to want them and imagine them, to picture their hands and cocks and hunger as I lay across my bed, eyes closed and back arched, rubbing the middle finger of my right hand across my own recently made clit and pushing the new dildo I'd trimmed to just the right size and shape deep into my own improbable, impossible cunt.

"Oh, my darling, this play is real," you wrote. "I do long to suck you, to take your courage into my mouth, both cunt, your flesh, and cock, your dream, deep into my mouth, and I do . . . She moans, moves, tries to watch, and cannot as the image overpowers her . . . and then she reaches down and slips the cock into me . . . I fall over her . . . I am pounding the bed, her arms, anything I can reach. How dare you do this to me, how dare you push me beyond my daily voice, my daily body, my daily fears. I am changing; we are dancing. We have broken through."

And I wondered if I would ever break through, as I wandered through one-night stands and short-time lovers, remembered the details of their bodies but not their faces, their technique but not their words. I actively avoided the kind of woman who turned me on, brushed aside their gaze, saw them in bars and left. Each time some hidden place inside me burned with a pain I forbid myself to touch or explore, desires and needs which are well described by words like "many-layered" and "complex," but which are far more distressing and aching than the crisp, black letters on the flat white pages containing them.

The truth is, I had used sex but could not submit to it, and the truth is I could come but I could not be present in my body nor use it to express vulnerability or surrender. Sex was something I exchanged for safety or shelter or companionship. Sex was something to attract a lover who wasn't sure if she wanted a transsexual, and later sex was something to bind her to me through the shit she would take from friends. And after it was over, sex was a way to be a child again for an hour, maybe two, in warm, safe arms.

Sex was a way to humiliate myself and my lovers, to suppress and yet simultaneously revisit again and again those childhood nights when the humiliation was mine and mine alone and the hot breath on my neck and back belonged to a complete stranger who only looked like my father and whom I met only in the dark. For the truth is, every time I tried to make love, the image of my father hovered above whatever bed I was in like some kind of demented crucifix hung on the wall over our heads, and the path I had tread so long back to my sexuality, my body, and my lesbian self led in a beeline as long and straight and narrow as the lane line down a flat-back Kansas highway right through to my father.

Incest is a word too ugly and short to do justice to something which is much more than simply ugly and too often not blessedly short. Incest is a daily thing, like the news, like dinner, like brushing your teeth. You can carry it around like a stick of gum in your pocket. It marks your body like a cancerous mole or a burn from hot cooking oil. It colors your thoughts like a drop of ink in a glass of water, and it poisons your life like shit down a well.

There is the nice, simple kind that comes accompanied by clear, sharp snapshot memories developed by Polaroid. They are terrifying, but at least they have defined shapes, colors and dimensions, and at least they are known. Then there are those as hard to grasp as smoke, invasions and violations not captured on neat Kodachrome squares, the kind which later in life announce themselves with only vague and confusing physical and emotional memories, welling up without warning or reason from unknown and uncharted underground springs, from acts carried out at an age so tender there were no words to frame and recall them; or perhaps a little older still, when words were at the ready and nearby, but quickly buried so well and far away they have no known latitude or longitude now but still manage to wake you from the dark in that familiar sweet sweat with your perpetrator's smell all over them and your inner child screaming with fear and rage like a wounded banshee in the close night air.

And there is another kind of incest, a kind no one even names. This is the transsexual kind and it is a symphony of abuse. It is the Bach and Beethoven, the Haydn and Mozart of incest. It is orchestrated and complex, with woodwinds and strings, brass notes, and deep, bass rhythms. It involves forcing female children to live as boys, withheld hormones and medical treatment, and quick, vicious punishment by those people you love and trust the most for the slightest omission or infraction in dress or behavior. Its terrors and confusions culminate in a second puberty in the full glare of midlife adulthood, followed by a gaudy, baroque crescendo of doctors and scalpels and stitches and blood which, however good the surgery, still leaves you feeling violated and broken inside somehow and never quite sane in your body again.

And I am thinking of this, of your words and my life, as I feel his hands on me from behind now, warm and dry, rubbing gently on my buttocks, moving in widening circles until they pause and then dip between my legs, finding and then caressing the pink skin whose origins and construction I still cannot imagine. A single finger pauses at my cunt, stroking just inside my vagina and then tunnels slowly inward, so slowly in fact that I cannot refrain from pushing back, surprising myself with a soft moan which sounds vaguely ridiculous, even to me. Even to me, who has walked the halls of this place many evenings, just listening to the sounds of women caught in the distress of their own lust, their overheated cries and whimpers clutching at my damp insides like a strong hand or running clean through my body like an ice pick through warm butter.

His finger slides out of my pussy now and I feel the first taut nudge of his cock. Holding it in his right hand, he searches patiently for my open, wondering vagina. After a year of work, my own dance is about to begin: you have helped to bring me here. I wonder: what will you think reading this? Will you be able to see the lesbian in me, in my experience? Have I come through so many rejections to face another? And if you cannot read this, and read in it other lesbian lives and identities and appetites and passions, then who will? I have heard my own echo in your voice. Will you hear yours in mine?

Our lives become the enactment of those things we can think, the erotic acts and petty daily defiances of the fears which haunt the borders of what we will confess to desiring, what we can imagine ourselves wanting to do with our own bodies and those of our lovers. The borders are not drawn by us, but by our fears, lines drawn in the sands of our need by rape or shame or abuse, imaginary lines in shifting sands we dare not cross. And standing beyond those lines are the women who have gone before, who have stepped past and returned to tell us what lies beyond, and about the parts of our lives we have lost, whose words we can read but not yet write, whose stories, at once terrifying and exciting, we carry around for years, running them over and over in our minds like old movie reels until at last we recognize them as our own, coming back to us like prodigal children returned in the night or the echoes of our own voices, thrown back at us from a cry of desire uttered so long ago, and in such pain, we neither recall it nor recognize its origins as our own.

He finds my vagina and gripping my hips, he uses both of his wide hands to pull me back onto his cock. I feel my body parting to take him in, a familiar-strange feeling of pressure-pleasure as he enters me confidently, until at last he is in my flesh up to the hilt. I am struggling to take all of him now, and to stay connected as well: feeling him, testing myself, tightening obscure muscles somewhere far up inside my vagina. He pulls me back, the air forced from my lungs as if someone has struck lightly at my stomach, and just as I catch my breath he begins to move, accelerating now, the apex of his thrusts going off like some liquid explosion deep in the center of my pelvis. I am filled with a kind of wonder now, my body showing me things novel and unsuspected.

In slow motion I close my eyes and collapse into his wife's waiting arms. She knows it is my first time, and gently gathers me in, her hands cradling my face, pulling it down and in between her legs. I begin to lick her thighs, her groin, her clit, anything my hungry little mouth can reach, the sweet-smelling hair of her bush containing the sounds now coming from my throat. She laughs, a quick, easy sound, as I raise my hips to take more of her husband's cock inside me. Her plump, butter-smooth hips are tightly encircled, my arms gathering her whole cunt onto my mouth. I suck on it viciously, teething like an infant with bottle while another part of me concentrates on withstanding each delicious withdrawal and fresh, fierce entrance. I am in a kind of heaven, and for the first time in my life I am present in my body and unafraid and I am on wings.

And nice as his maleness is, it is neither female nor what I want and I begin to play with my head a little, imagining he is a woman and his dick, a dildo strapped on with a soft butch's contradictory, perfectly masculine arrogance. Pleased and emboldened by the effect she is having, she uses her knees to lever my legs further apart. "Is it okay for you, honey?" she taunts, holding me like that for long seconds, pressing into me, pushing relentlessly forward and down, purposefully using all her weight so I need my full strength to support us both. She leans far forward over the long muscles of my back, taking time to pinch each of my nipples, and then pausing to wipe the small beads of sweat which have collected at my temples. "What's wrong, baby, is it too much for you?" she purrs, and pulling me backward she enters me so deeply the O-ring of her strap is suddenly clear and cold on my butt. I catch a glimpse of her over my shoulder, wearing the smile she flashes like a hidden blade, her teeth gleaming in the dim light with pleasure as my face contorts with that far-away look as if I'd heard the whistle of a train, high-pitched and way off in the distance. Her free hand slips beneath me, trails along my belly, oblivious to my hips jerking sideways, avoiding her, knowing her intent. She searches diligently for my clit, finds it, and begins to worry it, rubbing patiently from side to side with practiced, entirely successful fingers.

I am completely still now, holding my breath to deny her the reward of further response. Until something deep inside me just snaps, bursts clean; and groaning with rage and lust my back arches, a proverbial cat in heat, and she, laughing out loud, answers. Strong, veined hands grip my hips, and she makes the first, killing thrust that begins her final motion, and I know now that she will come fucking me, shouting hoarsely and thrusting into me just as hard as she is able. The warm honey-butter-blood begins to flood the cradle of my cunt and I realize that for once, my father is nowhere to be seen, no, nor my fear of masculinity and submission, of penetration and vulnerability, and closing my eyes to surrender to the first delicious tugs of orgasm, I know for the first time and with a certainty beyond simple trust that I am free.

Killer in Love

Sarah Schulman

(*Two women in a bedroom. KILLER speaks to the audience and to TROY. TROY only speaks to KILLER.*)

KILLER (*To audience*): It is a very strange thing but the lesbian community is a community of liars. Liars and believers, tops and bottoms, butches and femmes, doers and wannabes, yuppies and deadbeats, mommies and daddies, enemies and friends. It's all so dynamic. (*To TROY:*) Troy?

TROY: Yeah?

KILLER: Honey, could you hurt me? Rough me up a little.

TROY: What do you want me to do?

KILLER: I don't know, slap me, tell me off, make me cry. I really need to cry.

TROY: Your head is a silk factory. Your eyes are like posies. Your mouth is a lamp. Your nose is Kamchatka. Your cheeks are bonanzas. Your timing is three quarters. Your chest is a radio. Your thighs can sing opera. Your belly is mellow. Your knees are blue kanten. Your ankles are imported. Your cerebrum came from Macy's. Your tongue stings of KY. Your waist told a secret. Your soft lips gave me pleasure. Your forehead is a plum.

KILLER (*To audience*): She was so handsome, beautiful, my boy, my sailor. Dirty, sexy blue eyes. Soft lips sink ships. It

was strange, what was happening. For so long I thought I was
pretending to be a lady killer but all the while being very usual
instead. Then, one day as Troy was loving me, I realized that
I was exceptional. I realized that I will never be alone for very
long. I will never be bored and I will always be loved. I had
to come to terms with the fact that I am sexy and I am easy
to love. (*To TROY:*) When did you first know that we were
in love?

TROY: I was riding on a Greyhound bus through New Jersey,
in January. Rolling industrial tundra where cancer is king.
Every day of their lives is nineteen sixty-two and the dairy
truck still rattles along a hard-working run-down street. Ken-
tucky Fried Chicken looks so old-fashioned in the graying
dusk from a passing bus. Ho-hum. New Jersey. Even the coun-
tryside is dreary. Stomping grounds for traveling oldies reviv-
als. The Marvelettes are sixty. Still singing "Mister Postman,
Please." Please bring me my social security check. I'm an
aging Marvelette passing through New Jersey. There's not one
person I envy in that entire state.

KILLER: And that's when you fell in love with me.

TROY: Honey, I'm going to the corner to get a cup of coffee.

KILLER: Get me one too. (*TROY gets out of bed, steps off stage
and returns immediately with two cups of coffee.*) What happened at the store?

TROY: Saw a rat. Then I was upset and wanted something
special so I asked the storekeeper if he had Diet Cherry Seven-
Up or Wild Cherry Diet Pepsi. But he only had Crystal Cola
Clear Pepsi. Not even Diet Crystal Cola Clear Pepsi. He
did have Diet Doctor Pepper, Diet Mandarin Orange Slice,
Caffeine-Free Sprite and Grape Gatorade. So, I got a box of
doughnuts instead. I mean we could sit around eating hearts
of palm and blood-red cherry tomatoes, if you wish.

KILLER: What do hearts of palm taste like?

TROY: Like canned asparagus. Baby, choose your desirable
state of choice from the following list.

KILLER: Okay.

TROY: Mixture. Tundra. Beaucoup. Remo. Remoulade. Satay.

KILLER: My Way.

TROY: At least you're honest. Your turn.

KILLER: Okay Troy, pick a phrase from the following list.

TROY: I'm ready.

KILLER: Shark shards glistening. Lava raven so fine. Voodoo mixture Rambette.

TROY: Oooh baby, be mine.

KILLER (*To audience*): I ate three doughnuts in a state of deep shame. I don't have very much money for food right now. It is not that I don't eat. I do. I just don't have enough money for a free choice of food. I have to eat a lot of the same thing. I don't end up hungry at the end of the day but I do spend a lot of time imagining different tastes and treats. Like a piece of cake. A piece of cake filled with white cream. (*To TROY:*) Last year I had a scare in the middle of April where I was living on a $2.50-a-day food budget.

TROY: Rice omelettes?

KILLER: Yeah, and banana omelettes and rice and beans and bean omelettes and beans and bananas and bananas and rice. And tea in coffeeshops with lots of sugar and lots of milk.

TROY: That is very hard to live with.

KILLER (*To audience*): Something about her kindness and the coffee turned me on. How strange to have sexual fantasies about your lover while she's actually there pleasing you.

TROY: Tell me what you want to do to me and I'll let you. Tell me that you want to fuck me and I'll let you fuck me. Tell me that you want me to come and I will come.

KILLER (*To TROY*): I like it when it hurts. Vaginal trauma is what I live for. Skeletal friction first and then my skin is the softest skin. When you comfort me I love the comfort. When you hurt me, I love the pain. When you control me I love the capitulation. When you service me I love the intent. Coming out is not the end of insanity, you know. It is only the beginning.

TROY: Call me satan.

KILLER: I'll call you satan. You're not evil.

TROY: All Americans are dangerous, Killer. We destroy the earth, mind and lymph node and then market that destruction. We make it sound groovy. I have a lot of predictions about the future of America. Predictions that could have already come true.

KILLER: Like what?

TROY: I predict that there will be a new kind of cancer and advertising executives will name it Lymphomania. I predict T-shirts that say "I want to rape you." I predict haphazard memorial services at every hour of the day and night because too many people are dead. I predict that homeless people will piss on bank machines like storefronts lined with urinals.

KILLER: And personally?

TROY: First I lost my country. Now I predict that my country is going to lose me. Hmmm, I'm suspicious.

KILLER: Of what?

TROY: You.

KILLER (*To audience*): Troy's mouth is wired for sound. She is penetration in public places. She is unisex to me.

TROY: Well, I'm just Joe Lesbian on the street. I'm in love with you and I want to be with you. This is what Billie Holliday sings about. It's that dangerous netherworld called really living. Hey, I just thought of the first line of a poem.

KILLER: What?

TROY: Roses are dead.

KILLER: What kind of women do you usually like?

TROY: I used to have a stock answer. I like women who are not too pretty, kind of insecure, good in bed and butch enough to do me.

KILLER: That's about ninety percent of the lesbians in New York City.

TROY: God bless New York City. There was a really beautiful Puerto Rican woman in the store this morning. She also saw the rat. How come Spanish women look divine in something that would make any white girl look like trash? One of the things I love is a hot summer night. A hot winter night. The sound is blowing in your hair instead of breeze. There are two candles—purity and passion, and purity burns out while passion is just getting started. It's exciting.

KILLER: I'm excited. I think I had too much coffee.

TROY: Here baby, smoke a cigarette. It helps drain some of the oxygen away.

KILLER: Alone has such a different feeling now. It is all about waiting for you. There's jazz on the radio, I have a quiet glass of water. The clock says eleven o'clock and I'm waiting for the phone to ring announcing that you've been to work, been home and am now ready for me. It is a different kind of anxiety, this emptiness. Surrounded by my papers, my mementos, tchotchkes, all artifacts from my life before you. I wait, never patiently, as you take your time. Where are you, Troy? Your touch works on my flesh like a respirator, like Vick's Vapo-rub. Like a samba when you're feeling free enough, or the sun without boredom or one final glass of beer. Speaking love the same way to the same girl night after day.

The radiator whistles. There are holes in the walls of these old tenements. When it really chills outside I can't get warm. Night creeps in from all corners. You're the kind of woman that girls want to own. It's so obvious, the possession. You've got a permanent black collar around your neck. Keeping way too busy is the only form of escape that you know. Can I please be your wife? Even if only for a few days. Then I'm sure to be filled with regret and try to set you free, unwillingly. I'm older now and yet restraint is so hard to muster. Hey, girlfriend, where are you? My jaw is locked in anticipation. Phone? Ring? Ring? Why don't you. Your arrival is obvious, why can't I just relax and wait for it? Ho-hum. Yours is the last phone call every night. And it's a guarantee.

Okay, you called. You're on your way. At least a half hour from the store on 39th Street unless you take a cab. What else to do but clean out my supplemental dictionary or else try to figure out how to alphabetize on my 1980 IBM computer. How can I figure out anything if I don't know what "field" means. Oh, you're here. Hooray.

I can smell you when you're only halfway up the stairs, but even that warning doesn't anticipate the delight at your appearance. We embrace, sit together, chat softly. I bring you something, something to drink. I have been holding onto an emotion, trying to figure out how to offer it—to offer you a tip of an iceberg as bait to my life. Finally it comes out carefully, seems to appear haltingly. I wait for some recognition but there's an associative silence instead. Whatever it was I said only reminded you of your own sadness. It brought up something hidden which is now occupying your mind.

What is it, baby. Come on, just tell me. Because I want so desperately to be close to you. I'm trying every way I can.

God, my apartment looks so shabby. I'm ashamed of it. My clothes are all hand-me-downs. I'm deeply ashamed. Where is my father? I haven't heard from him since April. He and my mother came over to the house, we were sitting around watching the TV news. I felt so abandoned.

I am waiting for my female boyfriend. It is a beautiful night.
BLACKOUT

An American in Chiapas

Nisa Donnelly

Every December, as they have for generations and for generations even before that, the women of Celestun dress the mother goddess in red velvet and white satin, and carry her through the dirt streets of this village that smells of the sea and echoes with silence and the songs of women and flamingos, their voices joined in shimmering cries in the limp salty air. Around the dusty zocalo, where hungry dogs loll, pink tongues lapping at flies and crumbs, past the houses, where doors gape against the afternoon sun, welcoming the faint breeze, the true believers carry tradition in a solemn procession. Children, dressed in crisp colors and lace, march somber in their importance down the highway, past the wide swamp flats where the johnboats bob and wait for tourists. No one comes here to see the procession; tourists come to see flamingos. At dawn and again at dusk, hundreds of thousands of the giant birds streak the sky in shades of living pink, sending flames dancing across the green, mossy water. The flamingos do not fix their black beady eyes on the somber little parade, pay no mind to the songs carried on the wind that ruffles the skirts of the women of the children of the goddess, too.

Finally, at the intersection, the processional pauses, waits, voices softer now, half listening for the songs from the neighboring villagers, approaching, carrying a figure not unlike their own precious Maria. The women speak the name given their goddess by the conquerors four hundred years ago; they have forgotten her old name, the name she wore a thousand years or more. And here, under a Yucatan sun, under a sky streaked pink with flamingos, in the shadow of the twentieth century, the goddess meets her lover. The watchful eyes of the pious gleam with tears and devotion. The blind eyes of the statues stare straight ahead. The women and children whisper frantic prayers that catch on the wind. They call to heaven. Heaven does not answer. The goddesses smile their painted-on beatific smiles. Unflinching. Only the white lace rustles in the wind. After a time, the processions begin their march back home.

La Ruta Maya

December 31, 1993: It is cold here in the mountainous village of San Cristobal de las Casas, the colonial jewel of the Mexican state of Chiapas. Tourist books written especially for European and the fewer American tourists like us who find their ways here to the pit of the Yucatan peninsula, call this small, pitiably poor excuse for a city "reminiscent of Paris in an earlier century or Santa Fe, New Mexico." You wonder Paris of which century. It is too hungry. Too cold. The streets of Paris and Santa Fe are not filled with barefoot Mayan women, young but their eyes looking already older than the oldest woman you've ever seen, dragging children through the streets. Too many children. Too thin. Too dirty. Eyes too desperate. Hands outstretched. "Help me, help my child." But they do not say this, at least in no language the tourists understand. They, like us, speak only enough Spanish to get by, only enough to conduct the simple business transactions in the marketplace. We do not speak Tzotzil.

"Chiapas is not Mexico." Walking these narrow streets, I recall the words of my Spanish teacher. Faced with the formidable task of teaching a half-dozen San Franciscans enough of his language in eight weeks for us to survive as tourists, he would entertain us with tales of a wild ride through the mountains of Chiapas and Guatemala, sleeping in hotels with buggy beds for a quarter a night, trading his Hard Rock Café T-shirt for tamales. I have no gift for language, but I will learn because here even Spanish is the second language. Chiapas is not Mexico. He was right.

Ellyn and I are here on holiday, following *La Ruta Maya*, that loops through the Yucatan, connecting one city to the next in the Mayan world of a thousand years ago. Our map is marked with red and green circles indicating archaeological sites and the villages of indigenous weavers, reputedly the finest in the world.

Mérida, with its cosmopolitan grace and sophistication spoiled us. In the *Plaza de la Independencia*—site of the ancient Mayan city of Tho until the Spanish came and destroyed the temples and pyramids—are Christmas lights and politics. Talk of secession. Tourism and oil and NAFTA that are sure to bring untold riches to Yucatan, Campeche, Quintana Roo. But what about Chiapas, one of the men in the crowd wanted to know. The speaker's face contorted, he spat, a dull sound like bird droppings on the sidewalk. "Chiapas? They have nothing but poor people. Let Chiapas go back to Guatemala." Laughing, nodding, they ignore the American tourists with their dictionaries, their strange accents, imagining that we do not understand. In a way, they are right; in a way, we will never understand what we are about to witness.

The Road South

Leaving Mérida, we press south, tourists and some of the Mexicans wealthy enough to travel by the luxury buses that are a part of this country's class system. We are the only Americans. The rest must be content to stay in the resorts of Cancun, we tell each other, pleased, arrogant with independence. First, to the ruins of Palenque, then on to San Cristobal de las Casas for New Year's Eve. On the daylong bus trip, we talk of ruins, of jungles, of the people who by night steal into the park, the ancient city of their ancestors. "There are 500 or so Lacandones people left," I tell Ellyn. "They do not allow themselves to be photographed. Only the men interact with tourists and at that just to sell their arrows.'' The guidebooks have made us walking encyclopedias of trivia.

We arrive at Palenque a few days past the winter solstice, the time when the sun appears to set into the tomb of Lord Pacal, the centerpiece of the site. Not that we would be allowed to stay and witness this miracle of engineering and astronomy; tourists are scuttled out long before sunset, when it again becomes the domain of the Lacandones, the white-robed, long-tressed, barefoot, jungle-dwelling people, who kept the sacred site free of overgrowth for generations. They live much as they always have, planting corn by gouging holes with sticks, hauling water from streams, casting darkly mistrusting eyes on the tourists that they tolerate, but just barely. They are rumored to still use the site on religious holidays, moonlight washing over their white robes, over the white-rocked tombs and temples. We are the intruders. We know this without any guidebook having to tell us why.

This jungle, which sprouts leaves larger than any person, which guards the secrets of a people as ancient as the land itself, is giving birth to a revolution. We do not know this yet, do not know that the revolutionaries are training here, even as we climb the Temple of the Inscriptions. All we know is that we want to come back, want to feel the peace of this place that is more beautiful than any place imaginable. Yes, we tell each other, we will go on to San Cristobal, then stop here again when we come back. When we come back.

The next morning we are again the only Americans on the bus that leaves Palenque for the more than five-hour trip required to travel fewer than 100 miles on roads that curl like ribbons through the mountains. Eventually, we will reach 7,000 feet.

Finally grinding to a stop at a dusty crossroad village called Ocosingo, the bus waits to take on a few more passengers. I stand on a dirt street, watching a livestock auction. A few children stop to stare. *Alemana*, they speculate. No, I tell them, *Americana*. They shake their heads in disbelief. They see few American women here, apparently fewer still standing outside a bus smoking cigarettes. In the coming weeks, we will be increasingly mistaken for Germans. Back on the bus, Ellyn rouses from a Dramamine-imposed stupor and asks, "Anything here?" No, I tell her, nothing to see, just a marketplace across the road and some men auctioning off a pig. She passes me the Dramamine. The bus lurches on. It is the next to the last day of 1993. The next time we will hear of Ocosingo will be when we see newspaper pictures of boys not much older than the ones who mistook me for a German, dead in that marketplace, their blood staining the dirt and concrete.

The Revolution

"When I write of this revolution," I tell Ellyn on New Year's Day, "I will say that it came with hot water." We are on the roof of our hotel, sitting next to the large solar water heaters and reduced to telling bad jokes, any jokes at all to try to break up the boredom, to dispel the fear of not knowing what will come next. She smiles, turns her face toward the sun, listening for helicopters. They have been buzzing over the hills for the last twelve hours, maybe more; we can no longer remember. They remind her of the war, she says, meaning the Vietnam footage on the evening news twenty years ago. Neither of us has ever been to Vietnam. Neither of us has ever been to a war before. Now. "Do you think the embassy will send helicopters in to get us out? I've seen that on television," she says, "the tourists getting on helicopters." I don't answer. We are Americans, but the American Embassy is far away in Mexico City. There is nothing here the Americans would want; our government would not be interested in rescuing tourists like us.

The zocalo, a half block from our hotel, is filled with guerrillas, who appear to be nothing more than poorly armed boys. The streets are alternately deserted and filled with terrified men and women. I do not tell her that this morning when I ventured out of the hotel's colonial courtyard, I saw a knot of men carrying a screaming woman through the streets, her leg broken, her face contorted. How had that happened? I don't know anyone to ask. The few questions I manage are met with silence, distrusting stares. The women and their children from the day before are gone, huddled in their cardboard and stick shanties on the outskirts of the town. In their place are the guerrillas. The guerrillas watch the tourists with bored eyes.

Outside the sacked city hall, where the day before we were reading announcements of plays and poetry readings, a press conference is going on. We will find out later that the main speaker is Subcommandante Marcos, the EZLN's charismatic, ski-masked leader. We come as close as we dare, careful not to disturb the local residents who have gathered to carry away city files. A couple on a nearby park bench puzzle over an upside-down map of the city's sewer system; two boys push each other through the street on a rolling desk chair. The guerrillas watch with unamused eyes. The tourists' cameras click click and whir against the afternoon.

The women, the ones dressed in the identifying colors of the small mountain towns that gave birth to this revolution, no longer haunt the streets, surrounding tourists with their outstretched hands, selling folk art, small weavings, dolls, resin fashioned to look like amber. Perhaps they and their children are huddled in their cardboard and stick shanties that dot the hillsides of San Cristobal, across the highway that is closed by the revolution. The finest indigenous weavers in the world live in Chiapas, selling their art in the shops, in the market by the old convent. But the shops are closed and the market empty.

Following the cobblestone streets, we work our way toward the marketplace. Hansel and Gretel have gone before us, leaving behind their markers of banana peels and orange skins. Mayan women, dressed in the sky-blue blouses and rough black woolen skirts that identify their village as San Juan Chamula, sit in front of stalls with warm oranges and thick-skinned melons. They talk only to each other in subdued voices. They have nowhere else to go, except maybe back to their shantytown. Their village has turned them out for their religion. In their world, there is only one way to dress, one way to pray. Now, they survive by selling oranges and melons, embroidered blouses and small, finely crafted woven scarves. Some let tourists take their photographs

—for a price. The world has stolen their dignity, they are desperate enough to sell bits of their souls to the cameras of pale strangers. An aging American couple, the woman in the kind of tailored linen suit that belies position and power, is attempting to buy a few oranges with American cash. Worthless here. The vendor reclaims her oranges, shaking her head no. Who knows when the money changer will ever be open again? The husband opens his wallet displaying the greenbacks. He offers her a five, then a ten. She shakes her head again, turns away. He looks at her in disbelief. We stumble on, past the mostly closed stalls, the stench of rotting fruit rising up around us, forcing us back to the street, deserted except for tourists like us. There is no way out.

The next morning, the guerrillas are gone and in their place is the Mexican army, equipped with modern American-made war toys. The soldiers are less kind, less tolerant. They hold large guns loosely. They smile at tourists. We do not smile back. We are looking for other Americans, for answers, for a way out of this city. A low-level bureaucrat from the American Embassy has finally arrived. We find him in a bookstore. "Are you Americans?" the bookstore owner asks in Spanish. The bureaucrat offers to contact our parents—and tell them what, we wonder. He does not offer us a way out of San Cristobal. There is no safe way out. Some tourists have hired private cars to take them north. The road to Palenque is open, we hear. Some go, driving into the heart of guerrilla strongholds. They are the unlucky ones, they will have to run again. All of Chiapas is in a state of war. Go west to Tuxtla Gutierrez, the men who run our hotel tell us; they do not tell us how. The television cranks out endless reruns of 1960s American movies. The city is emptying of tourists, filling with journalists. We are too ignorant to be afraid.

"NAFTA" we hear whispered as we pass through the streets, "NAFTA is to blame for this." On the wall of the bank opposite the zocalo is the last of the handbills, the Zapatistas' declaration of war, pasted up on New Year's morning. I translate for Ellyn in my faltering Spanish: "After 500 years of oppression by the North Ameri" is all that remains. The rest has been torn away.

"I guess that would be us," I say. We trudge the streets, careful
to avoid the guns of the soldiers. We no longer correct anyone
who calls us Germans. In a small *tienda* I have found a saint
painted on a board. Which saint, I wonder. I ask the shopkeeper,
but my accent is too harsh. She misunderstands, tells me it is
from a village in the mountains. I recognize the name of the
village, still do not know the name of the saint. We pick through
the crafts market outside the convent, but the whir of sound and
color of a few days ago is hollow. An old woman approaches
with a white-on-white embroidered huipil. Delicate, intricate,
many hours of work, she tells me. I recognize the pattern as one
from the temples. The patterns pass down from generation to
generation, reaching all the way back to the Mayan ancestors of
more than a thousand years ago. I show her the saint, a gift for
a dying friend who has found strength in God. She crosses herself and points toward the church.

Dark and rough-hewn, the floors covered with pine needles
and the wax from the long, white tapers used by the Mayans in
prayer, the old church is cold and solemn, thick with smoke from
copal and candlewax. Saints with gaunt faces and haggard eyes
peer down on us. A Mayan family kneels in front of a trio of
saints with bloody faces. The men pray loudly, the women sway.
At the far end of one alcove is a figure of Jesus, a rope around
his neck, being led by a pair of conquistadors. "Doesn't need a
whole lot of translation, does it?" Ellyn asks, motioning me
toward the far side of the church where, in shadows, another
figure of another Jesus is laid out in a glass coffin, paraffin hands
crossed over its velvet covered chest, in death. A woman with
angry eyes rolls toward us, cluck-clucking, shooing us toward
the door, fanning her skirt behind us the way my grandmother
herded chickens.

The Road Back

It is Wednesday, the fourth day of the revolution, the last day
San Cristobal will be open. Determined to leave, we finally have
found a way out thanks to a taxi driver who has brought jour-

nalists into San Cristobal and is looking for a return fare to
Tuxtla.

On the highway, hundreds of tanks filled with Mexican *federales* pass us, heading toward the town we are fleeing. We are
stuffed into a Volkswagen beetle that bounces past hillsides dot-
ted with poor villages. Mayan houses of thatch and stick, with
dirt floors and no doors, but built in the style of the royal cities,
cluster at the bottom of steep hills. Barefoot women and children,
dressed in the colors of birds and rainbows, walk along the sides
of the road, oblivious to the passing tanks, gather sticks that they
carry on their backs. Sparse stalks of corn struggle for life on
craggy hillsides. Men lounge on the steps of a public building,
drawing patterns in the dirt, their white trousers and shirts shining like lost moons. There is no work for them, has not been for
a long time. The finest indigenous weavers in the world sell work
that takes weeks to make for pennies. And those are the lucky
ones, who are able to sell anything at all. "What will become
of them now?" Ellyn asks. "Who will buy their weavings? How
will they live?" I watch the landscape. I am trying to see it all,
trying to forget nothing, trying to understand. Two women and
three children follow the edge of the highway in a raggedy parade of life. I am a spoiled American; I have more of everything
than these people will ever have. Suddenly I feel dirty and very,
very cold.

We pass through another security checkpoint, our sixth in two
days, but this time instead of ordering all the men off the bus,
the soldiers board. Their guns slap against the torn, dirty seats.
Across the aisle, an old woman coughs. Coughs, coughs. Tu-
berculosis is rampant in Chiapas. We know this, we try not to
think about it. A pair of soldiers shine a flashlight into the faces
of the Mayan boys sitting in front of us, then turn their attention
to the couple behind us. These are the refugees. They speak only
to each other and to the soldiers when pressed. The couple behind us has 200 pesos, they tell the soldier. How will you live,
he asks. We do not hear the answer as he pushes them off the
bus. We hold up American passports. The soldiers are not interested in us; they smile at our stupidity. We wait. Ten minutes

pass. Then fifteen. How long will the bus wait for the couple? We strain to see, but only our own faces are visible in the dark glass. I doze; imagine I see guerrilla encampments in the mountains. Finally, the couple returns. The bus lurches on down the mountain.

The first newspapers we see are terrifying. The boys who had sat on the bus with us huddle close in the station in Villahermosa, carefully dissecting the pages before them. They read slowly, the way the near-illiterate do, the way we do, piecing the words together, focusing more easily on the photographs. Color pictures of the dead in the Ocosingo marketplace; of guerrillas or maybe just those believed to be guerrillas being held in makeshift prisons, their faces bruised and bloodied; stories of villages bombed, of house-to-house searches conducted by the *federales* in San Cristobal the day we left, of guerrillas routed from the jungle and mountains. Already, rumors are beginning to spread of torture: prisoners forced to drink urine, hoods loaded with hot chili powder used to asphyxiate the captive, skin burned by cigarettes, cut by knives, lacerated by pins.

They were children, we tell each other, no older than those boys on the bus. We saw the guerrillas and they were just hungry-looking kids armed with sticks and machetes and old hunting rifles held together by rope. We were in San Cristobal on New Year's morning; we saw Subcommandante Marcos. And if that was the seat of the rebellion, if those were the elite of the guerrilla fighting unit . . . The thought is difficult to finish. We put the newspapers away. The boys from the bus have disappeared.

San Francisco Redux

We are no longer the kind of women who attend revolutions. Middle age has tamed us poorly but nonetheless well. But because we were there, we try to sort out what it all meant. Means. So when a meeting is announced about the revolution in Chiapas, we go.

It is February. In an overheated, sparse hall we sit with a

hundred of the revolution's sympathizers listening to the rhetoric
of the Left. We children of the Vietnam protests, of women's
rights and gay rights and a dozen other causes we've endorsed
and fought for over the years, have heard it all before. Men who
have never been to Chiapas rant from the stage; a woman who
has just returned spins a story that makes so little sense to us,
we wonder if she was really there at all.

"We are the only people in this room who were there when
it happened," I whisper to Ellyn. She shushes me, nods toward
the stage, her eyes flashing, focused on the speaker, who is talking of the indigenous weavers: "Women from their villages
come to San Cristobal and are forced to sell trinkets to tourists."
The woman's voice pitches indignantly. Ellyn snorts softly.
"She doesn't even know who those women are. And they *do
not* sell trinkets. It's folk art. Some of the finest in the world."
A man behind us clears his throat, jostles our chairs with his
foot, urging us silent. The lights dim, the video we have come
to see plays. On the screen, the streets of San Cristobal roll out
before us, and the women of San Juan Chamula, the women who
were turned out of their village, who have nowhere else to go
but a cardboard shantytown on the hills outside the tiny city,
scuttle past the camera. A young girl hoists her baby onto her
hip, turns away from the camera. The baby looks over her shoulder, smiles. The film cranks on, documenting atrocities. We
struggle for glimpses of the women. Occasionally, we are rewarded. They have survived, at least for now. I recall the opening line of an anthropological paper about the women of
Chiapas: "Now the world is broken." I found the paper in a
bookstore on the streets of San Cristobal the first day of the
revolution, it was written more than two years before. Their
world is broken by more than revolution, but they survived. I
have the sinking feeling that for these women, the revolution
will change very little.

Just as the lights come up, we slip away into the night. Tourists still.

Family Reunion

Ann Allen Shockley

Ed took a night flight to Montgomery from San Francisco, then the afternoon Greyhound bus for the fifty miles to Tipperwannah. The bus was partially filled with people occupying seats in a checkerboard fashion, dependent upon who wanted to sit by whom, a window, or aisle. Most were black.

How things have changed, Ed reflected, eyeing the mahogany bus driver. Unlike the passengers, the driver tried not to stare too hard at her closely cut hair, short stocky figure dressed in gray pants creased to perfection, and white tailored shirt open at the throat as she climbed aboard with a shopping bag of gifts. They couldn't see her eyes behind the sunglasses. But she was aware of their stares. One of the three young black males sprawled on the backseat whispered something to the others that caused derisive laughter among them.

I can just about guess what you said, Ed's glance flashed at them while choosing a seat beside a matronly looking brown woman in a peach shirtwaist dress that smelled of drying in the sun. A sweater was neatly folded across her lap, cushioning a worn black leather pocketbook. Ed sat down, placing the bag between her feet.

"No drinking alcohol, smoking dope, cigars or pipes on this

bus. If you listening to the radio, use earphones,'' the driver chanted mechanically. ''First stop, Tipperwannah.''

Ed settled back in the seat, feeling jet lag catching up with her. Eyes closed, she sensed the woman looking in her direction. After a while, she heard her say: ''My, my. You sure do look familiar.''

''Used to live around here—years ago.''

''That so? Where?''

Nothing beats that peculiar trait of black southern inquisitiveness, Ed observed, opening her eyes to the woman's questioning face. ''Tipperwannah.''

''Hum-m-m,'' the woman murmured, inspecting her closer. ''You kin to them Joneses at Owen's Corner? Kind of favor them.''

''No. I'm a Crawford.''

The woman's thinning eyebrows made a slight dent in her forehead. ''Don't know no Crawfords. I live in Hopkins myself. That's a piece down the way from Tipperwannah.''

''I know.'' Ed shut her eyes again, hoping to signal to the woman that she was tired.

Noting the California shopping bag, the woman continued: ''You comin' back for a visit?''

''Family reunion.''

The woman perked up, smiling as she shifted the pocketbook closer to her. ''Well, well! Ain't that nice? We had one last year in South Carralina. Didn't know we had so many kinfolks. Ever'body so happy to see each other.''

Happy to see each other, Ed repeated in her mind. The way she had found out about it was through a xeroxed letter that somehow reached her.

''You sure do look like them Joneses—'' she heard the woman murmur, before she dozed off to sleep.

''Tipperwannah!''

The driver's blaring announcement awakened her. She got up stiffly. It had been ages since she had taken a bus trip. When a college student at Alabama State, it used to be all the time, back and forth from Montgomery to home.

"Have a good reunion!" the woman called after her.

The only one to get off, the sticky Alabama heat struck her body like a searing hot flash. She had forgotten how hot it could get. "That one—" she instructed the driver, pointing to her bag beneath the bus.

Where the bus stopped was a combination grocery store and filling station on the outskirts of town. She looked around. A white farmer was pumping gas into a truck with two calves. She didn't see anyone else. Maybe they didn't get her note, or they must feel the same way. Hadn't Lorna warned her about coming? *Why do you want to go? Nobody's written or called you since you left. Not even a Christmas card.*

"Edwina—"

The man's voice startled her. No one called her Edwina anymore. Just Ed. She turned to see Robert. He had the same tall straight body, only now his stomach held a small pouch under his T-shirt, and his face had ragged crevices in cheeks the color of his khaki pants.

"Robert!" She smiled at him, glad to see this man who had always been somewhat of a stranger to her. Quiet, aloof, but kind.

"I'm parked 'round back," he said, taking her bag. She followed him to a dusty black pickup truck. Carefully he set the bag in the carrier. "Kinfolks visitin' for the reunion borrowed the car. Otherwise I'd a drove it. Would've been better ridin' for you."

She climbed into the cab. The worn vinyl seat, hot from the sun, warmed her backside. "How's mom?"

"Fine. She's home cookin' for the big picnic Sat'day." Shifting gears, he moved onto the road. "You lookin' good, Edwina."

"Life's been good to me out there, Robert." Better than it had been here.

"You still drawin' them funny pictures?"

"Cartoons, Robert," she laughed, looking out the window at the passing rural landscape of cotton fields, lean-to shotgun shacks surrounded with chickens and half-naked black children playing in the dusty yards. This, she could never make satire out of.

"You kin make a livin' doin' *that*?"

"Sure. Enough for me. I'm syndicated with the National Negro Press Association and I also do freelancing."

"Somebody sholt me the picture where you had Nixon sittin' on top of the White House blowin' taps for a crowd of Negroes below. Had it in the white paper in Montgomery," he chuckled.

"Yeah—" she smiled. "Pretty good, hun?"

They rode the rest of the way in silence. Robert never was much of a talker. Long time ago, she tried to figure out why her mother had married him. Five years after her father died, Robert came into the house as her stepfather when she was fifteen. He drove a truck for an egg company. She supposed he offered another male figure in the house.

"Here we are."

She took off her sunglasses to get a better view. The old two-story frame homestead glistened with fresh white paint. When she went up the steps, she saw that the porch had been done over with new planks painted gray. There was even another glider replacing the old one where she and Lorna used to sit in the summer evenings and dream.

A tide of memories inundated her as she stepped into the living room that her mother referred to as the sitting room. The shades were partially drawn at the windows to keep the midday sun out. A standing floor fan purred in the corner. There was a different flower-patterned blue rug on the floor, but the same heavy furniture protected by white doilies crocheted by her mother was still holding up, for the room was hardly used. Family pictures adorned the walls and tables, but she did not see her own. Friends hardly congregated here, preferring the kitchen where now she could hear voices and smell of baking odors coming from it.

"You wait here while I go git your mama."

As she stood in the middle of the room, she felt her body tense, not knowing what to expect. Ed, brace up. *You're a forty-two-year-old woman now, and not the twenty-two-year old who left.*

Like a whisper, her mother came upon her. Silently they gazed at each other. It was hard to believe her mother was seventy-five. Gazing into the dark-skinned face, she saw her own strong features and wide-spaced eyes. Only her mother's face had altered with age. Her once thin body heavier, hair completely white, carelessly knotted in a bun on her neck. Warmth invaded Ed with a flush of tenderness.

"Hello, Mom—" Automatically she reached out to hug her, feeling the other's body stiffen in her embrace. "I brought you a present." Ed took out a colorfully wrapped box from the shopping bag.

Her mother looked beyond her. "Set it on the coffee table there."

"It's a robe. I thought you could use one," Ed said, following her directions.

"You'll have to sleep in the little room. Your Cousin Rosetta from Memphis and her husband are goin' to sleep in yours when they git here."

"Sure, Mom. That's okay." Why had she expected her to save her old room for her?

Suddenly her mother blurted out: "What happened to your hair? Fall out?"

"No, Mom," she laughed. "I just had it cut like that."

"Humph! Looks terrible. Can't tell you from a man."

"Zepth—" Robert came into the room, "I'll take her bag up."

Ed turned to him. "Robert, I brought you a present too." She handed him the package.

"Well, suh! Thanks, Edwina," he smiled gratefully. "Mighty nice of you!"

"Smells like somethin' burnin'," her mother remarked, abruptly going toward the kitchen.

The little room by the stairway that as a child she called the cabin held a small cot covered with a white spread and small white painted dresser. The closet was like a shoebox. She went to push the window higher to relieve the room of its heat and mustiness. People in these parts were homegrown to the steamy temperature, hardly bothering to buy fans or air conditioners.

She opened her bag and got out the picture of Lorna in a small gold frame. Lorna's beige dimpled face smiled out at her, bringing some cheer to her and the room. "You were right, honey," she said to the picture. "It's not going to be easy."

Taking off her clothes, she slipped into a robe and stretched out on the narrow bed. Within a few minutes, weariness claimed her and she went fast to sleep.

The sun had cooled when she was aroused by a loud knocking on her door and a voice calling out to her: "Edwina!"

Before she could answer, the door swung open and a tawny-colored striking woman in a splashy red skirt and sleeveless blouse barged in. "Hi, sweetie!"

"Shay!" Ed felt arms enveloping her in a big hug. "*You* are *here*?"

"Sure am. I'm the one who sent you that letter. With your being on one end in California and me on the other in New York, I figured this would be a good time for us to see each other again. Before we got *too* old," she added laughingly.

Ed smiled happily. "Oh, Shay, it's so good to see you." Shay was her cousin, the daughter of her mother's youngest sister, who, her mother complained, had married too early in life. Growing up, Shay had been like a big sister to her.

"How do I look for a fifty-five-year-old woman?" she asked, pivoting in a model's quick swirl, hands on hips, a leg thrust forward.

Ed took in the auburn tinted hair once black, flashing light-brown eyes and red-curved lips. "Great, as usual."

"Owning a beauty parlor helps too," Shay quipped.

"Shay, how long has it been?"

"Long, long time since I left this place. I'm just sorry that I missed all the Civil Rights action. Would have been right there

in Montgomery in the midst of it like you," she said, sitting on
the bed. "Things sure in hell are different now. You should have
seen me eyeballing a brother directing traffic yesterday when I
got to Montgomery."

"Me, too, when I saw one of us *driving* a Greyhound."

"The great seventies. Com'on, get up. We got some roaming
to do. Look over the old hometown. I rented a car. I'm staying
at the Southern Inn, seven miles out. Can you imagine? I remember the time when the only blacks they let in were the
maids, cooks, and waiters."

Shay drove slowly down the deserted streets. It was evening
and the stores had closed. Home lights shown out at them. Look-
ing around, Shay said: "Well, things haven't changed *that* much.
White folks still on one side of the tracks, and we on the other.
White folks in the big houses, and we in the little ones. Civil
Righteousness hasn't reached too far down *here* yet."

She stopped at a red light on Front Street. "I could take this
light and no one would know the difference," she laughed.
"Say! I *did* see a black girl at the cash register in the Piggly
Wiggly grocery store. That's an advancement when white folks
start letting us take the money."

Ed listened and relaxed to Shay's easy prattle and laughter.
Shay was more outgoing than she. Lorna always told her to
loosen up. She and Shay were alike in one way, rebellious, following their own stars.

"Let's stop by Harry's and get a drink. Providing he's still in
business," Shay suggested. "Lord, did I used to have fun there."

Harry's remained the one entertainment site for them at the
end of the black district where the back road out of town began.
It was a low, red-roofed cinderblock building with smudged,
slanted windows. When they went in, Marvin Gaye was singing
something about being chained to loving. The inside was dim
and cooled by an ancient air conditioner behind the bar. Two
men sat there lazily nursing beer and talking to the bartender
who had an Afro the size of a blown-up balloon. Seeing them,
the bartender came over to their table.

"Where's Harry?" Shay asked.

The man looked at her in surprise. "Harry died 'bout six years ago. Son's got the place now."

"Sorry. We've been away for quite a while."

"Welcome back. What'll it be?"

"Vodka and tonic okay with you, Edwina?"

"Fine." When the bartender left, Ed said: "Just call me Ed, Shay. I'm not Edwina anymore."

A frown appeared then quickly left Shay's face. "All right. I like Ed better anyway."

The bartender set the drinks on the table. Ed touched her glass to Shay's. "To our own mini-reunion."

Shay tasted her drink. "Your mother looks well. Wonder what mine would have looked like by now, if she had lived."

"Probably like an older sister," Ed smiled.

"I know Auntie Zepth was happy to see *you*—her only child."

Ed twirled the stirrer in her glass. "She didn't seem too happy. She apparently hasn't gotten over it, even after all these years."

The music stopped and the men's voices could be heard at the bar. Shay looked confused. "Over what?"

"Me and Lorna. Haven't you heard?"

Shay's eyes dropped. "In a way. Through the family grapevine."

"That's why we had to leave. The speculations—gossip. It came to a head a year after we finished State. Rumors floated all the way down from Montgomery about us. Mom got mad, ordered me to stop seeing Lorna. So, we left and went as far away as we could. Best decision we made, or we wouldn't be together now."

"How is Lorna?"

"Wonderful as ever. She works with a children's center and loves it." Ed finished her drink. "Shay, Mom hates me."

"No she doesn't," Shay replied quickly. "It's just that she doesn't know how to deal with you and Lorna. Some old people get set in their ideas about life. How it should be. Then, there are others who change with the times."

Seeing their empty glasses, the bartender came over. "Two more?"

"Right. Only this time, easy on the tonic," Shay cautioned.

"Mom will never change," Ed said, shaking her head.

"Maybe seeing you again and thinking about all the empty years without you could make her," Shay said softly. "In any case, she might as well start hating me too. I found similar roots in New York, so to speak."

Ed stared at her aghast. "Shay—you too!"

Shay nodded slowly. "The co-owner of my beauty parlor," she laughed. "Don't worry, sweetie," she soothed, patting Ed's hand. "You got company."

"Here you are, ladies." The bartender set fresh drinks before them. "These are on the house. We treat our old hometowners good."

Smiling, Ed lifted her glass in a toast. "To our sisterhood!"

The next day, Ed got up early to avoid the bathroom traffic, trying to ignore the door closed to her once room. Her mother was already in the large old-fashioned kitchen with the green cabinets stretching from counter to ceiling. Robert sat at the long, square table drinking coffee out of a thick white mug.

"Morning—" she smiled at them.

"Sleep all right on that cot?" Robert asked with concern.

"Yes, I did." Actually, it had been a humid, uncomfortable night.

"I sure do like that tie and hank'chief you give me. Goin' to wear 'em to church Sunday."

"Mom, did the robe fit? If not, I can—"

"Don't know. How you want your eggs?"

"It doesn't matter."

"Don't know how to fix them kind."

"Scrambled, I guess."

Robert refilled his cup from the coffee pot on the stove. "How come Lorna didn't come with you? Y'all such good friends. Left here together. Seems like only yesdiddy. I know she ain't *blood* kin, but it was just *like* she was. 'Round all the time."

Ed heard her mother slam the refrigerator door shut. The grapevine hadn't reached him. That kind of talk was for women's ears in the family.

"Robert!" Almost a shout from Zepth. "You want bacon?"

He looked at her puzzledly. "No, Zepth. I'll just finish this coffee and be on my way. Got to go to town for gas."

Shortly afterward, there were only the two of them. Her mother was busy at the stove, back to her. Eventually Zepth said: "You ought to go and buy a wig for the picnic tomorrow."

"What?" Ed almost dropped the cup she had gotten from the cabinet.

"You heard me. You can't be 'round kinfolks from all over lookin' like that. A *man*! If you want to be one, you got to have more'n short hair. I ain't goin' to be shamed."

"Mom! How are you going to be shamed? It's *my* hair," she retorted angrily. "This is the way *I* like it. It's not a matter of trying to change genders."

" 'N put on a dress. Skirt or somethin'. Them overalls look a mess."

"These are *jeans*, mom. Everybody wears them."

Ed poured coffee in the cup that matched Robert's. Shakily she reached for the sugar, then sat down at the table. Imagine telling her at her age how to dress and look. *Mamas forever going to try to rule their daughters, Lorna had philosophized one day. Long as you are the daughter and she's the mama. No matter how old you get, you will still be younger than she. And mamas don't forget that. Mine didn't before she passed.*

She shouldn't have come. But after all the years, she wanted to see her mother again. The woman who had helped her through college by working in the school cafeteria. Even stood by her when she got in the Montgomery student sit-in trouble singing "We Shall Overcome" on the courthouse steps.

"Mom, aren't you glad to just see me?" she asked quietly.

"Not lookin' like that." Zepth put a plate of bacon and eggs on the table.

"If I'm an embarrassment, I'll leave."

"Leave?" Shay barged into the kitchen, looking high-spirited in a bright yellow sundress. "Auntie Zepth, Robert left the front door open again."

"So I see," Zepth mumbled under her breath.

"Where you leaving to?" Shay looked at Ed.

"Home." Ed pushed the half-eaten food away.

"Ridiculous! The fun hasn't started yet. Why, you should see all that *food* folks are preparing for tomorrow. I just left Cousin Lottie's and her husband's been barbecuing all month, mind you. Nellie's got collard greens and—" Shay stopped to get a cup of coffee. "And, your mama's got a freezer out back loaded with sweet potato pies and cakes!" Shay pulled a chair next to Ed at the table. "Now, you know where *we* come from, soul food like that is hard to come by. First place, neither you nor I ever were much good at cooking."

"You got that right," Ed agreed, thinking how Lorna would spend hours in the kitchen experimenting with recipes.

"Say, Auntie Zepth, speaking of cooking, I'll have sausage, eggs over light, and those homemade biscuits you used to make for *my* breakfast," Shay ordered, playfully slapping Zepth on the rear.

"Shay! You stop that now! Lord, you still as crazy as ever." For the first time, Ed saw a fleeting smile on her mother's face.

"Also, Auntie Zepth," Shay went on, stirring her coffee, "save some time today for me to style your hair. That knot's got to go with all those hairpins sticking out like porcupines. For you, it's free. In New York, I'd charge forty dollars."

Zepth got out the biscuit board and rolling pin. "Wish you'd give somebody else one," she grunted.

"Like who?"

"Me," Ed broke in.

"Why nothing's wrong with Ed's hair."

"Her name is Edwina. That's what I give her when she came into the world," Zepth snorted, vigorously sifting the flour mixture.

"Now, now, Auntie Zepth, we don't always keep what we came into the world with. Time changes the world and its people," Shay answered, facetiously wagging an admonishing finger. "Back to Ed's hair. If that's the way she likes it, fine. Besides, she's not the only one with a haircut like that. Don't you read *Essence* magazine?" Shay burst out laughing, winking at Ed.

Zepth silently kneaded the dough, mouth pinched tightly.

"Ed, you're going nowhere. You're staying right here." Shay blew on her coffee.

"You ain't in this, Shay," Zepth said, slamming the rolling pin over the dough.

"Just *put* myself in it, Auntie Zepth," Shay rebutted. "What's wrong with you anyway? A late, late change of life? Why, you ought to be happy. Your only child comes all the way here to see you and meet a bunch of unheard of relatives from all around. And *you*, Auntie Zepth, carrying on about *hair*, while we're all here trying to find out about our *roots*. Isn't that what Alex Haley's ballyhooing about? Black folks finding their roots?"

As if the words had bounced off her, Zepth said in a low voice, almost like the words were meant to be only for herself, "I tolt her when she left with that—that Lorna that she wasn't no mo' daughter of mine."

"I don't care what you told her, Auntie Zepth, she's your daughter by birth and nothing can change that. People have different lifestyles—make different choices. It's something they can't help. It's just a *part* of them."

Zepth stopped cutting out the biscuits to turn and glare at Shay. "Oh, is that so? 'N how *you* know?"

Shay's eyes opened wide. "Because, Auntie Zepth, of what I am too."

Zepth swayed as if she were going to faint. The kitchen was deathly quiet like the world had died around them. "What you sayin', Shay?" Zepth's voice cracked like dry leaves.

"Auntie Zepth, I can't be more explicit."

"Who would've thought— *You!* Lord, God, have mercy!" Zepth knocked over the flour can as she sank down in the rocker by the stove. Tears formed in her eyes like shards of glass.

"Mom—." Ed felt helpless watching her.

Shay got up to put her arms around Zepth. "It's not all that bad. Look, see, Auntie Zepth. I have the same face, hands, body. I'm no different than I was a few minutes ago."

"No *dif'frent*? My own *sistah's* chile! It's a *curse* on this fam'bly."

"Auntie Zepth, get a hold of yourself," Shay pleaded gently, handing her a paper towel to dry her eyes on. "Ed and I love you, and we want you to love us too. *Please?*"

Ed got up, strength claiming her to bond with the woman who had given birth to her. Bending over the rocker, she smelled the freshness of her mother's morning clothes mixed with the faint odor of frying food. Softly, she brushed her lips against her cheek. When was the last time she had kissed her mother? She, too, felt like crying, but for a different reason.

"Mom, I love you," she said, squeezing her tightly. She knew Lorna would say: *That's right. Hold her tightly. Real tight, and the tightness will let her know.*

Zepth's eyes locked closed, like she was trying to shut out all that was happening around her, blot out the words and feelings reaching out to her. The morning's sun sharply nudged itself into the room, warming Zepth's back like a plea stroking her from beyond the grave. This was a family reunion. A coming together.

In what seemed like worlds of time later, Zepth's hand lifted to graze Ed's face. As if her body were a great weight, she slowly drew herself up out of the rocker, eyes swallowing the two of them into her own—into her life. Then she looked around at the spilled flour dusting the counter and flecking her apron. A smile spread across her face as she said: "Shay, might know *you'd* be the one wanting biscuits for breakfast."

Ed saw the smile on her face and knew that she was home now.

Author Biographies

Lucy Jane Bledsoe is the author of *Sweat: Stories and a Novella* (Seal Press, 1995) and a children's book called *The Big Bike Race* (Holiday House, 1995). She is also the editor of *Heatwave: Women in Love and Lust* (Alyson, 1995). She teaches creative writing in Bay Area literacy programs.

Rebecca Brown is the author of numerous works of fiction published both here and in England. *The Terrible Girls* (City Lights, 1992) was a finalist for the Lambda Literary Award. *Annie Oakely's Girl* (City Lights, 1993), was a featured title of the Quality Paperback Book Club and a finalist for its fiction award. *The Gifts of the Body* (HarperCollins, 1994) won the Pacific Northwest Writers Award and was a finalist for *The Boston Book Review* for Fiction and the Lambda Literary Award. Her work has been translated into Dutch, German, Danish and Japanese and adapted for theater in the United States, Scotland and England. She lives in Seattle where she teaches part time and works at a soup kitchen. She is looking for a patron.

Clover LaTonia Anasazi Cannady is an African-American poet and certified crystal therapist, who has worked in the healing arts for more than ten years. She is currently studying pyramid construction and developing a holistic massage system. Clover lives in Brooklyn, New York.

Mary Beth Caschetta is a freelance health writer in New York City. Her nonfiction writing has appeared in *The Seicus Report*, *The New England Journal of Medicine* and *The Journal of the American Medical Women's Association*, among others. This is her first published fiction.

Michelle Cliff is the author of the novels *Free Enterprise*, *No Telephone to Heaven* and *Abeng*, as well as the short-story collections *Bodies of Water* and *The Store of a Million Items*.

Nisa Donnelly, a San Francisco writer, is the author of two books, *The Love Songs of Phoenix Bay* and *The Bar Stories: A Novel After All* (winner of the 1990 Lambda Literary Award for Lesbian Fiction), both from St. Martin's Press. Her essays and short fiction have appeared in various anthologies, magazines and journals.

Leslie Feinberg is the author of the award-winning novel *Stone Butch Blues*. Her nonfiction book, *Transgender Warriors: A History of Resistance*, will be released from Beacon Press on March 1, 1996. Feinberg is a contributing editor to *Workers World* weekly newspaper and *Liberation* and *Marxism* magazine.

Ellen Frye is the author of *Amazon Story Bones* (Spinsters Ink) and *The Other Sappho* (Firebrand, 1989). She has been published in *Calyx*, *Short Fiction by Women*, *Room of One's Own* and *Caprice*, as well as several anthologies. "Flossie's Going" is the first chapter of a novel in progress set in Vermont in the early part of the century.

Naomi Holoch is coeditor of the series *Women on Women* (Plume/Penguin), the author of several short stories and a novel. She teaches French, Italian, and Lesbian and Gay literature at SUNY-Purchase, NY.

Frankie Hucklenbroich, born in 1939 of second-generation working-class parents, grew up in a solidly Catholic German/ Irish neighborhood in St. Louis. When she was 18, her parents —horrified at her sexual orientation—invited her to leave home for good. Since then, she has rocketed around the country, from Miami to Los Angeles, from San Francisco to Las Vegas, from Denver to San Diego working as a carhop, waitress, carnie barker, factory worker, bar owner, college graduate. She knows what jail is like and what it is to live alone for a year on top of a mountain.

Ann E. Imbrie is Professor of English at Vassar College, where she teaches literature, creative writing, and women's studies. *Spoken in Darkness* represents the first major revision of her life as a writer, daughter, friend, woman. She is looking forward to the next incarnation. She lives in Poughkeepsie and New York City.

Melanie Kaye/Kantrowitz is the author of *The Issue Is Power: Essays on Women, Jews, Violence and Resistance* and of *My Jewish Face & Other Stories* (both published by Aunt Lute Foundation). She coedited *The Tribe of Dina: A Jewish Women's Anthology* (Beacon Press), and is the former editor of *Sinister Wisdom*, one of the oldest lesbian/feminist journals. She earned a Ph.D. in Comparative Literature from the University of California at Berkeley, and has taught writing and women's studies all over the country, most recently at Brooklyn College and the University of Washington. She has worked as an activist in social-justice movements since the early sixties, and currently serves as Executive Director of *Jews for Racial and Economic Justice* in New York City.

Sarah Lane grew up in Madrid, Spain. After attending Carelton College in Minnesota, she moved to Chicago where, for ten years, she taught writing to high-school and college students and worked for a number of publishing houses. Recently, she and her family moved to an island in Puget Sound.

Jenifer Levin is the author of *Water Dancer*, *Snow*, *Shimoni's Lover* and *The Sea of Light*. She has recently completed a non-fiction work on lesbian sexual archetypes, *Power and Surrender*. Her short stories have been widely anthologized and she has written for the *New York Times*, the *Washington Post*, *Rolling Stone*, *Ms.* and many other publications. Having lived and worked in the Middle East, she currently lives in New York City with her lover and their son.

Catherine Lewis is the author of *Dry Fire*, a novel published by W. W. Norton, and is currently completing a second novel for the same press. She has worked as a police officer in Florida.

Cynthia Lollar recently turned her hand to fiction after more than fourteen years as a writer and editor in magazines and public relations. With various degrees in journalism and anthropology, she continues to earn her living as a science communicator and freelance writer/editor. In 1995, she received a Maryland State Arts Council Individual Artist Award in fiction. Previously she was a resident of the Ragdale Foundation in Illinois and the Virginia Center for the Creative Arts, where the first version of this story was written. She lives with her partner of nine years, Greta McVey, in College Park, Maryland.

Kate Millett, artist, author, teacher, has written eight books about women, including the groundbreaking study, *Sexual Politics*, in 1970 and her most recent, *The Politics of Cruelty*, in 1993. In 1978, she founded an art colony at her farm in Poughkeepsie, New York, for women artists.

Hilary Mullins grew up in Vermont dairy country and now lives in Oakland, California, with her partner and their growing clan of cats. Her first novel, *The Cat Came Back*, won a 1993 Lambda Literary Award. Her work has also appeared in various anthologies, including *Sleeping with Dionysus*, *Uncommon Heroes*, and *Tomboys! Tales of Dyke Derring-Do*. She is currently at work on a screenplay.

Elana Nachman/Dykewomon was an editor of *Sinister Wisdom* for eight years and is now happily writing and loving in Oakland, California. She has a new book of poetry, *Nothing Will Be as Sweet as the Taste*, just published by Onlywomen Press (London) and a novel in the works. *Riverfinger Women* contains the first Jewish Lesbian characters in the Second Wave.

Joan Nestle, author of *A Restricted Country* (Firebrand Books), editor of *The Persistent Desire* (Alyson Publications) and coeditor with John Preston of *Sister and Brother: Lesbians and Gay Men Talk about Their Lives Together* (HarperSanFrancisco), is cofounder of the Lesbian Herstory Archives and a teacher of writing in the SEEK Program at Queens College, CUNY. In 1995, after thirty years of teaching, she retired and is now working on a new collection of her own work, *A Fragile Union*.

Gerry Gomez Pearlberg's fiction and poetry have appeared in numerous publications, including *Calyx*, *Global City Review*, *modern words*, and *Sister and Brother: Lesbians and Gay Men Write About Their Lives Together*, edited by Joan Nestle and John Preston. She has edited *The Key To Everything: Classic Lesbian Love Poems* (St. Martin's Press), and is currently editing an anthology of erotic lesbian verse. She lives in Brooklyn with Otto, her beloved boxer muse.

Leslie Pietrzyk's short stories have appeared in many journals, including *The Iowa Review*, *Epoch*, *Gettysburg Review*, *The Seattle Review*, *The Journal*, *Literal Latte*, and *The Nebraska Review*.

Minnie Bruce Pratt's second book of poetry, *Crime Against Nature*, chosen as the 1989 Lamont Poetry Selection by the Academy of American Poets, was also nominated for a Pulitzer Prize and received the American Library Association's Gay and Lesbian Book Award for Literature. Her other books include *We Say We Love Each Other* and *Rebellion: Essays 1980–1991*. She is presently working on a series of narrative poems, *Walking*

Back Up Depot Street. Her book of stories about gender boundary crossing, *S/HE*, was released by Firebrand Books in spring 1995. She lives in Jersey City, New Jersey.

Susan Fox Rogers is editor of *Sports Dykes, Stories from on and off the Field* (St. Martin's Press) and *Another Wilderness: New Outdoor Writing by Women* (Seal Press). She lives in the mid-Hudson Valley, New York.

Lexa Roséan is a playwright, poet, and priestess. A resident of Manhattan's East Village, her plays *Sweeter Than*, *The Prisoner*, *Lesbians In The Bible*, and *I Married A Lesbian Witch* have all been produced at the WOW Cafe. Her book of poetry *Elements* was printed in 1991 and Lexa is featured in "The One Hundred Greatest Poets of All Time," the NuYorican Poetry Symphony CD Live at the Knitting Factory. Raised as an orthodox Jew, in 1981 she converted to paganism and is now a high priestess of the Wicca. "Lexa's Lesbian Love Signs" is featured on Dyke TV. Her book *Supermarket Sorceress* was released by St. Martin's Press in October, 1995. *A Kosher Megila* is an excerpt from *Spinoza's Daughter*, a novel in progress chronicling the author's excommunication for being a homosexual.

Sapphire, who lives and works in New York City, is a poet, writer and performance artist. Her work has appeared in numerous journals and anthologies, including *City Lights*, *Review*, *Bomb*, *The Portable Lower Eastside*, *Queer City*, *Downtown*, and *High Risk 2: Writings on Sex, Death and Subversion*, edited by Amy Scholder and Ira Silverberg, *Critical Condition: Women on the Edge of Violence*, edited by Amy Scholder and *Aloud: The Nuyorican Poet's Cafe Anthology*, edited by Miquel Algarin and Bob Holman. She has performed in bookstores and universities throughout the women's, black and lesbian and gay communities in the United States, Great Britain and South America. Her newest book is *American Dreams* (High Risk).

Sarah Schulman is the author of six novels: *Rat Bohemia* (1995), *Empathy* (1992), *People in Trouble* (1990), *After Delores* (1988), *Girls, Visions and Everything* (1986), *The Sophie Horowitz Story* (1984) and one nonfiction book *My American History: Lesbian and Gay Life During the Reagan/Bush Years* (1994).

Ann Allen Shockley is the author of the novels *Loving Her* and *Say Jesus and Come To Me*, and a collection of short stories, *The Black and White of It*. She edited the anthology *Afro-American Writers, 1746–1933*, and co-edited *Living Black American Authors* and *Handbook of Black Librarianship*.

Barbara Smith coedited *Conditions Five, The Black Women's Issue* with Lorraine Bethel (1979) and *All the Women are White, All the Blacks are Men, But Some of Us Are Brave: Black Women's Studies* with Gloria T. Hull and Patricia Bell Scott (The Feminist Press, 1982) and edited *Home Girls: A Black Feminist Anthology* (Kitchen Table Press, 1983). She is cofounder of Kitchen Table: Women of Color Press. Her essays exploring the connections between race, gender and class have appeared in many publications, including *Gay Community News*, *The Nation*, *Black Scholar* and *Ms.* She is currently working on the first book to fully explore the history of lesbian and gay African-Americans in the United States.

Linda Smukler's first book of poems, *Normal Sex*, was published by Firebrand Books (Ithaca, NY, 1994). Recently, she received awards from the Astraea Foundation and the New York Foundation for the Arts. She has been widely published in anthologies such as *Gay and Lesbian Poetry in Our Time* (St. Martin's Press, edited by Larkin and Morse) and literary journals such as *The Kenyon Review*, *The American Voice*, *Ploughshares* and *The Prose Poem: An International Journal*.

Lydia Swartz is a bisexual polyamorous sadomasochistic technical editor, essayist, writer of smut and recovering poet who lives in the Pacific Northwest. Published in *Ecce Queer*, *Libido*, *Northwest Gay and Lesbian Reader*, *Herotica 2* and *3*, *The Poetry of Sex*, *The 100th Boyfriend*, *Good to Go* and numerous community publications. Her hobby is giving pieces of fiction to publications that cease publishing before they can be published.

Sheila Ortiz Taylor, Chicana novelist and poet, is Professor of English at Florida State University, where for more than twenty years she has taught creative writing and women's literature at the graduate and undergraduate levels. A native of California and a graduate of UCLA, her novels—*Faultline* (1982), *Spring Forward/Fall Back* (1985), and *Southbound* (1990)—all use Southern California as setting and subject matter.

Lu Vickers lives in Florida, and her fiction has appeared in *Hurricane Alice*, *Common Lives*, *Applachee Quarterly Review*, *Kalliope*, *Calypso* and other publications.

Riki Anne Wilchins is a lesbian or bisexual, transsexual or transgendered, man or woman, living in Greenwich Village or New York City. Her hobbies include the Transsexual Menace, the Lesbian Avengers, attacking false binary economies and any other political system which oppresses her or just really pisses her off.